# Eighteenth-Century Novels by Women

Isobel Grundy, Editor

# THE DELICATE DISTRESS

### Elizabeth Griffith

Edited by
### CYNTHIA BOOTH RICCIARDI
AND
### SUSAN STAVES

THE UNIVERSITY PRESS OF KENTUCKY

Publication of this volume was made possible in part by a grant from
the National Endowment for the Humanities.

Scholarly publisher for the Commonwealth, serving Bellarmine College,
Berea College, Centre College of Kentucky, Eastern Kentucky University,
The Filson Club Historical Society, Georgetown College, Kentucky Historical Society,
Kentucky State University, Morehead State University, Murray State
University, Northern Kentucky University, Transylvania University,
University of Kentucky, University of Louisville,
and Western Kentucky University.

*Editorial and Sales Offices:* The University Press of Kentucky
663 South Limestone Street, Lexington, Kentucky 40508-4008

01 00 99 98 97   5 4 3 2 1

**Library of Congress Cataloging-in-Publication Data**

Griffith, Mrs. (Elizabeth), 1727?–1793
    The delicate distress / Elizabeth Griffith : edited by Cynthia
Booth Ricciardi and Susan Staves.
        p.   cm. — (Eighteenth-century novels by women)
    Previously published in 1769 as part of a set of Two novels, the
second, The gordian knot, writen by her husband, Richard Griffith
— prel. p.
    Includes bibliographical references.
    ISBN 0-8131-2014-4 (alk. paper). — ISBN 0-8131-0925-6 (pbk. :
alk. paper)
    I. Ricciardi, Cynthia Booth, 1959–   .  II. Staves, Susan, 1942–
.  III. Title.   IV. Series.
PR3505.G43D45   1997
813'.1—dc21                                                    96–50890

Manufactured in the United States of America

# Contents

~

# INTRODUCTION

~

Elizabeth Griffith's *Delicate Distress* was first published in London in 1769 in a most unusual format. Her novel was one of two published together in a matched set: *Two Novels In Letters. By the Authors of Henry and Frances. In Four Volumes.* Volumes one and two of the set contained *The Delicate Distress;* volumes three and four offered a second novel, *The Gordian Knot.* The characters and setting of *The Delicate Distress* and *The Gordian Knot* are quite different, although both novels tell stories of unhappy marriages, fidelity and infidelity, and disappointed lovers who struggle with the question of whether a first love can be followed by a second.

Contemporary readers understood that the authors of these new novels were a husband and wife, Richard and Elizabeth Griffith, who had already made themselves famous by publishing *A Series of Genuine Letters between Henry and Frances.* The first two volumes of the *Genuine Letters,* appearing in 1757, had covered the tense courtship between Richard, writing as "Henry," an Irish gentleman, and Elizabeth, writing as "Frances," an actress on the Dublin stage, but not a woman prepared to become merely a gentleman's mistress. Four subsequent volumes of *Genuine Letters* published after their marriage offered letters in which the two discussed their common reading, ideas about morality and the world, and, occasionally, plans for literary projects one or the other of them intended to undertake.

As far as we know, no other husband and wife have ever published their novels simultaneously in the fashion of the Griffiths's *Two Novels.*[1] Richard and Elizabeth Griffith were conscious of presenting themselves as exemplars of the possibilities of happy marriage; both criticized contemporary libertinism and cynicism about marriage and did their best to contribute to making anti-marriage attitudes archaic. Indeed, Richard ventures to guess in *Genuine Letters* that "We are . . . the most extraordinary viii / I<small>NTRODUCTION</small>

Couple that ever lived; and our Loves will hand us down to Fame, though our Wit should Fail."[2] Later, he playfully suggests that the two of them "open an Academy in London forthwith, *at the Court End of the Town,* to teach this charming Science, and stile it the *Bon ton* of domestic *Life"* (*GL* 6:48). As J. M. S. Tompkins noted in a pioneering essay on *The Genuine Letters,* Richard in his own writings often quotes and praises Elizabeth's work, and in *The Gordian Knot* introduces a Mr. and Mrs. Sutton who attempt to found just such an academy.[3] Both Richard and Elizabeth were also professional writers aware that novelty, including novelty of presentation, had its own appeal on the market.

Before the publication of *Genuine Letters,* Elizabeth Griffith had appeared as a professional actress, first in Dublin and then in London.[4] In a period when women were denied access to the formal literary education available to gentlemen, Griffith's professional familiarity with the plays in which she appeared was a useful preparation for her later career as a writer. Her father, Thomas Griffith, was himself an actor who became a manager at two Dublin theaters, although he died in 1744, before Elizabeth's stage career began. She made her debut at the Smock Alley Theatre in Dublin as Juliet in Shakespeare's *Romeo and Juliet* on 13 October 1749, at the age of twenty-two. Her other important roles included Cordelia in *Lear,* Andromache in Ambrose Philips's *Distrest Mother* (an adaptation of Racine's *Andromache*), and Calista in Nicholas Rowe's *Fair Penitent.* Not surprisingly, some of her allusions in *The Delicate Distress* are to plays in which she appeared, notably to Milton's *Comus,* in which she played the virtuous Lady. (Although originally a court masque, *Comus* was reinvented for the commercial stage in the eighteenth century by John Langhorne and Thomas Arne, who added new songs and music to Milton's text.)

Griffith was playing Ismene in Aaron Hill's *Meropé: or, the Princely Shepherdess* on the Dublin stage the day before she married Richard on 12 May 1751 in a private ceremony. She took the eminently sensible precaution of having Margaret Hamilton, the Countess of Orrery, as a witness should Richard ever later attempt to deny the marriage had taken place.

Elizabeth's next appearance as an author was as the translator and editor of *The Memoirs of Ninon de L'Enclos. With her Letters to Monsr. de St. Evremond and to the Marquis de Sevigné* (1761). According to the *Genuine Letters,* Richard first suggested this as a good project and then countered Elizabeth's scruples about the propriety of her translating the words of one of the most notorious French courtesans and female libertines of the late seventeenth century. While it is surprising that a woman who in the *Genuine Letters* positions herself as an icon of morality and marital virtue would suddenly proffer cynical French libertinism, Richard was nevertheless correct in believing that there was a contemporary market for translations from the French and also correct in supposing that this translation would not harm the reputation of his wife. Most professional women writers in the eighteenth century did some translation, usually from the French, since women were much more likely to have learned French than Greek or Latin, and since, as Richard calculated, there was a strong English market for translations and adaptations of contemporary or near contemporary French works. Just as professional acting offered Elizabeth useful literary training, so her translations from the French necessitated the kind of close and disciplined attention to language that also helped compensate for her exclusion from serious schooling. Throughout her career, Griffith continued to translate and to adapt contemporary French works, including plays and novels. Some of the French writers she translated or adapted are now considered minor, but she was also seriously interested in the major French writers of her day, including Marivaux, Beaumarchais, Diderot, Rousseau, and Voltaire.

*The Memoirs of Ninon* was a useful book for a would-be epistolary novelist to translate, because, in addition to the witty letters of Ninon and St. Evremond, Griffith also translated what purported to be authentic letters between Ninon and the Marquis de Sévigné.[5] These letters, however, were actually an historical epistolary novel, probably written by Louis Damours and first published in 1750, long after Ninon's death. Moreover, *Lettres de Ninon de Lenclos au Marquis de Sévigné* is a good epistolary novel, one that anticipates Choderlos de Laclos's *Les Liaisons dangereuses* (1782), but less cynically respects the virtue of the young widow whom the young marquis attempts to seduce, at first with the advice of the much older Ninon. Damours demonstrates how the epistolary novel can be a particularly good vehicle for the analysis of behavior and manners, and how small actions, observed by an intelligent letter writer, can be made to seem problematic, worthy of protracted debate between correspondents. The English novelist Samuel Richardson had, of course, also demonstrated the power of the epistolary novel in *Clarissa* (1749) and *Sir Charles Grandison* (1753–54), but we think it fair to say that, compared to Richardson, Griffith shows more French influence. She uses worldly, unsentimental women to critique contemporary manners, and even, as with Lady Straffon in *The Delicate Distress,* as sympathetic and authoritative characters.

Griffith's first independent and original publication, however, was not a novel but a verse drama, *Amana. A Dramatic Poem* (1764). It is the only tragedy, the only verse drama, and the only unperformed play she ever published. Basing her plot on an oriental tale by John Hawkesworth, Griffith, like many of her contemporaries, used the oriental tale and the figure of a sultan with his seraglio to develop patriotic contrasts between oriental despotism and British liberty. The virgin heroine remains faithful to her lover; rather than lose her chastity to the decadent sultan, she drinks poison. The more villainous male characters make negative statements about the female sex, which the play then shows are untrue "libels" on women. What are women? the sultan asks:

> the very sport of nature;
> Formed solely for our use, like the fair flower
> That blooms but to be cropt, then cast away.[6]

In *The Delicate Distress* and in Griffith's later novels, as in *Amana,* men who express contempt or disdain for women are seen as bad and dangerous, either doomed to be villains or in need of reeducation before they can enjoy decent lives.

Griffith is aware of living at a time when the nature of women is being debated and does her best to portray male expressions of sexism as wrong, unattractive, and foolish. Sultan-like or libertine attitudes, expressed by a character like Sir James Thornton in *The Delicate Distress,* she tries to defeat by argument, ridicule, and education. At the same time, Griffith is aware of the heavy weight of the tradition that figures women as lustful temptresses who have the capacity to spoil men's lives and to introduce evil into the world; the reader will note throughout *The Delicate Distress* allusions to Pandora, Calypso, Circe, and Eve.

That a relatively uneducated actress should attempt her debut as a playwright with a verse tragedy shows surprisingly high literary ambition. After *Amana,* however, and for the rest of her career as a playwright, Griffith turned to comedy, a genre in which she was to have more success. Her first comedy and her first play to be produced, *The Platonic Wife* (1765), is based on one of the elegant stories of Jean-François Marmontel, "L'hereux divorce" ("The Happy Divorce") from the popular *Contes moraux (Moral Tales)*. The female protagonist, Lady Frankland, makes such extravagant demands for romance of her husband that she forces a separation. While separated, she attempts to show that a married woman can have male friends, but the lesson of the play is that such platonic friendship is impossible. *The Platonic Wife* yields a double moral: overtly, Lady Frankland must learn that she is not entitled to have her demands for romance within marriage met and that she requires the protection of her husband to live with happiness and reputation; covertly, however, the play suggests that as soon as a good woman relinquishes her demand for romance within marriage as an entitlement, her husband will give her romance, indeed, romantic adulation as a free gift. Despite his initial resistance to Lady Frankland's demands for romance, the hero of the comedy, Lord Frankland, is like the heroes of *The Delicate Distress:* fundamentally virtuous, intelligent, sensitive, capable of strong feeling, and able to adore a woman. While they are separated, he spends hours gazing at her portrait; when she attempts a reconciliation by having the portrait repainted to show herself a penitent, he understands its meaning instantly and rushes to her.

Griffith's use of Marmontel as a source in *The Platonic Wife* and her continued involvement with contemporary French literature during her career are symptomatic of the closeness of French and English literature during the mid-eighteenth century. In drama and fiction, writers in both countries tried to create new kinds of works that would be more "natural," less "artificial"; more engaged with representations of "ordinary" domestic life and less concerned with public events; and more committed to the exploration and representation of "virtue." Philosophically, the Neoplatonism of the third Earl of Shaftesbury was further developed into progressive enlightenment ideologies that emphasized human capacity for good and argued that an important function of art was to provide representations of virtue that could provoke further ethical exploration and inspire imitation.

*The Platonic Wife* is very much in the spirit of contemporary French drama, which was interested in domestic subjects, moral problems, and characters of refined sensibility, but Griffith's next play, *The Double Mistake* (1766), was a more old-fashioned comedy of courtship and intrigue. *The Double Mistake* is Griffith's only experiment with the Spanish *capa y espada* play, being ultimately based on Calderón's *No siempre lo peor es cierto* (1652), probably through the mediation of George Digby's loose translation, *Elvira; or the Worst Not Always Certain* (1667). As happened all too often in commercial plays written by women, and despite her own eagerness to learn about the classics, Griffith here indulges in incidental satire directed at a learned lady interested in ancient Greek and Hebrew. When mistakes lead the hero to suspect, wrongly, that the heroine is unfaithful, he renounces any further "serious connection with any of the sex" and spouts misogynistic common-places: "damn'd smiling mischiefs all!—I will, henceforth, see, and admire the pretty baubles, as I wou'd a fine piece of China, but no more attribute worth and honour to them, than malleability to that . . . ."[7] Events show him his errors, and the heroine, Emily Southern, makes his trusting her honor a condition of their marriage, a condition he is, by the fifth act, happy to accept. For her part, Emily has wanted marriage all along; she articulates an understanding of woman's proper role that seems to reflect Griffith's own: "by nature and by providence design'd, our helpless sex's strength lies in dependence; and where we are so blest to meet with generous natures, our servitude is empire . . . ."[8]

Thanks to the *Genuine Letters,* we know more about the composition of *The Delicate Distress* than is usually known about the genesis of an eighteenth-century novel. Richard and Elizabeth were living apart during most of the composition of their *Two Novels,* Elizabeth in and near London, Richard in Ireland or travelling to and from Ireland on various legal and electioneering matters. With rare exceptions, the letters in *Genuine Letters* are not dated, but they occasionally refer to events that can help establish dates, and they can also be correlated with the surviving correspondence between Elizabeth and David Garrick, the famous actor and theater manager, in which her letters are dated.[9]

Elizabeth seems to have begun writing *The Delicate Distress* in 1766 and to have continued working on it almost until its publication in June of 1769. During these years, she was also trying to establish herself as a playwright, proposing various projects and submitting several scripts to David Garrick, not always with success. She certainly completed a version of Diderot's *drame, Le Père de famille* (1758), which Garrick rejected, and almost certainly at least one other play, neither performed nor published. More happily, with Garrick's assistance, she finished a successful adaptation of Beaumarchais's first play, *Eugenié,* first performed as *The School for Rakes* at Drury Lane on 4 February 1769. Elizabeth discusses her progress on these dramatic projects and on her novel in letters to Richard published in *Genuine Letters,* volumes five and six.

During the process of composition, Richard encouraged Elizabeth to finish her novel by praising her abilities, by offering to help promote it, and by engaging in friendly competition over whether husband or wife would finish first. Not too long before Richard's birthday, on St. Patrick's Day 1767, Elizabeth announced that she had finished volume one, but lamented that "the Booksellers will give nothing worth taking for it. . . . They say that they do not dispute the Merit of it, but that while the Public continue equally to buy a bad Thing as a good one, they do not think an Author can reasonably expect that they will make a Difference in the Price" (*GL* 5:15). To this despondency, Richard replies from Dublin with the news that he has "printed Subscription proposals already" and the observation that, given the disappearance of literary patronage, "this is the only Way of publishing in the present Times" (*GL* 5:17). *Two Novels* was eventually published by subscription, although it was also dedicated to the Duke of Bedford, who, with the Duchess of Bedford, did seem to keep the couple's hopes alive that literary patronage was not yet utterly extinguished.

The practice of publishing by subscription arose in the late seventeenth century, at first as a way to provide up-front capital to pay for the production of expensive books (like scholarly books that required Greek or Hebrew type or scientific books that required illustration) which were likely to have small readerships. Authors or others on their behalf collected money from individual subscribers before the book was printed and gave the money to the printers, who were thus insured against a large loss. Copies were then printed to be delivered to subscribers and anyone else who could be induced to buy them. By the mid-eighteenth century many more ordinary books were published by subscription; on occasion, subscribers complained of having been induced to part with their money on behalf of writers who never produced the promised books. Lists of subscribers, printed in the resulting books, were also a form of advertising. Names of the socially prominent or recognized literary names added cachet; like twentieth-century puffs printed on dust jackets, famous names were supposed to assist sales. Some subscription campaigns for books by women writers were designed more as genteel charitable relief than as ways of financing the production of books readers especially wanted.

Griffith's sensitivity to these realities of subscription publication is evident in her reply to Richard's news. Although she is encouraged by his support, she adds: "I dislike the Idea of *Subscriptions*. I spurn Contributions, though even voluntary. This but adds to the *Title* of my novel, by encreasing *The Delicate Distress*" (*GL* 5: 18–19). Despite her scruples, *Two Novels* appeared with a list of 227 subscribers, many Irish or residents of Ireland, like the Bishops of Clogher, Corke, and Cloyne; 59 subscribers were women. Among the notable subscribers were David Garrick, Mrs. Clive (probably Kitty Clive, the gifted comic actress), Dr. Goldsmith (probably Oliver Goldsmith), Edmund Burke, and Doctor Samuel Johnson.

Despite Griffith's unease over the prospect of subscription publication, her spirits were high enough that she jokingly invented a more lucrative marketing strategy: having their little daughter translate *The Delicate Distress* for her French lessons, then sending the French translation "to be printed at Geneva, or the Hague, with an advertisement, setting forth, that it was *forbid to be published in France*, on *Pain of the Bastille.*" Dangerous French books were frequently published in Switzerland or Holland, or in France with false imprints that claimed they had been published in Switzerland or Holland. Like many authors of edifying works, Griffith chafed at the realization that scandal and sensationalism were more valuable to the market than edification. Her marketing scheme, or *"ruse d'Auteur,"* she speculated, would at least make *The Delicate Distress* sell on the continent, "upon a Supposition that it contains nothing but Blasphemy or Treason; which may make a comfortable Portion for our little *Mademoiselle*" (*GL* 5:19).

By late 1766 or early 1767, Richard writes that he has almost finished *The Gordian Knot;* he notes "from the Number of pages" Elizabeth sends him, that she is proceeding more slowly; and urges her on: ". . . I don't care to publish without you. Hand in Hand, as Heart in Heart, let us march together through Life—Amen!" (*GL* 5:39). Both of them complain of various illnesses. Elizabeth laments that she holds her pen with pain (*GL* 5:112) and has difficulties with her eyes that make reading and writing impossible (*GL* 5:138, 165). She is also depressed by Garrick's resistance to her translation of Diderot's *Père de famille* and by objections to her "Tragedy" (*GL* 5:124). Garrick actively disliked French *comédie larmoyante. Père de famille,* though very important in the development of Diderot's dramatic theory, was ill-suited to the commercial stage in either France or England. Nevertheless, Elizabeth rather grimly resolves to complete her novel, writing to Richard: "I will follow your Example, and do every Thing, likely or unlikely, to serve my Family; and if all my Efforts fail, I must e'en let Posterity shift for itself. . . . There is a kind of Pleasure even in unsuccessful Efforts made towards Duty" (*GL* 5:124).

Like many women writers at mid-century and also like several of the more retiring male poets and sentimental writers of the day, Elizabeth disclaims ambition for fame and confesses timidity at the consequences of publication:

> I never was designed for an Author, and feel no Pride in Fame—
> therefore nought but Profit ever shapes my Quill. I have none of that
> charming, flattering Enthusiasm about me, that should support one's
> Spirits when their Works are left to the Mercy of the Public. On the

contrary, I shrink into nothing on such Occasions, and the Woman feels the Mortification that the Writer fears.

This may proceed possibly from one of two Causes. I am either too nice a Critic to be satisfied with my own Works, or else too proud to bear any other Person's Censure . . . . [*GL* 5:124–25]

A writer would not have to have been especially sensitive to have been mortified by *The Critical Review*'s scornful dismissal of *Amana:* the writer "seems to have a fine lady's disease, the vapours; as appears by her fancying herself a POETESS, and her performance a dramatic poem."[10] Richard's income apparently was not sufficient to support his small family (which included Elizabeth, a small daughter, and a son they were trying to place in the East India Company or in a bank), so Elizabeth's determination to work for money in one of the very few genteel occupations open to women is natural enough. Yet, in addition to what we believe was a real and not unintelligent deference to the views of gentlemen possessed of better education (like her husband) or more extensive professional experience (like Garrick), she also, on occasion, considered her own work superior to that of some of her male rivals, and—perhaps ill-advisedly—was prepared to argue with Garrick over matters theatrical.[11]

*Two Novels* was announced in *The St. James's Chronicle* and in the *London Chronicle* as "This Day Published" in London on 3 June 1769. The title page advertised *Two Novels. In Letters. By the Authors of Henry and Frances. In four volumes* and offered an epigraph from the description of rumor's house and the crowds of people who gather there in Ovid's *Metamorphoses,* "Hi narrata ferunt alio: mensuraque ficti / Crescit; et auditis aliquid novus adjicit auctor" (Book 12, ll. 57–58). ([Some fill idle ears with stories,] others go far-off to tell / What they have heard, and every story grows, / And each new teller adds to what he hears.)

The "delicate distress" at the center of Elizabeth's novel is that the heroine, Lady Woodville, comes to believe that her husband, Lord Woodville, to whom she has been married for only a few months, has again fallen in love with a French marchioness he loved before he knew his wife. The situation of a wife who suspects that her husband may be unfaithful was a well-established topos in bourgeois drama and the sentimental novel, familiar, for example, in Colley Cibber's play, *The Careless Husband* (1704) or in the second part of Samuel Richardson's *Pamela* (1742), in which an Italian countess appears as a rival to the newly-married Pamela. Literature and contemporary conduct books agreed that good wives, in such circumstances, ought never to upbraid their husbands, but instead, ought to suffer in silence, praying that displays of their own self-control and virtue—coupled with the likelihood that the husband would eventually become bored with his mistress—would ultimately recall husbands to their obligations to their wives. In the refined and "delicate" version of this plot that Griffith develops, Lord Woodville's errors are emotional rather than physical; he yearns for the marchioness, but never commits adultery. To an "insensible" ordinary reader—say, one like Fielding's Squire Western—Lady Woodville therefore has no problem and nothing of which to complain. But for readers of sensibility and delicacy, for whom states of mind may be more important than material realities, her suffering—and his, since he is a gentlemen of refinement and scruple—is worth taking seriously.

While many male writers were also interested in characters of sensibility, for women writers the values of sensibility had particular ideological appeal, and, often, a combative edge in the war between the sexes. Sensibility, from this perspective, expressed utopian longings like those earlier expressed in romance, longings which some women writers believed ought to be gratified and which a few women writers even hoped would be gratified. What for some women novelists of sensibility were serious representations of desirably sensitive men and admirably high-principled women often seemed to more "common-sensical" male reviewers absurdly unrealistic and silly characters.

Griffith's title suggests her awareness of contemporary debates over sensibility and delicacy, debates in which conduct that for some demonstrated admirable scrupulosity for others seemed, at best, foolish affectation, and, at worst, entanglement in dangerous and destructive illusion. The conduct of the characters in Rousseau's *La Nouvelle Héloïse* (1761), one of the greatest of the novels of sensibility, was debated throughout Europe. Some agreed with Rousseau that Julie and her lover St.-Preux were superior people, gifted with exquisitely feeling hearts and extraordinary capacities for virtue, others found their examples absurd, grotesque, dangerous, or evil (in various combinations). While none of Griffith's plots go so far as Rousseau's in depicting the return to virtue of a woman who has knowingly been guilty of fornication, the women characters in *The Delicate Distress* express sympathy for "the unhappy victims of love" (170) and Griffith describes Rousseau as "sensible, tender, ingenious, and philosophic. He is, in my Mind, a fine Writer in many Particulars, and is possessed of a Species of Enthusiasm that serves to ripen Virtue" (*GL* 6:27). The debates over sensibility and delicacy were as lively in England as in France. Griffith's fellow Irishman, Hugh Kelly, for example, capitalized on them in his comedy *False Delicacy* (1769), in which a young widow, scrupulously and romantically faithful to her first love, falls in love with Lord Winworth, but rejects his suit.

The structure of *The Delicate Distress* reveals both its descent from the French romance and Griffith's engagement with the new bourgeois art championed by Richardson, Rousseau, and Diderot. In both seventeenth-century French romance and in the new novel as practiced by Richardson and Rousseau, plot was often subordinated to discussion of urgent questions: amorous, social, ethical, and philosophical. Characters exist not merely to have adventures, but to express opinions and to debate issues. Diderot praises Richardson for having written novels that make his readers' conversation "all the more interesting and lively," that prompt readers to discuss and to analyze "questions concerning morality and taste."[12] In *The Delicate Distress* Lady Straffon advances a proposition the truth of which is still worth debating: "The passions of the human mind, are, I fear, as little under our command, as the motions of our pulse:—you have, therefore, just as much reason to resent your husband's becoming enamoured of another person, as you would have to be offended, at his having a fever" (145). The idea that passion is an involuntary affliction was common to such very different seventeenth-century writers as Racine and Aphra Behn, yet, by the mid-eighteenth century, particularly for women writers, neither Lady Straffon's first claim that passions are not controllable nor her deduction from it that wives are therefore not entitled to resent their husbands' unfaithfulness could command untroubled assent. Some of the questions to be debated in *The Delicate Distress* are transhistorical, for example, Is women's curiosity productive of good or evil? Others more directly reflect the social dilemmas, particularly the social dilemmas of women, in the period: Ought a wife to risk the health of her children by inoculating them against smallpox without telling her husband? Ought a woman who has been wronged by a man tell her male relations of her injury, knowing that they will feel obliged to defend her honor by dueling and thus risk their own lives? Are children ever justified in marrying when their parents oppose their choice?

As in the French romances, in *The Delicate Distress* intercalated stories offer variations on the plight of the principal personages and more "adventures" that in one way or another bear on the central questions of passion and reason and the duties of children, wives, and husbands. Sometimes, in the mode of the older romances, a story is told by a mysterious stranger encountered by the protagonists. Thus, the Italian Lady Somerville, offering hospitality to some of the protagonists when they are stranded by a carriage accident, tells how she came to marry an English lord against her parents' objections and of how that choice led her to a rural retirement. More often, in a more eighteenth-century mode, the intercalated stories are those of women in Lady Woodville's immediate circle and are presented as "memoirs" or "histories."

Like Richardson in *Clarissa* and Rousseau in *La Nouvelle Héloïse,* Griffith in *The Delicate Distress* conducts her epistolary narrative by having groups of correspondents with different points of view and quite different access to information. The very different concerns of the masculine world and the feminine world are dramatized by the contrasts between, on the one hand, the letters between Lord Woodville and his friend Lord Seymour, and, on the other hand, those between Lady Woodville and her older sister Lady Straffon. Although Griffith's French contemporary Madame Riccoboni in her epistolary novels almost always preferred the simpler approach of having only one principal letter writer whose letters are addressed to another whose letters do not appear, we think Ernest Baker in *The History of the English Novel* was nevertheless reasonable in calling Griffith "a follower of Madame Riccoboni," who "could handle conflicts of feeling with restraint and delicacy."[13]

Like Griffith, Riccoboni began as a professional actress; she then, in 1751, began publishing epistolary novels, many of which had English characters. Riccoboni's *Lettres de Mylady Juliette Catesby à Mylady Henrietta Camply, son amie* (1759) features a fiancé, Lord Ossory, who two years earlier inexplicably deserted the heroine to marry another woman. Eventually we discover that he has done so because, despite his love for Juliette, in a moment of infidelity, he had impregnated a girl he then felt obliged to marry. (This novel was promptly translated by Frances Brooke as *Letters from Juliet, Lady Catesby, to her friend, Lady Henrietta Campley* [1760] and influenced Frances Brooke's own fiction, although obviously Griffith was able to read Riccoboni in French.) In *Lettres de Mylady Juliette* and *Histoire de Miss Jenny* (1764)—the story of an ill-used illegitimate heroine—Riccoboni uses letters from the heroines that are in some respects like memoirs; sometimes the heroines quote or enclose key letters from others. Like Richardson and unlike Riccoboni, Griffith has a significant number of letters written by male characters, but like Riccoboni and like earlier, mostly non-epistolary, women novelists including Delarivière Manley and Eliza Haywood, Griffith concentrates on the dilemmas and sufferings produced by love and offers a copious catalogue of the injuries men are capable of inflicting on women. Lady Straffon in *The Delicate Distress* observes, "When I was very young, I used to be surprized that so many tragedies, and novels, were founded on the perfidy of men: but I have, for some years past, been perfectly convinced, that most of the miseries in this life, owe their being to that fatal source" (47).

The settings in *The Delicate Distress* express the mid-eighteenth-century delight in rural elegance and belief in the healing power of natural spas. Like Rousseau's Monsieur and Madame de Wolmar, although with less practical involvement in gardening and farming, Lord and Lady Woodville and the other virtuous characters in *The Delicate Distress* much prefer the innocent pleasures of their country estates to more corrupting urban entertainments. They ornament their grounds with rustic or classicizing buildings, sing and dance out of doors, and plan *fêtes champêtres* only slightly more robust and homely than those depicted in François Boucher. Perhaps the quintessential entertainment in the novel is that devised by Lord Woodville for his wife and house guests. Grateful for the services of the wet nurse who cared for him when he was an infant, he has provided an idyllic cottage on a river in the neighborhood for her and her family. One fine day, he conducts his new bride to pay a courtesy call on this humble family, introduces her to the silver-haired widow and her daughter, then contrives a dinner composed of rustic food provided by the cottagers and wine and cold provisions provided by himself. The wet nurse sheds tears of sentiment at Lord Woodville's thoughtfulness, but Lady Woodville writes her more explicitly feminist appreciation that Woodville condescends to concern himself with wet-nursing, "a point, which the foolish lords of the creation, generally think below them" (66).

Even in London and Paris, which the characters visit more out of necessity than desire, the preferred sites are the famous urban pleasure gardens of the day, Ranelagh in London or the Tuileries in Paris. At Ranelagh, visitors could combine walking in formal gardens with listening to music, either outdoors or in a large rotunda contemporaries compared to the Roman Pantheon. Many of the entertainments were of popular theater music and pageants, but visitors in June of 1764 would have heard Mozart, then eight years old, playing his original compositions on the harpsichord and the organ. Lord Woodville in *The Delicate Distress* decides to make an excursion to the north of England to attend the horse races, another fashionable diversion. According to *The History and Antiquities of the City of York* (1785), by 1753:

the resort of the nobility and gentry to York during the races was so considerable, that a subscription was opened by them for erecting a grand Stand on Knavesmire [the pasture ground outside the city where the race course was located] for the purpose of conveniently seeing the horses run. A considerable sum of money being raised, a building proper for the purpose was accordingly designed . . . and was completed in the year 1754. On the ground floor are convenient offices and rooms for the entertainment of the company; above which, on the second floor, is a large room for all the company to meet in, which is surrounded by a projecting mirador upwards of two hundred feet in length, supported by a rusticated arcade fifteen feet high above ground, from which mirador the company can command a prosect of the whole race-ground.[14]

The most delicate characters shy away even from the public pleasure gardens, preferring private houses or the spas that contemporaries believed had healing powers. Attempting to recover from his loss of Charlotte, Lord Seymour repairs to Bristol Hot Wells; Lord Woodville similarly thinks to take Lady Woodville there after her trials and illness. The spa at Bristol was smaller than its more famous neighbor, the spa at Bath. The chief spring gushed from an opening at the foot of St. Vincent's rock and was visible at low tide at ten feet above the water level of the Avon river; the temperature of the water was seventy-six degrees. Pumps raised the water into Hotwell House, built on a small rocky ledge jutting out into the river. Physicians were inclined to believe that only they could properly prescribe the appropriate uses of spa waters for the many diseases for which they were thought to have therapeutic value; contemporary scientists tried to analyze their composition, as, for example, Alexander Sutherland, a Bristol physician, did in The Nature and Qualities of Bristol Waters, Illustrated by Experiments and Observations with Practical Reflections on Bath Waters Occasionally Interspersed (London, 1758). The waters were thought to be more efficacious when drunk direct from the pump, but the water was also bottled to be sold in the streets of Bristol and to be shipped to more distant locations. (Richard Griffith, seeking relief from his own ailments at the Scarborough spa at one point during the composition of Two Novels, wrote to Elizabeth, "I have sent you a Hamper of this Spaw, and shall flatter myself, the next Week, with an idea of our both drinking out of the same Font together, at the same Time" [GL 2:75].) The fashionable procedure for drinking the waters directly was to ride in a carriage to the Pump Room, drink the prescribed number of glasses, and then sit chatting and listening to the music of a small orchestra. There was a tree-lined promenade along the bank of the Avon for strolling; sailing on the river and horseback riding on the Downs were also available for those whose health permitted.[15]

The sturdy twentieth-century reader may become impatient with *Delicate Distress* characters whose constitutions seem to respond so often to disappointments in love with obscure but dangerous and supposedly life-threatening fevers and wasting syndromes. While fevers were regularly resorted to by sentimental novelists, it is also useful to remember that in the eighteenth century many diseases, infectious and otherwise, could not very successfully be diagnosed or differentiated from one another. Moreover, a sufferer was fortunate to be treated with an innocuous remedy, like spa water, most of which at least did no harm, rather than with one of the other standard treatments, like bleeding or mercury, that might well make him or her sicker and weaker than the disease itself. Almost no therapeutic interventions of the day did much good and, for all a sufferer knew, what we dismiss as an inconsequential cold or the flu might be the beginning of a fatal illness.

Of the *Two Novels, The Delicate Distress* has fared a bit better with the original reviewers and with posterity than *The Gordian Knot.* Neither of the two major monthly magazines that reviewed novels at mid-century were inclined to take novels very seriously. The long lead reviews in both *The Critical Review* and *The Monthly Review* in 1769 featured volumes of Catherine Macaulay's *History of England,* Robertson's *History of the Reign of the Emperor Charles V,* and the *Philosophical Transactions* of the Royal Society; novels, considered a lightweight genre, were relegated to briefer notices at the backs of the magazines. Novel reviews in this period normally offered little more than plot summary, sample quotations, and very brief evaluative judgments. Reviewers often expressed annoyance at having to plough through yet another trivial or sentimental novel and used arch or condescending tones. Whether a novel had a morally improving tendency for impressionable young minds was apt to be a more significant issue for reviewers than any consideration of what we might now discuss as narrative technique. Reviewers, however, did quite vigorously attempt to police the representations of novels by denouncing certain characters or situations as improbable or not "natural." Such reviewers were especially likely to be hostile to sentimental male characters. One complained, for example, that in *True Delicacy: or the*

*History of Lady Frances Tylney and Henry Cecil, Esq.* (1769), "Cecil, Sir William Revil, and Col. Tylney, possess all the delicacy of sentiment becoming petticoats . . . ."[16]

The *Critical Review* took the usual condescending tone toward *Two Novels,* though concluding, "It would look like ill-nature to throw out any more animadversions upon compositions which, in many places, have real merit, and, through the whole, discover a virtuous tendency."[17] The reviewer finds Lord Woodville early in the novel "excessively fond" of his wife and complains that "the reader . . . foresees that he is to be served up with the old puppet-shew of a combat between love and duty" (*CR,* 133). He also dislikes the number of novelists who find "the Roman catholic, much more convenient for their purpose than the protestant, religion" (*CR,* 133), apparently because he considers Roman Catholicism irrelevant to the real concerns of English life and because novelists use it for a kind of cheap sensationalism inappropriate to serious fiction.

While it is true that English novelists at mid-century did have recourse to Roman Catholicism well before the rage for convents and monasteries in gothic fiction, it is also true that religion was an important issue at mid-century; that Griffith came from Ireland, a country in which the overwhelming majority of people were Roman Catholics; and that confinement in convents and monasteries was what we might now call a hot human rights issue throughout Europe in the 1760s. Characters and readers alike debated the propriety of the agreement between Richardson's hero, Sir Charles Grandison, and his Italian and Roman Catholic fiancée, Clementina, that sons of their marriage should be brought up as Protestants and daughters as Roman Catholics. Voltaire, who was denied permission to live in France, campaigned on behalf of a Protestant father accused of murdering a daughter who had been detained in a convent, escaped, and then committed suicide (*Avis au public sur les parricides,* 1765). Voltaire also semi-officially adopted a young girl he rescued from a convent and married to the Marquis de Villette.[18] Griffith's use of convents partly reflects this progressive horror at the fact that French families and officials had the power to confine women in these institutions against their wills.

At the same time, like other women writers, including Mary Astell and Sarah Scott, Griffith could imagine that beleaguered women could use some form of convent or "Protestant nunnery" for voluntary refuge and self-cultivation. The heroine in Griffith's later novel, *The History of Lady Barton,* supposes another woman character can only be safe in a convent:

You are sufficiently acquainted [w]ith my sentiments on the subject of monasteries, to know how very unwilling I should be to recommend a state of seclusion to any creature I either love or esteem; yet, in her unhappy situation, I see no other resource. . . .

Not but that I should approve extremely of an establishment of this kind, in our own country, under our own religion and laws; but equally free from tyranny—An asylum for unhappy women to retreat to—not from the world, but from the misfortunes, or the slander of it—for female orphans, young widows, or still more unhappy objects, forsaken, or ill treated wives, to betake themselves to, in such distresses. For in all these circumstances, women who live alone, have need of something more than either prudence or a fair character, to guard them from rudeness or censure.

Now some sort of foundation, under the government of a respectable matronage, endowed for such a purpose, would certainly be an institution most devoutly to be wished for, as a relief in the difficulties of those situations I have just mentioned. Here women might enjoy all the pleasures and advantages of living still in the world, have their conduct reciprocally vouched by one another, and be screened from those artful and insidious essays, which young or pretty women, when once become helpless adjectives of society, are generally liable to.[19]

Moreover, without endorsing the theology that supports the election of a cloistered life, Griffith deeply respects the capacity of women for heroic renunciation. She knew Madame de Lafayette's great novel The Princess of Clèves, which ends with the heroine, despite her attraction to a man who has offered her the prospect of adulterous passion and then offers to marry her when she becomes a widow, instead electing to enter a convent. That a woman, in order to preserve her own dignity, self-respect, and fidelity to what she believes to be a high standard of virtue, might refuse a legal and socially acceptable marriage to a decent man made sense to women writers like Madame de Lafayette and Elizabeth Griffith, but was likely to befuddle male critics. Charlotte Beaumont in The Delicate Distress rejects Lord Seymour's proposal of marriage and determines to enter a French convent as a nun. Not only has she learned that she is illegitimate, but she has also vowed that if God will allow her brother to live after he has been wounded in an unfortunate duel with Lord Seymour, she will become a nun (her brother does live). Refusing to recognize Charlotte's motives, the writer in the Critical Review registers the clash between the perspectives of sentiment and those of common sense, describing Charlotte as a young lady, who, in the novel-stile, has exquisite beauty, sensibility, and delicacy, as well as virtue; but whom in the language of common life, we should be apt to call foolish, fantastic, and hare-brained. This paragon shuts herself up in a convent, to seclude herself forever from his lordship, whom she passionately adores, for no manner of reason that we can see, but to give the author an opportunity of throwing upon paper a profusion of impracticable reveries, in the disguise of religion and sentiment.[20]

*The Monthly Review,* in a much shorter notice, and after jocular persiflage about the two authors as like two riders in a skimmington, pronounced *The Delicate Distress* an "interesting tale, embellished with an agreeable variety of characters . . . some very affecting incidents; and . . . natural easy language." *The Gordian Knot* it found "less sprightly and less pleasing," though it recognized Richard as "a good moralist, and man of sense."[21]

The London edition of *Two Novels* was followed later in 1769 by a Dublin edition: *Two Novels. In Letters. By the Authors of Henry and Frances* (Dublin: P. Wilson, J. Exshaw, H. Saunders, W. Sleater, B. Grierson, D. Chamberlaine, J. Potts, J. Hoey, and J. Williams). This may have been the edition about which Richard wrote cheerfully from Ireland: "Your Novel is in great Request in this Country. The Bishop *speaks of it*. A very pretty Miss Berkley sat up reading it all Night, and her Attention was so great, that she suffered her Cap to take Fire, but said, that she *quenched it with her Tears*" (*GL* 6:211). Both novels were quickly translated into French, hers as *La Situation critique, historie intéresante traduite de l'anglois* (Amsterdam and Paris, 1770), his as *Le Noeud gordien* (Paris, 1770). After 1769, more successful than *The Gordian Knot, The Delicate Distress* appeared alone, once as *The Delicate Distress. A Novel, in Letters: In Two Volumes* (Dublin: T. Walker, 1775), and later as *The Delicate Distress; A Novel. In Letters. By Frances* (Dublin: Printed by Brett Smith, for the United Company of Booksellers, 1787). In 1775, in Richard Brinsley Sheridan's comedy *The Rivals,* Lydia Languish sends her maid to fetch a list of books she wants from the Bath circulating libraries or booksellers. *The Delicate Distress* is among those books so popular as to be unobtainable on the day of this errand; Lydia has to settle for *The Gordian Knot,* Sterne's *Sentimental Journey,* and a few others the maid has been able to procure.

We have chosen the London edition of 1769 as our copy text. The Dublin edition of 1769 appears to have been set from this London edition;

the Dublin 1775 from Dublin 1769; and Dublin 1789 from Dublin 1775. In general, the text becomes progressively corrupt in the succeeding editions. There is no clear evidence of authorial revision, although some small stylistic revisions in Dublin 1769 may go a little beyond what one would expect of printers' corrections. Elizabeth was in and around London in 1769, but the possibility exists that Richard was in Dublin and made some small changes in the Dublin edition, changes she would probably have accepted had he made them. But, since we believe that it is more probable than not that all the variants in the Dublin editions are the work of the printers, we have considered them as suggesting possible emendations but have not treated them as having authority.

This critical edition text incorporates all the revisions published in the London 1769 lists of errata and also makes a variety of emendations to correct other errors. We have not normalized English spellings nor have we modernized the system of punctuation in the London 1769 edition. Variations in spellings of the same word were still normal and generally acceptable in the 1760s, although the movement toward invariant spelling had begun. Griffith certainly used variant spellings of the same word, and the compositors who set *The Delicate Distress* also appear comfortable with variant spellings. Believing that the principle "to regularize is to modernize" is still relevant for this text of 1769, we have not attempted to regularize spelling. Moreover, recent work on language has emphasized how radically different from our modern rules earlier principles of grammar and punctuation were. In earlier periods, written English was closer to being understood as a representation of various spoken Englishes rather than as a regularized "correct" representation of a standard, logical English. Earlier grammars explaining punctuation presented the several symbols of punctuation mainly as markers of pauses of varying lengths in utterances: punctuation was not earlier understood "to signal the grammatical or structural units of discourse."[22] Especially in theatrical texts, with which Griffith was of course very familiar, heavy use of punctuation, or "pointing," constituted directions to actors about where to breathe as they delivered their lines. In editing Griffith, there is a temptation to emend away a considerable number of commas in the copy texts as frank errors, for example, those commas that separate subjects and verbs, in violation of one of our modern rules. Gradually, however, we developed an appreciation of the different procedures of these and other contemporary texts and learned to abstain from such emendations. It should be emphasized, however, that what we have preserved in these accidentals cannot be claimed to represent Griffith's practice in the manuscript of *The Delicate Distress* (which has not survived), but only contemporary professional practices to which we believe she consented. We follow the London copy text in all cases of what we consider indifferent variants, but we have tried not to let our decision against modernizing make us craven about emending actual errors in the English text.

In treating French words and phrases, we have been more aggressive in emending and normalizing the spelling to acceptable 1760s French spellings because we believe the authority of the London text to be weak here. We observe that both the English and the Irish printers had particular difficulty with the French phrases in the text and we believe Griffith would have wanted her French to be correct. French spellings were closer to being normalized in the 1760s than English spellings were. We have used Abel Boyer's *Dictionnaire Royal François-Anglois et Anglois-Françoise* (London, 1764 and Lyon, 1768) as our authority in dealing with French words.

*The Delicate Distress* contains a significant number of quotations, which we have done our best to identify, although we have not been entirely successful. In cases where we believe misquotations are accidental, we have emended by correcting substantives from a source to which Griffith could have had access. In cases where she altered others' texts to fit her own purposes, we have, of course, not interfered. As contemporary practice made no effort to reproduce accidentals of quotations, we have not done so either.

All of our emendations to the London 1769 copy text are recorded in the list of emendations printed at the back of this book. Certain non-textual features of the London copy text have been silently altered: long *s*, printing of initial word or words of paragraphs in capitals, marking quotations with quotation marks flush left on each line. A fuller textual apparatus, including textual notes, historical collations, and word division lists will appear in Cynthia B. Ricciardi's forthcoming Brandeis dissertation. Her textual notes will also contain discussion of the problems raised by the simultaneous presence in the text of 1) French words used as French words, 2) French words that were on their way to becoming English words or that had recently become English words, and 3) French words that might have seemed to some in 1769 to be becoming English words but that failed to do so.

## NOTES

1. The only analogue we have discovered is the private publication at their Hogarth Press of *Two Stories Written and Printed by Virginia Woolf and L. S. Woolf* (Richmond: Hogarth Press, 1917).

2. *A Series of Genuine Letters between Henry and Frances* (London, 1770), 5:280. Vols. 1 and 2 were first published in 1757; vols. 3 and 4 first published in 1766; and vols. 5 and 6 in 1770. Subsequent references to *Genuine Letters (GL)* will be cited in the text.

3. J. M. S. Tompkins, *The Polite Marriage* (Cambridge: Univ. Press, 1938), pp. 26–27.

4. Philip H. Highfill Jr., Kalman A. Burnim, and Edward A. Langhans, *A Biographical Dictionary of Actors, Actresses, Musicians, Dancers, Managers and Other Stage Personnel in London, 1660–1800* (Carbondale: Southern Illinois Univ. Press, 1973–93), s.vv. "Griffith, Elizabeth," "Griffith, Richard" (brother), "Griffith, Thomas" (father). For corrections to the "Elizabeth Griffith" entry, see the later entry for "Miss Kennedy."

5. See Susan Staves, "French Fire, English Asbestos: Ninon de Lenclos and Elizabeth Griffith," *Studies on Voltaire and the Eighteenth Century* 314 (1993): 193–205.

6. [Elizabeth Griffith], *Amana. A Dramatic Poem* (London, 1764), p. 45.

7. Elizabeth Griffith, *The Double Mistake. A Comedy* (Dublin, 1766), p. 17.

8. *Double Mistake,* p. 8.

9. *The Private Correspondence of David Garrick. . .,* ed. James Boaden, 2 vols. (London, 1831–32), prints both Griffith's and Garrick's letters, although *The Letters of David Garrick,* ed. David M. Little and George M. Kahrl, 3 vols. (Cambridge, Mass.: Belknap Press, Harvard Univ., 1963) offers more authoritative versions of the Garrick letters. Griffith's manuscript letters have also been microfilmed by the Victoria and Albert Museum.

10. *Critical Review* 19 (Mar. 1765): 235.

11. Note the discussions of the Garrick/Griffith correspondence in George Winchester Stone and George M. Kahrl, *David Garrick: A Critical Biography* (Carbondale: Southern Illinois Univ. Press, 1979), pp. 598–99, and Betty Rizzo, "'Depressa Resurgam': Elizabeth Griffith's Playwriting Caree r," in *Curtain Calls: British and American Women and the Theater, 1660–1820,* ed. Mary Anne Schofield and Cecilia Macheski (Athens: Ohio Univ. Press, 1991), pp. 120–42. We are inclined to be more sympathetic to Garrick's concerns and to the limitations circumstances placed on the time and attention he had to spare for Griffith than either Griffith herself or Rizzo.

12. Denis Diderot, "In Praise of Richardson" (1762), in *Selected Writings on Art and Literature,* trans. Geoffrey Bremner (London: Penguin, 1994), p. 88.

13. Ernest Baker, *The History of the English Novel, Vol. 5, The Novel of Sentiment and the Gothic Romance* (London: H. F. & G. Witherby, 1934), p. 149.

14. Quoted in Charles Barton Knight, *A History of the City of York,* 2d ed. (York and London: Herald Printing Works, 1944), p. 543.

15. Vincent Waite, "The Bristol Hotwell," in Patrick McGrath, ed. *Bristol in the Eighteenth Century* (Newton Abbot: David and Charles, 1972), pp. 109–26.

16. *Critical Review* 29 (1770): 151.

17. *Critical Review* 28 (1769): 142.

18. Robert Niklaus, *A Literary History of France: The Eighteenth Century, 1715–1789* (London: Ernest Benn, 1970), p. 162.

19. Elizabeth Griffith, *The History of Lady Barton,* 3 vols. (London, 1771), 2:55–57.

20. *Critical Review* 28 (1769): 133.

21. *Monthly Review* 41 (Sept. 1769): 232–33. An additional review appeared in the *London Chronicle* 26 (1770): 233, which only added to plot summary its approval of the writer's "just and natural reflection on the impropriety of that enmity which subsists in the breasts of the worshippers [Protestant and Roman Catholic] of the same merciful and benevolent God and Saviour, whose doctrines tend to promote happiness and goodwill on earth."

22. Michael Vande Berg, "'Pictures of Pronunciation': Typographical Travels through *Tristram Shandy* and *Jacques le fataliste,*" *Eighteenth-Century Studies* 21 (1987): 21–47. See, e.g., The Rev. John Entick, A.M., "Grammatical Introduction," *The New Spelling Dictionary, Teaching to Write and Pronounce the English Tongue. . .* (London, 1765).

# CHRONOLOGY OF EVENTS

# IN

# ELIZABETH GRIFFITH'S LIFE

~

| | |
|---|---|
| 1721 | Thomas Griffith, Elizabeth's father, an actor and a manager of Smock Alley Theatre, Dublin, appointed Master of the Revels in Ireland; holds the post until 1729. |
| 1727?, 11 Oct. | Birth of Elizabeth Griffith to Thomas Griffith and Jane Foxcroft Griffith, daughter of Richard Foxcroft, rector at Portarlington, Ireland. |
| 1734, 9 Mar. | Thomas Griffith and colleagues open Aungier Street Theatre in Dublin; Thomas also acts. |
| 1736, 8 Feb. | Thomas Griffith, in financial difficulties with Aungier Street Theatre, applies to Jonathan Swift for financial assistance. |
| 1744, 23 Jan. | Thomas Griffith dies at age 63 in Dublin. |
| 1749, 13 Oct. | Elizabeth debuts as Juliet in *Romeo and Juliet* at Smock Alley Theatre, Dublin; continues in various roles this season and the next. |
| 1750, 18 Sept. | Elizabeth's brother Richard debuts as Barnwell in Lillo's *London Merchant* at the Theatre Royal, Drury Lane, London; subsequently also appears at Bath, Winchester, Dublin, and Edinburgh. |
| 1751, 11, 18 May | Elizabeth appears as Ismene in *Meropé* (a tragedy adapted from Voltaire by Aaron Hill) at Smock Alley, Dublin. |
| 1751, 12 May? | Elizabeth marries Richard Griffith in a private ceremony. |

| | |
|---|---|
| 1752, 10 June? | Birth of a son, Richard, to Elizabeth and Richard. |
| 1753, 19 Jan. | Richard executes a will in favor of Elizabeth and his infant son. |
| 1753 | Richard's Irish linen mill fails. |
| c. 1756 | Birth of a daughter to Elizabeth and Richard; the Griffiths settle in London. |
| 1757 | Vols. 1 and 2 of *A Series of Genuine Letters between Henry and Frances* by Elizabeth and Richard published in Dublin and London. |
| 1760 | The Duke of Bedford secures a customs post for Richard; a second edition of *Genuine Letters . . . Revised, Corrected, Enlarged, and Improved* published in Dublin. |
| 1761 | Elizabeth's translation of *The Memoirs of Ninon de L'Enclos, with Her Letters to Monsr. de St. Evremond and the Marquis de Sevigné* published in London. |
| 1764 | Elizabeth's first play, *Amana. A Dramatic Poem,* published in London, but never performed; Richard's *An Extract of the History and Genealogy of the Noble Families of the Earl and Countess of Northumberland* also published. |
| 1765 | Elizabeth's comedy, *The Platonic Wife,* opens at the Theatre Royal, Drury Lane, London (24 Jan.); her brother Richard appeared in *The Platonic Wife* as Sir Harry Wilmot; play subsequently published in London and Dublin; Richard's novel, *The Triumvirate: or the Authentic Memoirs of A., B. and C.* (an imitation of Lawrence Sterne's *Tristram Shandy*), published under the pseudonym "Biographer Triglyph." |
| 1766 | Elizabeth's comedy, *The Double Mistake,* opens at the Theatre Royal, Covent Garden, London (9 Jan.); subsequently published in several editions in London and Dublin; *A Series of Genuine Letters between Henry and Frances,* vols. 3 and 4, by Elizabeth and Richard published; Richard, Elizabeth's brother, becomes manager of the Norwich theatre, continuing until 1780. |
| 1769, 4 Feb. | Elizabeth's comedy, *The School for Rakes,* opens at the |

|  | Theatre Royal, Drury Lane, London; subsequently published anonymously in London and Dublin in several editions. |
|---|---|
| 1769, June | *Two Novels. In Letters. By the Authors of Henry and Frances,* 4 vols., containing *The Delicate Distress* by Elizabeth and *The Gordian Knot* by Richard, published in London by T. Becket and P. A. De Hondt. |
| 1770 | Elizabeth's translation of *Memoirs, Anecdotes, and Characters of the Court of Lewis XIV,* by Marie-Marguerite, marquis de Caylus, published in London; *A Series of Genuine Letters between Henry and Frances,* vols. 5 and 6, by Elizabeth and Richard, published in London, all six vols. now available as a set; Richard's *Posthumous Works of a Late Celebrated Genius, Deceased* or *The Koran: or the Life, Character and Sentiments of Tria Juncta in Uno* (purporting to be the autobiography of Lawrence Sterne), published under the pseudonym "M.N.A., or Master of No Arts" in London; Richard, Elizabeth's son, appointed Bengal Writer in the East India Company. |
| 1771 | Elizabeth's *The History of Lady Barton, A Novel in Letters* and her translation of *The Shipwreck and Adventures of Monsieur Pierre Viaud, a Native of Bordeaux, and Captain of a Ship* by Jean Gaspard Dubois-Fontenelle both published in London. |
| 1772 | Elizabeth's comedy, *A Wife in the Right,* also known as *Patience the Best Remedy,* opens at the Theatre Royal, Covent Garden, London; subsequently published in London; Richard's *Something New,* with a preface signed "Automathes," published in London with an admission that *The Koran* not by Sterne. |
| 1773–79 | Elizabeth writes thirteen short stories published in *The Westminster Magazine, or The Pantheon of Taste;* subsequently collected in *Novellettes, Selected for the use of Young Ladies and Gentlemen,* along with two stories by Oliver Goldsmith and one by Mr. McMillan, published in London in 1780 and in Dublin in 1784. |

| | |
|---|---|
| 1775 | Elizabeth's *Morality of Shakespeare's Drama Illustrated* published by T. Cadell in London. |
| 1776 | Elizabeth's *Story of Lady Juliana Harley. A Novel. In Letters* published by T. Cadell in London and by a conger in Dublin. |
| 1777 | Elizabeth edits *A Collection of Novels, Selected and Revised by Mrs. Griffith,* 3 vols., published in London by G. Kearsley; Elizabeth's translation of Noel Desenfans' *Letter from Monsieur Desenfans to Mrs. Montagu* (a letter complimenting Montagu for her work on Shakespeare and defending Fenelon against Lord Chesterfield) published by T. Cadell in London. |
| 1778 | Son Richard promoted to accountant at Patna in the East India Company. |
| 1779, 2 Dec. | Elizabeth's comedy, *The Times,* opens at the Theatre Royal, Drury Lane, London; subsequently published in London and Dublin in 1780. |
| 1779–81 | Publication of *The Works of Voltaire,* ed. by William Kenrick, in 14 vols.; Elizabeth translated *The Spirit of Nations* in 4 vols.; Richard translated *The Age of Louis XIV* in 3 vols.; both contributed to the vol. of miscellanies and *The Annals of Empire.* |
| 1780, 1 Sept. | Son Richard marries Charity, daughter of John Bramston, Esq., of Oundale, Northamptonshire. |
| 1782 | Elizabeth's *Essays, Addressed to Young Married Women* published in London by T. Cadell and J. Robson. |
| 2 Feb. | Richard's *Variety, a Comedy,* acted at the Theater Royal, Drury Lane, London. |
| 1783–90 | Son Richard Griffith represents Askeaton in the Irish parliament; Elizabeth and Richard settle with son Richard at Millicent, County Kildare, in 1780s. |
| 1786 | A new edition of 6 vols. of *Genuine Letters* published by J. Bew in London. |
| 1788 | Death of Richard Griffith; *Gentleman's Magazine* obituary gives his first name as "Henry" (vol. 58, p. 271). |
| 1789, June | Death of Charity Griffith. |
| 1793, 5 Jan. | Death of Elizabeth Griffith, at Millicent, County Kildare. |

| | |
|---|---|
| 1793, 24 Feb. | Son Richard marries Mary, daughter of Walter Hussey Burgh. |
| 1795 | Elizabeth's *School for Rakes* published in *Bell's British Theatre,* vol. 30. |
| 1820, 30 June | Son Richard dies and is buried at Millicent. |

# THE
# DELICATE DISTRESS,

~

## A NOVEL.
## IN LETTERS,
## BY FRANCES.

L'amour ne peut jamais subsister, sans peine, dans une ame délicate, mais ses peines mêmes, sont, quelquefois, la source de ses plus doux plaisirs.

Recueil Anonyme.[1]

# To
## His Grace the
## Duke of Bedford.[2]

Sir,

     If a private suffrage could add fame to a public character, we should be the foremost to express our opinion of your Grace's merits; "for they who speak thy praise secure their own." But as a compliment is always intended, in an address of this nature, we shall assume the sole honour of it to ourselves, by declaring to the world, that we are some of the many, who have reason to subscribe themselves,

With respect and gratitude,
Your Grace's,
much obliged, and
most obedient servants,

Henry and Frances.

# Preface.

~

The following work is submitted to the perusal of the public, with infinite timidity, and apprehension, as it is a species of writing, which I had never attempted before, from a consciousness of my deficiency, in the principal article of such compositions, namely, invention.

The generality of NOVEL READERS may, therefore, probably, be disappointed in not meeting with any extraordinary adventure, or uncommon situation, in the following pages; while persons of a more natural taste, will, I flatter myself, be rather pleased at finding the stories and incidents, here related, such as might, for I affirm they did, and most of them to my own knowledge, certainly happen, in the various contingencies of real life.

But though I have not attempted to feign any fable, I acknowledge that I have endeavoured to conceal some truth, by changing scenes, and altering circumstances, in order to avoid too marked an application, of the several stories and characters, to the real persons, from whom I have taken my drama. We have no right, over other persons secrets, come they to our knowledge through whatsoever medium of intelligence, they may.—Accident confers none, and confidence forbids it.

As there is no fictitious memoir here related, neither is there any factitious moral displayed, to the incredulous reader, amongst all the various sentiments of this recital. I write not of puppets, but of men. I have endeavoured to describe the feelings, nay the foibles, of the human heart, such as we are naturally conscious of, in ourselves; but meddle not with *the wires of the stoics,* which only render us *machines,* by helping us to *perform a part,* of which we have *no sensation.*

I know not whether the novel, like the *épopée,*[3] has any rules, peculiar to itself—If it has, I may have innocently erred against them all, and drawn upon myself the envenomed rage of that tremendous body, the *minor crit-*

*ics.*—But if I have spread a table for them, they shall be welcome to the treat, and let them feed upon it, heartily.—Sensibility is, in my mind, as necessary, as taste, to intitle us to judge of a work, like this; and a cold criticism, formed upon *rules for writing,* can, therefore, be of no manner of use, but to enable the stupid to speak, with a seeming intelligence, of what they neither feel, nor understand.

L'Abbé Trublet,[4] in his essays, on literature and morals, says, *"Si un ouvrage sans défaut étoit possible, il ne le seroit qu'à un homme médiocre.*[5] And in another place, *"Il n'y a rien de plus différent, qu'un ouvrage sans défaut, & un ouvrage parfait."*[6]

I shall only add, that I sincerely wish the subsequent pages had fewer faults to exercise the good, or ill nature, of my several readers; but I must, now, throw myself, and my book, *with all its imperfections on its head,*[7] upon the indulgence of the public, from whom I have received many favours, and to whom I am a truly grateful, and

Most obedient servant,

FRANCES.

# VOLUME I.

~

## LETTER I.

### *Lady* WOODVILLE, *To Lady* STRAFFON.

Tell me, my dear philosophic, wise sister, why those gloomy mortals, stiled moralists, take so much pains to put us out of humour with our present state of existence, by declaring that happiness is not the lot of man, &c. &c.? Do they think these dogmas enhance the value of felicity, as unexpected blessings are most prized? or is it that themselves, soured by mortifications and disappointments, which their vanity or caprice have occasioned, they are unwilling to acknowledge that degree of perfection, in any state, or being, which they do not themselves enjoy? But why do I argue, where I can at once confute? by declaring your Emily blessed to the utmost extent of her most romantic wishes; and feeling, if possible, an addition to her felicity, by knowing that you share it.

Our journey was delightful; even the sun, which had not appeared for some days, shone forth on us, in its full lustre: creation smiled; the gladness of my heart gilded every object; I thought the birds sung hymeneals,[8] and I was sorry when even Miss Weston's fine voice interrupted their still sweeter notes. My lord was—himself. I cannot say more, to express all that is tender, elegant, and polite.

Lady Harriet, who, you know, is of the gentle kind, looked assent to our happiness; yet frequent sighs escaped her. Why should she sigh? I have heard people say they do so from habit, without sensibility, or sensation. Time and use may possibly work such an effect, but this habit must certainly have had its rise, either from sickness, or sorrow. Perhaps lady Harriet may be in love. If unhappily so, how truly to be pitied!

It is impossible I should yet be able to give you any idea of this fine old seat, nor do I think I shall ever attempt it. I had much rather you should see, than read its beauties. I hate flourishing descriptions. Modern writers over-dress nature, as ill-judging women do themselves. They give her parterres[9] for patches, hanging woods for lappets,[10] and embroider her beautiful green gown, with all the colours of the rainbow. I flatter myself that your taste (for it is elegant) will approve whatever my lord has planned; and I shall not insist much on your admiring the works of his ancestors. The closet,[11] in which I am now writing, is charmingly situated. It commands—but after what I have just said, let me command my pen.

My lord, ever kind and attentive to me, wrote to his sister, lady Lawson, who lives eight miles off, to defer her visit, till this day, as it was probable I might have been fatigued with my journey. He speaks with such extreme tenderness of this lady, that I begin to love her, already, by anticipation.

But hark, her carriage rolls into the court-yard, and my heart steps forth to meet her; but returns again to assure my dear Fanny, that I am

her truly affectionate sister,

E. WOODVILLE.

## LETTER 2.

### Lady STRAFFON, To Lady WOODVILLE.

May my dearest Emily ever continue an exception to those opinions, which, notwithstanding her present felicity, have too surely their foundation in this world's experience. The bitter ingredients of life, are, however, more sparingly scattered in the potions of some, than others; and I believe there may be many who have passed through life, without feeling one natural misfortune.—But then, these favourites of heaven, unworthy of its bounty, are apt to create afflictions for themselves, and mourn over ideal, for want of real distress.

This is a failing I am not at all apprehensive of your falling into, at least for some years to come; but as I have ever acted as a mother to my dearest Emily, or at least, endeavoured, as far as it was possible for me, to supply that loss to her infant years, let me now, with the same maternal tenderness, warn her against the contrary extreme, that of being too much elated, with her present joys, "lest while she clasps, she kill them."

And now, my Emily, a truce with moralizing, which I confess, would have been improper at this æra, but that you brought it on yourself; and I only appear in the character of the slave, who attended the triumphs of the Roman conquerors, merely to inform them they were mortal. Gracious heaven! that such an information should be necessary, to any of thy frail creatures! But I find myself relapsing, and will learn from you, to command my pen.

Poor lady Harriet! I am sorry she should have cause to sigh; for I agree with you, that sighing may be *incidental,* but not *accidental.* I hope the gay scene of receiving and returning visits, &c. in which she will be engaged with you, may help to dissipate the cloud of her chagrin. I rejoice in the acquisition of your new sister; she must be amiable, if lord Woodville loves her. What a compliment to my Emily! but let it rather make her grateful, than vain.

I fear I shall not have an opportunity of approving my taste, by admiring lord Woodville's improvements, for some time. Sir John, who is not a little jealous of your not having mentioned him, purposes going, for a couple of months, to Paris. Do not grow jealous, in your turn. I do not intend to accompany him, to that gay scene, which would have fewer charms for me, than the rational, and rural pleasures, of Woodfort. But I design to inoculate[12] my little Edward and Emily, during his absence. I shall not acquaint him with my intention, till it is over. I know he wishes it done; and I would spare him the anxiety of a fond father, upon such an occasion. I know too, he will be vastly obliged to me, for laying hold of this opportunity; for it is an invariable maxim, that all men hate trouble, of every kind, and choose to be out of the way, when there is any disagreeable operation to be performed.

My sister Straffon, who you know is to be married to Sir James Miller, has determined to take her chance, with my children. She says she could not answer it to her conscience, to marry Sir James, who seems to be enamoured of her face, till she has put her features beyond the common danger of an alteration. I went with her, last night, to Ranelagh[13]—as she said, to take leave of it: I hope but for a short time.

The attention of the whole assembly, was taken up with a beautiful foreigner, the marchioness de St. Aumont. I think I never beheld so much vivacity and sweetness joined, before, in the same countenance. I have just looked up at your picture, and thought it tacitly reproached me, for having so soon forgot my Emily's face. I'll look again. Her eyes have more vivacity, I must confess, but yours a greater sweetness. Hers are black, yours blue. The advantage, which each of you have, over the other, in this particular, may be more owing to colour, than expression.

The marchioness has been a widow, about a year, and does not appear to be above twenty. I am certain that if I were a man, I should be in love with her. I am glad she has left Paris, before my *Straffon* goes thither—you may read *Strephon,*[14] if you please. I shall take care to keep him out of danger, while he stays in London; or perhaps, she might keep him sighing, at home, and so mar both his scheme, and mine. The very best of these men, my dear Emily, have hearts nearly resembling tinder, though they would have us think they are made of sterner stuff—a sparkling eye sets them all in a blaze.

Lady Sandford, who doats upon foreigners, has already engrossed her; perhaps she may engage her to go with her into the country. If so, you will, probably, meet her, at York races; and if that should happen, it will be absolutely necessary for lord Woodville to arm himself, *cap-à-pie,*[15] with constancy, and for you also, to rivet the joints of that armour, with unaffected complacency, chearfulness, and love.

Lucy and Sir James Miller are in the drawing-room. I fancy she is tired of a *tête-à-tête,* as the fondest lovers sometimes are; for she has just sent your little name-sake, to request my company. I must, therefore, quit you, to attend her summons. I shall expect a particular account of all occurrences, at Woodfort, as the most minute matter, that relates to you, must ever be of consequence to your affectionate

FRANCES STRAFFON.

P.S. As I have yet time enough to send my letter, I shall acquaint you with the occasion of my being called from it. Lucy had just informed Sir James that she intended to be inoculated. He opposed it, with the utmost vehemence, and told many stories, upon that subject, to intimidate her. In vain; she continued firm to her purpose.

He then intreated that they might be married, before the operation, and he would give his consent to her undergoing it, in ten days after. This she absolutely refused; and, I think, with good reason. The altercation grew warm, on both sides; I was chosen umpire;[16] and gave my opinion, in favour of Lucy's arguments. Sir James said I was a partial judge, and quitted us, soon after, with some little warmth.

I was sorry to perceive a starting tear, in Lucy's lovely eye, and rallied her, on being low-spirited. She confessed she felt a kind of foreboding, that the union between Sir James and her, would never be accomplished; and yet said, she had not the least apprehension that her death would prevent it. I told her that I foresaw nothing else that could, as her beauty was even less in danger from this experiment, than her life.

She replied, that they were both of them but transient blessings, and she had, happily, brought her mind to such a state of resignation, as to be fully prepared for the loss of either. But she owned that she had not yet accustomed herself to the thought of resigning Sir James: however, if she was to lose his affection, she could better sustain that affliction, before marriage, than after.

Here her eyes streamed again, and while I was endeavouring to dissipate these gloomy vapours, Sir John luckily came in, to the relief of us both, as it put an end to the subject of inoculation, which I told you before, he is not to receive the least hint about, for the present. Both Lucy and he are affectionately yours, and rejoice with me in your happiness.

Once more, adieu, and good night.

F. STRAFFON.

## LETTER 3.

### *Lady* WOODVILLE, *To Lady* STRAFFON.

My dear Fanny,

I did not insist upon the permanence of human felicity. I said only, that there was such a thing as perfect happiness, and, I hope, with a truly grateful heart, acknowledged myself in possession of that rare treasure. However, your letter has given a little alloy to it, and rendered it less pure, and unmixed.

I feel for you, on your childrens account, and for Lucy, on her own. She has long determined on inoculation: she mentioned it to lady Harriet, before I was married, and made her will, the day after she became of age. I admire her fortitude, but fear I should not be able to imitate it.

Your description of the marchioness, is really alarming, and has already made me jealous, not of lord Woodville, but of lady Straffon. If you should ever become acquainted with her, she will certainly rival every body, but Sir

John, and the dear little ones. Perhaps Lucy's heroism may still preserve her some place in your heart, but the poor absent Emily will be totally forgotten, when you already begin to stand in need of her picture, to remind you of her.

My lord, and lady Harriet, both knew her, in Paris, and both agree that the charms of her person, are inferior to those of her mind; and that she was still more admired, as *un bel esprit,* than as *une belle dame.*[17] Won't you give me credit for the utmost generosity, in furnishing you with this account of my rival, that is to be?

I hope she may come to York races, that I may have an opportunity of examining this phœnix, with a critic's eye; but it shall not be like the modern ones, who are, generally, so intent on spying defects, that they are apt to overlook the most striking beauties. This, however, may sometimes proceed, rather from a want of taste, than a spirit of malevolence, and I am always inclined to pity those unhappy people, who never seem to be pleased.

Charming lady Lawson! What an engaging countenance, what a quick sensibility in her looks, what an irresistible smile! I am not under a necessity of looking at my bracelet, to remind me that this portrait resembles lady Straffon: but lady Lawson is taller, thinner, and more of the brunette. She is two years younger than my lord, and has been, married six years, to Sir William Lawson, who seems to be what they call a jolly, good-humoured man. He hates London, loves fox hunting, and has, they say, no exception to a chearful glass, or a pretty lass. I fear poor lady Lawson was thrown away; though Sir William is generally esteemed, what they call, a good husband. He behaves outwardly well to his wife, merely because she is so, and would have treated her chambermaid, in the same manner, if he had happened to marry her. What a mortifying situation, to a woman of delicacy!

The meeting between her and my lord, was truly affectionate, and tender. She had not seen him since his return from making the grand tour.[18] She thanked him, in the most graceful manner, for increasing her happiness, by ensuring his own, and she also hoped, that of so amiable a person, she was pleased to add, as lady Woodville. My lord replied, that if any thing could add to his felicity, it must be her approbation of his choice, which he was certain would increase with her knowledge of his dear Emily. He then joined our hands, bowed, and withdrew. How kind in him to bespeak her favour for me! But I shall endeavour to deserve, what she seems so ready to bestow.

Lady Harriet's dove-like eyes glistened with pleasure, at her cousin's politeness. She said there was a nearer relation between lady Lawson and me, than what my lord had given us, for we had kindred souls.

Here the arrival of a great deal of company, put an end to all conversation. Is it not surprizing, sister, that where there are most words, there is generally the least sense?[19] And yet, it is always the case; for I never remember to have met with any thing like rational discourse, in a company that exceeded five or six.

Lord and lady Withers, their two daughters, the eldest a fine woman, and once intended as a wife for lord Woodville. The point had been settled between their fathers, but the death of old lord Woodville, happily for me, left the son at liberty, to chuse for himself. She appeared to be in some confusion, when he saluted[20] her, and I felt myself a good deal distressed, on her account.

Women are not such wretches, as men misrepresent them. Conquest, I own, is pleasant, but I detest a triumph. It sinks one, methinks, below the vanquished. Her sister is pretty, young, and modest. I think the whole family amiable, and agreeable.

Sir Harry Ransford, and his lady—What a pair! He old, gouty, and peevish—she young, handsome, and vulgar. His son, by a former wife, polite, and sensible, with a well-made, genteel person. My lord and he were intimate, abroad. I wish he would fall in love with our dear lady Harriet. Nay, he certainly will do so. I can't possibly see how he can well avoid it.

Mr. Watson, Mr. Young, Mr. Haywood, &c. What a croud! You would have pitied me, Fanny. Though I have been four months married, I was so be-brided, and wished joy, that it made me downright sad. Lady Lawson was very useful to me, in assisting to entertain the company. She has, in her manners and address, a great deal of that graceful, and courtly ease, which I always admire, in others, without having ever been able to obtain, in myself. But all farther endeavours after this perfection, are, henceforward, at an end with me, and I hope now to be able to preserve my *mauvaise honte,*[21] during life; for after twenty, it is rarely to be overcome, without *paying too dear,* for the conquest.

In the afternoon, the younger part of my lord's tenants, appeared in the avenue, neatly dressed, and adorned with all the honours of the spring, and forming a long dance together. My lord proposed our going out to see them; I found this had been designed, as there was a large carpet spread on the lawn, and seats already prepared for us.

When we were seated, they passed by, in couples, chanting a rustic hymn, in praise of Hymen,[22] and strewing flowers before me. At length, they presented me with a beautiful, and fragrant wreath, which I immediately placed on lord Woodville's brow, while the villagers retreated singing, and forming themselves into a rural dance, infinitely more agreeable to me, than any of the *grands ballets*,[23] at the opera, or theatres. We left them at their sport, and returned into the house.

After tea, my lord proposed our following the example of his merry peasants. This was readily assented to, by every one, but Sir Harry Ransford, who told us he never lay within ten miles of his own house, after the twenty-fifth of March;[24] and insisted upon lady Ransford's going away with him, that instant, as he said they should hardly be able to reach home, by his usual time of going to bed, at nine o'clock, summer and winter.

We all intreated that he would permit lady Ransford to stay, which he peremptorily refused, saying, it would be setting an ill example to the bridegroom, to let women have their way. She said every thing in her power to prevail, but when she found it in vain, and that he would force her away, she was provoked, at last, to call him methodical *monster.* He replied, that it was better to be *one,* by his own *method,* than hers, and hobbled into his coach. She followed, with the face of a fury. What a delightful tête-à-tête must theirs be!

Mr. Ransford staid, and danced with me. I think him the best dancer I ever saw. Our little ball got the better of all disagreeable reserve; and, at supper, we appeared like old acquaintance, perfectly at ease, and quite chearful. My lord was in remarkable good spirits, and even lady Harriet seemed gay. The Withers's are a charming family; both the young ladies play on the harpsichord, and sing finely.

We had an agreeable concert, the next day; they staid till late in the evening. Sir William and lady Lawson went home, this morning. We are to return their visit, to-morrow. Mr. Ransford is still with us. He is a great lover of music: I fancy there is not much harmony, in his father's house, and where the instruments of a matrimonial concert, do not sound in *unison,* the discord is most grating.

I shall long, impatiently, for every post, till I hear that all your patients are out of danger. Lucy's presages, with regard to Sir James, are only the effect of low spirits. I never saw any man, I think, more in love, than he appears to be. I cannot, however, bear the thoughts of his consenting to her being inoculated, in ten days after their marriage. Selfish wretch! Don't let Lucy see this paragraph.

I have now shewn my obedience to my dear motherly sister's commands, by entering into a minute detail of every thing that has passed at

Woodfort. I am disappointed at not having the pleasure of seeing her here; yet I highly applaud the disposition of that time she promised to bestow on her affectionate,

E. WOODVILLE.

P.S. Sir John has no reason to be jealous, while I can, with truth, declare I love but one man in the world, better than him.

## LETTER 4.

### *Lady* STRAFFON, *To Lady* WOODVILLE.

I am much obliged to my dear Emily, for the entertaining detail of her amusements in the country. I am charmed with your account of lady Lawson, and am not, like my dear spoiled child, the least inclined to be jealous. I thank you for the flattering likeness, you have drawn of me; may there be a still stronger resemblance between us, in our love and esteem for lady Woodville.

I think you extremely happy in meeting with such an amiable friend, in so agreeable a neighbour. She will, I doubt not, be kind enough to inform you of the *Carte du Païs,*[25] where you are situated: and what is of infinitely more consequence to your happiness, she may, perhaps, acquaint you with the particularities of her brother's temper; for be assured, all charming as he is, that he has some, the knowing, and treating of which properly, may be the surest basis of your future felicity.

Sir John set out, for Paris, last Monday, and, in an hour after, Mr. Ranby inoculated Lucy and my dear children. Though I have the firmest reliance on the goodness of Providence, and the fullest conviction of the general success of this operation, the mother could not stand it. I was forced to retire to my closet. I repented my not having acquainted Sir John, with my design, and thought, that if any misfortune should happen to either of the children, even his grief would seem a constant reproach to me.

In this situation of mind, I poured forth my soul in fervent prayer, before the throne of mercy. My apprehensions vanished, the rectitude of my intentions confirmed my resolution, and I felt myself perfectly calm, and resigned. Amazing efficacy of true devotion! But indeed, my dear Emily, there is no other resource for the afflicted. No other balm to heal the wounded soul. By this, and this alone, we are enabled to triumph over pain, sickness, distress, sorrow, even death itself.

The children are in a fine way, and have received the infection. Lucy, it is thought, has not. She insists upon being inoculated again, to-morrow. Sir James supped with us, on Sunday night; and told us, with a grave face, that he should not see us again, till this affair was quite over; for if he visited here, he could go no where else. I laughed, and bid him stay away, if he could.

Though I did not think him serious, he has hitherto kept his word, but sends a formal card, every day, to inquire our healths. I see that his behaviour hurts Lucy, though she affects not to take notice of it. I hear he spends all his time with Miss Nelson. She is artful, and agreeable. I begin to fear poor Lucy's presage may be verified.

Adieu, my dearest Emily, I shall not write to you, again, till I can congratulate you on the perfect recovery of our invalids. Till then, and ever, I am,

most affectionately, yours,

F. STRAFFON.

## LETTER 5.

### *Sir* JA. THORNTON, *To Lord* WOODVILLE.

The devil's in it, if the honey moon is not over yet, and you near half a year married. This is carrying on the farce, too far, and looks as if you wanted to make us infidels believe, that pleasure was to be found, in the sober and virtuous scheme of matrimony.

I allow your wife to be handsome. I will suppose her lively, and agreeable, too; but then, have you not had time enough to be tired of all these perfections? and whenever that happened, the more merit a woman has, the greater our dislike.

I should never forgive a wife that did not supply me with a reason for hating, when I grew weary of her. But I fancy I need not be in any manner of pain, on that account; for the precious creatures have, generally, a *quantum sufficit*,[26] of foible and caprice, to answer that end; at least, all those I have ever conversed with, appeared to be compounded of nothing else, after one month's intimate acquaintance.

You will, perhaps, tell me, that lady Woodville is a very different kind of woman, from those I hint at. It may be so; and I will admit it. But prithee, Harry, is she not your wife? And in that comprehensive term, are not restraint, care, limitation of pleasures, and squalling brats, included? But love her, if you will, and as long as you can: but, believe me, the only way to keep such a sickly flame alive, is by the fuel of absence.

Therefore, order your horses directly, and leave her, where she should ever remain, fixed to the freehold; while you shine forth, once more, among your old friends, at the Shakespear.[27] I write this, by order of the society, from which you will be excluded, if you do not appear, upon this summons, from

Your's, &c.

J.T.

## LETTER 6.

### *From Lord* WOODVILLE, *To Sir* JAMES THORNTON.

Dear Thornton,

I received your lively letter; but wish you had chosen a fitter subject to display your wit upon, than the old common-place topic of matrimony. Were I not perfectly acquainted with your writing, as well as your humour, I should have thought your letter a counterfeit. You are no libertine, Thornton, and yet seem to take pleasure in adopting their gross, and contemptible sentiments.

Their general abuse of women, is truly ridiculous: they pretend to know them, without having ever conversed with any, but that unhappy species of them, whose minds and manners are a disgrace, not only to their sex, but to human nature, itself. Profligates first betray to infamy all the women they can deceive; and then, by a double injustice, judge of the sex, from the examples they have made.

But come, my young friend, and convince yourself, that happiness is to be found in a virtuous connection with an amiable, and agreeable woman.

Order your horses, directly, I say; and leave your gross errors where they should ever remain, in Covent Garden.[28]

I never was a member of any society at the Shakespear, though I have spent some evenings there, both pleasantly and innocently. I love chearfulness, wit, and humour, wherever to be met with; and when Sir James Thornton shall be added to our society at Woodfort, I shall not have occasion to go in pursuit of any of them, elsewhere. As a farther inducement, we shall go to York races. I know you have horses to run there. Hasten then, to
    Your's sincerely,

WOODVILLE.

## LETTER 7.

### *Lord* SEYMOUR, *To Lord* WOODVILLE.

My dear Lord,

I arrived in London, the day after you left it: how unfortunate to have missed the friend of my heart! to whom I have a thousand things to communicate, that will not bear the cold, slow forms, of narrative letter-writing.

But one sad truth I must pour into your bosom, from mine, that almost bursts whilst I repeat it. The lovely, the angelic Charlotte Beaumont, has fled from these fond arms, and taken refuge, in a convent! I beheld her, renounce the pomps, and vanities, of that world, which she was born to adorn. None but her kindred angels ever appeared so beautiful as she, when led, like a blooming sacrifice, to the altar.

As she advanced up the isle, she caught *my eyes;* she stopt, and sigh'd; but quickly recollecting herself, turned *her's* to heaven—then with a ray of that ineffable tenderness, with which we may suppose angelic beings look on mortal woes, she turned them full on me—but ah! too soon recalled them, and passed along, with all the dignity of conscious virtue!

How I got out of the convent, I know not: my senses vanished, with her.—I was fifteen days delirious; and but for the officious kindness of Wilson, should not now feel those poignant agonies, that rend my heart. O Woodville, to lose such a woman, by my own folly! That fatal duel, in what misery has it involved me! When I am calm enough, if that should ever be, I will copy her *last letter,* and send it to you: I would not part with the original, for worlds, though it has destroyed my peace, in this.

Will you forgive your wretched friend, for breaking in, one moment, on your present felicity? I hear you are completely blessed—This is the only ray of joy, that ever can, or shall pervade the gloom, in which my fate is involved. Happy Woodville! to triumph over an unhappy passion, and now to feel the transports of successful love!

But let me intreat you, as you value your future peace, not to see the marchioness. Your wounds are not long healed, and may all bleed again. She is a true Calypso:[29] therefore, my friend, shun her ensnaring wiles! and remember you are accountable for the happiness of an amiable, and innocent young woman:—what a breach of honour, even to hazard it!

This single consideration will, I am certain, be a more powerful preservative to your generous heart, than all the philosophic reasonings, in the world; which too well I know, were never yet proof against strong passion.

Adieu, my friend: that you may continue to deserve, and possess, every happiness this world can give, is now the warmest wish of your unhappy

SEYMOUR.

## LETTER 8.

### *Lord* WOODVILLE, *To Lord* SEYMOUR.

My dear, unhappy Friend,

I am truly sorry that I had left London, before your arrival.—Had you given me the least hint of your intentions to return, I should certainly have staid to meet you: and I would, at this moment, fly to pour the balm of friendship, into your wounded bosom, but that Sir James Thornton, whom I have invited to spend some time with me, at Woodfort, and go with me to York races, came here, last night.

He is quite a stranger to lady Woodville, and all this family, and would certainly consider it as the highest breach of hospitality, if I were to leave him in the hands of a parcel of *virtuous* women, which are a race of beings, that he is totally unacquainted with. He is young, has a very large fortune, and many amiable qualities; but his education has been so shamefully neglected, that he is in imminent danger of becoming a prey, to sharpers,[30] and prostitutes.

Even you must have smiled, to have seen this young man, who is made up of frolic, and vivacity, look as frighted and abashed, before lady Woodville, who is gentleness itself, as a young country lady, who has never been out of the family mansion, when first presented at St. James's. But I hope this timid aukwardness will wear off, in a few days: and as I know nothing that can refine the sentiments, or polish the manners, so much, as the conversation of elegant women, I wish to keep Sir James, for some time, amongst us.

My cousin, Lady Harriet Hanbury, is here; and a very lively girl, miss Weston, a near relation of my Emily! Your old friend, Ransford, spends much of his time with us, also. What would I not give to tempt you hither? You shall retire when you please; read, walk, and muse, alone: and when you are disposed, my Emily shall play to you, some of the sweetest, softest airs, the very food of love,[31] accompanied with the sweetest, softest voice, you ever heard. Harriet, who is of the melancholy cast, and, I fear, unhappily in love, shall sigh, in concert with you; and Thornton, and miss Weston, shall sometimes make you smile.

I confess to you, my dear Seymour, that I was both shocked, and sorry, when I heard that the marchioness was in England. Lady Woodville was the first person who informed me of it: but, utterly ignorant of there having ever been any connection between us, she did not perceive my emotion, at her name.

Cruel woman! does she wish again to disturb the peace of a heart, which she had well nigh broken! but I defy her power.—In lady Woodville, I have found all that is amiable in the most lovely sex; sensible, beautiful, gentle, kind, and unaffectedly good.

True, she is not mistress of those lively sallies of wit, that dazzle the understanding, and captivate the heart. Her form, though lovely, has not the striking elegance, the nameless, numberless graces, that wait on every motion of the marchioness!

But why do I suffer myself to dwell upon her charms? or make a comparison injurious to the amiable woman, who deserves my love? why can I not say, who possesses it! Ah, Seymour! it is impossible to regulate the emotions of the human heart, by the cold rules of reason. Not all the charms of the whole sex combined, can ever render mine susceptible of those agonizing transports, it has already known. Yet let me boast, that it is as impossible for her, who first occasioned, to revive, as for any other woman, to inspire them.

If this was not the case, I should have made a worthless present to my Emily, when I gave her both my hand, and heart: and tho' I allow the latter not to be an adequate return for hers, she shall never be able to discover its deficiency, by any word, or action, of my life. This I can safely promise.

I have purposely avoided mentioning your lost, your lovely Charlotte! When you are more at ease, I know you will acquaint me with the particulars of your distress. Why may not that happy æra be hastened, by a reliance on all the tender cares of friendship, which you may certainly depend on, from

      Your ever affectionate

WOODVILLE.

P.S. You have a house, within a mile of York; where we have spent many happy days—"Days of ease, and nights of pleasure."[32] Who knows but we may there recover our juvenile tastes and passions? impossible! As well, when advanced in life, might we hope to regain our youth, *in those fields, where we once were young.*—But is that house untenanted? Will you be our host? or have you let, or lent it?

## LETTER 9.

### *Lord* SEYMOUR, *To Lord* WOODVILLE.

My dear Woodville,

Your letter has added to the affliction, I am already involved in. I think I am fated never to possess any of those blessings, without which, life is a burthen. The object of my fondest, tenderest wishes, already torn from my bleeding heart, there remained yet one consolation; a generous, and affectionate friend; and he, inhuman suicide! is going to rob me of himself! what an hard lot is mine! all that I ever loved, devote themselves; and by their misery, I am twice undone!

But stop, my friend! and let my warning voice prevent your rushing down the precipice! you must not, shall not, see the marchioness. I will go to

Woodfort, though heaven knows how unfit to mingle in society, merely to prevent your going to York races.—The Syren[33] will be there.—

I went, last night, to pay a visit to my sister, lady Sandford, and there I met your lovely enemy. She asked many questions about you, but many more about lady Woodville, and wanted me to draw her picture. I told her that I had not seen her, for some years; that she was then extremely young, but had, I thought, a very near resemblance to her ladyship, which was pronouncing her a perfect beauty.

I said this, to prevent her finding fault, which she certainly would have done, had I attempted a particular description. She saw through my design, but would not let me triumph in the success of it, then smiling said, "Like me! perhaps that was the reason he chose her.—Constant creature! this is a compliment, for which I think myself more indebted to him, than for all the fine things, he ever said, or wrote to me."

I hope, madam, his lordship had other motives. "O fye, lord Seymour, how you love to mortify? but pray let me indulge my vanity, a little. As the man is married, and to a perfect beauty, too, there can be no danger in avowing my sensibility of his regards. This, you know, I never did, while he was single, and I might have hopes. But women have strange caprices.

"However, I can assure you I have not the least design, upon his heart. It would be the height of vanity, indeed, to attempt rivalling this *perfect beauty*." It would be the height of cruelty madam, but to wish it. "I declare I cannot see it in that light, my lord; for such a woman can never want adorers." Our married ladies, madam, seek for that character, only in their husbands. "Nay now, my lord, you want to impose on me, as I am a stranger; but you cannot deceive me, for I know numberless instances to contradict your assertion, and not one to prove it. And I really think that London is as much the seat of galantry, as Paris."—

The arrival of other company, gave the conversation a general turn; but what I have repeated, is, I think, sufficient to make you fly from a woman, who audaciously owns her designs against your peace. As she talked of going to York, my sister, who is to accompany her, requested I would let her have my house, which I readily assented to; but were it unemployed, I would refuse it to my dear Woodville.

You see the snare is laid, and will you self-devoted rush into it; I know you, Woodville, you cannot live with loss of honour, and it is impossible to preserve your's, if in your present situation, you can be again drawn in, to doat upon this.—But I will not abuse her. I shall set out for Woodfort, to-morrow, and there enforce every argument I have used, to preserve you from yourself.

Till then, adieu.

SEYMOUR.

## LETTER 10.

### *Lady* WOODVILLE, *To Lady* STRAFFON.

I cannot tell my dearest Fanny how much her last letter affected me; nor can I sufficiently express my admiration of that happy turn of mind, that enables you to triumph over every difficulty and distress, and to rise so far superior to what any one might reasonably expect, from the gentleness of your nature, on every trial.

How happy is it for your poor weak Emily, that she has had nothing to struggle with! she would have sunk beneath the slightest weight, and given a loose to tears, and to complainings. But let the goodness of that all-wise Providence, who proportions our trials to our strength, fill my heart with the warmest gratitude, and let me "ever bless, and praise his name."

I have no sort of doubt but you are eased of all a mother's fears, by this time, and that the dear little ones are prattling round you, with their usual chearfulness; while you feel, even an additional tenderness from recollection, of the danger they have past.

I have very uneasy apprehensions, for poor Lucy: I almost wish she may not receive the infection.—There have been numberless instances of persons who never had the small-pox; and I think it is like forcing nature, to make a second effort.

I detest Sir James Miller; and hope, with all my heart, he may never be married to Lucy, as I am very sure he never will deserve her.

Our family party has received some very agreeable additions, since I wrote last. There is a most delightful contrast, between our visitors. Sir James Thornton, lively, boyish, with a good natural understanding, totally unim-proved, without the least idea of good breeding;—and yet, that want is amply supplied, by what I call natural politeness. But if "good breeding is the blossom of good sense,"[34] we ought to find out some other term, for that species of form, which is only to be acquired in courts. There was such an aukward reserve, about poor Thornton, for the first three days he spent at Woodfort, that I looked upon him as a Hottentot:[35] but that rough cast is now worn off, and he is really agreeable, and entertaining.

Lord Seymour, our latest guest, is, really, an accomplished gentleman; an elegant form, and affable countenance, bespeak your favour, at first sight, and his every word and action insensibly engage your regard. Yet, lavish as nature has been to him, there seems to be something wanting to his happiness. There is a tender air of melancholy, diffused over his whole form, with such a softness in his voice, and manner, as is rarely natural to the gay sons of prosperity. His fortune is ample, and his birth high; it must then be that source of the most poignant sorrow, ill-fated love, that has disturbed his peace. Yet, I think, he could not love in vain, unless there was a prior prepossession. I long to know his story: I feel myself interested, as for a brother.

He acquainted my lord with his intention to visit us, the night before he came. We were all engaged to dine at Sir Harry Ransford's, the next day; and her ladyship had got the old knight to consent to her having a ball. My lord remained at Woodfort, to receive his guest. I accompanied the young folks, to Sir Harry's.—After tea, I intreated lady Ransford to excuse my leaving her, without taking any notice of it to the company. She was so obliging as to consent, and I drove home, directly.

My lord seemed surprized, and pleased, at seeing me; and, as he handed me from the coach, said, with an air of the utmost tenderness, I am much obliged to you for your attention to my friend; and can with truth assure you, that your company is the only agreeable addition, that could be made, to our present society. My little heart exulted, at the kindness of this compliment; as to please, or oblige him, is, and ever will be, its highest ambition. Notwithstanding this, I thought my company was a restraint on them, and therefore retired, soon after supper.

It was four o'clock, when my lord came up stairs.—I was miserably apprehensive he was ill, as he sighed often, and was uncommonly restless. But my fears are now fled, like a morning dream.—He seemed perfectly well, at breakfast. Lord Seymour and he are gone into the gardens.

The coach is just returned, with the boys and girls; and Thornton is, this moment, come into my dressing-room, to tell me *all about it,* as he expresses himself: but he is too civil to speak, till I leave off writing. I must, therefore, impose silence on myself, to relieve him from it; and so bid my dear sister,

Adieu.

E.W.

## LETTER 11.

### *Lady* STRAFFON, *To Lady* WOODVILLE.

I was vastly pleased with my dear Emily's letter.—There is infinitely more merit, in looking up to the Almighty, in our prosperity, than adversity. Praise is surely the noblest, and, of course, the most acceptable sacrifice, that a human creature can offer, to the great Author of good. Mr. Addison, very justly observes, that "the mind that hath any cast towards devotion, naturally flies to it in its afflictions."[36] We then feel our own insufficiency; we are humbled by sorrow, and perhaps only then, deduce real satisfaction from a thorough conviction, that there is a superior being, whose aid is graciously promised, to those who sincerely seek it. But, surrounded by the delights of life, youth, fortune, gaiety, and dissipation, we too frequently become forgetful of the source, from whence our blessings flow;[37] and while we are indulging all our appetites, in the delicious stream of happiness, it becomes impregnated with the qualities of Lethe,[38] and renders us unmindful of its fountain.

But let me be truly thankful, that the sister of my love, the child of my care, is not only blessed with the insignia of happiness, but with a heart capable of the first virtue, gratitude; which, I hope, will ensure to her the long, and full possession, of all earthly good.

I now can tell my dear prophetess, her hopes are accomplished.—The mother's fears are lost, in the happy certainty of my children's perfect recovery.—But the friend still suffers: poor Lucy continues extremely ill, though, thank God, this day pronounced out of danger. The small-pox was as favourable to her, as possible; but the emotions of her mind, on account of that wretch, Sir James Miller, have thrown her into a violent fever.

He is, this day, to be married, to Miss Nelson! This she is yet ignorant of: but on the first day that she sat up, she received a kind of leave-taking letter from him, excusing his perfidy, by her want of complaisance to his request. Said, "he had reason to apprehend, that a lady, who seemed so little inclined to oblige him, before marriage, would not make a very complying wife;—that he was glad to hear her beauty was out of danger, as there was no doubt, but it would procure her a better husband, than him; and that he should endeavour to look out for a wife, who was less anxious about her features." Was there ever any thing so provoking! This is adding insolence, to baseness!

If Sir John was here, I am sure a duel would ensue.—I know not how to act, in this affair.—I cannot bear the thoughts of his triumphing in his villainy; nor yet can I think of hazarding Sir John's life, to punish such a scoundrel. Swift says "the *occasions* are few, that can induce a man of sense, and virtue, to draw his sword." I am certain, were he living, he would allow this to be a justifiable *one*.

But as a wife and mother, I most sincerely hope, Sir John may never hear of his infamous behaviour: but what excuse to invent, for breaking off the match, I know not. Sir John is jealous of his honour, and will inquire minutely into the affair. I will refer it all to Lucy's prudence: she loves her brother, and is a christian.

You are an admirable painter. I should have known lord Seymour's picture, if you had not set his name to it; all but that shade of melancholy, which you have thrown over it. He was extremely lively, when I knew him; but I have not seen him, since his return to England.

You have made me perfectly acquainted with Sir James Thornton: I saw his precipitate stride into your dressing-room, and his short stop, on finding you were writing. It reminded me of the snapping of a watch-spring. Have you ever had one break in your hand? Lucy has just awoke, from a refreshing sleep; and, on being told I was writing, she desires to see me immediately. I will return to you, again.

What an affecting interview! That odious idiot, Sir James Miller, has,

> Like the base Indian, thrown a pearl away,
> Richer than all his tribe.[39]

When I went into Lucy's chamber, she desired every one to withdraw: then taking my hand, and pressing it to her lips, What infinite trouble must I have given to the compassionate heart of my dear lady Straffon! but I hope you do not despise me: it was the weak state of my body, that overpowered my mind. But now, that I have recovered my senses, I am amazed how I could be affected, by the loss of such a man.—Did I say loss? then, I fear, I rave again. But I grieved for an ideal character; and am much obliged to Sir James, for removing the mist from before my eyes, and shewing himself in his native colours. How happy, the delusion vanished, so soon! Had it continued but a little longer, I should have been a wretch, indeed! What a misery, to despise the man, whom it is our duty to love and honour! Yet such might have been my fate! Should I have been unpardonably criminal, my dearest sister?

I intreated her, not to think upon the subject, but to calm her spirits; and that I would converse with her on any other topic, that she pleased.— She begged my attention, for a few minutes; said, she had wandered from her purpose, and asked my pardon for detaining me. You are writing, lady Straffon; perhaps, to my brother. Then raising herself on her knees, in spite of my efforts to hinder her, Let me, in this humble posture, intreat you, my dearest sister, not to mention what has passed, to Sir John. I know his natural bravery, joined to his love for an only sister, would tempt him to call Sir James Miller to an account.[40]—Good God! what might be the consequence! He has done me no wrong; and should any misfortune happen to my brother, from this event, I could not answer for my senses. And were even the aggressor, for such indeed he is, to fall, I never should know peace again.

Here she was quite overcome by weakness, and sunk down, in a flood of tears. I said every thing in my power, to assuage her grief; and gave her the strongest assurances, that I neither had, or would mention a syllable of the affair, to Sir John. She told me then, I had restored her tranquillity; and she should soon be well, and able to contrive some plausible pretence to her brother, for breaking off the match: and as this would be the first falsehood she had ever told him, she hoped it might be considered as a *pious fraud,* only.

After this conversation, she grew perfectly composed; I left her retired to rest: but, I fear, she has disturbed mine, for this night. What an amiable heart is her's? While yet smarting with undeserved wounds, she would preserve the cruel wretch who inflicted them! I will religiously keep my promise to her; yet cannot help sincerely wishing, that his crime may be his punishment; and, I think, he bids fair for being overpaid, in kind.

Miss Nelson, now lady Miller, is at least twenty-nine, and has been a remarkable coquette, these ten years; yet never could catch a poor unguarded fly in her net, till Sir James rushed in.—She was perfectly acquainted with his attachment to Lucy; had requested to be her bride-maid; yet could think of separating them, for ever! May they be mutual avengers of each other's perfidy!

I feel myself in an unchristian mood; I cannot help it; I pity folly, but detest vice! Alas! my Emily, I am too severe; for they are, in general, synonimous terms. I will, in charity, wish you good night; for, if I write on, I shall rail more: therefore,
Adieu.

F.S.

## LETTER 12.

### *Lady* WOODVILLE, *To Lady* STRAFFON.

My dear Fanny,

I am so violently provoked, at the insolent baseness of that abominable Miller, that I cannot find words to express my resentment. I do not think you seem sufficiently rejoiced at Lucy's escape, from such a monster. For my part, I am delighted at the thoughts of his being married to such a woman, as miss Nelson.—May she render him just as miserable, as he deserves to be.—His greatest enemy could not wish him worse.

But there are more wretches in the world, than he; and Lucy is not without companions in affliction. The willow grows on purpose for our sex; and were it to be watered, only by the tears drawn from beauteous eyes, by the perfidy of men, it would need no other moisture. Poor lady Harriet! an accident has discovered the cause of her too frequent sighs.

Yesterday morning, after breakfast, when the gentlemen had retired to their separate amusements, lady Harriet, miss Weston, and I, were in my dressing-room. Lady Harriet took up Prior's Poems, and was reading his Henry and Emma,[41] to Fanny, and me, who were at work; when in rushed lady Ransford, in a riding-dress, and begged I would permit her to introduce a gentleman, an acquaintance of her's, whom she had accidentally met on the road, as she was coming to spend the day with me. She concluded, he was a particular friend, whom she had not seen, for a long time. I immediately consented; and said, I was sorry my lord was not at home, to receive the gentleman.

She ran out directly, and led in captain Barnard.—While she was presenting him to me, the book fell from lady Harriet's hand, and she sunk motionless upon the couch. As soon as the captain cast his eyes on her, he appeared almost in the same condition: the colour forsook his lips, and he could hardly breathe. Lady Ransford looked with a spiteful kind of astonishment, and cried out, What can all this mean! Is she subject to fits? Fanny, and I, were engaged in trying to recover lady Harriet, I began to fear, in vain.—Life seemed, for some minutes, absolutely fled.—The wretched captain looked the picture of despair.—The moment she opened her eyes, he bowed, left the room, mounted his horse, and rode off.

We conveyed lady Harriet to her chamber, and laid her on the bed;—when a plentiful shower of tears seemed to have relieved her. I left Fanny Weston with her, and returned to lady Ransford. She seemed in a violent passion, that the captain was gone.—What had he to do with lady Harriet's faintings? She was very sure it was only an air she gave herself. She thanked God, she was not subject to such tricks. She never fainted in her life, and was quite certain she never should, &c. &c.

I congratulated her on the goodness of her constitution; said, lady Harriet's was extremely delicate, and that she had not been well, for some time. This did not satisfy her; and she continued out of humour at the captain's desertion, the whole day. Several times repeating, I do not suppose he ever saw her before; of what consequence was her fainting, to him? I encouraged her in this opinion, though far from believing it.

I said, his retiring was a mark of politeness, as the presence of a stranger, must increase the confusion we were in. Nothing that I said could pacify her. I therefore suffered her to mutter out her dissatisfaction, without replying, for the remainder of the time she staid, which was not long after dinner.—She said, she should be afraid to ride with only one servant, after it was dusk.

I never was better pleased, with the departure of a guest. I longed to see poor Harriet, who had not left her room, and flew to her the moment lady Ransford was gone. She looked abashed, and held down her lovely eyes, which were yet bathed in tears, when I approached her;—but the tenderness with which I inquired her health, seemed to reassure her.

You are too good to me, my dear lady Woodville; such weakness as mine, scarcely deserves your compassion: and I can only presume to hope for it, by the most unbounded confidence, which I should long since have re-posed in your friendly bosom, but that I thought it cruel, even for a moment, to interrupt that happiness which you so well deserve. But as the accident, which happened this day, must convince you, that there is a secret sorrow, which preys upon my heart, I will readily acquaint you with the cause of it, lest the tenderness of your nature, should make you imagine me more wretched, than I really am.

You must suppose, my dear, said I, that your situation, this morning, alarmed me extremely; but I have long thought there was some secret source, for that soft melancholy, which you vainly endeavour to represent as con-stitutional. But do not let this remark make you think yourself under a ne-cessity of disclosing your secrets to me. I am far from desiring to pry into them: but should rejoice at having it in my power to do any thing, which might alleviate your distress. And if my participation of your sorrow, can soothe it, but for a moment, it will more than repay me, for what I feel, in knowing that you are unhappy.

She said, she was not then capable of making the least return to my kindness, though perfectly sensible of it; but that, as soon as she was able, she would write out her short story, for me, and lady Straffon. She said, Lucy knew something of it, but not the whole; and desired she might see it, as a kind of consolation, under her present circumstances.

As soon as I receive it, I will send it to you. Pray present my love to Lucy; and tell her, I intreat her company at Woodfort, whenever she is able to travel. Change of air, and objects, will forward her recovery. Why cannot you, and the little ones, accompany her, and complete the wishes of,

Your affectionate,

E. WOODVILLE?

# LETTER 13.

## *Lady* WOODVILLE, *To Lady* STRAFFON.

My dear Sister,

I, this morning, received the inclosed, which has engaged my attention, ever since; I have but just time to send it to you, without the smallest comment; but, as it may remain longer in your hands, I shall expect it to be returned, with notes *variorum*.

I have absented myself, from our family party, (which is indeed a charming one) except during dinner, this whole day; I shall return to it, with double gust, from a certainty, that amiable as they who compose it are, in their manners, and persons, their hearts are still more valuable. Haste then, my dearest Fanny, and Lucy, to partake, and perfect, the most delightful society, in the world,

sincerely prays your

E. WOODVILLE.

## *The Memoir of Lady* HARRIET HANBURY

As the strongest mark, of my sincerity and gratitude, to my dear lady Woodville, for all her kindness to me, I sit down to fulfil the voluntary promise I made, of acquainting her with the few events of a short life, whose duration has only been marked, by sorrow; and as, "to mention, is to suffer pain,"[42] I chose to save her gentle heart the uneasiness, of seeing the distress, which, the recollection of unhappy circumstances, must ever revive, where the sufferer is the relater. I must now, like all Biographers, step a little back, to give you some account of the authors of my being, and then proceed with a plain narrative, submitting my weaknesses, and follies, without the least reserve, to your friendly eye.

My father, was eldest son, to the earl of G———. During my grandfather's life, he became passionately in love, with my mother, who was a daughter of colonel Stanley's, and reputed one of the greatest beauties, of that time. My father well knew it would be in vain, to hope for the earl's consent to his marrying, without a large fortune, let the merits of the lady be ever so great; as his estate was extremely involved,[43] and that he had four children, by a second wife, unprovided for.

My mother's portion[44] was only four thousand pounds, but her father, who considered her birth, beauty, and accomplishments, as full equivalents to any fortune, when he found the earl was not acquainted with my father's courtship, forbad his daughter ever to see her lover more, as his pride would not have suffered him to have matched her with a prince, clandestinely.

The lovers, reduced to this unhappy situation, after much fruitless sorrow, had recourse to the usual alternative, and married, without consent, on either side. The affair, was not long kept secret, and the earl, whose rage was without bounds, accused the colonel of being privy to the marriage, and of drawing in his son—he also lavished every kind of abuse, upon my mother, and stopt the allowance he had, for some years, given to my father.

The colonel, though highly offended with his daughter, resented the cruelty and injustice of the earl's behaviour towards her, and sent him a challenge.—The duel was prevented, by my father's address, but, the most implacable hatred ever remained, between the old gentlemen; which communicated itself to every branch of the families, except my father and mother, who were the most perfect patterns of conjugal tenderness.

Notwithstanding my father's increasing fondness for his lovely wife, the unhappy feuds, which she thought herself the occasion of, preyed on her tender mind, and, so much weakened her delicate frame, that, in giving me life, she lost her own;—fatal exchange for her unhappy orphan! My father was quite distracted at her loss, and the colonel, who had been reconciled to them both, for some time, was obliged to restrain his own affliction, to endeavour to console my father, and engage him to preserve his life, by frequently presenting me before him.

"Yes, he would then say, I will live, for the protection, of that only transcript of my angel Harriet. I will watch over her rising virtues, and endeavour, to restore to the world, some part of that perfection, my cruel father has deprived it of." For four years, his fondness for me, *was* unabated, and I appeared to be the sole object, of his attention, or regard.

About that æra, the earl wrote to him, and a reconciliation soon ensued; the terms of which were, that as my father had gratified himself, by his first marriage, he should oblige the earl, and serve his family, by a second. My father, whose nature was gentle, was soon induced to comply, and, as I believe his real fondness for my mother, had rendered all women indifferent to him, the choice of his future lady was intirely left to the earl, who, you may suppose, would rate her value, only by her fortune. My father paid his addresses, in form, and even without the least degree of liking, on either side, the match was concluded.

The perpetual scenes of discord, which succeeded to this ill-suited marriage, are but too public, and I have great reason to apprehend, that, to this constant source of domestic misery, I owe the loss of my unhappy father. The first cause of disgust, which my step-mother gave him, was her absolutely refusing to let me be brought into the house, politely adding, that she would not suffer a *beggar's brat,* to be brought up with her children, who were at least, intitled to a fortune, by their mother's side; and, that those who had nothing, but their blood to boast of, should be bred humbly, to lower their pride. This one specimen is, I think, sufficient to give you a perfect idea of my poor father's unhappiness, and I shall say nothing more, of one, who has the honour, to bear his name, and title.

I remained at my grandfather's and was his principal favourite. My father continued to see me, frequently, and, notwithstanding his family was increased, by the birth of a son, and two daughters, his fondness for me, appeared undiminished—but neither his lady, nor the earl, ever took the least notice of me—my father's sister, lady Woodville, was extremely kind to me, and, even pressed my grandfather to let me live with her, but he refused to part with the only joy he had on earth, and she died before him.

When I was about fourteen, I was deprived of my affectionate, and tender parent, the good old colonel.—Before he died, he recommended me, in the most affecting terms, to my father, who promised every thing in my favour, that he could desire; but, seemed offended, that the colonel should think it necessary, to plead, for his dearest, best loved child, the child of his affection, the child of his ever-adored, and lamented Harriet. Fully satisfied with these assurances, the good old man resigned his soul, in peace, leaving me all his personal fortune, which amounted to about six thousand pounds; his paternal estate being entailed,[45] on a male heir.

Lady Anne Westrop, who was a distant relation of my mother's, invited me to live with her, and in the society of this agreeable woman, I began to recover my natural chearfulness, which had been totally absorbed, by the grief I felt, for my grandfather's ill health, and death.—During a year, that we passed intirely at her seat in the country, I knew not one moment's uneasiness—my mind was like a peaceful ocean, whose every motion was uniformly gentle, without one ruffling breeze to disturb, or deform it; yet sufficiently actuated, to prevent languor or disgust, the stagnation of the soul.

How often have I looked back, with regret, upon this pleasing calm! which was, alas! too soon succeeded by impetuous storms, where all my peace was shipwrecked. About the end of this happy æra, captain Barnard came to pay a visit to his sister, lady Anne; he is youngest son to the earl of W———. He was designed for the navy, and his father was, at that time, soliciting a ship,[46] which he soon obtained for him. I shall not take up your ladyship's time, by giving you an account of our childish courtship, but tell you, at once, that,

A mutual flame was quickly caught,
  Was quickly too reveal'd,
For neither bosom lodg'd a wish,
  That virtue keeps conceal'd.

What happy hours of heart-felt bliss,
  Did love on both bestow!
But bliss too mighty long to last,
  Where fortune proves a foe.[47]

In the midst of these truly Arcadian[48] pleasures, the earl, my grandfather, died; which I can by no means say disturbed my happiness; but, alas! it was to be interrupted by a severer shock; for my father survived him, but eleven days; the six thousand pounds, which colonel Stanley, had bequeathed to me, was in my father's hands, his estate was all settled upon the issue of his second marriage, and his debts amounted to rather more, than his personal fortune; so that there remained not a shilling for me,[49] even of my grandfather's legacy, without going to law with the countess, my step-mother, who had possessed herself of every thing my father left.

I grieved only for his loss, that of my fortune appearing, then, of no consequence; my lover, seemed to redouble his tenderness for me, but thought, circumstanced as I then was, it would be prudent to conceal our passion, as it was highly probable his friends might oppose our union. I acquiesced in his opinion, and rested all my hopes of happiness, on him,—unworthy guardian of that sacred trust!

When the time for his leaving West-hill, arrived, I then discovered that I had never known sorrow, before; it was impossible to conceal my anguish, and lady Anne Westrop, who had taken great pains to comfort me for the death of my father, and imagined, not without reason, that my grief had subsided into a calm, and gentle melancholy, seemed astonished, at the violence of my affliction; but, I might have answered her, with the words of Helena,

        I think not on my father,
    And these great tears grace his remembrance, more,
    Than those I shed for him.[50]

However, I thought it very lucky, that my late misfortune appeared a sufficient cause, for my present melancholy, which I indulged to such an excess, as soon affected my constitution, and I was ordered by my physician, to Bristol.[51] Lady Anne, ever kind, and affectionate, towards me, accompanied me thither, and Mr. Westrop went up to London, to consult lawyers, about the recovery of my fortune.

The frequency and tenderness, of captain Barnard's letters, contributed much more, to the restoration of my health, than all the waters of those salubrious springs; and lady Anne expressed such sincere joy, at my recovery, that I, romantic as I was, thought myself bound in honour, to acquaint her with the real cause of it. I thought concealing any thing, from such a friend, was *acting a lye,* and, in the fulness of my gratitude, I poured forth all the secrets of my heart.

She heard me, with that sort of coldness, with which one listens to a twice-told tale, yet, at the same time, assured me, she had never suspected any attachment, between her brother and me; said she wished, for both our sakes, we could conquer our passion, for she was certain, it could only be productive of misery, to both.

I was equally picqued at her manner, and expression, and replied, with some warmth, that, as I considered myself under very great obligations to her, I would not entail misery on any part of her family, let my own fate be what it would. She applauded my resolution, with the same *sang froid,* with which she had heard my story, and I retired from her apartment, to my own, more humbled, and mortified, than I had ever been, in my life.

I passed a most restless, miserable night, sometimes resolving, from the highest generosity, to break with captain Barnard,—the next moment, repeating vows of everlasting love—but, at all events, I determined, to quit lady Anne; yet, whither should I go? where fly to? a wretched orphan, without friends, or fortune!

The agitation of my mind, at length subsided, and towards morning, I fell into a profound slumber. As I slept much longer than usual, I found lady Anne's woman by my bedside, when I awoke, who said, she came from her lady, to inquire my health, and to request that I would go to her, immediately.

I obeyed the summons, instantly, and, while I was hurrying on my cloaths, flattered myself, that she had relented of her unkindness, and wished again to restore me, to that sisterly affection, which she seemed so long to have felt for me, and yet to have lost, in one moment; possessed with this imagination, I ran, or rather flew, to her apartment; but, on opening the door, was surprized to see lord N——, who appeared very earnest in conversation with her ladyship.

This gentleman, had been very particular to me, ever since our residence at Bristol; he was young, polite, and master of a large, independant fortune; but, these advantages had made me rather decline, than encourage his acquaintance, lest the busy tongues of men, or rather women, might have pronounced him a lover—an epithet, which is, of all others, most hateful, to a delicate, pre-engaged heart.

On my entrance, the conversation became general. Lady Anne affected to treat me with her usual tenderness, but, I too plainly saw, that she only affected it. After some little time, she withdrew, abruptly, and left me alone, with lord N——. A thousand disagreeable things rushed into my mind, at once, but above all, I feared a declaration of love, from his lordship, which, though I was determined to refuse, must have distressed me, extremely, as I could not, to the world, assign any justifiable cause, for my refusal.

I rose from my seat, with trepidation, and rang the bell, for breakfast. I hoped this would be a hint for his lordship to retire—on the contrary, he said, it was very fortunate for him, that I had called for tea, as he had not touched any thing, but a glass of water, that day, and should have absolutely forgot that eating was necessary, if I had not reminded him of it; but since I had, he hoped I would allow him the honour of breakfasting with me.

I coolly bowed assent, and the moment the tea-table was removed, said I must retire, to put on my riding-dress, as I had promised to meet a lady on the Downs,[52] and feared I should keep her waiting. Lord N—— saw my confusion, pitied, and relieved it, by saying he would not trespass farther, on my leisure, but hoped I would permit him the honour of paying me a visit, in the afternoon: he did not wait for my reply, and I thought myself infinitely obliged to him, for even postponing the embarrassment, in which I knew I should be too soon involved.

As soon as lady Anne and I were alone, after dinner, she congratulated me, with a serious air, on the important conquest I had made, enumerated the great advantages of such a match, and said, she was rejoiced to find, by the ease, and propriety of my behaviour, that the silly prepossession I had talked of, the night before, had not rendered me so romantically absurd, as to reject happiness, and lord N——, or to persist in embracing misery, and captain Barnard.

Though I had, in some measure, prepared myself, to hear her speak on this subject, yet I could not avoid feeling the utmost surprize, at her want of delicacy, in mentioning the man whom I professed to love, at the same instant, that she approved my accepting of another.

As soon as I recovered myself, I told her that I was neither intitled to her congratulation, or approbation, as lord N—— had never said any thing upon such a subject, to me, and that I hoped he never would, as I should be very sorry, to give him the mortification of a denial; but, at the same time, that I fled from what *she* called happiness, I hoped I should find, what I thought so, in the consciousness of having acted right; for though I never could divest myself, of the tenderest attachment, to captain Barnard, yet I could sacrifice my hopes of any future connection with him, to his advantage, and her desire.

Lady Anne took me at my word, praised my generosity, and intreated I would take time to consider, before I refused lord N——. I assured her, that delay was unnecessary; and as I had a very high esteem for his lordship, and was sincerely grateful, for the honour he intended me, I could not think of trifling with his peace, or meanly accepting a heart, because set in gold, when it was absolutely impossible for me to make the only return, which such a valuable present deserved. She called me, dear, romantic, generous girl; said she had no doubt, but time, and reason, would conquer my childish passion, and that she should rejoice to see me happy, with some worthy man; but, still intreated me, not to act precipitately, with regard to lord N——, as she feared I might never have such another offer.

This kind of conversation, lasted till lord N—— came to visit us, and I now wished for his making that declaration, I so much dreaded, in the morning. I was determined, on the conduct I should pursue towards him, and secretly triumphed, in the sacrifice I should make, to my truly disinterested love for captain Barnard. However, her ladyship took care that we should not so immediately come to an explanation; for she never left us, the whole evening. Lord N—— appeared to be chagrined; and I was also extremely mortified that the affair was not brought to a conclusion.

The next day, I received a letter, from Mr. Westrop, informing me, that my step-mother had consented to give me four thousand pounds, rather than stand a law suit for the six, which my grandfather left me. In consideration of this sum, I was to relinquish all farther claim, to my father's fortune, and to receive it as a present, from her bounty. These terms I thought extremely hard; but to attempt carrying on an expensive suit, without money, appeared impracticable. It is true, Mr. Westrop, in the most friendly manner, offered to advance any sum I might have occasion for; but I already felt the *weight* of my obligation to lady Anne, and determined not to increase *the load.* I, therefore, complied with these severe conditions: but as I was not of age, Mr. Westrop became security, for my part of the contract; and the interest of this splendid sum,[53] was allotted for my maintenance.

On this occasion, lady Anne behaved with the utmost kindness towards me; begged I would consider her as my sister, and never think of quitting her house, till I went to one of my own. She made me several valuable presents, which I received with the utmost reluctance; yet could not refuse, as her manner of bestowing them, was peculiarly polite, and tender. In short, she did every thing in her power, to conciliate that true esteem, and affection, which her conduct, with regard to captain Barnard, had, for a while, restrained.

Lord N—— soon found an opportunity, to disclose his passion to me; and I, as quickly, put an end to all his hopes. He thanked me for the generous frankness of my conduct, and earnestly intreated to be admitted to see me as a friend, though I had denied him as a lover. I readily consented to his request, and have ever found him a most amiable, and worthy man.

I had not received a letter from captain Barnard, for near a month.— He was stationed in the Mediterranean: and though determined, as soon as he returned to England, to take an everlasting leave of him, I grew impatient at his silence, and longed to return to Westhill, to retrace those paths we had trod together, and woo sweet echo[54] to repeat his name. I knew lady Anne received foreign letters, frequently, some of which I supposed were from captain Barnard; but as she was silent, on the subject of them, I did not think it proper to appear inquisitive; and some weeks elapsed, without suffering that name to pass my lips, which was but too deeply engraved, on my heart.

At length, the time for our departure, came, and we arrived at Westhill.—The morning after, I rose, very early, in order to indulge the fond idea of revisiting those woods, and lawns, where I had spent so many happy hours.—I did not imagine any of the family were stirring, and went softly into lady Anne's dressing-room, where all the English poets lay, to take a book with me into the gardens. I started, at finding her there. Her surprize at seeing me, equalled mine: but quickly recovering herself, she talked of the fineness of the morning, which she said had tempted her to leave her bed, so soon; but that finding the dew was not off the grass, she had sat down to write letters.

A propos, said she; I have had one in my possession for you, these ten days; but as I did not know whether the contents might be perfectly agreeable to you, I chose to defer delivering it, till we were quite free from observers. I flatter myself, madam, said I, that your precaution was unnecessary, if, as I apprehend, the letter comes from captain Barnard. Lady Anne replied, Do not be too sanguine, my dear; we feel our disappointments, in proportion to our expectations. True, madam, I returned; but as the height of mine, at present, extends only to knowing that your brother is well, and happy, do not protract my anxiety, on that account, but be so good to let me have my letter.

She then presented it to me, saying, I believe you had better retire to your own apartment, before you read it. I willingly obeyed: but though all this preparation was sufficient to alarm me, yet at the sight of those dear, well-known characters, I forgot all that lady Anne had said, and broke the seal with the highest transport. But before I had read half the following lines, I, in reality, suffered the transformation, which Ovid feigned for Niobe:[55] my limbs were petrified: nor was there the least sign of life, or motion, remaining in me, but my flowing tears.

### *To Lady* HARRIET HANBURY

Madam,

The ingratitude, and unkindness, of your behaviour towards me, deserve such reproaches, as I am incapable of making, to a person I once truly loved. I ought to be thankful for your having cured me of that folly; but the manner of your doing it, takes away the merit of the obligation.

Unworthy Harriet! you might have ceased to love, without betraying, and exposing the wretch, who doated on you. Lord N——'s superior rank, and fortune, were temptations, I scarce could hope you should withstand. But why, ingrate! should you despise, and ridicule the fondness, of that heart,—where, though you have planted daggers, there still remains the warmest wishes, for your future happiness.

It is now above two months, since I have heard from you. This cruel, this alarming silence, filled my fond bosom with the tenderest sorrow. I had a thousand fears for my loved Harriet. I feared some fatal accident might have befallen her. I feared every thing that could befall, except her breach of vows! The fidelity of my own heart, prevented that suspicion.

But I have done, for ever, on this subject; nor will I longer interrupt your felicity, than to intreat, as my last request, if you have thought my letters worth preserving, that you will immediately deliver them, to my sister. If ever I return to England, and you desire it, I will restore your's, dear as they once were to my faithful heart, which wants not memento's of the faithless Harriet.

I have got another ship, and shall use all my interest, to prevent my returning to England.—Amidst all the perils, to which my situation daily exposed me, I wished to preserve my life, for your sake, only; but your perfidy has now rendered it of as little value to me, as it ever was to you: and to die nobly in the service of my country, is, at present, the most earnest wish of,

The unfortunate,

WM. BARNARD.

I had remained, for some hours, in the situation I have already described, when lady Anne sent her woman, to call me to breakfast. On finding my eyes fixed, and my whole frame immoveable, Mrs. Atkins screamed so loud, that lady Anne, and Mr. Westrop, ran into my dressing-room. I was immediately put into bed, and every care was taken for my recovery. A slow fever ensued, which I daily hoped would terminate my life, and misery; but it pleased Providence that I should be reserved, for greater woes.

As soon as I was capable of reasoning, I found captain Barnard had been imposed upon, and felt even more for his sufferings, than my own.—But who could have deceived him? it must be lady Anne. But as I was not in a situation to resent such cruelty, I thought it most prudent to acquiesce, in silence, and wait till time, the great expounder of mysteries, should clear my innocence. She frequently observed, that as I was determined to break with him, it would be better to let him remain in his error, than to come to an explanation, that could answer no end, as we were to part, for ever. To this I could, by no means, agree. But, alas! it was not in my power to oppose her pleasure. I neither knew the name of his ship, nor his place of destination; and I continued, for near twelve months, a prey to the most cruel suspence.

At this time, lady Anne, and Mr. Westrop, purposed making the *petit tour,* and insisted on my accompanying them.—I gladly accepted the offer; for I might truly say, "I had such perpetual source of disquiet, in my own breast, that rest was grown painful to me, and a state of agitation, only, could afford me ease, by rescuing me, as it were, from myself."

Though we spent a month, in London, to wait for the conclusion of the peace,[56] I knew not where to make any inquiry after captain Barnard; nor had I a friend, to whom I could venture to repeat his name; and I set out for Paris, much more inclined to enter into the most gloomy solitude, than to partake of the pleasures of that gay city.

There I became acquainted with lord Woodville, and there I also met Mrs. Bolton, who was nearly related to me, by my mother.—We had been acquainted, from our infancy, and had a real friendship for each other; but her living in Ireland, where her husband had a very large fortune, had prevented our meeting, for three years before. She was in a very declining state of health, and was going to Montpellier,⁵⁷ on that account, when Mr. Bolton was obliged to set out for Ireland, on the death of a near relation.

As lady Anne was constantly engaged in the *grand monde*,⁵⁸ I spent much of my time with Mrs. Bolton, and with real sorrow saw that amiable woman growing worse, every day.—Her physicians, at length, had her removed, to Fontainbleau.—Just then, lady Anne grew weary of Paris, and resolved to pursue her route. Poor Mrs. Bolton shed a flood of tears, when I talked of quitting Paris, and intreated me not to leave her "a helpless stranger in a foreign land." Even her own maid, had married one of the *gens d'armes*,⁵⁹ and left her, so that she had not a creature about her, that had the least regard, or tenderness, for her. She said, a few days would put an end to the arduous task she required from my friendship, that of closing her dying eyes: but that, if Mr. Bolton should return, before that happened, her carriage, and servants, should convey me to lady Anne, or wherever I desired.

There was no resisting her importunities; and lady Anne, though dissatisfied at my stay, applauded the nobleness of my friendship, and took a very affectionate leave of me. I saw her get into her carriage, with sincere regret. I considered myself, as torn from one who had been the friend, and protectress of my youth. Her cruelty was forgot; and every act of kindness she had ever shewn me, returned with double force, into my memory; and my heart and eyes overflowed, with grateful tenderness.

I was waiting, in this situation of mind, for Mrs. Bolton's chariot, to carry me to Fontainbleau, when captain Barnard entered the room! I will not pretend to describe the emotions of my heart;—in short, they were too strong for my reason, and suspended all its powers.—Never sure was such a meeting! The extremes of love, surprize, resentment, joy, all operated on me.

He was all penitence, and love; kneeled at my feet, and bathed my hand with tears; pleaded the violence of his distracted love, in excuse for the cruel letter he had wrote, when he believed me false; and uttered the most solemn vows, that if I would again receive his heart, which never had strayed, one moment, from me, no power on earth, should ever part us more: but if I refused to accept his love, he would instantly give up the command of his ship, and retire to some part of the world, where he should never be heard of.

I will frankly confess, that all my tenderness for this unworthy man, returned; and I even thought I loved him better, than I had ever done, before.

He was then of age, and master of himself: there remained, therefore, nothing to oppose *our* wishes, for I own them mutual, but the obligations I was under, and the voluntary promise I had made, to lady Anne. This objection he treated as romantic; but said, he would gratify my delicacy, in this particular; and engaged to obtain her free consent.

He attended me to Fontainbleau, and visited me there, every day, during two months, that my amiable friend continued to languish.—At the end of that time, she was released, and left me in sincere affliction. Mr. Bolton returned, a few days before her death; and, some time after, made me a present of part of her jewels, to the amount of two thousand pounds.—I would have declined so valuable a gift; but it was my dear Mrs. Bolton's dying request, that I should have them.

At captain Barnard's earnest intreaty, I returned to Paris, where he still continued to sollicit our marriage, and I to refuse, till he had fulfilled his promise, with regard to lady Anne.—At length, he extorted one from me, that even her opposing it, should not prevent our union; and, in an oblique manner, confessed, that she had been the cause of that letter, which had given me so much pain, by her misrepresentation of my conduct at Bristol. He that can please, is certain to persuade; and I, at last, acquiesced in his request.

He would not hear of my returning to England, till we were married. I had no parent's consent to ask, and he had wrote to the chaplain of his ship, to come and marry us. Seemingly possessed with the tenderest passion, that ever warmed a human heart, he set out for Aix la Chapelle, where we supposed lady Anne to be; but, unluckily, she had left it, two days before captain Barnard arrived, and was then returning to England. Thither the captain followed. I was extremely concerned at his disappointment; but it was only on account of the additional trouble, and fatigue, he was to undergo.

He wrote to me, every post; nay, I was sometimes so happy, as to receive two or three letters, wrote at different times of the same day, filled with the language of love, with fond complaints of absence, and vows never to leave me more.

However, blinded as I was by my own passion, I could not help perceiving, that when he had been some time in England, the stile of his letters began to change, though he continued still to complain of the cruel necessity that detained him; but not in that charming, plaintive stile, which used, at once, to soften, and delight my heart.

Three months passed away, in this manner, during which time, I received a cold, but civil letter, from lady Anne, congratulating me on the constancy of my lover, and thanking me for the needless compliment I had paid her, as she was perfectly convinced we were too much in love, to follow any person's advice, but our own.—Notwithstanding this, she very sincerely wished my happiness, whether I should, or should not become her sister.

As I found captain Barnard's return was still protracted, by his father's ill health, and many other reasons, that did not appear to me sufficient, I began to be uneasy at my situation.—A single woman, without friends, or relations, in such a place as Paris, was, by no means, in an eligible state.— I had some acquaintance, and those of distinction, who received me, on lady Anne's account, without inquiring into the motives of my stay: but I felt a consciousness, that their civilities were more the effect of politeness, than esteem: which rendered me unhappy; and I wrote to captain Barnard, requesting his permission to return to England, if he did not intend to come to Paris, immediately.

My letter lay sealed, and directed, on my dressing-table, when lord N—— came to make me a visit; and casting his eyes on the letter, said, I might spare myself the trouble of sending it to the post-office, as he had, that moment, met captain Barnard, in a very fine equipage. My heart sunk in me, at this news.—Yet I still flattered myself, that Lord N—— might mistake some other person for him, and was earnest in persuading his lordship, that he was deceived, when the captain's servant brought me the following card.

> If lady Harriet H——, will be at home, and alone, this evening, captain Barnard will, if agreeable, do himself the honour of waiting on her, at six o'clock.

The surprize I had been in before, was augmented, by this extraordinary message. I, however, sent word I should be glad to see him; and passed the intermediate hours in endeavouring to prepare myself, for that fatal change, which was already but too visible, but which I was utterly unable to account for.

At the appointed time, he came, and endeavoured to assume a sort of formal tenderness, accompanied with an air of gravity, and mystery. I could not long endure such a cruel state of suspence, and pressed to know, what it was that affected him? he told me, he was the most miserable man breathing, that all his schemes of happiness were blasted, but that he never could have resolution to tell me, how they were so—called me, dear, suffering angel! kissed my hand, and wept.—

I cannot describe the emotion of my heart; I longed, yet feared, to know what all this meant; and, at length, told him, that if he did not wish to make me extremely unhappy, he would explain this enigma. He said, he had great reason to fear, that satisfying my inquiries, would render me, yet more wretched, even than doubt could do; and if the secret could be kept, for ever, from me, he would die, rather than reveal it. But I must know it, and he who was a sharer in the misfortune, would tell it, with most tenderness.

He then conjured me, to summon all the love I ever had for him, that it might incline me to pity, and pardon a wretch, that had undone himself! in short, he told me, that his friends had prevailed on him to marry Miss S———, whom he unfortunately met, at Aix la Chapelle, and accompanied to London—that at the moment he received her hand, the icy one of death, would have been more welcome; that his heart did, and ever should, adore me, and only me; and that he lived for me, and me, only.

He had knelt by my side, while he told this fatal story, and when he finished it, wept extremely. To his amazement, not one sigh, or tear, escaped me. I rose immediately, and wished him joy, then rung the bell, to order my chariot; he remained immoveable, I begged he would rise, before the servant entered—he obeyed; but implored me not to leave him; said it was impossible, that I could really be so indifferent, as I appeared; that he was prepared to meet my anger, or my sorrow, but could not bear contempt.

I told him, that was, at present, my predominant sentiment, and the sooner he retired from it, and put an end to this interview, the better, and which I would take care should be our last. He vowed he would never leave the spot, where he again prostrated himself, till I pronounced his pardon. I told him this was adding insult, to injury, but since he would not quit my apartment, I should.

I threw myself into my carriage, and suffered myself to be carried to the marchioness de St. Aumont's—there I met lord Woodville, and lord N———; who both remarked, that I looked extremely ill, and advised me to leave the assembly, and return home. And I soon found myself so really so, that I was obliged to follow their advice.

I went immediately to bed, without speaking a syllable, even to my maid, who observing so sudden a change in my manners and appearance, sat up in my dressing-room. The heroism of my conduct, towards captain

Barnard, had flattered my pride, and kept up my spirits, while he was present, but I was no sooner alone, than I felt all the weight of my misfortunes; and the agitation, and distraction of my mind, threw me into convulsions. My maid had immediate help for me, but all the art of the best physicians in Paris, could not restore my senses, for fifteen days—happy interval! delightful recess, from agonizing sorrow.

At length, their cruel kindness triumphed, so far, as to restore my reason—but, good God! in what a shattered plight, did it return! and to what a poor, defaced, and wretched habitation? my disorder was generally believed to be a malignant fever, but, doctor L——, who understood the maladies of the mind, as well as body, and was acquainted with my attachment to captain Barnard, contributed to the recovery of the latter, by administring consolation to the former, much more, than all the art of medicine could have done. I soon discharged all my physicians, but him, who only knew the source of my complaint; and to his skill, and tenderness, am I indebted, for the preservation of this wretched being.

During my illness, lord Woodville, and lord N——, behaved like brothers to me—they both visited me daily, and endeavoured, but in vain, and unknowing of the cause, to dissipate that melancholy, which will for ever prey upon my heart. My mind was so much weakened, that I determined to go into a convent, and flattered myself, that in that calm retirement, I should find peace, and rest. I fancied I might there retain the tenets of my own religion,[60] only conforming, externally, to theirs.

I communicated my project to doctor L——, who soon convinced me, that peace dwells not in a cloister, but that even those holy retreats, are filled with vain wishes, and tumultuous passions; and that it would be making a mockery of all religion, to pretend to embrace theirs, unless I could do it, sincerely.

While I remained in a very weak, and languishing condition, a gentleman called frequently to inquire my health; but as he refused to leave his name, I guessed it was some person sent by captain Barnard, and was therefore not the least inquisitive about him. At length he desired to be admitted to see me, saying, he had something of importance, to communicate.

I consented; and after the common civilities were over, he took a pacquet out of his pocket, and presenting it to me, said he hoped that would be an acceptable present. It was directed, in an unknown hand; but as I hesitated about receiving it, he said I had nothing to fear, from the contents, and he would call for my answer, the next day; and instantly left the room.

The pacquet contained a long letter, from captain Barnard, filled with vain excuses for his falsehood, and passionate intreaties that I would again suffer him to plead his pardon, at my feet—he expressed the most poignant sorrow for my illness, and begged I would at least permit him to repair the injuries he had done me, as far as it was possible, by accepting an unlimited power over that fortune, to which he had sacrificed his love, honour, and happiness; and as a proof of my forgiveness, requested I would receive an inclosed bill, for five hundred pounds; but if my pride should still reject his penitence, he desired I would return his letters, by the gentleman that was the bearer of that.

This fresh insult roused all my resentment against him, and I passed a restless night, counting the clock, and with impatience, waiting for the hour when I should restore his insolent present, with the scorn it merited.

At length, his ambassador arrived, and either was, or seemed to be surprized, when I acquainted him with the purport of the letter he had brought me; and made many apologies for having unwittingly offended—said the affair between captain Barnard and me, had been represented in a very different light to him; that he understood there had been a slight quarrel between us, and that the letter he brought, was to be the means of reconcilement.

Cruel Barnard, merciless man! was it not enough to make me wretched! why should he endeavour to make me infamous, also! I returned the note, and put the letter which had inclosed it, into the fire. As to those I had formerly received from captain Barnard, I told his friend I would readily part with them, when he should have restored mine; but as I had no reason to have the least reliance on his word, I would not give them out of my possession, on any other terms. He applauded my resolution, and retired.

I longed, impatiently, to leave Paris, and fancied I should recover my peace, by quitting the scene of my unhappiness—I was obliged to part with some of the jewels, which Mrs. Bolton had left me, to defray the expences of my illness, and journey; and in a state of the lowest weakness, both of mind, and body, I returned to London.

On my arrival, I found that a maiden aunt of my father's, who had never taken the least notice of me, during her life, had bequeathed me her whole fortune, ten thousand pounds, merely because I was her namesake, and unprovided for, by my father. This was a very happy addition to my confined circumstances; but I was incapable of joy, and continued to live like a recluse, till lord Woodville's return to England.—He soon found me out, and did me the honour to present me to lady Straffon, and his lovely Emily.

In this charming society, I began to recover my tranquillity, and flattered myself that it was well nigh established, till the unlucky accident, which brought captain Barnard to my sight, convinced me, that there is no cure, for ill-fated love; since neither the cruelty I have experienced, nor time itself, have yet been able to conquer it.

I will not now, my dear lady Woodville, take up more of your time, by apologizing for the weakness of my conduct, through this unhappy affair; for

> With thee, I scorn the low constraint of art,
> And boast the graceful weakness of my heart.[61]

## LETTER 14.

### *Lady* STRAFFON, *To Lady* WOODVILLE.

I have a thousand thanks to give my dear Emily, for the pleasing, though melancholy entertainment, which lady Harriet's history has afforded me.—When I was very young, I used to be surprized that so many tragedies, and novels, were founded on the perfidy of men: but I have, for some years past, been perfectly convinced, that most of the miseries of this life, owe their being to that fatal source. And were there but a window in every fair bosom, in the cities of London, and Westminster, we should discover numberless hidden traces of the barbarous triumphs, of those doughty "Heroes, famous and renowned, for wronging innocence, and breaking vows:" and among this detestable corps, I think captain Barnard might lead the van, and Sir James Miller bring up the rear.

You may see, by this disposition, that I think worse of the captain, than the baronet, as I think lady Harriet much more unhappy, than Lucy. However, I sincerely hope they may both surmount their afflictions: for time, and reason, can do more, in these cases, than the sufferers are willing to allow. They are patients that do not wish to be cured; and find a degree of pleasure, in indulging their malady.

I am of opinion, that when disappointed love subsides into a calm, and gentle melancholy, its sensations may, not only be pleasing, to the persons that feel it, but render them more amiable, than they would otherwise be, by giving a peculiar softness, both to their form and manners. I think I should be more apt to fall in love, with a person so circumstanced, than with one who had never felt *la belle passion.*[62]

I have great pleasure in telling you, that Lucy daily gains strength, both of mind, and body; and I, by no means, despair of a perfect cure. The most favourable symptom is, her not having mentioned Sir James, these two days; yet have I not once restrained her on the subject, as she has lately spoke of him with great calmness. I have not yet shewn her lady Harriet's memoir.— Tenderness, like sorrow, is contagious; and the similitude of their situations, might call forth tears, which, though set down to the account of friendship, would certainly flow from her own sympathy.

It is utterly impossible for me to have the pleasure of visiting Woodfort, this summer.—I expect Sir John, in a very few days.—As soon as he arrives, we shall go into Essex.—I do not think Lucy sufficiently recovered, to quit her nurse, as she calls me.—My little Emily, and Edward, are quite well, and surprizingly grown, since their illness.

I long to know what became of captain Barnard, the day he left you; and what connexion he could have, with lady Ransford; who, from your account, seems not to be one of those, who were born to weep over the willow.[63]

I suppose you will soon set out, for York.—The lovely marchioness is to be there.—Is lady Lawson to be of your party? I could wish she were; as, I fear, my dear Emily may not be sufficiently attentive, to her present situation.— Let me entreat you not to ride, and to dance, but little. My true love attends your lord; and, with good wishes to all your party, I am, affectionately,

Your's,

F. Straffon.

## LETTER 15.

### *Lady* WOODVILLE, *To Lady* STRAFFON.

I am not half satisfied with my dear Fanny's *no comment*, on lady Harriet's affecting story.—By making the case general, you seem inclined to lessen the calamity.—But a plague is a plague, though ten thousand, or only one thousand, die of it; and, by extending its dominion you increase the fatality, without abating our compassion for particular sufferers.

Again, and again, I say, what a blessed, happy creature, is your Emily! Had my dear lord, after gaining, trifled with my heart, his triumph would soon have been complete; for I really think the first wound must have subdued it. But he, who has penetration enough, to see the softness of my nature, has also generosity sufficient, to prevent my very wishes; and seems to have no fear, but want of power to gratify them. This is a theme, on which my grateful heart could dwell, for ever: but, not to tire you, I shall change the subject.

I find lord Seymour vastly averse, to our going to York.—He has taken so much pains to dissuade me from it, that if I had not promised Fanny Weston, and Sir James Thornton, whose hearts are set on going, I should find great pleasure in sacrificing my own inclination, to his lordship.—Yet he gives no solid reason, for our declining this party.—I perceive that *my* lord looks grave, when the subject is mentioned; of course, it is immediately dropped: and, I find, the boys and girls, will be conquerors.—Even the grave lady Harriet, and Mr. Ransford, seemed to be alarmed, while the matter appeared doubtful.

I think I have as little curiosity, as any of my sex, yet I confess myself anxious to know lord Seymour's motive.—He is a man of such excellent understanding, and true politeness, that I am astonished at his thinking differently, even upon this trifling subject, from *my lord!* But avaunt! thou first female vice, curiosity! I will not suffer thee to harbour, one moment longer, in my breast, thou inhospitable tenant! disturber of the peaceful mansion that receives thee!

Lady Lawson will not accompany us, to York: she has been confined to her chamber, for some days, with a fever on her spirits. A young lady, whom she took into her house a distressed orphan, five years ago, and treated with the utmost tenderness, has just left her. This is unlucky, as she is ill, and alone. Sir William set out, for London, yesterday, without calling upon us.

The moment I have quitted one dear sister, I shall fly to the other, and spend as much time, as I possibly can, with her. Should she continue ill, it will prevent my going to York. I shall only be sorry for the occasion, for I have lost all relish for the party.

I know not what became of captain Barnard, the day he left us; but, I hear, he is a constant visitor, at Ransford-Hall.—The old knight is laid up, in the gout; and her ladyship acts in the double capacity, of master, and mistress, of the family.

I hope Sir John is, by this time, returned to you, full of love, and joy, and admiration, at your amazing, and successful prowess, with regard to his children; and that you are all as happy, as you deserve, and I wish.

Amen, and adieu.

E. Woodville.

A thousand loves to Lucy.

## Letter 16.

### *Lady* Woodville, *To Lady* Straffon.

My dear Fanny,

As I have been used, from my infancy, to your tender participation of all my pains, and pleasures, I could not resist my inclination of sending you the inclosed, which afforded me the most charming *mélange* of both, that I have ever met with. I am proud, and pleased, that the writer was a woman; but cannot help lamenting, that such noble sentiments, such an elegant turn of mind, and above all, such tender sensibility, should be buried in a cloister.

Now for the means, by which I obtained this treasure.—Yesterday evening, after tea, the conversation turned on the subject of letter-writing. Lord Seymour advanced, and was seconded by *my lord,* that ladies, in general, wrote better, in the epistolary stile, than men.—As I looked upon such a declaration, rather as a compliment paid to the present company, than their real sentiments, I took up the argument: and though they mentioned several instances of charming female scribes, all of whom I admire, as much as they, yet would I not allow the merit general:—for those very persons, whom they quoted, are, or ought to be, as much distinguished from the rest of their sex, for their superior talents, as lady C——, or the duchess of H——, for their uncommon beauty.

Lord Seymour politely called me an heretic, against self-conviction; said, he had observed my frequent use of the pen, and was persuaded, that no person, with half my understanding, was ever fond of writing, who was not conscious of writing well. I told his lordship that if the conversation became particular, there must be an end of the general argument. He bowed, and went on with repeating some passages, from female letters, which did honour to his taste, and with which we were all charmed.

He then told us, that he had a letter in his pocket, which he looked upon to be the *chef d'œuvre*[64] of female eloquence; that he had found it, as he was, one morning, taking a solitary walk, in the Tuileries;[65] that he would permit me to read it, provided I would candidly give him my opinion, whether I thought any man living, could dictate such a letter. On my promising to be sincere, he took it out of his pocket-book, presented it to me, with a trembling hand, and left the room.

When we met, at supper, I was lavish in its praise, and declared, that I doubted whether even Rousseau,[66] could have wrote more tenderly. He seemed delighted at my conversion, and immediately complied with my request, to suffer me to take a copy of it, for you, and you, only.

I impatiently long to know something more of the lady's history.—I cannot be persuaded, that it was mere accident, which put it into lord Seymour's hands.—But I will not detain you from the perusal of it, by my vague conjectures.—I shall, however, satisfy your curiosity, in a more material point, by letting you know lady Lawson is better.—I am to dine with her, *tête à tête,* to-morrow.

I shall claim great merit, for this volunteer. I hope Lucy continues well. I earnestly wish to know what apology you have made, for that worthless ideot, Sir James Miller, to Sir John. Pray write very soon, a very long letter, to

    Your's, very sincerely,

E. WOODVILLE.

## THE LETTER.

After a conflict of four months, the mildest moment of which sad time, was infinitely more painful, than that which shall separate this feeble frame from its perturbed spirit, I sit down to bid an everlasting adieu, to him, who was far dearer than the first, and long maintained the scale in equal balance, with the latter. Did I say *was?* alas! he is, and ever will be, dearer, than my life! which I would sacrifice, a thousand times, rather than wound his heart, as now I must.

Unhappy Henry! what pangs, what anguish, will now rend thy bosom, when thou shalt be convinced, thou never hadst a rival, in thy Charlotte's love! Even heaven itself, yielded its claim to thee; and my fond heart adored the Maker, in his most perfect work, thy charming self! Such, in thy Charlotte's eyes, didst thou appear, till thy relentless jealousy pursued, and would have robbed of life—no rival, Henry! but thy Charlotte's brother!

How will amazement strike thee! My sad heart bleeds for thine. Involved in mystery, and misery, from my birth, this truth could not have reached you, sooner; nor could I possibly reveal the secret, and brand with cruelty, and guilt, the authors of my wretched being.

Recall the fatal evening to your mind, when that accursed jealousy infused its venom first into your bosom—what pains did I not take to counteract the poison! how was the innocent young man astonished, at your behaviour! remember the last words I ever uttered to you.—*My dearest Henry, let not appearances disturb your mind, I can, and will, account for every action of my life, to you—let your servant attend, at the grate, to-morrow, for a letter from me, and you shall be fully satisfied.*

Ah! Henry, how could you doubt her truth, who never yet deceived you! by what you now must feel, judge what I felt, when word was brought me, you had killed my brother! that he survives, for your sake, and my own, I bow my heart to heaven. Ah! what uncommon misery were mine, were I compelled to hate you! No, Henry, I am not so wretched; I may love you still, without a crime; most truly love you; and every prayer that I address to Heaven, may waft petitions for your true felicity!

To-morrow, I renounce the world; vain ceremony! Alas! I have renounced my Henry, before.—This is my last adieu.—May every saint, and angel, bless, protect, and guide you, to that heaven, where we may, once more, hope to meet!—Till then, farewell, for ever—

# LETTER 17.

## *Lady* STRAFFON, *To Lady* WOODVILLE.

I am vastly obliged to my dear Emily, for her two last letters—her volunteer was delightful—that angelic nun has almost broke my heart—it is impossible she can be happy, in a cloister, and I very much doubt, whether those fine feelings, which she seems to have, would not have rendered her rather more miserable, had she remained in the world. May she soon arrive at that place, where the highest sensibility must be productive of the highest happiness!

You will, perhaps, think me cruel, for wishing her death; but indeed, my dear sister, there is scarce a man living, who could deserve such a heart as hers; not even lord Seymour, to whom I believe it devoted. If I read aright, I am truly sorry for his misfortune; he has sustained an irreparable loss.

I dare say your lord is acquainted with the whole story; and as I am persuaded that lord Seymour is incapable of a base, or mean action, he may, perhaps, be prevailed on, to satisfy your curiosity—but if he once declines it, press him no farther. As you value his peace, and your own, never lay him under the painful necessity, of refusing any thing, to the woman he loves; nor let him ever see you have a wish ungratified. Believe me, Emily, more women lose their husbands hearts, by what they call carrying their point, and teizing a good-natured man into compliance, than any other way.

The first part of this letter, like the Gazette,[67] has been devoted to foreign affairs; now for domestic.—Sir John returned, last week, in perfect health and spirits, from Paris. I did not suffer the children to appear, till I acquainted him with my bold undertaking—at first he looked surprized, and terrified; but immediately recollecting himself, said, that from his Fanny's countenance, he was certain our joint treasure must be safe. At that instant, the little animals flew into his arms; I cannot describe the charming scene, but it was, as you say, all "love, and joy, and admiration."

Lucy came next; she had summoned all her spirits, to meet her brother, but in spite of all her resolution, a wayward tear stole down her lovely cheek. To our mutual surprize Sir John took not the least notice, of her soft confusion, nor asked a single question, about Sir James Miller. Lucy was vastly happy, at his seeming inattention; but it alarmed me, much more, than if he had spoken upon the subject.

A little time after, he withdrew into his closet, and wrote a letter—his servant returned, as we were sitting down to dinner, and told him the gentleman was not at home. During our meal, I felt the utmost anxiety, but durst not speak. Lucy was the exact resemblance of Shakespear's patience on a monument, "smiling at grief."[68] Sir John appeared to be perfectly at ease, chearful, and lively.

I observed to him, that he talked much, and eat little. He pressed my hand, with unaffected tenderness, and said the joy he felt at seeing us all, had quite absorbed any thought of himself, but that nature would soon return to its old bent; and bid me beware of my beef and mutton, to-morrow.

I knew the loss of appetite, to be a common effect of joy, and therefore endeavoured to persuade myself that all was well. When we arose from table, he said he had some business to transact, for a gentleman in Paris, but that he should return to tea, and desired Lucy, to have her voice and harpsichord, in tune, to sing him some new songs; he then put on his sword, and walked briskly out of the house.

Lucy and I remained for some moments, petrified; we could neither speak, nor look at each other—at length, she arose, and with a slow pace, and down-cast look, advanced to where I sat, then fell upon her knees, before me, and bathed my hand with her fast-falling tears. I could not bid her rise, but sunk down by her, and joined in fervent prayer, for my husband, and her brother's safety.

A thousand times the dear unhappy girl implored my pardon, as though she were the guilty cause, of what I did, or might, hereafter, suffer. Her anguish seemed unutterable; and alarmed, and distressed, as I then was, I found it absolutely necessary to conceal my own fears, and speak peace to her distracted, tortured mind.

In less than an hour, Sir John relieved us from this shocking state—at the transporting sound of his voice, we endeavoured to compose ourselves—Lucy flew to open the door of the parlour, where we had remained, during his absence; she rushed into his arms, and fainted there. The strong transition over-powered her every faculty, and it was a considerable time, before she shewed any signs of life. I do not blush to tell you that Sir John wept, over his beloved sister.

As soon as she had power of articulation, she gazed intently on her brother, and exclaimed, Where is the unhappy man? and do I see my dearest brother safe, and unstained with blood?

My dear Lucy, Sir John replied, calm your spirits—you need have no apprehensions, either for Sir James Miller, or for me—he is fallen below my resentment; and you might have been assured, from the first, that any man who dared to treat a woman ill, must be a coward in his heart.

But did you meet? cried Lucy. No, said Sir John, and I will answer for it, we never shall, if he can avoid it; and I promise you, I shall not seek the wretch.

But pray, Sir John, said I, how came you acquainted with his ungenerous behaviour? As vice and folly are generally connected, replied Sir John, he was weak enough, to inform against himself, by a letter which he wrote me, to Paris, sometime after his marriage; and concluded it with presenting lady Miller's compliments, and hoping that, notwithstanding what had passed, we might still be friends, and live upon good terms.

In my answer, I told him that though fighting had formerly been my profession, I was neither a bully, nor a bravo,[69] and if he could acquit himself with honour, of a breach of faith to a woman of unquestioned merit, I was ready to accord him the friendship he desired; but as I looked upon that to be impossible, I hoped he would, at least, be ready to afford me the only satisfaction, that remained in his power to offer, or mine to receive. That I should leave Paris, in a few days, and call upon him, as soon as I arrived in London.

I saw his servant, near this house, when I alighted, and I have reason to think he was placed there, to watch my coming; as Sir James and his lady set out, in a few minutes after, for Paris. And I think there now remains nothing, but to wish my dear Lucy joy, of her escape, from such a contemptible animal.

I am, indeed, my dear brother, said Lucy, truly joyful—what a wretch should I have been, if any misfortune had befallen you, on my account! how could I ever have looked upon my more than sister, or her little angel babes. Sir John and I endeavoured to change the subject, but Lucy frequently recurred to it.

Ah, Emily! her wounds are not yet healed. We spent the evening in a kind of pleasing melancholy—though our hearts were at peace, our spirits were too much agitated, to be chearful. I proposed our setting out for Straffon Hill, next day, but Sir John seemed inclined to stay, for a few days longer. As I have now no apprehensions, from Sir James Miller, I can have no objection, though I confess I long for pure air, and peace; two charming things, which are never to be found, in a great city.

I congratulate you, on lady Lawson's recovery. How does poor lady Harriet? Have you civilized Sir James Thornton? I mean, has he yet fallen in love? What is Fanny Weston doing? I shall think her much to blame, if she does not make a conquest—the country is the place, to inspire sentiment— in London, we think of nothing, but outward shew—*happiness* is intirely out of the question. May *it* long continue to reside, at Woodfort, sincerely wishes
    Your

        F. STRAFFON.


P.S. What an amazing long letter! but I am never tired of conversing with you—Sir John, and my Lucy, and my babes, all send you their loves.

# Letter 18.

## *Lady* Woodville, *To Lady* Straffon.

My dear FANNY,

You very aptly compare your last letter to a news paper, which records facts indiscriminately—how could you, possibly, think of the charming nun, however engaging, or affecting her situation, and thence proceed to a sober lecture on matrimony, before you mentioned events so interesting, as those which related to Sir John, Lucy, and yourself? You are certainly a perfect stoic, and I begin to fear you will soon be above "life's weakness, and its comforts too."[70] You see how gladly I lay hold of the first opportunity, I ever had, to criticise on you. I have no doubt but you will explain away all my objections, by next post; but, in the mean time, I shall fully enjoy that *self-given* consequence, and superiority, which we all assume, when we take the liberty of condemning another person's conduct.

But to be serious, both my lord and I are charmed with Sir John—his tenderness for his amiable sister, sets his bravery in the strongest light—and you really did not blush to record it! my dear Fanny must have a great deal of effrontery, notwithstanding her modest countenance, and her meek air. I am in such high spirits, at the happy conclusion of this disagreeable affair, that I cannot command my pen to write one rational line.

Yes, it shall tell you, that all this family congratulate our dear Lucy, and you, but more particularly her, on her lucky escape from that contemptible wretch, Sir James Miller; and though we all hope, and believe ourselves to be very good christians, there is not one of us would lament his untimely end, if he should be detected in picking pockets, in Paris, and make his exit, at the *Grève.*[71]

And so my dear wise sister very prudently warned me against teazing my lord—it was a proper caution, and I shall use it—am not I very obedient? but she left me at full liberty, to torment anyone else—I shall use this latitude, also. To begin: I must inform you that I am in full possession of the history of our lovely nun, and unrestrained from communicating it to you; yet shall I not gratify your curiosity, which I am certain is as great as mine, until you are brought to confess it; and provoked to say, Psha, Emily, how can you be so teizing?

I must now hasten to your queries, as we are going to dine at lord Withers's, four miles off. I have prevailed on lady Lawson to be of the party;

Sir William is not returned from London, yet. I do believe Sir James Thornton is in love, though we cannot guess with whom. He is lately become thoughtful, and reserved; we rally him on his gravity, and tell him he is "proud and melancholy and gentleman-like:"[72] though he has lost his chearfulness, his good humour is invincible, and he strives to laugh, whenever he thinks we wish he should.

I much fear that Cupid has played at cross-bow, amongst our young-folks, and dealt out left-handed arrows. I fear poor Fanny Weston is a stricken deer, and am apprehensive, that the hand which gave, will never heal the wound. She sits, whole evenings, alone, in her chamber, listening to an Æolian harp,[73] and sometimes looks as if she had been in tears. She says she will go to London, from York; but I fancy she may as well return to Wood-fort, as all our male inmates will have left us.

Lord Seymour talks of going to the hot wells, at Bristol, in a few days; and Sir James Thornton goes from York, to his own seat, in the West. Lady Harriet continues pretty much the same, except when captain Barnard is mentioned; which happens, too frequently, as he still visits at lady Ransford's.

Adieu, dear Fanny, the coach is ready, and Sir James Thornton waiting in the ante-chamber of the dressing-room, to hand me to it. I cannot help laughing, at the idea of his grave face. A thousand loves attend Sir John, Lucy, and the babes.

Once more, adieu.

E. WOODVILLE.

# LETTER 19.

## Lady STRAFFON, To Lady WOODVILLE.

Straffon Hill.

It is a remark, much to the honour of human nature, that happiness creates benevolence. I am, therefore, pleased with illustrating it, by telling you, that the calm and rational delight I receive, from my present happy situation, has rendered my mind so placid, and serene, as to prevent my re-senting your ladyship's sarcastical comment, on my last letter. *Au contraire,*[74]

I am pleased at your becoming a critic; as I think you want a little of that *self-given* consequence, which is sometimes necessary, to give us weight with others.

But now to prove to you, that I am not stoic enough to be indifferent about your good opinion, I must inform you, that the first part of my last letter, was wrote a few minutes before Sir John's arrival, the remainder, the day after. And, as I know my dear Emily's weak spirits are too apt to be alarmed, I chose to proceed in continuation, in hopes, that by seeming to treat the matter lightly, I might prevent her apprehensions: and this remark-able instance of my delicacy, has her pretty little ladyship construed into a total want of feeling. But you love *faire la guerre*,[75] and now, look to yourself.

I never pretended to be devoid of curiosity; it is a passion inherent to our natures, and, properly conducted, may be productive of every good.—It is the source of knowledge; and, in my mind, the strongest mark of distinc-tion, between the rational, and brute creation.—It is our birth-right, de-scended to us from our first mother.[76]—You will, perhaps, say, it is an inheri-tance we might have dispensed with, as it has certainly cost us too dear; yet, as I have already said, if well cultivated, it is, a fruitful soil; but, in the hands of the weak, or idle, it can bring forth nothing but weeds, or thorns.

Against this kind of produce, I warned my Emily, and still will warn her, lest they, at any time, should wound her tender heart. I frankly confess myself interested in the fate of your lovely nun; but, instead of saying, as you would have me, Psha, Emily, how can you be so teizing! I shall say, Pray, Emily, do not be teizing, but write me a full and true account, of every cir-cumstance you know, relating to the charming vestal; and of every thing else, that you think can afford any entertainment, to

> Your affectionate sister,

> F. STRAFFON.

## LETTER 20.

## *Lady* WOODVILLE, *To Lady* STRAFFON.

What a triumph, for such a little, insignificant animal as me, to be able to ruffle the calm dignity of a female philosopher! I shall begin to think myself of some consequence; rather of more weight, than *the fly upon the chariot wheel.*[77] For, indeed, my dear Fanny, notwithstanding your efforts to disguise it, you were a little chagrined, at the small attempt towards pertness, which I ventured to make, in my last letter; and, in truth, you wise ones, when once thrown off your guard, make as foolish a figure, as any of us simpletons.

I have heard it said, that a person who never learnt to fence, shall be able to disconcert the greatest master of that noble science; nay more, may possibly kill him, by a random pass, while he stands in the best posture of defence, and is aiming at his antagonist, in all the profundity of quarte, or tierce.[78] Just such a scrambling combatant have you to deal with, who, without the least skill in the art of logic, presumes to enter the lists with your wise ladyship.

And so, Fanny, curiosity is now become a virtue, "productive of every good, the source of knowledge, the distinguishing mark of rationality, an inheritance descended to us," &c. And yet poor Emily is not to be allowed the use of this treasure, but to be deprived of her birth-right, and treated as an absolute alien to our grand-mother Eve. Is not this a little hard?

But now what says *my philosophy,* to this severe treatment? I think I see you laugh, at that expression. But pray, madam, is not the great use and end, of that exalted study, to render us happy, by perfectly acquiescing in our own lot, and wisely contemning all those advantages, that are denied us? Grant me but this, and I will immediately prove myself a philosopher, by shewing you how differently we think, in regard to this same treasure, called curiosity, which I am not permitted to have any share of.

And first, I absolutely deny, that it ever was, or can be, productive of good. *Au contraire,* I have scripture on my side, to prove, that it was the original cause of every physical, and moral ill, that has happened in this world, for I know not how many thousand years. You say, "it is inherent to our natures." Fie, Fanny! Could the Author of good then have punished dame Eve, and all her descendants, merely for following the bent of that nature, he had himself endued her with?—Impossible!

I say, it was the devil, who first introduced it into Paradise, and infected poor Eve; for it certainly is contagious, and never to be eradicated. From her, then, it has descended to all her offspring, not as an inheritance though, but rather as an uncancellable mortgage upon their natural patrimony.

You say, "it is the source of knowledge." There again, my dear, you are unluckily mistaken.—Pride is, undoubtedly, the first motive; for not *to be wise,* but to be *thought wiser,* than our neighbours, is the great reward. "A distinguishing mark of rationality." You are really no philosopher, lady Straffon.—Have you never seen a dog, or cat, raise up their ears, and listen, with all the avidity with which an old maid hearkens to a scandalous report of some blooming beauty of eighteen? Indeed, my dear, you must have observed this, frequently; and I am firmly persuaded, that those animals I have mentioned, are just as instinctively curious, as any duchess in Christendom.

I think I have now fairly demolished all your arguments, in favour of this precious commodity: but as you *boast* the possession of it, which I believe no woman ever did, but yourself, I will shew myself the paragon of good nature, and gratify the weakness I condemn, by telling you the history of our amiable nun.

How unlucky now, for your poor dear curiosity! Lady Ransford has this moment alighted.—I must fly to receive her, and bid you
    Adieu.

                                                                E. WOODVILLE.

## LETTER 21.

### *Lady* STRAFFON, *To Lady* WOODVILLE.

And so, my pretty little Bizarre, you are really delighted, at having ruffled a female philosopher; and from thence are determined to derive self-consequence: *Hélas, ma pauvre enfant!*[79] How grieved am I to mortify, by undeceiving you? for I cannot help informing you (though I know it to be cruel) that I have never been so much pleased, with any of your letters, as your two last.

You have been brought up, from your early infancy, with a high deference for my opinions, which, for some years past, I have wished you to shake off, lest it should prevent the free use of your own understanding, and occasion your receiving notions upon trust, without giving yourself the trouble of examining them. I am delighted to find that my dear Emily will, though in pure *badinage,*[80] exert her reason, and argue, if not logically, at least ingeniously.

Go on, my lively opponent, and push the mock war between us, as far as it will go; though, indeed, you have left me little to say, on the subject of curiosity, except, that it certainly was the original source of knowledge, however unmeritorious, as it first induced Eve's trespass, in tasting the forbidden fruit: but, I think, we have fairly exhausted this thesis, and now, for *quelque chose de nouveau.*[81]

Sir John has received a letter, from Sir James Miller, wherein "he intreats that Sir John will not banish him his native land, by keeping up any resentment against him. He implores Lucy's pardon; and is mean enough to give hints, that his crime has been his punishment." Poor abject wretch! Sir John has assured him, that he can never feel resentment for a person he despises; so that he may return to England in perfect safety.

This last contemptible *manœuvre* of Sir James, has, I think, completed Lucy's cure. Her faded charms begin to recover their former lustre; and I had the pleasure of over-hearing her singing a very lively air, as she walked, just now, under my window. Are not these good symptoms, my fair philosopher?

No friendly visitant has broke in upon me, to interrupt the tediousness of this epistle; but the clock has just reminded me of an appointment I made with my Edward, and Emily, to take them to our park. Exact punctuality should ever be preserved, in promises made to those, who are not capable of judging of the reasons, which might be given for a breach of it.—I, therefore, must fly to them, and bid my dear Emily
> Adieu.

> F. STRAFFON.

## LETTER 22.

### *Lady* WOODVILLE, *To Lady* STRAFFON.

My dear Fanny,

I am heartily glad that the mock war, as you call it, between us, is at an end, as I should, at present, be totally unable to support my share in the combat, and, of course, must fall before the conqueror. I have been unusually dispirited, and languid, for these two days.—I feel, as if I had cause to be

"The Disappointment," a song sung by Lord Woodville, words by William Shenstone, music by Thomas Arne. Reproduced from the facsimile edition of Arne's *Agreeable Musical Choice. A Pastoral Collection of Songs Sung at the Publick Gardens. Composed by Mr. Arne* (London, 175?), published by King's Music, Huntingdon, Cambs., England [c. 1990]

She fmil'd and I cou'd not but love, She was faithlefs and I am undone.

**2**

The Sweets of a dew-fprinkled Rofe,
The found of a murmering Stream,
The peace which from Solitude flows,
Henceforth fhall be CORIDON's Theme.
High Tranfports are fhewn to the Sight,
But we are not to find them our own;
Fate never beftow'd fuch delight,
As I with my PHILLIS had known.

**3**

Ye Woods, fpread your branches apace,
To your deepeft recefses I fly;
I wou'd hide with the Beafts of the chace,
I wou'd vanifh from every Eye.
Yet my Reed fhall refound thro' the Grove,
With the fame fad Complaint it begun;
How fhe fmil'd, and I cou'd not but love;
Was faithlefs, and I am undone.

For the German Flute

Poco Largo

So

melancholy, and yet endeavour to persuade myself that I have none. This is a state not to be described: and to you, who, I dare say, have never experienced it, may appear ridiculous; and yet, believe me, it is a painful situation.—But I flatter myself, I have rather caught, than bred this malady.

Lord Seymour left us, this morning; and, for some days before he set out, he seemed to have acquired an additional degree of melancholy softness. Love he can never feel more.—Besides, *my* lord seems infected with the same disorder; looks grave, and sighs. Tell me then, Fanny, is it possible that male friendship is so much more delicate and tender, than ours, that their mutual sadness could arise from a separation, for a few weeks, or perhaps, months. If this should be the real cause, I shall blush for my own want of sensibility.

I should think lord Seymour in such a state of mind, that no slight, or trivial misfortune, could possibly affect him; for they who have once felt real anguish, may bid defiance to future ills. The arrows of adversity, may glance against, but cannot wound a heart, already broken. From sympathy alone, such minds can suffer.—But, Oh! far, far be the thought, from Emily's fond bosom, that lord Woodville's sufferings should cause lord Seymour's sorrow! It is impossible! I am sorry I have expressed such a thought, even to you, my sister. I would blot it from the paper, if I could erase it from my mind.

We had, last night, a concert, in a temple dedicated to Apollo,[82] in the garden.—My lord, whose voice is harmony itself, was singing one of Shenstone's elegies. I accompanied him on the harpsichord, and lord Seymour on the violoncello.—At the words,

> She was fair, and I could not but love,
> She is faithless, and I am undone,[83]

I saw lord Seymour fix his eyes on lord Woodville's face, which, in a moment, became suffused with crimson; his voice faultered so much, that he could scarce finish the song.

The moment it was ended, he quitted the temple. I felt myself alarmed: I feared he was taken ill, and went immediately towards the house. As I crossed the parterre, I saw him walking briskly, in a path that leads to the wood: this quieted my apprehensions for his health, but left my mind in a state incapable of thinking.—I retired to my chamber, and continued to muse, till summoned to supper.

There was no notice taken, of what had passed.—We parted earlier than usual, all but lord Seymour, and my lord, who continued together, till near four o'clock. I could not sleep, and wished to have risen, and either walked, or read; but was unwilling to discover my restlessness, to him who caused it. When we met, at breakfast, Mr. Ransford, who was just arrived from London, asked my lord, in a low voice, if I had been ill, as he observed that I looked much paler, than usual.

What a flutter am I in! Just as I had wrote the last word, my dear lord opened the door, and said he came to request the pleasure of my company, to see a new improvement he is making; and, with the most engaging affability, added, that he feared he had disturbed my rest, by sitting up so late, but thought an airing would do us both good.

His behaviour has made all the foregoing part of my letter, appear a vision to me. Do not reply to it, my Fanny, till you hear from me again; and I hope, by next post, to have forgot I ever wrote it.

Adieu, adieu, that I may fly indeed, to the most amiable of men.

E. WOODVILLE.


P.S. You shall have the little history of the nun, with my next.—I rejoice at Lucy's recovery.—Happy, happy, may you all be!


# LETTER 23.

## Lady WOODVILLE, To Lady STRAFFON.

My dearest Fanny,

The cloud that hung over my mind, is totally dispersed, and my happiness restored, with my reason. What a visionary must you think me! but do not chide me, my loved sister, lest, by endeavouring at a justification, I should fancy I had found reasons, to support my folly.

I never spent so delightful a day, as the last on which I wrote to you. During our airing, which was about six miles, my lord appeared, if possible, more amiable to me, than ever. There was a peculiar air of tenderness, diffused through his voice and manner; perhaps the parting from his friend, had softened his already gentle nature. Perhaps—but why pry into his bosom, in search of a cause, which might render the effect less pleasing?

In less than an hour, we arrived at the neatest, and most elegant cottage, I ever beheld. It was seated on the declivity of a hill, and defended from the North winds, by a small wood, so beautifully variegated, that even in this leafy season, summer, autumn, and winter, seemed to vye in the luxuriancy of the different shades, which their several periods produce.

Before the house a pendant lawn, covered with sheep and lambs, reached to the river, which winded in the most beautiful mazes, round the hill. Over the broadest part of it, was a Gothic bridge, of one arch, with a watch tower in the center; and on the other side of the house, stood a small nursery and shrubbery—I was never more agreeably surprized, than with this lovely scene. I really think if I was to meet with any severe affliction, that I should like to retire to this delightful solitude, and pass my days in it.

I frequently saw my lord's eyes sparkle with pleasure, at that which I expressed. As I neither saw nor heard a human creature, but ourselves, I begged to know who were the happy owners of this lovely spot? said I wished to see, and congratulate them, on their taste, and felicity.—He said he would immediately comply with my request, and by so doing, increase the happiness of its possessors. He then led me to the house, which was as simply elegant within, as without—I think I never saw perfect neatness, before—and presented me to his nurse,[84] an extreme good looking woman, about fifty—she knew not in what manner to receive me—humility and joy seemed to struggle in her countenance—I stepped forward, and embraced her—my lord seemed delighted, at what he was pleased to call my condescension.

The good woman has been a widow, for twelve years; her husband was first gardener to my lord's father, and her son-in-law is now in the same station, with us. Her daughter is a very pretty woman, about two-and-twenty; and ready to lye in,[85] of a second child. I never beheld such a cherubim, as the first. My lord said, archly, he hoped his foster sister[86] and I should be better acquainted, and that she would undertake the same good office for me, that her mother had done for his.

The poor girl blushed, and curtsyed; I felt my cheeks glow, and walked to the window—I confess I was charmed with his attention to such a point, which the foolish lords of the creation, generally think below them. He then inquired for his nurse's mother, and the finest old woman I ever saw, came into the room—I saluted her also—her hair was perfectly silver, and her skin like down—she blessed, and embraced my lord, while tears of joy, and gratitude, ran down her fair, unfurrowed cheek.

My lord was affected, and saw me so; and in order to change the subject, told the good woman of the house, he was come to dine with her.—She looked amazed, and so should I, had I then thought him serious.—But I found he was so, when he told her she could certainly give us good bread, butter, rashers, and eggs, and a sallad; and that he would take care of the rest.

I smiled assent; but said we should send home, to prevent the company's waiting. He said, there was no necessity for it, as he was quite satisfied that our friends at Woodfort, would sit down to dinner, at the same instant that we did, without hearing from us. I then supposed he had left orders that they should not wait, and was pleased with the idea of our simple rustic meal. But I was to be still more surprized; for in about ten minutes, the coach arrived, with lady Harriet, Fanny Weston, Sir James Thornton, and Mr. Ransford. A sumpter car[87] followed, with wine, and cold provisions.

The beauty of the scene, the fineness of the day, the unpremeditatedness of the scheme, all conspired to render us more chearful, than we should have been, perhaps, in any other place, on earth; and we all returned home delighted with our little expedition, and full of gratitude to my lord, for the pleasure it had afforded us.

This is an enormous long letter, but you taught me to rise early; I can, therefore, spare time to my absent friends, as well as those about me; and I can never think that time better employed, than in proving to my dearest Fanny, that I am

Her truly affectionate sister,

E. WOODVILLE.

P.S. I fear I have delayed the history I now send you, too long; perhaps your curiosity may be as much palled, as one's appetite sometimes is, by waiting for a second course; which, though elegant in itself, cannot repair the damage done by the delay. But if you are a true epicure, and like the feast, you will feed heartily, though the tediousness of the cook, be ever so teizing to you.

## The HISTORY of Miss CHARLOTTE BEAUMONT.

As the chief circumstances which relate to this lady, refer more to others, than herself, we must look back, to the first causes of those effects, which seem to have marked her fate. Unhappy, in the very article of her birth, though descended from a noble family, it will be necessary to give some account, of the authors of her being.

Her father, the present general Beaumont, was the youngest son of one of the most antient, and illustrious houses, in France: but, as is generally the case with the superfluous branches of great families, of that nation, he was possessed of no other patrimony, than his high birth, a graceful person, and his sword.

The church, and the army, are the only provisions, which seem to be designed for the cadets of the noblesse. To the latter, our young soldier of fortune, applied himself, and soon obtained a genteel post there. In this situation the then duchess dowager of H——saw, and was captivated, with our young hero.—Though her age more than doubled his, her person was still pleasing, and her fortune so infinitely superior to his most sanguine hopes, that he did not long hesitate to accept such a splendid establishment.

They passed some years together, with that polite indifference, which distinguishes the married couples of high rank, in that gay nation. At length, the duchess began to grow weary, of treading the same dull circle, for so many years, and proposed to the general, that they should visit one of her estates, in *Languedoc*,[88] and pass a summer there. Though he was, by no means, tired of the *grand monde*, nor could possibly form any very delightful idea of retirement, with such a companion, as her grace, he, politely, assented to her request.

When they had been, some time, in the country, the duchess hinted a desire of sending for a young lady, who was a distant relation of her first husband's, and whom she had formerly placed in a convent. This proposal was perfectly agreeable to the general. The most desirable *têtes à têtes,* sometimes grow languid; but the intervention of a third person, in such a situation as theirs, was most devoutly to be wished for.

Her grace set out, the next morning, for the convent de ————, which was about five leagues from her seat, and returned, in the evening, accompanied by the too lovely Charlotte D'Etree.—The general, though well accustomed to the power of beauty, became suddenly captivated.—Never had he beheld such a face, and form, before—such simple elegance, such unaffected grace, the beauties of Venus, with Dian's modesty.[89]

The lovely Charlotte felt, at least, as much surprise, at the sight of him. We have already said, his person was remarkably graceful, his air at once engaging, and commanding; nor was any outward ornament neglected, that could set off such a form to the best advantage.—What an amazing effect must such a figure have, upon a girl not yet seventeen! who had been bred in a cloister, and had never seen, or at least conversed, with any man who did not wear a *cowl.*

The duchess attempted to apologize for Charlotte's astonishment, by observing, that the poor girl had been brought up in absolute ignorance; but hoped, when she had been some time with her, that her aukward amazement would wear off. She might have talked, for ever, without interruption. The general had neither speech, nor hearing; his faculties seemed all absorbed, in one; and through his eyes alone, his heart was, for the first time, taught to feel a real passion.

The little wanton god, too much the general's friend, soon inspired the innocent, and fair D'Etree, with the same sentiments. Never did the tyrant reign more absolute, than in the hearts of these his willing slaves. Whole months passed away, in all the delights of mutual fondness, seemed to the lovers, but a day; and when, at the end of autumn, the duchess talked of returning to Paris, it appeared to them like being doomed to banishment.

Charlotte was to accompany the duchess thither; but the general knew their interviews must be less frequent, and more liable to interruption, than in the charming solitude of *Belleveüe.* After every excuse was obviated, and every possible contrivance of delay exhausted, they were forced to submit; and the once gay and lively Charles Beaumont, set out for the metropolis, with infinitely more regret, than he had ever quitted it. The duchess was, happily, not of a jealous nature; and the enamoured pair behaved with so much circumspection, that she never seemed to have the least suspicion, of their mutual attachment, to the last hour of her life.

The natural consequences of their guilty love, now began to make Charlotte taste the bitter ingredients of that intoxicating cup, of which she had drank so deeply. Infamy stared her in the face; and, though a criminal passion had triumphed over her chastity, her modesty was not yet extinguished. Sleepless nights, and days of anguish, now became her portion. She detested herself, and all the world; all, but the guilty author of her misery. How often did she wish, she never had quitted the cloister; but there, like the desart rose, have bloomed, and died unseen, in innocence and peace.[90]

The general, whose fondness, if possible, was encreased by her situation, said every thing in his power, to console her, by promising to secure her fame. Many were the expedients he thought of, but none of them seemed sufficient, to satisfy the delicate apprehensions of the unhappy Charlotte. At length, she recollected, that there was a young woman, in the convent where she had been bred, whose father and mother were dead, and had left her in such low circumstances, that she could neither afford, to live in the world, or pay her pension, where she remained; and was, therefore, under the painful necessity of taking the veil, contrary to her inclinations, or of going into the world, as a dependent.

This person, then, she fixed on, as a confidante; and immediately wrote to her to come to Paris, with ample promises of taking care of her future fortune. Mademoiselle Laval was overjoyed at such a summons, and instantly obeyed it. In the mean time, the general hired a very neat furnished house, for her reception, and appointed servants, and every thing proper, before her arrival.—She was informed, that she was to personate a lady whose husband was just dead, and who was come from a distant part of Normandy, to prosecute a law-suit, and lye in, at Paris.

The unhappy situation of this young woman's circumstances, made her readily acquiesce in every thing that Charlotte required; and she entered her house, with all the melancholy solemnity of an afflicted relict. In a few days after her arrival, the real mourner, the poor, wretched Charlotte, went to visit her; and, after shedding floods of tears upon her bosom, acquainted her with her unhappy situation, and implored her assistance.

Mademoiselle Laval, naturally good-natured, and softened by the unhappy condition of her friend, promised every thing she could desire;— endeavoured to soothe and comfort her affliction; and, at last, settled matters, in such a way, that the moment Charlotte found herself ill, she was to go there; that every necessary preparation should be made, and every tender care taken of her, and her offspring.

Every thing happened to their utmost wishes: she was taken ill, as she was dressing to go to a ball, at the English ambassador's. The duchess was luckily prevented from going, by a slight cold; and Charlotte, when she got into the carriage, had no one to oppose her being set down, where she pleased.—She went directly to her friend's house, and was there happily delivered of a son, and daughter, who were immediately baptized, by the names of Charles, and Charlotte.

In as short a time as was possible, after this event, the general, and one of his particular friends, carried Charlotte home, in a sedan chair. She said she had been taken ill, at the ball, and went directly to bed, where she continued, for some days: and, to carry on the deceit, mademoiselle Laval confined herself to her bed, and went through all the forms, of a real *accouchement.*[91]

This great event so well over, the general thought himself the happiest man living.—He doated on his children, and perfectly adored their lovely mother.—But she continued to appear gloomy, and dejected; and, at last, declared, she should never know peace, while the living witnesses of her shame, continued in the same kingdom with her. She seldom saw them, and when she did, expressed abhorrence, rather than tenderness, towards them. She behaved with the utmost coldness, to the general, and affected to be infinitely more miserable, than she had ever been before.

The general was almost distracted at her conduct, and, at length, consented to the removal of the children. It was agreed that Laval should go over to England, take upon her the name of Beaumont, and educate them as her own, till the duchess died—as soon as that should happen, he promised to marry Charlotte, and receive them, as the orphans of a near relation.

In the mean time, he settled a very handsome income on Laval, and the little innocents set out for London, with their fictitious mother, who felt, however, infinitely more tenderness for them, than their real one seemed to have done.

Nothing remarkable happened, during their infancy. Mademoiselle Laval, by the general's recommendation, became acquainted with many families of distinction, and though quite unacquainted with the world, behaved herself so properly, that she was as much esteemed, as known, and her lovely children universally admired.

When they were about seven years old, the duchess died, and in as short a space, as decency would admit of, the general fulfilled his promise, to his still adored, and beautiful Charlotte. On this occasion, mademoiselle Laval, who really doated on her amiable charge, felt the tenderest concern at the thoughts of parting with it—but she might have spared her sorrow, for madame de Beaumont was, by no means, inclined to rob her of it. On the contrary, when the general proposed the children's return, she grew outrageous, and declared she would never see him more, if he attempted to bring them into any part of France. She was born to rule his fate, and he submitted, though reluctantly, to her inhuman, and unnatural commands.

In about ten months, after their marriage, she brought him a son, which, in some measure, consoled him for the loss of his other children; and, in another year, presented him with a daughter. In a little time, his fondness was wholly transferred to the objects of her adoration—never was so fond a mother; and madame de Beaumont was looked upon as the pattern of maternal affection, while she not only abandoned, but detested, her former offspring.

The general's letters to Laval, became less frequent; and though he punctually remitted her income, he seldom mentioned those, for whose use it was designed. In vain poor Laval endeavoured to awaken the tender feelings of a father, in his heart, by boasting the amazing beauty of his Charlotte, or mentioning the fine parts, and accomplishments, of his amiable Charles. Nature seemed dead in him, as much as in their cruel mother.

At length, worn by the perpetual remonstrances of the humane, and generous Laval, he obtained a commission for his son, who was then about sixteen, in a regiment that was to embark from Dunkirk, for America; but sent strict orders that he should not go to Paris, and conjured Laval to keep him still ignorant of his birth.

Poor Charlotte almost died away, at the thoughts of being separated from her brother. It was the first cause she had ever known for sorrow, and nature seemed inclined to make them both amends, for the loss of parental affection, by bestowing a double portion of fraternal love, on each.

Our young soldier, whose ardor for glory, was extreme, was all gratitude to his supposed mother, for suffering him to follow the bent of his inclination; and, at the appointed time, he quitted London, with a heart filled at once with bravery, and tenderness.

In order to divert the melancholy which affected Charlotte, for her brother's absence, lady Sandford invited the feigned madame de Beaumont, and her supposed daughter, to pass some time, at her seat in the country. The invitation was readily accepted, and there Charlotte, now in her seventeenth year, first saw lord Seymour.

Her beauty was then only in its dawn, but even then, like Aurora[92] breaking through the clouds, it gave a promise of the brightest day. The tender regret she felt for her brother's absence, gave an additional softness to her voice, and manners; and the expressive sensibility of her large hazel eyes, seemed encreased, by her gentle distress.

Such an amiable object could not fail of inspiring passion, in a heart less susceptible than lord Seymour's, or indeed, in any heart, that was not guarded by a pre-possession. He soon felt the most ardent, and sincere affection, for her, nor was he the only person who was sensible of the power of her charms. The young duke of B—— saw her, at a ball, at Northampton, and became instantly enamoured—He waited on lady Sandford, in a few days after, and with all the precipitancy of youth, high rank, and fortune, proposed himself to madame de Beaumont, for her daughter.

Whether Charlotte's delicacy was really hurt, by such a proceeding, or whether she then felt a preference for lord Seymour, she instantly rejected the duke's proposal, with an air of *fierté*,[93] unknown to her before. Madame de Beaumont, who tenderly loved her, acquiesced in her determination, and resolved not to acquaint her real parents, that such a match had been proposed.

Charlotte was transported, at her feigned mother's kind condescension, and promised the most implicit obedience, which indeed she had ever shewn, to all her commands. She began now, to recover her spirits, was all chearfulness, and vivacity; and from this pleasing transition, she acquired, if possible, new charms; and each, and every day, lord Seymour became more, and more enamoured.

The two happiest months of Charlotte's life, were now passed, and madame de Beaumont talked of returning to London. Before they set out, lord Seymour found an opportunity, of disclosing his passion to Charlotte. She received his declaration, with that frankness, and candour, that ever dwell with generous minds; but, at the same time, told him, that she considered herself under such obligations to her mother, for her conduct towards her, in regard to the duke of B——, that she would never listen to any persons addresses, who had not the sanction of her approbation.

The enamoured Seymour, whose passion was as truly delicate, as the fair object that inspired it, was, now, at the summit of felicity—he threw himself at Charlotte's feet, and poured forth his soul, in the warmest expressions of gratitude, for her generous, and, unaffected behaviour; and, at the same time, obtained her leave to apply to madame de Beaumont for her consent, as soon as they should return to London.

He was permitted the happiness of attending them, thither, and the day after their arrival, waited on madame de Beaumont, to intreat her leave, to pay his addresses to her lovely daughter. True love is ever timid, and conscious as lord Seymour was, that the advantage, of birth, and fortune, were on his side, he felt, perhaps, more apprehensions, on this occasion, than a young ensign would, at addressing a lady of the highest rank.

All that he knew of Charlotte's circumstances, or condition, was, that her mother passed for the widow of a general officer, that her fortune was small, but sufficient to support her little family, genteelly, with œconomy;

and that she had maintained an unblemished reputation in London, for near seventeen years.

But how were the generous, and disinterested Seymour's fears increased, when Madame de Beaumont told him she was highly sensible of the honour he intended her daughter, but that she thought her yet too young to marry, and that she had laid herself under an engagement, never to dispose of Charlotte, without first consulting her father's family, and friends! she conjured him, as a man of honour, not to mention his passion, to Charlotte, as by inspiring her with a mutual one, he might, perhaps, render them both miserable.

Lord Seymour instantly told her it was out of his power to obey her injunction, as it was by Charlotte's permission, he had then the honour of intreating her consent, and that he neither could, nor would desist, from endeavouring to gain a heart, on which all his happiness in this life, depended. Madame de Beaumont was moved, even to tears, at the unhappy situation of the lovers. She, too plainly, saw the obstacles that must prevent their union, but generously promised, and resolved, to do every thing in her power, for their mutual happiness.

Lord Seymour ventured to remonstrate to her, that with regard to the duke of B——'s proposal, she had acted as sole parent, and guardian of her daughter, and he could not see the necessity of farther consultation, for accepting, than refusing a lover. She owned her tenderness for Charlotte, had, in that case, triumphed over her promise, but she had, even then, only assumed a negative power, which was more in right of her daughter, than herself, for she never could think it just, that either parents, or friends, should ever persuade a person to marry, contrary to their own inclinations. She told him she would write, immediately, to France, and represent his lordship's birth, fortune, and person, in the advantageous light in which she beheld them.

Exalted as his ideas were of the object of his passion, he had great reason to flatter himself, that his alliance would not be contemned, by any family in France; and when he considered that the exquisite perfection of his charming Charlotte, must be unknown to those persons, who were to be consulted in the disposal of them, his fears would sometimes vanish, and his fond heart beat, with all the transporting hopes of successful love.

Charlotte, who had never heard madame de Beaumont talk of her father's family, till now, considered the difficulties that were started, in another light, and fancied she only meant them to protract the marriage, till she should be eighteen, which she had often heard her say, was full early for a young lady to marry. However, without inquiring, she perfectly acquiesced in her supposed mother's conduct, and while she had the happiness of seeing and hearing the tenderest of lovers and most charming of men, she knew not a wish ungratified. Madame de Beaumont fulfilled her promise, by writing immediately, to the general, and mentioning lord Seymour, in the justest, and, of course, most pleasing light.

It happened that the general, and his lady, were, at that time, at Aix la Chapelle, where he had been seized with a violent fever; and though the letter was forwarded to him, as the characters of the superscription were known by his lady, it lay, for some time, unopened.

During this interval, the fictitious madame de Beaumont was attacked by the small pox, which appeared of so malignant a sort, that her fate was quickly pronounced, by her physicians. As soon as she was acquainted with her disorder, she forbad Charlotte to come near her, as she had never had it; but in vain she commanded, or lord Seymour entreated her, to absent herself, a moment, from her bedside. She said it was her first, and should be her last act, of disobedience; and for that reason, she hoped her dear, and tender parent would pardon it.

Overcome by her filial piety, they suffered her to undergo such constant and violent fatigue, as, at any other time, would have destroyed her delicate, and beauteous frame. But she supported it, with such a tender alacrity, and attention, as amazed and affected every one who saw her: even lord Seymour's love was encreased, by his admiration of her virtues, and rose almost to adoration.

When madame de Beaumont was informed of her danger, which was but a few hours before her death, she desired to be left alone with Charlotte.—After embracing, and imploring blessings on her, she told her, that neither her time, nor strength, would permit her revealing a secret, that was of the utmost consequence to her. But as she had ever endeavoured to be prepared for the tremendous event, that was now come to pass, she had kept a journal of her life, from the time she quitted the convent de ————, to the moment of her illness; that in those papers she would find her own history included, and that of *her real parents*.

Charlotte, though drowned in tears, was all attention, till those astonishing words, *her real parents!* smote her ear.—She then cried out, Ah, madam! will you not only abandon, but deny me? Alas! what has your Charlotte done! Be comforted, my more than daughter, she replied; I was not worthy of such a blessing.—Yet still, I hope, more worthy, than they who possess so rich a treasure, regardless of its value. But if their hearts, so long hardened to your blooming virtues, at length relent, and give you to the worthy Seymour, you will have no cause to regret their past neglect, or court their future protection. May you be happy! This key (taking one from her bosom) will explain what I cannot. And now, adieu, for ever!

The sudden effects of surprize, joined to those of grief, quite overcame the afflicted Charlotte.—She fainted, and was conveyed, senseless, to her own apartment. Madame de Beaumont continued to breathe, till she heard Charlotte was restored to life; then yielded up her own.

The next day Charlotte was seized with convulsions; and immediately after, the small-pox appeared, but of a safe, and gentle kind—the malignity of the disorder had spent its force, upon madame de Beaumont; and the low state, both of Charlotte's mind, and body, rendered its operations less powerful. Lord Seymour never quitted her apartment, though not permitted to enter her chamber; nor could he be prevailed on, even to rest himself on a couch, till the physicians pronounced her out of danger.

As soon as it was possible, she saw him: he appeared more altered, than herself. Never was such an interview between two lovers. Their present loss of beauty, seemed to augment their fondness; and each felt more real tenderness for the other, than at any former instant of their lives. Lord Seymour, though he lamented the death of madame de Beaumont, very sincerely, now thought that every bar to his happiness was removed; and as Charlotte appeared to be the mistress of her own fate, he had no apprehensions that his could be unhappy.

She had laughed at madame de Beaumont's superstitious attachment to distant relations, whom she had not seen for many years, he therefore could not suspect her being infected with the same caprice. The mother said, she was bound by solemn engagements to the family of Beaumont; the daughter could have entered into none, as she left Paris, when an infant. He had, therefore, no reason to imagine, that any power on earth could oppose his felicity; and indulged his fond imagination with perspective views of fancied bliss, which he was fated, never to enjoy!

The small-pox had been so favourable to Charlotte, that she had not been affected with the least mark, or alteration of feature; and the natural whiteness of her snowy skin, soon triumphed over the transitory redness, which is the common effect of that always disagreeable, and sometimes fatal, disorder.

But though her beauty had returned, her chearfulness seemed buried in madame de Beaumont's tomb. Her affliction for her, as a parent, would, perhaps, have subsided, into a calm and gentle melancholy; but her last words had raised a tumult in her bosom, which she had not resolution sufficient to conquer. She frequently endeavoured to persuade herself, that her dear mother had raved, in her last moments; but the strength of her expression, and calmness of her manner, opposed that fond belief.

After her recovery, whole weeks elapsed without her having courage to open the cabinet, where the mystery of her fate lay concealed. She feared to meet with new obstacles, to that happiness, which she had promised herself, by being united to lord Seymour.

His delicacy had yet prevented him from expressing his ardent wishes for their union, as the cause of her amiable distress, was yet too recent; and many months might possibly have passed away, in the same irresolution, if the receipt of the following letter, had not precipitated this point, to a more immediate crisis.

### To Madame de BEAUMONT.

Aix la Chapelle.

Never was amazement equal to mine, at perusing your last letter! What, you! wretch as you are, raised by my hand, and supported by my bounty, presume to dictate to me, in the disposal of my child! And who is this lord Seymour? is he not an heretic?[94] if so, that is a sufficient objection, were he a prince.

But surely, madam, since you take upon you to inform us of intended marriages, and act as plenipotentiary, between our daughter, and ourselves, you should have informed us of the duke of B——'s proposal, and no more have dared to refuse, than accept, a lover, for Charlotte Beaumont.

The young duke, himself, has informed me of his simple attachment to the silly girl, and of the insolence, with which his proposal was rejected. He inquired, whether she was of our family? I did, as I ever shall, disclaim her.

The general, who has been ill of a fever, by me commands you, on the receipt of this, to set out with Charlotte Beaumont, instantly, for Paris. He has devoted her to heaven,[95] and found out a fit retreat for

that purpose, in the convent of St. Anthony. Be it your business, as it is
your duty, to teach her an implicit obedience, to his will.

She is now of an age, to be trusted with the secret of her birth; but let
her also know, that when she relinquishes you, as a mother, she is not to
expect to find one, in

CHARLOTTE BEAUMONT.

P.S. The general, and I, shall return to Paris, in a few days, where we
expect not to see, but hear from you, and Charlotte.

The moment you arrive at the hotel Angloise, you are commanded to
send to the general; but, on no account, attempt to come near our
house.

The situation of the unhappy Charlotte's mind, upon reading this
letter, is not to be described. Who is this cruel woman, she exclaimed, that
thus disclaims an unoffending child? Oh! I will throw myself beneath her
feet, and soften that obdurate heart, with tears. My father too; I have a father
then! Sure he will raise me up, in his paternal arms, and bless me! They will
relent; and when they see my Seymour, and know his wondrous worth, his
wondrous love, they will be charmed, as their fond daughter is, and give me
to his wishes.

Full of these warm, and natural apprehensions, the half-distracted
Charlotte flew to the cabinet, which, like Pandora's box,[96] contained a thousand ills, and, with a trembling hand, unlocked it. The first objects that
presented themselves to her view, were miniature portraits, of her father and
mother.—She gazed, with joy and wonder. Never had she beheld such striking beauty, of both kinds; the manly, and the mild.

She kissed, embraced, wept over them; nay, knelt to them, implored
their pity and protection, and, in one moment, was inspired with more respect and tenderness, for those inanimate figures, than she had ever felt for
her supposed mother; though gratitude and esteem had answered all the purposes of filial affection, in her gentle nature.

She now sat down to search the book of fate, those fatal Sybil's leaves[97]
that told her doom; and while she read, felt every passion, that the human
heart is capable of.—Yet still her love, and reverence for her parents, remained predominant; and she determined to sacrifice herself, to their
unnatural commands, and pass her days in a cloister, if she could not prevail
on them to change their cruel purpose.

She quickly saw how improper it would have been to acquaint lord Seymour with her real situation, as he would, doubtless, oppose her returning to France, with all the eloquence of love.—Yet, to quit him, without making any excuse, or to descend to invent a false one, were equally repugnant, to her tender, and generous nature.

She had been bred in the Roman Catholic faith, but had never conversed with bigots, nor once thought that marrying the man she loved, could be deemed a crime, against any religion. The idea first shocked her, on her mother's pronouncing him an heretic; and she resolved to make the difference of opinions, a pretext, for postponing their marriage, till she could try to prevail on her parents, to give their consent; which she vainly hoped she should be able to obtain, from their tenderness, and his uncommon merits.

They know the power of love, said she, and will not, like vulgar, and unfeeling minds, attempt to oppose his uncontrolable decrees.—They will regard lord Seymour, for their Charlotte's sake; and his tenderness for me, shall appear, by that love and duty, that he shews to them.

Thus did the unhappy visionary fair one amuse herself, till lord Seymour came to pay his daily visit. He had been used, for some time past, to see her melancholy, and, at times, disturbed; but as soon as he then saw her, he perceived that her whole frame had been uncommonly agitated. And when he tenderly intreated to know the cause, she answered only, with a flood of tears; and begged he would not press her, on the subject.

Though his fond heart was alarmed by a thousand different fears, he chose rather to bear that cruel state of suspense, than distress the object he adored; and immediately desisted, from any farther inquiries. When he left her, that evening, he felt an unusual degree of anxiety, and was several times tempted to return, and beg to know the source of her distress; but he feared to offend, by disobeying her commands; and hoped, at their next meeting, her chagrin might be dispelled.

Lord Seymour was to go out of town, for a few days, to the nuptials of a near relation; and his loved Charlotte had bid him adieu, with more than usual tenderness. Charlotte resolved to lay hold on the opportunity of Lord Seymour's absence, to set out for France. She had found, in the late madame de Beaumont's cabinet, about two hundred pounds, in bills and money; out of this sum, she discharged all her servants, except her own maid, whom she determined to take with her. She ordered one of those she parted with, to remain in the house, till lord Seymour's return, in order to deliver him a letter, which she should leave for him.

She had now, she thought, settled matters in such a way, that nothing remained to obstruct her purposed journey.—But, alas! the most difficult part of her arduous task, was yet to come.—She was now, to bid adieu, to the man her soul adored. She knew not what passion was, till the severity of her fate, compelled her to wish to conquer it. A thousand times she attempted to write to him, who was now dearer, than ever, to her, but could not find words that were capable of expressing her complicated feelings.— Two sleepless nights, and miserable days, thus passed. She dreaded lord Seymour's return; and, on the third, while the chaise waited to carry her off, she wrote the following lines.

#### To Lord SEYMOUR.

With a heart, and eyes overflowing with the sincerest tenderness, at the sad thought of being separated from the only man, I ever did, or, shall ever love, I find myself incapable of taking even a transient leave of him. Oh! may it prove so!

My flight must appear extraordinary to you. Why am not I at liberty, to explain my motives? But, be assured, they are such, as your honour, and virtue would approve, though your fondness might oppose the effect. I fly then, my dear lord Seymour, to render myself more worthy of you; to ease my heart of some scruples, which, only, can prevent its being wholly yours.

If heaven smiles upon my purpose, you shall hear quickly from me; and surely innocence, and love, so pure as mine, may claim its care. But should it, for wise purposes, unknown to me, blast all my flattering hopes of happiness, and doom me to the lowest wretchedness, thy image still shall dwell within my heart, and shield it from dishonour.

I would say more, but cannot; the chaise waits to carry me—from whom! from thee! What agonies are in that thought! Nought but the hope of meeting, soon again, could now enable me to say,

Adieu.

CHARLOTTE BEAUMONT.

As soon as she had sealed her letter, she flung herself into the chaise, and pursued her journey; which she performed, without meeting with any uncommon accident.

In a few hours after she set out, her brother, who had been near two years absent, returned to London. His bravery had raised him to the rank of captain; and, as the war was then over, he had obtained leave to visit his friends in England.

He had not heard of madame de Beaumont's death, till he came to her house, and was at once informed of that, and Charlotte's abrupt departure. The amiable young man was extremely shocked, and grieved; and in the midst of his tears for madame de Beaumont, lamented the uncertainty of his loved sister's fate; and determined, as soon as it was possible, to pursue her steps, to Paris.

Just as he was quitting the house, his eyes swoln with tears, and his aspect impressed with the deepest sorrow, lord Seymour came to the door.— Young Beaumont issued out, regardless of a man he had never seen before; and lord Seymour, though at first surprized at his appearance, upon receiving Charlotte's letter, thought of him no more.

Indeed all traces of recollection, seemed to have been instantly erased from his memory, and he remained like a man suddenly transfixed by lightning. It was some time before he had power to ask, when she set out? or whither she was gone? And when the servant replied to his queries, he continued to repeat them, without seeming to receive the information he so earnestly desired.

He read her letter, a thousand times, yet would neither credit that, nor the servant's affirmation, that she had left the house.—He ran distractedly through every room, calling on his dear Charlotte's name; and crying out, It is impossible! she must be here!—O do not kill me, for thy sport, my love! But when he found his search was vain, he retired to his house, in a state very little short of distraction.

The moment our fair fugitive landed, at Calais, she wrote a letter, to each of her parents, filled with expressions of the humblest duty, and tenderest affection. She acquainted them with the death of her supposed mother, and mentioned her obligations to her, with the highest gratitude, and esteem. She implored their permission, to throw herself at their feet, and that they would allow her a happiness, she had been so long deprived of, that of receiving a parent's blessing.

In vain was her tender and virtuous mind, enriched with every noble and generous sentiment, that could do honour to humanity; her cruel parents were, literally, in the state of the *deaf adder:*[98] they shut their ears and eyes, to her perfections; and refused to receive the highest pleasure, that human nature is capable of, that of beholding an amiable, and accomplished child.

As soon as she arrived at the hotel Angloise, she found a servant waiting with a letter for her, which contained these words.

Charlotte Beaumont,

You are commanded to accompany the bearer of this, who will conduct you to an apartment, that is provided for your reception, this night. To-morrow, a carriage shall attend, to convey you to the convent of St. Anthony.—The general is too much indisposed to see you, at present;—when he is able, he will call on you, there.

An implicit obedience to our orders, which particularly enjoin the strictest secrecy, in regard to your connexion with us, can only prove the truth of those professions of duty, which you have made.

You are still to appear in the state of an orphan, which can be no great difficulty, to one who has so lately known that she has parents. If you have brought a servant, she must be dismissed, to-morrow, and sent back to England. If you have occasion for money, the bearer will supply you.

Adieu.

C. De Beaumont.

Upon reading this letter, all the tender ideas of filial affection, which had thronged about poor Charlotte's heart, seemed to vanish, and the poignant anguish she had felt, at tearing herself from her fond and generous lover, returned, with double force.

She, however, determined not to halt, at beginning the race; and turning to her conductor, with the utmost mildness and resignation, said she was ready to attend him; and hoped, when she was lodged for the night, he would do her the favour to wait, till she should write a few lines to madame de Beaumont.

He told her, he was ordered not to bring back any letter, or message, and hoped she would not take his refusal ill, as he durst not venture to disobey.—The tears now forced their way into Charlotte's eyes. She told the servant she would not be the cause of his disobedience, on any account; and that she was ready to follow him.

He put her and her maid, into a chariot, and directed the coachman where he was to go. When they alighted, she was shewn into a very elegant apartment; and her conductor, after inquiring whether she wanted money, or any farther assistance from him, being answered in the negative, bowed, and withdrew.

As soon as he was gone, the now miserable Charlotte gave vent to all her sorrows; she threw herself upon the ground, and washed it with her tears. Her affectionate servant, who had lived with her from her infancy, without knowing the cause of her distress, vainly endeavoured to console her; intreated her to return to England; and talked of lord Seymour's love and constancy.

Her every word struck daggers, to the unhappy Charlotte's heart.—As soon as she was able to speak, she told her maid she must part with her, the next day; that she had determined to go into a convent, for some time; and advised her to set out, immediately, for London. The poor girl, who truly loved her, was almost distracted, at seeing and hearing her mistress look and speak so: and positively declared she would never leave her, let her determination in life, be what it would.

Charlotte peremptorily insisted on discharging her, from her service; but told her she would support her, in Paris, while her money lasted, and that she might, sometimes, see her, at the convent. This, in some measure, quieted the poor servant's anxiety; but Charlotte's unhappiness increased, every hour.—She went not to bed, and the pearly drops remained on her fair cheek, when the sun had exhaled those of the dew.

She wrote a few lines, to let lord Seymour know, that she was going into the convent of St. Anthony; and, in her distraction, gave the letter to her maid, to deliver; without reflecting, that the faithful Nannette had resolved not to quit Paris, till her mistress's fate was determined.

In the morning she dressed herself, and endeavoured to assume an air of composure and tranquillity, with a breaking heart. About ten o'clock, the same person, who had attended her, the night before, came in a coach, accompanied by madame de Beaumont's woman, who presented her with the following letter:

CHARLOTTE,

Both the general, and I, are much pleased with the accounts we have received, of your behaviour. Any remonstrance against our commands, would be, at once, presumptuous and vain. Continue, therefore, to deserve our favour, by a silent and unlimited obedience.

You are already informed, that the general has devoted you to heaven.—Let not his will, who has an absolute power over you, appear severe. A convent is the only place, where true happiness is to be found.—That you may meet it there, sincerely wishes

C. De Beaumont.

P.S. You are expected to enter upon your noviciate, immediately.

Charlotte received this cruel sentence, with amazing fortitude. To her perturbed and wretched state of mind, the quiet asylum of a cloister, appeared not undelightful; and had not her passion for lord Seymour, revolted against the severity of her doom, she might have been led, like a lamb to the sacrifice, without a sigh, or groan.

Madame de Beaumont's last letter seemed less *farouche*[99] than her former one; and this encouraged Charlotte to hope, that time and her obedience, might possibly awaken the tender feelings of maternal love, in her hitherto obdurate breast. She again inquired, whether she might not be permitted to return her thanks, for madame de Beaumont's favour, in writing? and was again answered in the negative.

She took a most affectionate leave of her disconsolate maid, who followed the coach, at a distance, and saw her enter those gates, through which she was never to pass, again.

When they had arrived at the convent, madame de Beaumont's woman presented Charlotte to the abbess, as a willing victim. She was, therefore, received with every outward mark of esteem; and the grossest flattery was lavished by the whole sisterhood, on those charms, which they vainly imagined an acceptable sacrifice, to the great Creator of them.

Deluded mortals!—the heart alone is all that he requires! nor do the tender charities of life, the love of parents, husband, brethren, children, pollute the oblation, but render it more pleasing, in his sight, who first ordained, then sanctified, these natural ties.

Charlotte shewed not the least reluctance, at entering on her probation.—She knew that a year must elapse, before she could be compelled to take the veil; and still flattered herself, that fate would dispose of her, in another way, before that time should expire. She imagined, that by a seeming acquiescence, she might be able to lessen, if not intirely remove, any restraint they might otherwise have imposed on her.

She made no doubt, that lord Seymour's passion would prompt him to pursue her; and she fully determined to acquaint him with every circumstance of her life, if she should ever have an opportunity. For this purpose, she employed every leisure moment, she was mistress of, in framing a little history, from the papers she had found in the cabinet, with the additional circumstances, that had happened, from the time of her leaving London.

As she scarce ever appeared in the parlour, or at the grate, the sister-hood beheld her as the paragon of sanctity; and her edifying example was quoted as a pattern, for all the young ladies in the convent. The little task she had imposed on herself, by amusing her mind, kept up her spirits, so that she seeemed to have acquired a constant habit of chearfulness.

But when her work was finished, and two months had elapsed, without hearing from her father, mother, or, what was far more interesting, her lover, she fell into a lowness of spirits, which terminated in a slow fever. She now looked upon herself as abandoned by all the world; and the cruel suspicion of lord Seymour's inconstancy, perfectly reconciled her, to the gloomy prospect of perpetual seclusion.

Her faithful servant continued to see her, frequently, and, as often, mingled her tears, with those of her unhappy mistress. As she was, one day, musing on the uncommon miseries of her fate, her maid approached her with unusual chearfulness, and cried out, O, madam! he is come.

A transitory joy now sparkled in Charlotte's lovely eyes, and the soft bloom that had forsook her cheek, returned with added blushes. Where is he? she replied; and ah! how could he stay, so long! Didst thou see him Nan-nette, and has he mourned my absence?

At that instant, one of the lay-sisters came to inform Charlotte, that a gentleman desired to see her. She flew to the grate, but how was her surprize increased, when instead of lord Seymour, she beheld her brother?

If any thing could have abated her joy at seeing him, it must have been the disappointment she felt, at not meeting lord Seymour. But though her ex-pectation had been highly raised, with the pleasing hope of such an interview, she was sincerely rejoiced at the unexpected sight of her much-loved brother.

He immediately began to expostulate with her, on her quitting England; and earnestly intreated her to leave the convent, and put herself under his pro-tection. She told him that was not, at present, in her power, as she was then in her noviciate, but promised not to take the veil, without his approbation, which she was certain would follow every action of her life, when he was ac-quainted with their motives; and, in order to explain, both her situation, and his own, she would send him some papers to peruse, which were of the utmost consequence, to them both.

Captain Beaumont was astonished at the mysterious manner which ac-companied his sister's words; but, as he had the highest opinion of her honour, and understanding, he, for the present, suppressed his curiosity, about the secrets she hinted at, and retired to his lodgings, to wait till Nannette should bring an explanation of the mystery, in which he found his innocent and unhappy sister involved.

Captain Beaumont had left London, the day after his sister, and easily traced her through the progress of her journey; but when he arrived, at Paris, as he had no clue to guide him, he wandered, near three months, in pursuit of her, and but for the accidental meeting of Nannette, in the street, he might have spent as many years, in the same fruitless inquiry.

Lord Seymour, whose ardour and impatience to recover his lost fair one, was even more sanguine than a brother's could be, was not so early in his pursuit. The agitation of his mind, upon receiving Charlotte's letter, had thrown him into a violent fever, and it was above three weeks, before he was able to follow his fair fugitive.

When he came to Paris, he was as much at a loss to direct his inquiries, as her brother had been—he had heard of her, along the road, and also of captain Beaumont's following her; and from the description he received of him, had no doubt of his being the same person he had seen at her house, the day she left it.

Love and jealousy are twins, and it is impossible to defend the heart, from one, if you admit the other. It was apparent to him that this person, and Charlotte, were connected; and his never having seen or heard of him, increased his apprehensions of his being a favoured lover. Yet why! if that were the case, should Charlotte continue to deceive him? why write such a tender and affectionate adieu? He knew not, unless it were to lull his fears to sleep, and prevent his endangering her lover's safety. Thus did the unhappy Seymour increase his own calamities, and drag about a wretched, lifeless form, to every public place, in Paris, in the fond hope of meeting those transcendant charms, that were now buried in a cloister.

The sight of her brother, had raised poor Charlotte's spirits, by reviving her hopes of getting out of the convent. Yet of what use, would she exclaim, is liberty, without love? Seymour abandons me, and the world itself is now become a solitude to me, more gloomy, even than this cell. But grant his love and constancy should still subsist, and that he is, this moment, as wretched as myself, could he receive into his family, the *natural,* and *rejected* daughter, of such cruel parents! No, there is no resource for me, on earth; these walls, for ever, must confine this hapless frame; my heart alone is free, and flies, of course, to him!

As soon as she had leisure, she inclosed mademoiselle Laval's papers, her father and mother's pictures, with a letter from herself, to her brother, acquainting him with every thing that had passed, since her arrival in France, and intreating him not to mention the affinity between them, at the convent, lest it should give offence to their parents, and occasion their being restrained from seeing each other, for the future. She earnestly implored his protection and assistance, toward releasing her from the state she was in, and promised to be guided by him, in every action of her life.

Notwithstanding the inhuman treatment, that Charlotte had met with, on perusing the papers, captain Beaumont was transported, at finding himself so nearly related to the general—the pride of blood is inherent; and the sanguine hopes of preferment, from such a high descent, dazzled his reason. He flew directly to his sister, and told her, with the precipitancy natural to a young man, that he was rejoiced at this discovery, and would go, immediately, and throw himself at his father's feet, without having the least doubt of a favourable reception.

In vain Charlotte remonstrated against such an unadvised proceeding, and mentioned the humility of her own conduct, and the severity of her parents, notwithstanding; in order to deter him, from making the experiment. She feared that his approaching the general, without any introduction, would be construed into want of respect, and that she should be condemned, for informing him that he had a right to do so—but he was not to be restrained.

She passed the night under the most gloomy apprehensions, yet would often say to herself, what have I to fear? can I be made more wretched? let me, then, receive the only consolation that remains for misery like mine, the knowing that any change must be for the better. Hapless maid! a change will come, that shall render your present state, by sad comparison, a scene of soft tranquillity and ease.

The next evening, on being informed that captain Beaumont was in the parlour, she flew to receive him; and after asking a thousand questions, with her eyes and tongue, she laid her cheek close to the grate, to listen to his answers. At that instant, she beheld lord Seymour entering the room. The agitation of her mind was now increased, almost to distraction: she knew not what she said, or did; and was utterly incapable of expressing the joy she felt, at seeing the dear idol of her soul. Her brother appeared dejected, and unhappy; and the mistaken Seymour attributed her confusion, and his melancholy, to motives, which their souls were strangers to.

We have already hinted, that jealousy had infected his noble nature; but his seeing the object of it, with the woman he adored, added a thousand stings; and he now felt, in the supremest degree, its poignant anguish. His behaviour to Charlotte, was constrained, and cold. He told her he was indebted to that gentleman, pointing to her brother, for the happiness of seeing her: as he could not easily forget his having met him, at her house, the morning she left London, he naturally supposed he could inform him where she was; and having accidentally seen him, just then, enter the convent, he had taken the liberty to inquire for her, and hoped she would pardon his intrusion. He added, that he should leave Paris, in a few days, and desired to know if she had any commands, to England.

Though Charlotte was astonished, at his behaviour, she had, however, penetration enough, to discover the cause, and said, she hoped she should be able to prevail on him to prolong his stay, as she flattered herself with the thoughts of returning to England, in a few months, and should wish to have him for her conductor.

He bowed, and replied, he should think himself happy to be of any service to her, provided he did not interfere, with another person's right; but, as he believed that gentleman was her chief motive, for visiting France, he was, doubtless, intitled to the honour of attending her to England, or wherever else she pleased.

Charlotte was rendered miserable, by lord Seymour's suspicions; yet, as there was other company in the parlour, she knew not how to obviate them, as she was yet ignorant, whether she might dare to own captain Beaumont for her brother. The latter was much surprized, at lord Seymour's manner.— He knew not of any connection, between Charlotte and him, and thought her rather too condescending.

The rest of the time they staid, was passed in a constrained, and difficult situation. However, Charlotte found, and seized an opportunity, of speaking the words, which are quoted in her letter to lord Seymour, already related [page 52, para. 3], before the gentlemen withdrew.

"My dearest Henry, let not appearances disturb your mind; I can, and will, account, for every action of my life, to you.—Let your servant attend, at the grate, to-morrow, for a letter from me, and you shall be fully satisfied."

Though Charlotte's mind was perplexed with a thousand doubts, and fears, both for her brother, and herself, the transport of having seen lord Seymour, triumphed over them all; and she, once again, enjoyed a transient gleam of happiness. She knew it was in her power, to remove all his suspicions: she neither doubted his love, nor honour; and was certain he would assist her in getting out of the convent, should they attempt to compel her to take the veil.

After writing a few lines to lord Seymour, and making up her pacquet for him, she lay down to rest, with a heart more at ease, than she had ever felt, since the death of mademoiselle Laval. But the bell had no sooner rung for mattins, than she was presented with the following note:

> My dearest CHARLOTTE,
>
> I die, by lord Seymour's hand;—some fatal mistake has caused this tragedy. If he is your friend, let him fly, to preserve the only one, you have now left. My cruel parents will rejoice at my fate, and I only lament it, for your sake.
>
> Adieu, I fear, for ever.
>
> CHARLES BEAUMONT.

Nothing, but the immediate loss of her senses, could have preserved her life.—She sunk, motionless, upon the ground; and nature, by being totally overpowered, afforded some little respite to her distracted mind. She remained in this situation, till the nuns, alarmed at her absence from chapel, came to seek her, in her cell. But when their cruel care had brought her so far back, as to shew some signs of life, she could neither speak, nor weep. She appeared like grief personified. She neither beat her bosom, rent her hair, or committed any act of outrage, but continued almost immoveable, till a letter was brought her, from madame de Beaumont, which contained these words:

> Accursed be the hour, that gave thee birth, and doubly cursed the moment, when thy pretended filial piety brought thee back to France, to ruin and destroy the peace of them, who had been blessed, if thou hadst never been born! Why, parricide, and fratricide in one, didst thou inform the unhappy wretch, who is now fallen a victim to thy vices, of his affinity to us? Thy father never will surmount the shock which he received from seeing him, and, with his latest breath, will curse thee, for being the cause of his, and thy brother's death.
>
> But thou, I doubt not, triumphest in thy wickedness, and fondly hopest to wed the murtherer of thy brother. But here thy crimes shall end.—Thou shalt, immediately, be conveyed to *La Salpêtrière*,[100] and made sensible of the unmerited kindness, thou hast hitherto received, by the severities thou shalt hereafter experience.
>
> C. B.

We might suppose, that when the unhappy Charlotte had read her brother's note, her miseries could scarce admit addition; but her inhuman mother's letter convinced her, that the cup of sorrow, though seemingly brimfull, is always capable of increase.

She was seized with inexpressible terrors, at the thoughts of being sent to *La Salpêtrière.* She was sensible that the abbess, and nuns, where she then was, had treated her with the utmost kindness: for, as they looked upon her as a voluntary victim, she had never experienced the least restraint, but what the common rules of the house prescribed. She had been accustomed to the tenderest treatment, all her life; and her present melancholy situation demanded it, more than ever.

After perusing the cruel anathema, that doomed her to still greater miseries, she flew into the abbess's apartment, and prostrating herself before her, with a flood of tears implored her pity, and protection. The good woman was moved, at her distress; and raising her from the ground, assured her that no authority, except the express order of the king, should force her from that house; and that if her enemies should attempt to procure a mandate, by any false representation, she would exert her utmost interest, to protect her.

Charlotte now considered the absolute impossibility, of any future connection with lord Seymour, and therefore looked upon her continuance in the convent, of *St. Anthony,* as an asylum, most devoutly to be wished for. She thanked the abbess, on her knees; and would, at that instant, have taken the veil, without repining, if they could have abridged the time of her probation.

She had now no longer any terms to keep, with madame de Beaumont; and therefore mentioned the misfortune her brother had met with, and entreated the abbess's permission, to send hourly, to inquire his health. Her request was granted; and she retired to her cell, in some degree less wretched, than she had left it.

But when her tortured imagination represented her still dear lord Seymour, as the executioner of her brother, her grief was without bounds. Yes, she would say, I am, indeed, accursed! well does my mother stile me so.—Yet are they cruel words, to pass maternal lips! Oh! had she but once blessed me, I could not be the wretch I am.

It is impossible to describe the various emotions of her distracted mind; yet still love remained triumphant; and she strove, in vain, to pursue what she thought the dictates of her duty, the hating of lord Seymour.

Captain Beaumont continued to languish, without hopes, for near three months; during which time, she received the following letter, from lord Seymour.

*To Mademoiselle de* BEAUMONT.

Convinced as I am, that I have given you cause to detest the name of him, who now presumes to address you, I would not, madam, intrude upon your sorrows, but to offer you the only atonement, which you can receive, from such a wretch as me.

I mean to inform you, madam, that I do not intend to fly from justice; I knew the severity of the laws, when I incurred their censure: and the moment that precious life is ended, which I have robbed you of, I mean to offer up my own, worthless as it is, in order to expiate, as far as is now possible, the crime of having rendered you unhappy.

But Oh, my dearest Charlotte! may I not hope, that when my blood has washed away my stains, exhausted as the fountains of thy beauteous eyes may be, with grief for my too happy rival, thou then mayst spare one tear, to the sad memory of the lost,

SEYMOUR.

There wanted but this last stroke, to render Charlotte the veriest wretch on earth. She had flattered herself, that lord Seymour had quitted *France,* immediately after the duel, and that his life, at least, was safe; and that, at some time, or other, she should be able to convince him of his error, and her innocence. But now she beheld him, wilfully devoting himself to the rack, and suffering torture, greater than even that can inflict, from his mistaken opinion of her inconstancy.

It was impossible that her delicate frame could longer support the complicated agonies, that assailed her mind. She fell into a raging fever: during her delirium, she raved incessantly, of racks, and gibbets, of snatching Seymour from them, and suffering in his place. At length, however, the natural goodness of her constitution, and her blooming youth, surmounted this dreadful disorder, and her reason and wretchedness returned, together.

The first gleam of peace, that broke through the horrors of her fate, were some small hopes, of her brother's recovery; and in consequence of those hopes, she, by a solemn vow, devoted herself to heaven, if it should be pleased to spare his life. But not all her religion and virtue, could prevent her as firmly resolving, not to outlive lord Seymour, should he suffer.

As soon as captain Beaumont was able to sit up in his bed, he wrote to his loved sister, congratulating her on his deliverance from death, and exculpating lord Seymour, as far as possible, by condemning himself, for not avowing the relation between him and Charlotte, before their engagement; but from a false punctilio, he had thought it beneath an officer, to use any argument in his defence, except his sword; and, therefore, by his manner, had rather confirmed lord Seymour in his error, of supposing him his rival, than undeceived him; for which he begged both his lordship's, and his sister's pardon.

He then gave her an account of the interview he had with his father, and of the disgust, and surprize, which the general expressed, at seeing him; and that he had, peremptorily, commanded him to quit Paris, and join his regiment, immediately; and farther informed him, that if he attempted to disobey, he would have him broke,[101] with infamy.

He said he had, however, reason to hope, that the misfortune he had met with, had softened his father's heart, as he had been attended, during his illness, by the first surgeons in Paris, who came to his assistance, unsent for, and unpaid, by him; and that if his sufferings had made his father relent, he should, for ever, bless the hand, that had inflicted them.

The pleasing hope of her brother's recovery, was the most healing balm that could have been administred, to Charlotte's wounded heart. She no longer trembled for his life, or what was dearer still, lord Seymour's; and she began, in some measure, to be reconciled to her fate, merely by reflecting, that it might have been more wretched.

Notwithstanding all her efforts to conquer it, her passion for lord Seymour, remained undiminished, and she would have given worlds, had she been mistress of them, to undeceive him. But though her faithful Nannette, had made the most diligent search for him, from the time that captain Beaumont was pronounced out of danger, she could not discover his retreat.

The time now approached, for Charlotte's fulfilling the vow she had made to heaven, by taking the veil. The cruel madame de Beaumont had made several fruitless efforts to prevail on the abbess to suffer her removal to another convent; but as she feared to appear publickly in soliciting it, lest the affinity between them, should be revealed, she, at last, contented herself with endeavouring to enforce the utmost strictness and severity, which their rules would admit of; with which the poor innocent sacrifice unreluctantly complied.

As soon as captain Beaumont was tolerably recovered, he wrote again to his sister, to inform her, that he had received an order from his colonel, to join his regiment, immediately; and, at the same time, a positive command from his father, to leave Paris, without seeing her. He conjured her, in the strongest terms, to renounce the veil, and fly to lord Seymour, for protection; and told her he was certain, that his lordship was still in Paris, as he had just then discovered, that he was the person, who appointed, and paid the surgeons, for their attendance on him.

The fair disconsolate was now so enured to affliction, that she bore this fresh mark of her parents inhumanity, with gentleness and resignation; but alas! there was a woe, superior far, to all they could inflict, and which, like Aaron's rod,[102] had swallowed up the rest. Lord Seymour thought her guilty, still!

She had preserved the pacquet she had made up for him, on the evening of their last interview; and on the day preceding that, on which she was to make her vows, she received the following lines from him.

### To Mademoiselle de BEAUMONT.

Though I approach you now, with less terror, madam, than when I last presumed to address you, still does my beating heart, and trembling hand, avow your power, and amply revenge your sufferings, on the wretch who dared to offend you. But, since it has pleased heaven, to repair the cruel injury I did you, by restoring my rival to your prayers, and wishes, will not the gentle Charlotte condescend, to pardon, and pity, the unhappy man, who once thought (fatal delusion!) himself honoured with her love?

I fly from Paris, madam, from the sad scene of all my sorrows; but they, alas! will be companions of my flight. Yet let me take one blessing with me, a last, if not a kind, adieu, from you.

As you talked of returning to England, I never will revisit it—the sight of the detested Seymour, no more shall shock your eyes, or damp your joys—but let me wander where I will, the warmest effusions of this still doating heart, shall, to its latest throb, be poured forth, in blessings on, Ah! I had like to have said, *my* angel Charlotte! My hand refuses longer to obey its wretched master, and I can hardly say,

Adieu.

SEYMOUR.

Affected as the tender heart of Charlotte was, at her loved Seymour's deep distress, she felt a momentary joy, at the thought of being able to recover his esteem, by proving herself worthy of his love. She instantly sat down, and with inexpressible anguish, wrote the letter [page 51], which has been already related, and inclosed it, with the narrative she had before written of her life, to lord Seymour.

This dreadful conflict past, she felt a dawn of peace, beam on her mind, and immediately gave orders, that no letter, or message, should be brought to her. She passed the night in fervent prayer, and at the break of day, summoned her young companions in the convent, to adorn her for the sacrifice, with all the dignified composure, with which a queen puts on her regal robes.

Her conduct, during the awful ceremony, has been already described, by lord Seymour; and sure a heart, more truly virtuous, or a form more exquisitely fair, were never offered up, at any shrine! And may that gracious power, to whom they are devoted, bless all her future days, with that "sweet peace, that goodness, bosoms ever."[103]

# LETTER 24.

## *Lady* STRAFFON, *To Lady* WOODVILLE.

That my dear Emily may not again reproach me, for attending equally to *foreign,* and *domestic* affairs, I shall answer her two last letters, before I speak my sentiments of the truly amiable, and unhappy Charlotte Beaumont. And first, of the first—Though you have desired me not to reply to it, I find the subject so very interesting, and alarming, that I cannot, in justice to you, or myself, comply with your request—

You certainly must have lived, some days, upon essence of tea, and reduced your nerves to the lowest state, imaginable, before your mind could be affected, by the circumstance you mention. Not that I would insinuate that lord Woodville's sudden confusion, was not the effect of a quick recollection, or consciousness of some former scene, which he, perhaps, might wish to have forgot. In all probability, it arose from the remembrance, of some disastrous love adventure, which obtruded itself, involuntarily, upon his mind.

This point, which you have barely hinted at, I shall take for granted; and then endeavour to shew you the absurdity of being alarmed, on such an occasion. Lord Woodville is now in his eight-and-twentieth year, and has lived, both in foreign courts, and at home, as much in the gay world, as any man in England.—And can my dear Emily really suppose, that she was the first object of his love?—Impossible! It is much more reasonable to imagine, that he had felt that passion, half a dozen times, at least, before she was out of her hanging sleeves.[104]

But all girls flatter themselves with the intire possession, of an husband's heart; which, if he happens, as in your case, to be seven or eight years older than her, is no more in his power to bestow, than youth or beauty. But if he generously grants you all that remains at that time in his gift, you have not the least right to complain; and this, I firmly believe, lord Woodville has done. Beware, then, my Emily, of appearing ungrateful for this present; nor let him ever see that you do not consider, even the remnant of his heart, as a full equivalent, for all your own. This I must confess to be a very unequal lot of affections; but the conditions of life, should be acquiesced in, without too much refining.—

There never was an higher instance of delicacy, than lord Woodville's behaviour to you, in consequence of the temple adventure; but do not give him too frequent opportunities, of exerting his galantry:—you are a musical lady; and know that a string may be strained, till it breaks. I am perfectly acquainted with the tenderness, and sensibility, of your nature; but you are not to judge of others, by your own fine feelings; or think your husband deficient in affection, if he is not so minutely attentive to trifling circumstances, as your delicacy may prompt you to expect.

*Les petits soins*[105] belong, most properly, to female life: the great cares of the world, are load sufficient, for the ablest man. I have now done chiding, I hope, for ever, as I never can be angry with my Emily, but when she wounds herself.

The description of your rural entertainment, pleased me much.—Whenever I go to Woodfort, you shall take me to see your *pocket Arcadia*—No, upon second thoughts, the scene would be incomplete, without a swain; I therefore desire you will present my compliments to Sir James Thornton, and tell him, that I appoint him my *Cecisbeo*,[106] for that party, if we should ever happen to meet at your house.

I am not at all sorry that lord Seymour has left you.—The constant anguish which he must ever feel, was sufficient to infect ye all. This naturally leads me to the charming nun.—I cannot forgive your want of ingenuousness, in not mentioning the million of tears, her story must have cost you—there never was any thing more affecting—Lucy and I, read, and wept, by turns—When one of us began to falter, the other endeavoured to relieve her; but there were many passages, that neither of us could repeat aloud, and only gazed silently on, through the dim medium of our tears.

It really requires a perfect certainty of the facts, to suppose there ever were such monsters, in nature, as the general, and madame de Beaumont. But Charlotte's unhappy fate is but too strong a voucher of their inhumanity. Yet miserable, as the lovely vestal is, I think lord Seymour much more wretched—Time, devotion, and a thorough consciousness of the rectitude of all her actions, may calm her sorrows; whilst his must, for ever, be aggravated, by knowing that he has rendered her unhappy. I think him truly to be pitied. Adieu, my Emily—Loves, and good wishes, from all here, accompany this to Woodfort.

F. STRAFFON.

## LETTER 25.

### *Lady* WOODVILLE, *To Lady* STRAFFON.

I have, at present, a house full of company; and therefore must content myself with barely acknowledging the receipt of my dear Fanny's friendly admonitions, which I frankly admit to be just, though I feel they are severe. Call me no more a spoiled child, when I so readily embrace the rod.

Lady Lawson has been here, these three days. There have been odd reports, about Sir William and the young lady I formerly mentioned to you, who went to London, a few days before him. But I am persuaded they are false, for on Sir William's return, last night, lady Lawson received him with the most genuine, and unaffected delight, that could be expressed, in looks, or words; and I hear that miss Fanning (that is the lady's name) is to return to Lawson-Hall, in a few days. The knight appeared a little embarrassed; but that might be owing to the meeting his lady in so much company: we were all assembled at tea, and knew nothing of his return.

You must not expect me to be a constant correspondent, from York: the fatigue of dressing twice, nay, perhaps, thrice, a day, will afford me but little time, for more rational entertainment. There are no moments which I think so totally lost, as those spent at the toilette; but the customs of whatever place we are in, must be complied with. Your Emily has not resolution sufficient to stem a torrent, and must, therefore, always be carried away with the stream. I will, however, keep a sort of journal of the occurrences of each day, and you must accept of that, in lieu of my letters.

My reason for not avowing how much I was affected, by the story of the nun, was to avoid taking off that surprize, which gives strength to every emotion.—When we are told that a tragedy is extremely tragical, we summon our resolution, to oppose the feelings of our hearts; and frequently suffer our pride to conquer its most graceful weakness: whereas, when we are taken by surprize, we give nature fair play, and do not attempt to combat with our humanity.

Adieu, my dear Fanny! Woodfort sincerely repays all the loves, and good wishes, of Straffon-Hill.

E. WOODVILLE.

## LETTER 26.

### *Lady* STRAFFON, *To Lady* WOODVILLE.

I ought, perhaps, to be more thankful to my dear Emily, for her last short letter, than for any other she has written to me. There is, certainly, the highest degree of merit, in giving pleasure to others, when the effort is attended with trouble, or difficulty, to ourselves. The bestowing a quarter of an hour, upon an absent friend, while we are surrounded with the chearful gaiety of present ones, should always be considered as an high compliment.

You may see, by this remark, that I set a proper value upon your kind attention; but I am still more charmed with your condescension, in admitting the justness of my arguments. Believe me, my dear, if we wish to be happy, we must make it a constant rule to turn away our eyes, even from the minutest failings of those we love; the suffering our thoughts to dwell long upon them, must insensibly lessen our affection, and, of course, our felicity.

There cannot, in my mind, be a more pitiable object, than a virtuous woman, who ceases to love her husband.—What a dreadful vacuity must she feel in her heart! How coldly, and insipidly, must her life pass away, who is merely actuated by duty, unanimated by love!

Where there never has been passion, there may, for ought I know, be a kind of mixed sensation, compounded of esteem, and mutual interest, that supplies the place of affection, to the insensible part of mankind.—If this were not the case, the generality of married people, could not live so well together, as they do.—But this wretched substitute will never answer, to a man, or woman, who has once truly loved.

I would, therefore, most earnestly recommend it to all those, who are so happy as to be united to the objects of their choice, to set the merits and attractions of each other, in the fairest point of view, to themselves, and never, even for a moment, to cast their eyes on *the wrong side of the tapestry.*

Your account of the kindness, with which lady Lawson received her wandering swain, very fully proves that she is an excellent wife; but is, by no means, a refutation of the reports relative to him, and miss Fanning. Your ignorance of the world, and its ways, makes such scenes appear extraordinary to you.—But, alas! they are too frequent, to be wondered at, in such times as these.

I shall not, my dear Emily, insist upon your writing, from York, if it is inconvenient to you: but as Fanny Weston tells Lucy, that you do not set out from Woodfort, this fortnight, every day of which, I dare say, she thinks a year, I may flatter myself with the hopes of hearing from you, perhaps more than once, before you go.

That surprize increases our emotions, I readily admit; but, as you had no reason to doubt the tenderness of Lucy's nature, or mine, you might have communicated your own sensations, without fear of abating ours.

Sir John is gone to London, for a short time; and Lucy and I are to spend the days of his absence, not in retirement, as you might possibly suppose, but in discharging a heavy debt of visits, which we owe to all the neighbourhood, for five miles round. I think there are few small evils that torture us so much, as what is generally called a good neighborhood, in the country.

Adieu, my dear Emily. I feel myself peevish, at the idea of squandering my time, with persons that I have not the least wish to converse with, and asking simple questions, without the smallest desire to be informed. But as the world is constituted, we must compound for spending some part of our lives disagreably, and endeavour to make ourselves what amends we can, by enjoying that portion of it, which is left to our own disposal.

Health, and her fair handmaid, chearfulness, attend my dearest Emily.

F. STRAFFON.

LETTER 27.

*Lady* WOODVILLE, *To Lady* STRAFFON.

My dear Fanny is extremely kind, in seeming to set so high a value upon my small, or rather no, merit, in writing to her; for, indeed, I can never claim any, for what is to me the highest self-indulgence.—So a truce with your compliments, my too civil sister.

Do not be angry, Fanny; but I really cannot think with you, that true affection should be founded on illusion, which must be the case, if we are to be totally blind to the failings of those we love.—On the contrary, I have always considered the raising our ideas, of the persons we are to be united to, too romantically high, as one great source, of matrimonial unhappiness. By that means, we become enamoured of a being, which exists not in nature, and feel ourselves mortified, and displeased, as at a real disappointment, when we discover that our imagination has exceeded the bounds of possibility.

But if absolute perfection were to be found on earth, it would wound our self-love; and whatever injures that, can never be, long, dear to us. In the imperfections of our most amiable friends, we find a consolation for our own, which forbids despair, and places the generality of mankind, pretty nearly upon a level. This equality creates confidence, and that, naturally, produces esteem, and love.

As these are my real sentiments, I think I may venture to tell you, that I am very sorry I have never yet been able to discover one failing, in my lord. I declare, Fanny, this is an humiliating situation, to a creature so conscious of a thousand weaknesses, as I am; and, instead of restraining me from searching for his faults, I desire you will, immediately, provide me with a magnifying glass, to assist me in discovering them.

What an horrid idea have you conjured up, of a woman who ceases to love her husband! There can be but two causes in nature, that are capable of producing such an effect—for I talk not of those animals, who never felt passion.—The first of these, must be a constant series of ill treatment, which I suppose may, at length, conquer the tenderest affection; and the unhappy sufferer who continues to act up to her duty, under such circumstances, deserves, in my mind, a much higher fame, than any Greek, or Roman, that ever yet existed.

The other cause must be owing to a shameful and vicious depravity of heart, commonly called inconstancy; which, to the honour of our sex, I think I may say, is not frequent, amongst us. But when this happens to be the case, there is, generally, some new object, in view; for that despicable wretch, "a woman of galantry, never changes her first love, till she is engaged in a second."

I thank heaven for my ignorance of the world, and its ways, as I hope, and believe, I shall never have any trial, that may render a knowledge of them necessary. I know not what to think, with regard to lady Lawson; but, for my own ease, I will hope the best, as it is impossible that I should be indifferent, to any thing that distresses her.

Sir James Thornton has had an ugly fall from his horse, and strained his right arm, but has not received any dangerous hurt, though he is confined to his chamber. Lady Harriet, and Fanny Weston are indefatigable in their attendance on him. I just now received a message from him, to inquire my health; which seems a kind of tacit reproach, for not having been to visit him.—My sister Lawson and I spent all this morning, in designing plans, for a woodhouse;[107]—but as we are neither of us partial to our own inventions, we have laid them by, and determined to be rather good copyists, than bad originals. We have both agreed, that it was impossible to devise any thing more truly elegant, than that on the terrace at *Taplow,* which is to be our model. I have barely time to finish this, to dress, and look in upon Thornton, before dinner. Adieu, my dear Fanny! I may hear from you again, before we set out for York.

Your's, ever,

E. WOODVILLE.

## LETTER 28.

## *Lady* STRAFFON, *To Lady* WOODVILLE.

My dear EMILY,

As I am perfectly convinced that, in the account of our correspondence, I am much your debtor, on the article of entertainment, I am pleased at having a little adventure to relate to you, though I cannot hope that the recital will afford you as much pleasure, as the action gave me; but you must make the same allowance as you do for a play, in your closet, and furnish out all the scenery, decorations, &c. from the store-house of your own imagination.

My tale runs simply thus—as Lucy and I were returning home, last night, from lady Vaughan's, about eight o'clock, the sky quite dark, and rainy, one of the hind wheels of our chaise, flew off; but as we were travelling, at a very slow pace, in a miry road, we received no hurt from the accident.—We were about three miles, from Straffon Hill, which was rather too far for us to walk, as we were, by no means, accoutred for Peripatetics; and just as ill qualified for an equestrian expedition; we, therefore, sent off the postilion, on one of the horses, to bring the coach to us—

We saw no friendly cottage near; but, at the distance of a quarter of a mile, in the fields, we perceived a light, which seemed to us bright "as the Arcadian star, or Tyrian Cynosure."[108] One of the servants discovered a path, that seemed to lead to the mansion, from whence these charming beams had issued.

We took him with us, and setting forward, soon reached the small, but hospitable dwelling. When we knocked at the door, a little neat country girl appeared, and after conducting us into a small parlour, said she would acquaint her young lady, that there were strangers there, but that her mistress was at her devotions. We annonced ourselves to the girl, and she retired.

I was surprized, at this young creature's mode of expression; she seemed greatly amazed at our appearance, but her astonishment could only be discovered, by her looks. In a few minutes, an elegant young woman, about eighteen, entered the room, and after saluting us, very gracefully, inquired to what happy accident she was indebted, for the honour of our visit?

The courtliness of her address, and the ease of her manners, were all new subjects of wonder, both to Lucy and me; which we could not help expressing, after we had informed her of the accident we had met with. She very politely offered us tea, or coffee—we declined both—but there was a much higher treat, in her power, namely, the gratification of our curiosity, which we could not, however, venture to propose.

When we had sat, about a quarter of an hour, the little servant came in, and said her lady was come out of the chapel, and would be glad to see us—we were immediately shewn into a room, the neatness, and elegance of which, it is impossible to describe; at the upper end of it, on a small sofa, sat a woman, with the finest form, though pale and emaciated, that can be imagined.

She rose to receive us, with such an affable dignity, as at once attracted our respect, and love; she was dressed in black, and appeared to be about five-and-thirty—though she spoke perfect good English, there was just so much of the foreign accent in her utterance, as must prevent your taking her for a native of this country.

Over the chimney, of the chamber, we sat in, was a picture of a very handsome young man, and at the other end of the room, there hung one of the lady before us, in all the bloom of beauty, with her daughter, then about four years old, by her side, and a boy that looked like a cherubim, seated in her lap.

As I gazed on every object round me, with looks of admiration, which the lady of the house could not help observing, she turned to me, with an engaging smile, and said, the surprize which your ladyship is too polite to express, in words, is so perfectly visible in your countenance, that it would appear like affectation, to seem insensible of it; and as there is no part, either of my past, or present life, that should cause a blush to glow upon my cheek, I am ready to gratify that curiosity, which the extraordinariness of my situation, seems to have raised.

It will, probably, be near an hour, continued she, before your carriage can arrive, and a much less time will serve to relate the few, though uncommon events, that have placed me in the circumstances you now see me. Both Lucy and I expressed our gratitude, for such an obliging offer, in the warmest terms, and entreated she would proceed—Without more ceremony, she began.

I am a native of Italy, and descended from one of the most ancient families, of the republic of Genoa.—About twenty years ago, I became acquainted with a young English nobleman, called lord Somerville, whose picture you see there (pointing her beautiful hand towards the chimney;) he was then, upon his travels, and under age.—He became passionately in love with me, and soon inspired me with more than gratitude; with honest heart-felt love.

With my permission, he applied to my father, for his consent to our marriage; well knowing that he could have no exception, to his birth, or fortune. We had not the least apprehension, of my father's refusal—but we had both forgot, that my lover was an *heretic*. This was deemed by him, so material an objection to our union, that he declared he would confine me to a convent, for life, rather than hazard my salvation, by such a marriage.—My lover was forbidden to repeat his visits, and I was sent about twenty leagues off, into the country.

Lord Somerville soon discovered my retreat, and got access to me. By the treachery or zeal of a servant, who was intrusted with the care of me, my father was informed of our interviews, and determined to send me, directly, to a convent, at Naples, where an aunt of my mother's, was lady abbess. A particular accident let me into the secret of my intended doom, and I no longer hesitated, to prefer love and liberty, to cruelty and confinement. After lord Somerville had given me the most solemn assurances, that I should preserve my religion inviolate, we were married, and set out, privately, in a felucca,[109] hired for the purpose, which conveyed us to Marseilles.

When we came to *Lyons,* we were obliged to wait there, for remittances from England, before we could proceed farther. After having long expected them, in vain, my lord received a very severe, and angry letter, from his father, accusing him with having stolen the daughter of an Italian nobleman, and commanding him to restore me to my parents, and return immediately, to England.

The distress of my husband's mind, upon this occasion, was not to be concealed; but it was a long time before he acquainted me with the real motives of his concern. Fondly and passionately, as I loved him, I would have torn myself from his arms, and gone into a convent, till his father's resentment might have been appeased, if my condition would have permitted it.

But I was then far gone with child, of that young lady before you, and he, in the tenderest manner, assured me, that not even the commands of a father, should have power to force him from me, till he had the happiness of being himself a parent, and of seeing me in a situation to support his absence, or able to travel with him.

We had lived in the utmost retirement, and privacy, from the time of our arrival at *Lyons.*—My lord had taken the name of Fortescue, and no creature, except his banker, knew who he was.—We were so perfectly happy, in each other, that we wished for no other society—my lord amused himself, with teaching me English—with such a tutor, I soon became a considerable proficient; and at the time that my Laura was born, I could read, and perfectly understand, the most difficult English authors.

As soon as I was quite recovered, we set out for Paris, where my lord purposed leaving me, while he went over to England, to pay his duty to his father, and to endeavour to reconcile him to our marriage. I will not take up your time, with attempting to describe our mutual sufferings, at our separation; such forms as yours, must have feeling hearts, and you can judge, better than I describe, what we endured.

My lord remained, above a year, in England, making repeated, but fruitless efforts, to conquer his father's resentment, against a person who had never in thought offended him; but, alas! my being a catholic, was as unpardonable a crime to him, as my dear husband's being a protestant, was to my father. Strange! that the worshippers of one God, and Saviour, whose doctrine was peace, and good-will to men, should feel such enmity, and hatred to each other!

At my lord's return to France, I could not help perceiving a visible change, both in his health, and spirits, though his fondness for me was undiminished; or, if possible, seemed to be increased, by his tenderness for his daughter, who was then near two years old. As my lord concealed a great part of his father's unreasonable aversion to me, I was not without hopes that time would conquer his prejudices; which, indeed, I only wished, upon my lord's account; for while I enjoyed the real happiness of his company, there was not a desire of my heart, ungratified.

In less than a year, that infant, whose portrait you see there, was born.—From the time of his birth, my lord's health and spirits seemed to revive, and I then certainly reached the zenith of human felicity; alas! how quickly did the wheel turn round, to lay me in the lowest state of misery? With what rapture have I seen him catch the infant in his arms, and say, this boy, this boy, my love, will plead our cause, with my obdurate father, and soften his hard heart? Would he were three years old!—but that blessed time will come; and we shall all be happy.—

While lady Somerville repeated the foregoing words, her countenance became more animated, than it is possible to describe; but a sudden gush of tears, soon dimmed the brilliant lustre of her eyes, and quenched the glowing crimson on her cheek. She rose, and, opening a small folding door, retired into the chapel.

The young lady sympathized, most sincerely, with her mother's sorrow; and Lucy and I, who were extremely affected, were scarcely capable of making proper apologies, for having been the innocent cause of renewing both the ladies afflictions. Miss Somerville said every thing that politeness could dictate, to make us easy; and, in a few minutes, lady Somerville returned, with such an air of calmness, and resignation, as amazed me.

I took the liberty of entreating that she would not proceed farther in her story, for the present. But as I could not avoid being extremely anxious, about every circumstance relative to so amiable a person, I requested she would permit me to wait upon her, the next day, or whenever it was most agreeable to her inclination.

She told me she was very sensible of the delicacy, and propriety of my request, which she readily assented to, as it promised her the happiness of another interview, with persons, for whose sensibility, and politeness, she had conceived the highest respect: said, she was a little ashamed, that her long acquaintance with grief, had not yet rendered her so familiar with it, as she might naturally be supposed to be; but hoped we would excuse the sudden emotion, which had, for a few minutes, transported her. She then intreated our company to drink tea, the next evening, and said she would, if possible, be more composed.

In about a quarter of an hour, the coach arrived, and we took leave of this charming unfortunate, with the most earnest desire to renew our visit, and the warmest hopes of being serviceable to her, and her daughter.

I am really fatigued, with this long letter; but I would not suffer oblivious sleep to steal any part of this extraordinary adventure, from my memory, till I had communicated it to my dear Emily. By next post, you shall have the remainder of the story; till then, and ever,

I am affectionately your's,

F. STRAFFON.

## LETTER 29.

### *Lady* STRAFFON, *To Lady* WOODVILLE.

Lucy and I set out, immediately after dinner, yesterday, and reached lady Somerville's elegant cottage, before five o'clock. As we approached it by day-light, we discovered many beauties that had been hidden from us, by the

dun shades of night; particularly, several small clumps of trees, that were en-
circled with woodbines, orange and lemon gourds, and intermixed with a
great variety of flowering shrubs:—a small, but neat garden, at the bottom of
which ran a rivulet, so clear, and sparkling, as to appear like liquid diamonds.

As we drove by the pales of the garden, we perceived a building in it,
that seemed to be fitted up for a gardener's house; and, to our great astonishment, beheld a man, of a very respectable appearance, about sixty years of
age, seated in an arbour, with a book in his hand. We were received by both
the ladies, with the same politeness and affability, as the day before. The
folding doors, which led to the chapel, stood open; and, indeed, Emily, there
is no describing the elegance, with which the altar is adorned.

I am an enemy to all devotional parade: yet I could not help considering the decorations, of this sacred spot, rather as the offerings of the heart, to
heaven, than a sacrifice to vanity, as all the ornaments that are placed there,
were the work of lady Somerville's, and her daughter's hands.

As soon as tea and coffee were removed, lady Somerville, without waiting to be intreated, proceeded in her narrative, thus.—When I mentioned
my having reached the pinnacle of human felicity, I forgot to inform you,
that my father had been reconciled to me, for some time; and, on the birth
of my son, had presented me with his picture, set with diamonds, and desired the portrait of my lord, and those of my children.

But, before this request could be complied with, I had the misfortune
to lose my only parent.—His death was sudden; and he died without a will.
This was the first real affliction I had ever known; and my lord, in order to
divert my melancholy, proposed our going to the south of France.

I acquiesced in his desire, on his account, more than my own; for, as
his constitution was become extremely delicate, I hoped the change of air,
might be of service to him. We lived at Montauban, for near two years,
during which time I had the constant anguish, of beholding my dear husband's health decline, daily.

As he was perfectly sensible of his own situation, he determined to take
his little family to England, and present his son to his unkind father. Every
thing was fixed for our departure, when Providence, to whose all-wise decrees
I bow myself beneath the dust, thought proper to recall the treasure he had
lent us, and took my little cherubim, to join the heavenly choir!

No words can express the affliction of my loved lord, nor describe the
wretched state, both of his mind, and body. Whole days he hung enamoured

over the pale beauteous clay that was his child, nor would he be prevailed upon to resign it to corruption, till weakness left him not the power of opposition.

From that time, he sunk into a state, nearly approaching to insensibility, towards every thing, except myself; but, to his latest moment, his tenderness for me, was undiminished. Why should I dwell longer, upon a scene, which, but to think of, now, strains every nerve, and makes the blood run backward to its source! My misery was completed by his death, in less than six weeks after that of my lovely boy!

> But I will stay my sorrows! will forbid
> My eyes to stream before thee, and my heart,
> Thus full of anguish, will from sighs restrain!
> For why should thy humanity be grieved
> With my distress, and learn from me to mourn
> The lot of nature doomed to care and pain![110]

You may suppose that lady Somerville was, for some time, deprived of speech; nor was there one of us capable of interrupting the melancholy silence, but by our sighs. She, however, soon dried her tears, and resumed her discourse.—I shall relate the rest of my story, said she, though totally uninteresting to myself, as it will account for my present situation.

I was about four months gone with child, at the time of my lord's illness; and his last request to me was, that I would, if possible, lye-in in England, and acquaint his father with my pregnancy, as soon as I arrived there. He told me, that if the child, I carried, should be a son, it would inherit the fortune and honours of his family; but if not, that there was no provision made for me, or any daughters I might have, as he was under age, at the time he married; and that the estate was intailed, upon a very distant relation. He implored me to preserve my life, for the sake of the poor Laura; and to throw myself, and her, into his father's protection.

As it is utterly impossible that I should give you an adequate idea of my situation, at that time, I will not attempt it; but endeavour to cast a veil over that scene of distress, which no pen, no pencil, can ever be able to describe.

I set out from Montauban, with my maid, my chaplain, and my child, and arrived safe in London. I obeyed my dear lord's request, and wrote immediately to his father. His lordship was then in the country. He answered my letter with great civility, mixed with an affectation of kindness: said, he should be in town, shortly; that he would then see me; and desired I would take care of myself, for the sake of the unborn babe, which he hoped would prove a son and heir.

In a few days after I had received this letter, I was informed that there were persons appointed to attend me, till I was brought to bed, lest I should impose a surreptitious child, upon the family. I knew not that such proceedings were usual in my case, and I wrote a letter to my father-in-law, complaining of such treatment, to which he never deigned a reply.

But all their apprehensions on my account, were soon over: I was delivered, in the seventh month, of a dead son; and from that time, I heard nothing farther, from my lord's father, or any of his family, for above six months. The little money I had brought with me into England, was now quite exhausted; and I was obliged to apply, heaven knows how unwillingly! to this inhuman parent, for some means of support, for his son's widow, and his grandchild.

In his reply to my letter, he told me what I knew before, that neither my daughter, nor I, were intitled to any thing, by law; that, therefore, he advised me to go back to my own country, and he would furnish me with money, to carry me there; provided I would leave Laura, in England, to his care. That if I should refuse these terms, I must even provide for myself, as it was not his purpose to offer me any others.

When the mind has been once totally subdued by sorrow, we flatter ourselves, that we are incapable of being wounded, by any new distress: but the idea of being torn from the dear remains of my loved lord, my only child, convinced me that there were still some arrows, in the quiver of adversity, that had not yet been pointed at my peace.

I did not hesitate, one moment, to determine that no consideration should make me consent to a separation, from all that was now dear to me on earth. I must, indeed, have been as absolutely void of humanity, as himself, if I could have resigned my child, into the hands of a man, who had never even desired to see her, before.

I wrote, immediately, to my brothers, at Genoa, and acquainted them with my distress. They very kindly assured me, that they would receive me, and my daughter, with open arms, at our return; but if it should be my choice, to remain in England, they would take care that I should not want a support, there. They, immediately, remitted me bills for a thousand *piasters*,[III] and agreed to settle the same sum, annually, upon me, or more, if I should have occasion for it.

At this instance of generosity and affection, my heart once more became expanded with gratitude, to the Almighty, and with true sisterly tenderness, to my benefactors. I now began to make the first efforts towards subduing the violence of my grief, and to be sensible, that I might have been rendered still more wretched, than I was, by the deprivation of my child, or our being reduced to slavery, for bread.

I soon fixed upon the plan of life, which I meant to pursue, and sent out my worthy chaplain, and my faithful maid, in search of a retirement, such as you now see. In this spot I have lived, about eight years; in which time, I have had no manner of converse, with any human creature, but my own family; which now consists of my daughter, my chaplain, and myself; my gardener, his wife, and the little maid, their daughter, whom your ladyship has seen.

The only additional misfortune I have known, in this place, was the loss of my faithful Maria: she died, about two years since; and as my daughter was then of an age, not to need her attendance, I have never attempted to supply her place.

Rusticated so long as we have been, you will not, I hope, ladies, be surprized at the simplicity of mine, or my daughter's manners.—Our situation is certainly a very extraordinary one, and must naturally have raised your curiosity, which I have endeavoured to gratify, by a plain and artless narrative.

I wish, for your sakes, as well as my own, that my story had been less affecting; but I shall not make any apology for having drawn forth the lovely drop of sympathetic sorrow, which glowed with brighter lustre on your cheeks, than the most costly brilliant.

Both Lucy and I poured forth our thanks, for her kindness, and condescension, in relating her story; admired the constancy of her resolution, in remaining so long in retirement, but seemed to hope that she might change her purpose. I saw she was displeased at such a hint; but, with great politeness, said it was the only subject she did not wish to hear us talk upon, as it would always give her pain to dissent from our opinion, which she must ever do, both in word, and deed, upon that subject.

I then ventured to ask her, if she wished that miss Somerville should pass her life, in such a state of seclusion? She said, by no means;—so far from it, that she had sent forth a thousand fruitless wishes, that some lucky accident might happen to introduce her to persons of sense, and virtue, and of a proper rank, to lead her gently into life;—that she had heard the characters of all the persons of fashion, in that neighbourhood, from her chaplain, who frequently mixed with the world, in order to transact her affairs;—that as she was above flattery, she was also superior to disguise, and frankly owned that her utmost wish, in this world, would be gratified, if lady Straffon would promise her protection, to her dear orphan.

I scarce suffered her to finish the latter part of her speech, before I flew to, and embraced her, and, with great truth, assured her, that my inclinations met hers, more than half way. I begged that, from that moment, she would do me the honour to consider me, as her sister; and that the lovely Laura might be henceforth deemed my niece.

Every thing, that delicate gratitude could dictate, was uttered, upon this occasion; and we all appeared to be infinitely happier, than we could have supposed it possible for us to be, in so short a time after having been so much afflicted.

Lady Somerville concluded with informing me, that her father-in-law had been dead, about four years, and had left miss Somerville six thousand pounds. We agreed that Lucy should bring Laura to Straffon-Hill, to-morrow; and I promised to convey her back to her ladyship, whenever she required her attendance.

You cannot, my dear Emily; yes, you can, conceive, the sincere pleasure I feel, at having it in my power, to oblige the amiable, and unfortunate lady Somerville. It must certainly be an infinite relief to her mind, to know that her daughter has a friend, and protector, in case Providence should be pleased to put a period to her woes, and take her to his mercy. But she must, necessarily, suffer a great deal, in being separated from her, till use shall have made it easy.

Laura is but just seventeen, though she looks rather older, from the gravity, and dignity of her appearance. I flatter myself you will receive some entertainment, from this narrative, which I have been as exact in, as my memory would permit; and, indeed, it has, for the time, so intirely engrossed my attention, that I am pretty sure I have not omitted a circumstance of any consequence.

I expect Sir John will return, from London, the beginning of next week.—I hope he will be charmed with our young visitor; and that lady Somerville will suffer him, sometimes, to spend an hour with her. Adieu, my dear Emily.

I am, as usual, affectionately your's,

F. STRAFFON.

# LETTER 30.

## *Lady* WOODVILLE, *To Lady* STRAFFON.

I most sincerely congratulate my dear Fanny, upon the acquisition she has made to her happiness, by her acquaintance with lady Somerville. There was something extremely romantic, in the opening of your adventure, and I almost began to imagine, that you had taken a trip, to Fairy-land; but every circumstance, though surprizing, at first, is very naturally accounted for, in the course of your narrative. I truly compassionate the unhappy lady's situation; and again felicitate you, on having it in your power, to remove a very material part of her distress, by affording your friendship, and protection, to her daughter.

Lady Somerville's misfortunes are of the hopeless kind; it is not in the power of fate, to restore her husband, or her son; and slight observers would, for these reasons, pronounce her much more wretched, than those who are led on, by a faint glimpse of hope, to wander through the thorny paths of life, in search of some imaginary bliss, which still eludes their grasp. But I think otherwise. When the grave closes on our joys, our prospects of this world, must all end there; we can no more deceive ourselves, or be deceived. We sink, it is true, and fall with the dear prop, which fate has torn away. Then reason, and religion, come to our aid; and, when the first wild starts of grief, are over, an humble acquiescence in the divine will, sooths our sad souls to peace; our hopes spring forward to another goal, and pierce beyond the stars.

But while vain doubts and fears torment the heart, while passion has possession of the soul, and still impels us forward, through a maze, where our bewildered reason finds no clue, where peace is lost, and keen disquiet fills its vacant place; where our desires are raised, but to be mocked, and cruelty repaid for artless love!—Sure, sure, this state is worse, far worse, than lady Somerville's! She feels the stroke of death; but lady Harriet feels a living torture! inflicted, too, by whom her soul adored!

I have been led into this reflection, by observing, that lady Harriet's health, and spirits, have declined, visibly, ever since her unlucky interview with captain Barnard; and I am certain, that his almost perpetual residence, at Ransford-Hall, increases her disquiet. In his first act of inconstancy, she might, with great reason, imagine that fortune only had turned the scale, in favour of her rival, and she had still the melancholy consolation of supposing herself beloved, though by a worthless man.

His present attachment can arise, only from choice, or galantry; and it is certainly much more difficult, to bear contempt, than injury. Had he died, at the time he left her in Paris, her grief for his loss, would, by this time, have been softened into a gentle melancholy, which, though it might for ever have barred her pretentions to happiness, would not have rendered her half so wretched, as she is, at this moment, and, I fear, will ever be.

Let not what I have said, upon this subject, make my dear Fanny think, that I am not extremely affected, with lady Somerville's distress.—I acknowledge that her sufferings have been great, but they certainly came to a period, when her husband died; and time has, I doubt not, insensibly lessened her affliction. I also hope, that there is yet in reserve for her, the felicity of seeing her daughter perfectly amiable, and happy.

Adieu, my dear Fanny; my lord, and all this family, salute you, and yours, most affectionately. I desire you will present my respects, to lady Somerville, and her daughter, both of whom I hope to have the pleasure of seeing, when next I am so happy, as to visit Straffon-Hill.

Your's, ever,

E. WOODVILLE.

## LETTER 31.

### *Lady* STRAFFON, *To Lady* WOODVILLE.

My dear Emily,

I am so sincerely charmed at the hope of your prophecy, in favour of lady Somerville, being immediately accomplished, that I can neither think, speak, or write, upon any other subject.—Sir John returned, from London, in two days after Laura had become our guest; she and I were just come back from paying an evening visit, to lady Somerville, when he entered the drawing-room, and introduced a young Italian nobleman, who had been recommended to him, by one of his most intimate friends, at Paris.

I never beheld a handsomer youth; tall, graceful, and finely made, with the strongest expression of sense and sweetness, in his countenance—as he cannot speak English, our conversation was intirely Italian, in which, though Lucy and I are tolerable proficients, we were greatly excelled by miss

Somerville, who has had the advantage of conversing with her mother, in that charming language, from her earliest infancy.

The first two or three days, that our young foreigner spent with us, we imagined that his devoting the largest share of his time and conversation, to Laura, was owing to the easy fluency with which she spoke his native language; but his motives remained not long doubtful; he became very particular, in his inquiries about her, to Sir John, who gave him the fullest information of her birth, and situation in life. He seemed charmed at the account of both, and from that time, his assiduity towards her appeared, less embarrassed.

Nor is the gentle heart of Laura, insensible to his attentions: her blushes, when he is mentioned, and down-cast looks, when he addresses her, plainly discover the state of her artless mind. She is really a very fine creature, Emily, and I am truly anxious for her happiness. She has a sensibility, a frankness, a delicate ingenuousness of nature, not to be found in those, who have had much commerce with the world, which she owes to her sequestered education, with a parent, whose natural softness has been increased, by a long acquaintance with affliction.

But, to the purpose—Last night, the enamoured Lodovico explained his sentiments, to Sir John, and intreated him to prevail on me, to introduce him to lady Somerville; though he confessed that he found Laura extremely averse to a proposal, which must for ever divide her, from the tenderest of mother's; but as she seemed to have no other objection, he flattered himself that this might be surmounted.

Sir John's friend, lord Mount Willis, who recommended Lodovico to him, informed him, that he is descended from one of the first families, at Genoa, that he is an only son, intitled to a very large fortune, and possessed of a still higher treasure—an unexceptionable character.

I needed not much persuasion, to enter upon such a pleasing embassy.—I waited on lady Somerville, this morning; she seemed a little alarmed at Laura's not being with me. I quickly removed her apprehensions, by explaining the cause of my visit. She heard me, with the utmost attention, but could not help dropping some tears, when I mentioned Laura's objection to quitting her.

Lady Straffon, said she, when I had finished my discourse, though my dear girl's affection awakens all my tenderness for her, I will not suffer her to sacrifice her welfare, to my selfish satisfaction.—The world contains but one object for me; let her be happy, and contribute to the happiness of a deserving husband, and I shall taste the only *joy*, my heart is capable of. And should that long absent *guest*, ever deign to visit me, again, it is to you, the blessed minister of Providence, to whom I am indebted, for its presence.

I endeavoured to restrain the grateful effusions of her generous heart, by assuring her, that I felt almost as much pleasure, as even she could be sensible of, from the prospect of Laura's future happiness.—We then agreed, that I should bring Laura and Lodovico, to wait upon her, in the afternoon.—The instant I return, I will acquaint you with the result of our visit; till then,
Adieu.

F. STRAFFON.

## LETTER 32.

### *Lady* STRAFFON, *To Lady* WOODVILLE.

(In continuation.)

Join with me, my dearest Emily, in rejoicing at the happiness, which opens to the view of our amiable friends. But I will not detain you from the events which create their present joy. I carried my two young guests, Laura, and Lodovico, this afternoon, to lady Somerville's cottage; she received us with her usual grace and elegance; but when I presented signior Lodovico, to her, I fancied I perceived a change of countenance, which I knew not how to account for. However, she presently recovered herself, and continued to entertain us, with the greatest politeness.

After tea, I took Laura into the garden, under pretence of admiring a little grotto, she had lately finished, in order to give the young gentleman an opportunity, of explaining his sentiments, to her mother. We had not been ten minutes absent, when the little country maid came running to us, and desired we should return, immediately.

We were not a little surprized, at this summons; but judge how our wonder was increased, on finding lady Somerville, with her eyes streaming, and Lodovico seated by her, with an air that spoke him a sharer in her emotions! The moment we entered the room, she started up, and taking her daughter's hand, Come, said she, come and embrace your cousin, the son of that friend, that more than brother, to whom we have been indebted for the means of life, so many years.

Poor Laura was unable to speak; but her eyes fully expressed the tender, and grateful sentiments of her heart. The enraptured Lodovico seemed totally absorbed, in the pleasure of gazing on her.—After some time, lady Somerville turning to me, said, You see before you, my dear lady Straffon, the only son of count Melespini.—The instant I saw him, I was struck with the resemblance of that much-loved brother—but how could I flatter myself, with the happiness of beholding his son!

And now, my dear children, continued she, though my consent awaits ye, be assured, that without the count's concurrence, this union never can take place; write to him, therefore, Lodovico, and let both him and you rest satisfied, that his will shall, in this affair, determine mine.

In the mean time, I hope, said she, your ladyship will dispense with Laura's attendance, at Straffon-Hill. Perhaps my brother may have other views, for his son; if so, it is best not to indulge an affection, too far, which may be productive of unhappy consequences: for be assured, that however deserving the object, however virtuous the attachment, no marriage can be truly blest, that pains a parent's heart.—A too energic sigh accompanied these words: but, added she, when lady Straffon honours me with her company, I hope my nephew will attend her.

It was very visible that Lodovico complied, reluctantly, with these conditions; and, perhaps, Laura, for the first time, found obedience difficult.—But as her ladyship seemed determined, a bow of assent, was the only reply that was made. Signior Lodovico, and I, returned home, soon after this conversation.

By the way, he accounted to me, for not knowing that lady Somerville, or Laura, were related to him, as he had always heard them called Statevilla, which is their name, in Italian.[112] I find he intends making as much use, as possible, of the privilege of attending me to lady Somerville's; so that I expect to pass much of my time, at the cottage.

He is now retired, to acquaint his father with the happy discovery he has made, of his relations, and his sentiments towards his fair cousin. I shall be truly impatient, for the count's answer.—I hope it will be favourable; if it should not, I fear all lady Somerville's precaution will be insufficient to prevent the attachments of the young people, though I believe it would be impossible to draw Laura from her obedience.

I have been so much engaged, in the affairs of the Somerville family, for these two days, that I have scarce had leisure to think of my own.—You must, therefore, excuse my not entering upon the critical distinctions you have made, on the various modes of misery, in your last letter. I heartily wish you would take the opposite extreme for your subject, and descant on your own happiness; which I believe to be as perfect, as this frail state will admit of. May it long continue so, sincerely wishes,

Your affectionate,

F. STRAFFON.

## LETTER 33.

### *Lady* WOODVILLE, *To Lady* STRAFFON.

I do indeed, my dear Fanny, sincerely rejoice at the pleasing prospects which seem to open to your new friends; I also congratulate you, on being, in so high a degree, instrumental to their happiness.—I think I may almost say, that Providence seems to interest itself, in the future fate, of the amiable Laura.

There is something very particular, in your becoming accidentally acquainted with lady Somerville, so critically.—Had your meeting with this charming woman, been deferred, but a month longer, the connection between ye, might, in all probability, have been only productive of unavailing good wishes, and mutual esteem;—but the lucky arrival of signior Lodovico, has made you a principal performer, in the great drama of Laura's life.

Though not an absolute predestinarian, I am apt to believe, that there is a sort of fate, in marriage; and, as one absurdity creates another, I find I must lean a little to the Manichean doctrine, to establish my thesis; by supposing that there is a good, and an evil genius, which presides, occasionally, at that great crisis, on which all the colour of our future lives, depends. I sincerely hope that Laura's union with the young Melespini, will be completed under the happiest auspices.—I do not feel one doubt arise in my mind, with regard to his father's consent.—The only cloud which I foresee, to intercept the brightest sunshine, will arise from the separation of lady Somerville, and Laura—but that, like a cloud, also, will pass away:—for though the tenderest affection for a husband, does not oppose the natural claims of parents, or relations, on our hearts, it, in some measure, lessens their force.—Our hopes, and fears, are directed to another object; and self-love strengthens our attachment to that person, on whom we find our happiness depends.

You see I have a passion for philosophizing upon every subject;—where incidents do not abound, it would be impossible to keep up even a monthly correspondence, without these little aids; I will not call them arts, for I detest the mean idea, which is conveyed by that expression.

I shall be glad to have my expectations gratified, by hearing of the count's immediate concurrence with his son's inclinations.—In the mean time, I beg you to present my compliments to lady Somerville, and her fair daughter, and to assure them, that I regret my not having the pleasure of being known to them.—Fanny Weston is quite transported, at the happy meeting of Lodovico and Laura; but says, she can scarce believe it true, be-cause it is likely to end, so fortunately.

I can perceive that lady Harriet has doubts, with regard to the event; but as she finds me sanguine on the subject, she suppresses them.—Sir James Thornton, with a sigh, exclaimed, what an happy man is Lodovico, to find the object of his passion, disengaged! This has left us more in the dark, than ever, with regard to his attachment, for I am pretty sure lady Harriet is not his object.

I cannot help remarking, upon this occasion, how much the particular-ities of our own situation, affect our judgments, with regard to others; and how much more than we are willing to allow, our opinions are warped, and biassed, by it, even in matters that appear indifferent to us.—Adieu, my Fanny!—True love from me, and mine, to you, and yours.

E. WOODVILLE.

# LETTER 34.

## *Lady* STRAFFON, *To Lady* WOODVILLE.

My dear Emily shall, from henceforth, be our augur.—Be her predic-tions fortunate, and be they ever verified!

The wished-for pacquet is, at length, arrived;—it contained a letter for Lodovico, and one for lady Somerville.—The moment he had read his, which was fraught with congratulations from all his friends, and the most plenary indulgence from his fond father, to his ardent wishes, he intreated me to go with him, instantly, to the cottage.—We almost flew there; and Lodovico, in the highest rapture, acquainted lady Somerville and his loved Laura, with the glad tidings.

Lady Somerville received the news, with tears of joy: conflicting passions warred in Laura's face; gladness and grief took turns. The bright suffusion of her cheek, the brilliant animation of her eyes, expressed her heart-felt joy: but when she turned those eyes upon her mother, their radiance was obscured by starting tears; the transient roses fled from her fair cheek, and left the lily mistress of the field.

Lady Somerville was affected by these sudden emotions, and retired to peruse her brother's letter.—She returned soon, and giving it into my hands, said, with a sigh, By this you may judge if I flattered my brother, by calling him the most generous of men. Alas! why must I appear unworthy of his kindness, by declining it? but when he knows my reasons for so doing, I hope he will acquiesce in them, and pardon me.

Upon reading the count's letter, I found, that after testifying his joy, at his son's attachment to Laura, he added, that it was from the mother's hand, he hoped to receive the daughter; and conjured her, by the friendship that had ever subsisted between them, to return to her native country, with her children, to hold the first place in his house, and to contribute, by her presence, to restore that happiness, which had been deeply wounded, by the loss of an amiable wife.

When I had finished the letter, which I read aloud, I feel myself unhappy, said lady Somerville, in not being able to comply with my kind brother's request.—It is long, much longer, than I thought it would be, since I devoted the remnant of my wretched days, to solitude.—Here I have lived, and here will pass that portion of my life, which heaven may yet allot me.

As she spoke, I thought I saw her expressive eyes fixed on her lord's picture, as if addressing her vows to him. But she had scarcely finished, when Laura, springing from her seat, fell at her mother's feet, and catching her hand, cried out, My more than parent! is it possible your love for me, should have so little power? and could you part, so easily, with her, whom I have often heard you call the living transcript of your dear dead lord? But Laura must not, cannot quit her mother! all pleasing prospects vanish, at that thought; which makes the world appear even more a solitude, than ever I found this cottage.

The parent's heart was touched.—No, my beloved child, said she, I will not bar your happiness.—Since you desire it, I will again behold the fatal place which gave me birth, and even strive to lose the sad remembrance of my griefs, in your felicity.—I owe this sacrifice to Laura's filial tenderness.— What would my child have more?

Tears and embraces supplied the place of language, or rather super-seded it, for some time; but when their emotions had subsided, the young pair expressed their joy and gratitude, at lady Somerville's condescension, in the most proper terms; and the evening was spent in such a manner, as could only be pleasing to those, who are blest with feeling hearts.

The count has accompanied his letter with a very noble present, to enable his sister and niece, to appear as the widow, and daughter, of lord Somerville.—There is something above pride, in that thought.

As Lodovico and I returned home, he entreated me to use my interest with lady Somerville, to consent to his being privately married, by her lady-ship's chaplain, before they set out for Genoa.—I think she can have no objection to this request.

I hope I shall be able, in a few days, to send my Emily an account, that this affair is happily concluded.

Till then, adieu.

F. STRAFFON.

## LETTER 35.

### *Lady* STRAFFON, *To Lady* WOODVILLE.

When the subjects are pleasing, I find narrative writing not so dull, as I once thought—I begin to fear I shall make but a poor figure, in the episto-lary way, when I have concluded my little novel; for I honestly confess, that my dear Emily beats me, all to nothing, in the moralizing strain.—Sorry am I, on this account, only, that I must now proceed to the denoüement, of my simple, yet interesting story.

Lady Somerville desired two days to consider of Lodovico's proposal; at the end of that time, she expressed her consent, in a most elegant letter to me.—She said, that as she had, on every occasion, concurred with my requests, she hoped I would not think her too presuming to make one to me; which was, that I would accept of her cottage, with every thing which it contained, except her lord's picture, and that, with my permission, she would fill its vacant place, with Laura's portrait.

I was both pleased, and distressed, at her politeness, and generosity.—I accepted her present.—In that charming *séjour*,[113] I shall spend many hours, in thinking of its amiable owner, and in reflecting on the inscrutable ways of Providence, who after so many trials, has been pleased to restore this valuable woman, to her country, and her friends.

Such characters as hers, were never meant to droop in obscurity; she owes herself to society, and will, I hope, recover some degree of that happiness, she thinks totally lost, in the exercise of those virtues, which in her retired state, she could never be called on to exert.

Slight as the preparations were for a wedding, which it was determined should be private, they took up every moment of our time, till yesterday morning; when Lodovico, Lucy, Sir John, my little Emily, and I, set out together, for the cottage, before breakfast.—We were received by lady Somerville, and the charming bride, with that graceful ease and politeness, which is the result of good sense, and operates equally upon all occasions. After breakfast, Sir John led Laura into the chapel. Lady Somerville presented her hand, to Lodovico; the priest and altar were prepared; Sir John had the honour of personating Laura's father, and had the pleasure of completing Lodovico's wishes, by bestowing her hand, where she had already given her heart. The fervour of lady Somerville's devotion, was truly edifying; when the ceremony was over, she endeavoured, in vain, to suppress her tears; but they were tears of joy.

Sir John presented the bride with a pair of ear-rings, and a cross of diamonds, and I had the pleasure of placing my picture in a bracelet, upon lady Somerville's arm. From the elegance of our dinner and supper, at the cottage, I apprehend that lady Somerville is one of those extraordinary characters, who do not think that the most refined understanding, or the most exalted sentiments, place a woman above the little duties of life.

The new married couple are to dine with me, this day. Sir John is gone to try if he can prevail upon lady Somerville, to accompany them. Next week, they set out, for *Genoa;* they are to occupy our house, in town, while they stay in London. May their voyage thither, and through life, be attended with prosperous gales! Amen, and adieu,

My dear sister,

F. STRAFFON.

## LETTER 36.

## *Lady* WOODVILLE, *To Lady* STRAFFON.

I sincerely congratulate my dear Fanny, on the fortunate denoüement of her pleasing and interesting narrative, and join in her good wishes for the happiness of lady Somerville, and the new married pair.—As you seem inclined to rally me, on my turn for moralizing, I shall not exert it, at present, though I think lady Somerville's story a very proper subject for it.

But to deal ingenuously, I have a stronger reason, for declining to expatiate on it, than what I have mentioned, which is my being stinted in time, as I am going to dine, at lord Withers's, where we shall stay, this night. On Thursday, we are to dine at Sir William Lawson's, and Friday is fixed, for our setting out, for York.

This short letter will, probably, be the last you will receive from me, till my return from thence. If I were mistress of myself, our correspondence should not be interrupted, on that account. If I were superstitious, I would not go to York, as I cannot help feeling a kind of præsentiment, against it. Why did lord Seymour attempt to inspire me with this disgust? I will not reason farther, upon the subject. "*Obedience* is better than SACRIFICE;"[114] but pray is not that, sometimes the greatest we can make?

Affectionate regards, and sincere congratulations, wait on the hosts, and guests, at Straffon-Hill, from all this house, and from

Your's, most truly,

E. WOODVILLE.

END OF THE FIRST VOLUME.

# VOLUME II.

~

## LETTER 37.

### *Lord* WOODVILLE, *To Lord* SEYMOUR.

York.

In justice to those friendly apprehensions, which you seemed to suffer, on my account, I think I ought to inform you, that the so-much-dreaded event, of an interview with the marchioness, is over, without my being sensible of the least ill consequence, from it. All lovely! all engaging, as she is! I had armed *my heart* with the remembrance of her former treatment; and though *the little rebel* did flutter, at her sight, I think its emotions were rather the effect of resentment, than a softer passion.

The worst symptom I discovered in myself (I will be perfectly sincere) was my being picqued, at the composure of her air, and deportment, when she first saluted me. Is it possible, Seymour, she can be really indifferent! or is it only the artifice of her sex, that makes her appear so?

As the room was very full, and she stood at some distance from me, before I could approach her, she was taken out to dance, by lord Bellingham. —When her first minuet was over, she desired I should be called out; and though I felt the utmost reluctance, to accept the compliment, it was impossible to refuse. I am certain I never acquitted myself so ill, in my life. You have seen her dance, and therefore know that the eyes of the whole company, were engaged by her, and my confusion passed unnoticed.

As I led her to her seat, she wished me *joy*, and asked if the fair cause of *it*, was in the room? I answered, yes.—She then intreated I would present her to lady Woodville, whom she longed to see, more than any person in England; as lord Seymour had told her, that she was a perfect beauty.

I made no reply, but led her to the place where lady Woodville sat, who received her with the utmost ease and politeness. I swear to you, my dear Seymour, that Emily never appeared half so lovely, in my eyes, as at that moment. The innocence, and gaiety of her heart, lighted up her charms; and

I flattered myself, that the marchioness's brow seemed overcast, with the pale hue of envy.

Lady Harriet, and she renewed their acquaintance: they all, soon after, joined your sister Sandford, and continued in the same party, for the remainder of the evening. I danced country dances, with one of the miss Broughtons, and returned home triumphing in the just preference, which my heart accorded to lady Woodville, on the comparison I had drawn, in the ball room, between her and the marchioness.

Fear for me, no longer, my too timid friend; but congratulate me on the most arduous of all victories, the having conquered myself.

Your's, ever,

WOODVILLE.

## LETTER 38.

### Lord SEYMOUR, *To Lord* WOODVILLE.

Hot-Wells, Bristol.

Dear WOODVILLE,

I thank you for the attention you have shewn to those apprehensions, which you seem to think groundless. I did not expect to hear from you, during your stay at York. The constant hurry and dissipation of the scene, would have been a sufficient excuse for your silence, both to me, and yourself, if you had not fancied you had good news to communicate.

I know you incapable of the smallest deceit, and am certain that you think your last letter a faithful transcript of your heart. But alas, my friend! you impose upon yourself, if you imagine your passion for the marchioness, extinct; or that it is possible for you, to give a preference, however justly deserved, to any other woman breathing. Therefore, for the truly amiable lady Woodville's sake, I conjure you to avoid all future comparisons, as I think it will be highly injurious to her merits, to put her on a level with that object, which your partiality has made you look upon as the standard of perfection.

After the confession of my own weakness, I condemn myself, for reasoning with you, upon this subject.—I know it is preaching to the winds.—Our passions make our fate; and we ought to suffer, without repining, those calamities we bring upon ourselves: but what philosophy shall enable us to bear the heart-rending agonies, of having involved the innocent, in our punishment, and rendered the amiable, and deserving, unhappy! Who can speak peace to my sad heart, when I reflect upon the miseries, in which I have plunged the ever-dear Charlotte Beaumont.

O, Woodville, fly, betimes, from horrors such as these! Imagine you now see your gentle Emily, whose peaceful bosom has never harboured an unruly guest, stung with the rage of jealousy;—see those sweet eyes inflamed by passion, their natural brightness quenched by flowing tears, her mind disordered, and her frame unnerved!—could you behold her in that state, and live!

I know this horrid image will shock your nature, and, for a time, you will shudder at yourself. But quickly say, these are the gloomy visions of Seymour's disturbed brain. I would not make my Emily, unhappy, for the world—then fly, directly, to the marchioness, to banish the sad thought.—But I have done, for ever, on the theme; for if this picture does not speak to your heart, I cannot paint more strongly.

My wishes, for your happiness, but without hope, except in flight, shall still attend upon you; and my highest esteem shall ever wait upon the lovely lady Woodville.

SEYMOUR.

# LETTER 39.

## *Lord* WOODVILLE, *To Lord* SEYMOUR.

My dear SEYMOUR,

I confess your last letter shocked me, extremely, but not from the motives you may possibly imagine. I am truly grieved to find your mind so overclouded, or ingrained, with the dark tints of melancholy, as not to allow your reason fair play. Answer me, truly, were you not just then returned from the methodist's chapel,[1] when you sat down to write? When I expected congratulations, songs of triumph, and the laurel wreath, how could you cruelly pop an old-fashioned prophecy upon me, of what never was, nor is, nor ever shall be!

But away with thy dismal presages, thou Pseudo-Magus![2] Have I not told thee, infidel as thou art, that no action of my life, should ever discover the real state of my heart, to lady Woodville, or make her think it was not all her own? Have I not been married, above eight months, and am I not, now, just as tender, and obliging, as the first day we were united?

Hadst thou real pity, or compassion, thou wouldst advise me to desist from my pursuit of the marchioness, on her account, rather than lady Woodville's. O Seymour! what a triumph would it be, if I could humble this proud beauty, and pay her scorn for scorn! again reduce her to that soft timidity, blushing confusion, and sweet trembling voice, with which she first uttered those dear sounds, *I love!*

Recal her image to your view, on the first night we met her, at the Bois de Boulogne.—What perfect beauty, amazing grace, and native modesty, beamed round her angel form!—There is a picture for you: and, I hope, much more to the life, than your Tisiphone.[3]

I have often thought of asking you, by what talisman, or spell, your heart was preserved, from becoming her instant victim? You did not know your Charlotte, then. Perhaps you felt the marchioness's power, and loved like me; but, in pity to your friend, endeavoured to suppress your passion. I should adore you, if I thought it were so.

I do not think her half so beautiful, as she was then, though her person is much improved.—She can be gazed at, now, without a blush; and wears rouge, I suppose, in order to heighten the finest complexion in the world.

We met, this day, on the race-ground. She has engaged me to hold a Pharo-bank[4] for her, at night; and begged me to prevail on lady Woodville, to be of the party.—She seems vastly charmed with her; but whenever she mentions her, assumes a peculiar air of sensibility.—I think I heard her sigh, when she pronounced the name.

What an odd mortal am I, to sit down to write, when I have scarce time to breathe. Sir James Thornton's mare was distanced: he has lost above five hundred pounds; but what is much worse, I think he has lost himself.— I never saw such an alteration, in any creature: I am almost sorry I brought him to Woodfort.

The ladies fancy he is in love, but I cannot get the secret out of the simpleton. Lady Woodville, and her nymphs, are much yours. I intreat you will drink half a dozen bumpers of Burgundy, before you sit down to write again, to

      Your's sincerely,

WOODVILLE.

## LETTER 40.

### *Lord* WOODVILLE, *To Lord* SEYMOUR.

Ah Seymour! what a tale have I to unfold to you! I am undone, for ever lost to virtue, relapsed again, to all my former follies—I doat, I die for love! Do not despise me, Seymour, but once again stretch forth thy friendly hand, and strive to save a sinking wretch. Alas, it is in vain! fate overwhelms me, and I must yield to the impetuous torrent. But hear my story, first, before you pronounce stern sentence on me, and guilty as I am, perhaps you will pity me.

For some days past, the marchioness contrived to throw herself perpetually in my way, and strove to engage me in the most interesting conversations, by hinting at particular scenes, in which we had formerly been actors. Fool that I was, the recollection charmed me, and my weak heart expanded with delight, at the repetition of its former follies.

Last night, your sister, lady Sandford not being well, declined going to the ball. The marchioness sent to lady Woodville, to desire she might attend her, to the rooms. Emily politely assented, and they went together—she returned and supped with us.

After supper, she said she hated being cooped up in a carriage, at the course, and asked if I could lend her a horse, for the next day. The ladies informed her that no woman of fashion, ever appeared on horseback, at a race. She replied, she had no idea of a *salique* law,[5] imposed by jockies; that she despised all vulgar prejudices, and would be the first to break through this arbitrary rule, if she could engage any lady to accompany her.

She soon prevailed on miss Weston, who rides remarkably well, to be of her party, and again applied to me for a horse. I told her I had not one, that had been used to carry a lady, but if she would venture on that which I usually rode, it should be at her service.

She accepted my offer, and after dinner, the next day, Fanny Weston, Ransford, and I, attended her at lady Sandford's; and sure there never was so lovely a figure as she made, on horseback!

> Diana, huntress, mistress of the groves!
> The charming Isabel, speaks, looks, and moves.[6]

When we came to the race-ground, all the company thronged round her, and though the horses were then running, she seemed to be the sole object, of every one's attention. She affected to be displeased, at the general gaze, and said if there was room in lady Woodville's carriage, she would get into it. We rode up immediately to it, but on perceiving that Emily was in the chariot, and lady Harriet with her, she would not suffer me to mention her design, lest it might be inconvenient to my wife, whose present condition is now very apparent.

Thornton was by the side of the chariot, talking to the ladies who were in it. He immediately retired, to make way for us to come close. A croud had followed us, and some one of their horses struck that on which the marchioness rode;—it immediately made an effort to disengage itself from the throng, and in spite of all she could do, ran away with her, with such an amazing swiftness, that it seemed to outgo all the racers.

I followed, instantly—O Seymour! judge of my emotions, when I saw her fall to the ground! when I came up to her, she was senseless, her eyes closed, and her face covered with blood and dust. I raised her in my arms, and held her to my breast; but unable long to sustain her weight, in that posture, I sunk down gently, held her on my knees, and gazed in stupid silence.

At that instant, numbers came up to us; among the rest, Thornton, and lady Woodville, who on perceiving blood upon my cheek, fainted.—She might have fallen to the earth, for me;—I was insensible to all the world! Thornton luckily caught her in his arms, and conveyed her to her chariot.

Notwithstanding all the applications, that were used, the marchioness seemed irrecoverable, and my despair is not to be expressed. A gentleman that was present, opened a vein in her arm. She then lifted up her languid eyes, and looking round her, closed them quick again, and whispered, as she lay upon my bosom, "I die, my lord; but ought not to repine, since I expire within your arms."

A crimson blush succeeded to her paleness, and a vast shower of tears soon followed. I know not what reply I made, but I have reason to suppose it must have been expressive of the complicated passions which affected me. I carried her in my arms, to lady Winterton's coach, and conveyed her, in that manner, to your sister's.

We had all the assistance this place could afford. My spirits are so extremely harrassed, that I cannot write more, than just to give you the satisfaction to know, that she is not in danger—would *I* could say as much.

Adieu, till next post.

WOODVILLE.

## LETTER 41.

### *Lord* WOODVILLE, *To Lord* SEYMOUR.

As soon as the fair invalid was laid on the bed, and the medical tribe who were summoned from all quarters, had performed their usual evolutions, of pulse-feeling, profound looks, and long perscriptions, I knelt by her bed-side, and tenderly inquired her health? She told me, that though much hurt, she did believe, the only incurable wound she had received, was given by herself, in the weak confession she had made, when she thought her situation had placed her beyond the necessity of longer disguising the tender sentiments, she felt for me. She would give worlds, to recal what she had said; but, as she knew that was impossible, begged I would not despise her, or meanly think her capable of a design, to rival lady Woodville; and that the moment she was sufficiently recovered, she should fly me, and England, for ever.

Think of my situation, Seymour! and forgive my weakness; while I tell you I poured forth all the fondness long concealed, even from myself, within my labouring bosom, and swore, with too much truth, I never had, one moment, ceased to love her. She sighed, and wept; I kissed her lily hand, and bathed it with my tears.

How much longer we should have continued in this situation, I know not, had I not been roused, by a message from lady Woodville, to inquire the marchioness's health, and an excuse for not making the inquiry in person, on account of her own indisposition. I started, Seymour—and recollected, that I had a wife.

I flew home, instantly; found Emily had been blooded, and put to bed.—I rejoiced at being able to avoid the sight of that amiable woman; said I would not disturb her, by going into her chamber, and ordered another bed to be got ready for me, against night.

Conscious guilt will make a coward, of the bravest man.—I could not bear my own thoughts.—I dreaded being alone. I went to the coffee-house, to drown reflection, in noise and nonsense. The conversation turned, intirely, on the accident that had befallen the marchioness, and I replied with the utmost complacency, to every trifling question that was asked, because it related to her.

I soon grew weary of this scene. I walked out, and found my steps insensibly straying towards the marchioness.—By chance I met Thornton, who with more liveliness in his looks, than I have seen, for a long time, told me lady Woodville was much better, and would be glad to see me; that she had expressed some uneasiness, at their not suffering me to go into her chamber, when I called at home, though she was then asleep.

I went directly back with him, and saw my Emily; she looked pale, and dispirited, questioned me with great tenderness, about the marchioness, and said the fright she had suffered, on her account, joined to her apprehension of my having received some hurt, had quite overpowered her; but she would endeavour to become a stouter soldier. Sweet gentleness! how thy soft looks, upbraid me!

I determined not to go to the marchioness, that night, but sent to know how she did, and sat down to write my last letter to you. In that, and this, are contained only the transactions of one fatal day.—Where my narrative will end, I know not! but the only relief, that is, at present, left me, is the pouring out my heart, to you.—I again implore you, to pity its weakness, and pardon its follies.

> Your's ever,
>
> Woodville.

## Letter 42.

### *Lord* Woodville, *To Lord* Seymour.

Too cruel Seymour! how am I to interpret such an obstinate silence? Am I so far sunk in your esteem, that you disdain even to hold converse, or correspondence with me? Now was the time, to have exerted all your friendship, and stopped me on the very verge of ruin.—But you disclaim the painful office of counselling an incorrigible, self-willed man; and I now triumph, in your cold neglect. Left to myself, in such a critical juncture, I have a higher pride, in being able, from my own conduct, to claim your friendship, and esteem, than I could have felt, had I acted conformably to your prudent advice, and declined the meeting of my most dangerous foe.

The morning after the date of my last, I was surprized to find lady Woodville in the dining-room, dressed, and waiting breakfast for me, when I came down stairs, between seven and eight o'clock.—I thought she looked paler, and more delicate, than I had ever seen her, with an air of resignation impressed upon her countenance, which, added to its natural sweetness, had rendered her one of the most interesting objects, I had ever beheld. The tenderness with which I inquired her health, seemed to animate her languid frame, and her eyes quickly recovered their native lustre.

After breakfast, she proposed accompanying me to see the marchioness. I was embarrassed, beyond measure; but knew not how to prevent her doing, what appeared to be so proper. Just then, Thornton, luckily, came into the room, which afforded me a moment to recollect myself. I told her I thought it would be better to send, first, to inquire how the marchioness had rested, and whether she was yet able to receive our visits? Emily seemed to blush at her want of consideration, and readily assented to my proposal.

Williams was dispatched with a card, and soon returned with a verbal answer, that the marchioness was much better, and should be glad to see us. I hoped she would have had address enough, to have saved me from the embarrassment, which such an interview must give me. But there was, now, no retreating; and Emily and I got into the chariot, together.

When we were shewn into the marchioness's apartment, she was lying on a couch, in the most elegant deshabille.—What a subject for an Apelles,[7] Seymour! It was with difficulty I could restrain myself from expressing the transports that I felt. She rose to receive lady Woodville, with such an air of graceful dignity, as queens might gladly learn. I saw that Emily blushed, and looked confused, at her amazing superiority, but was relieved by the entrance of your sister, lady Sandford.

The marchioness's behaviour towards me, was remarkably cold, and distant; and I thought she overacted her part so much, that any other woman in the world, but Emily, must have perceived something extraordinary, in the change of her manner; but, happily, lady Woodville is a stranger to suspicion.

You may suppose our visit was not a very long one, yet it appeared to me insufferably tedious; and I thought myself more obliged to Emily, when she rose to go away, than ever I had been to any one, in my life. I had the happiness to hear that the marchioness had received no hurt, from her fall, that could be of any ill consequence: the blood that appeared, was from a slight contusion in her nose.

Ransford came to wait on her, while we were there; and as he handed my wife to her carriage, and I was quitting the room, the marchioness, with the utmost *fierté,* though in a low voice, said, Lord Woodville, return instantly, or never!

The manner, with which she pronounced these words, astonished and confounded me. I then saw that her behaviour towards me, was the effect of resentment, not art;—yet how had I offended, how forfeited that tenderness, which she expressed for me, the day before? Inexplicable creature! mysterious woman! of all riddles, the hardest to be expounded by the boasted wisdom, of thy vassal, man!

I bowed, and withdrew, in the utmost amazement, at her conduct; and, by vainly endeavouring to account for it, I fell into such a profound reverie, that I did not even perceive the motion of the carriage, till it stopped at our lodgings.

I then felt myself ashamed, at not having taken the least notice of Emily, during our little journey; and, by way of saying something, told her I had been considering whether we might not set out for *London,* the next day, if it was agreeable to her. She smiling said, my will was hers; and though quite unprepared for such an expedition, as she did not know I purposed going so soon, she would be ready, at what hour I pleased.

I knew not what I said, when I talked of London, and had not the least intention of carrying her there; but my blunder was lucky, as it gave me an opportunity of paying a well-deserved compliment, to her complacency, and condescension, and also of paving the way to my going, without her, if the sovereign arbitress of my fate, should command me to attend her. I likewise appeared to have the merit of sacrificing my own inclination to hers, by readily consenting to her returning to Woodfort.

Upon these terms we parted, and I set out, with a slow pace, and a disturbed mind, to measure back the ground, I had just passed. During my walk, I reflected upon the disagreeable necessity, I had laid myself under, of acting the hypocrite, with a woman, whose amiable qualities compelled me to esteem her, and whose personal charms fully intitled her to the fondest affection, of an unengaged heart. Deceit cannot dwell long with honour; and I determined either to sacrifice my passion to my virtue, or, at once, to triumph over character, honour, and every other consideration in life, and act the villain, boldly.

Almost distracted with the struggles of my mind, I entered the marchioness's apartment. I found her lying on a couch, with a handkerchief close to her eyes, which she removed, upon my entrance, and shewed her lovely face, all bathed in tears. I advanced, with precipitation, and would have kissed her hand, but she withdrew it from me, with such an air of coldness, and disdain, as almost petrified me: then rising, briskly, said, is your wife with you?

I gravely answered, No. She then burst into a violent passion of tears, and exclaimed, Ah, Woodville! after what had passed between us, but a few short hours ago, how could you use me thus? How did you dare to insult me, with the presence of that object, whose *legal* claim to your affection, renders mine criminal?

I was so much alarmed, and confounded, at the vehemence of her voice, and manner, that I knew not what answer to make, but told her, it was lady Woodville who had proposed our coming together, and that I knew not how to avoid attending her, without running the hazard of giving her offence.

What, then, you fear, as well as love her, and you avow it, to my face!—I would not, willingly, madam, inflict unnecessary wounds, upon the victim I have sacrificed to you, nor add brutality, to perfidy.—Her colour rose to crimson.

So then, my lord, you vainly hope to keep a flame alive, in two such hearts, as mine, and lady Woodville's! to love *en Turk,*[8] and play our passions off, against each other, for your sport!—Amazing vanity! But know, it will not do, my lord; her soft, insipid nature might, perhaps, submit to be the loved sultana of the day, then yield her place to me, or any other, and meanly take it back again, from your caprice; but I will reign alone, or else despise that transitory toy, the empire of your heart.

You may remember, madam, there was a time, when more than you now ask, or I can give, my hand and heart, were offered at your feet: you then disdained to accept them; they are no longer free. For doating on you, as I do, with all the fervor of distracted passion, I cannot be insensible to the merits of unoffending innocence, and love; nor cease, one hour, to feel the anguish of remorse, for having injured lady Woodville.

If the frankness of this confession, madam, should exclude me, for ever, from your love, I have the consolation to know, that it must insure me your esteem.—Without some claim to the latter, I should be unworthy of the former. But if, under these unhappy circumstances, you still can condescend to feel that passion, which you have profest, let me, upon my knees, conjure you to tell me, how I may preserve my honour, without forfeiting, what is as dear to me, your love.

I had knelt at her feet, during the latter part of this discourse.—Her eyes had streamed.—I do not blush to own, that mine were not quite dry. She remained silent, for some minutes, and when I pressed her to speak, she replied, with a determined voice and manner: There is no alternative, my lord; you must fly with me, or never see me more.

I had dreaded such a proposal, yet could scarce believe she would make it, and, with the utmost agitation, cried out, Impossible! But before I could utter another syllable, she laid her hand upon my lips, and said, I command you silence.—You must not, shall not, answer me. I know you are to quit this place, immediately: would I had never seen it. But as you are, now, to determine the fate of one, whose love for you, has made her leap the bounds, prescribed to her weak sex, O do not reply, rashly! but, take the last moment that can be allowed, before you pronounce the doom of a fond wretch, who has placed more than her life—her happiness, or misery—in your power.

I rose, and bowed, totally unable to speak, or even to think, from the confusion of my ideas.—She took advantage of my silence, to tell me she would not receive any letter upon this subject, from me, but that she expected to see me, at twelve o'clock, next day; and smiling added, lest you should forget, I will present you with a little monitor, which will remind you of your absent friend.

She then gave me her picture, which I had, a thousand times, in our first acquaintance, solicited, in vain. I kissed it, with transport. See here, said she, and drew a miniature of me, which I had formerly given her, out of her pocket; and now take care that you preserve my image, as carefully as I have done yours.

Then looking at her watch, you must leave me; it is near lady Sandford's dining hour, and I must dress. How slowly will the miserable moments creep, till we two meet again! But I shall defy time, after that, as it can neither add to, or diminish from, the felicity, or anguish, which must then, irrevocably, be my portion.

I intreated her to spare me, on that subject, as she would not permit me to reply. You must withdraw, then, immediately, my lord, for I can neither think, or speak, on any other theme. She permitted me to kiss her hand, before I left her; and seemed to have conquered all those violent passions, which possessed her at my approach. I confess I quitted her, with infinite reluctance, and so I now must you.

WOODVILLE.

## LETTER 43.

### *Lord* WOODVILLE, *To Lord* SEYMOUR.

I parted from the marchioness, in a more irresolute, and confused state of mind, than I had ever before experienced. I well knew that all the colour of my future fate, depended on the resolution, I was compelled to make, within a few short hours. I found it absolutely impossible, to determine on any thing, from a consciousness of the importance, of my final determination.

Never, sure, had reason and passion a severer strife. One moment, I resolved to sacrifice every thing, to love; to fly with my adored Isabella, into some distant country, "and live in shades with her, and love alone."[9] The next instant, the image of the gentle Emily, obtruded itself upon my imagination, in her present situation; pale, and dying. Methought I heard her last soft sigh express my name; I felt myself a murderer, and started at my shadow.

In this distracted state, I had wandered, a considerable way, into the fields, and saw night coming on apace, without power, or inclination, to think of returning to York, when I heard the sound of a horse, galloping towards me.—The man who rode him, called to me, to desire I would direct him the nearest way to the town, and also, if I could, inform him, where lord Woodville lived.

The sound of my own name, surprized me, and I inquired his business.—The fellow quickly knew me; he instantly alighted, and told me he was a servant of Sir Harry Ransford's, and had been sent, express, to let his young master know, that lady Ransford had eloped, two days before, with captain Barnard; and that it was supposed they were gone, either to France, or Ireland. He added, that the poor old knight was almost distracted, for the loss of his lady, and wanted his son to pursue the ravisher.

The servant pressed me to mount his horse, and expressed his simple astonishment at my being by myself, in such a lonesome place, at that hour. I refused his offer, and we walked on, together. It was near eight o'clock, when I got home; and as it was the last night of the races, I did suppose Emily was gone to the ball—but I found her alone.

I thought she looked as if she had been in tears, though her eyes sparkled, when she saw me. This little circumstance had its full weight; and the unaffected joy she shewed, at my return, without seeming to be alarmed, at my absence, when contrasted with the violence of temper, which the marchioness had discovered, in the morning, so far turned the scale, as to determine me to remain a slave to the obligations I owe to my wife, and the world: and though I am persuaded, that I never shall be able to extract the arrow from my wounded heart, I will suffer it to rankle, there, in silence, and endeavour to derive fortitude, sufficient to bear the anguish, from the noble consideration of having sacrificed my pleasure—I must not stile it happiness—to my duty.—What would my friend have more?

My mind grew much calmer, after these reflections.—In order to prevent my relapsing, I locked up the marchioness's picture, in my writing box, and threw the key into the fire, that it might not be in my power to gaze away my reason, for that night, at least.

Emily was much surprised, at the account of lady Ransford, and captain Barnard—her own innocence keeps her a child.—She begged I would not mention the story, before lady Harriet.—I knew there had been an attachment between the captain and her, but thought it long since over—yet why should I imagine that time could conquer love? O! never, never, Seymour!

Lady Woodville and I supped, *tête-à-tête;* the young folks, as she calls them, though they are all elder than herself, staid late, at the ball.—I was impatient for Ransford's return, and had sent to the assembly room, to look for him, but he was not there.—I ordered every thing to be in readiness, for his setting out, immediately, on his filial errand.

When the ladies and Thornton came in, I retired to my chamber, to wait for Ransford. By frequently revolving my unhappy situation, in my mind, I began to consider it, in a new light; which at once increased my misery, and confirmed me in the justness of the resolution, I had before taken, of bearing it, in silence. Upon strict examination, I found I was the only culpable person, of the three; and, therefore, ought to be the only sufferer.—

Wretch, that I was, I had deceived myself; and in consequence of that error, had imposed upon another! How vain to imagine that the marchioness's cruel treatment of my love, her preferring age, and infirmity, to me, on account of superior rank and riches, had supplied me with arms sufficient to vindicate my freedom, and break her tyrannic chains. O Seymour! they are twined about my heart, and nought, I fear, but death, can loose them.

It was near three o'clock, when Ransford came in; he seemed in very high spirits—when I told him of lady Ransford's ill conduct, he said he was not in the least surprised; he had long known that his step-dame only waited for a galant, who had spirit enough to engage in such a frolic with her; and he thought his father had a fair riddance.

I was surprized to hear him treat the affair, so lightly, as I know him to be a man of nice honour. I then asked him, whether he intended going immediately to his father? he answered, no; said he was engaged in a pursuit of the utmost consequence, which he could not quit, and that he did not believe he should see Ransford Hall, for some time.

I told him I thought his father would have reason to resent his neglect, and pressed him to wait upon him, though but for one day. He persisted in his resolution, and we parted. I think it odd, that Ransford did not communicate his motives for acting in this manner, to me;—but what have I to do with other people's affairs? my poor tortured mind is sufficiently encumbered, with its own.

I think I need not tell you that I passed a sleepless night. —At breakfast, I told Emily that I should be ready to set out with her, for Woodfort, after dinner, if she pleased. She seemed delighted, and the carriages were ordered, at half an hour after four.—I intreated Sir James Thornton to return with us, for a few days; he made a thousand excuses; but, at length, complied, at lady Woodville's request.

I was now to enter upon the most arduous task, of my whole life; that of taking an everlasting leave, of the woman, whom I doated on—and in this highest act of self-denial, I must appear, to her, a volunteer! I am grieved, that Brutus should have said, "virtue was but a name."[10] O let me bend before her awful shrine, and pay my grateful vows, for the kind aid she lent me, in that hour of trial!

I endeavoured to assume an air of calmness, on my entering the marchioness's apartment. She fixed her eyes, her piercing eyes, in stedfast gaze upon me, as if to read my soul. A minute passed, in silence. I found she would not speak, and hardly seemed to breathe. You see before you, madam, an unhappy man, who dares not purchase transport, with remorse; and, therefore, turns self-banished from her sight, whom most his soul adores!

She quick exclaimed, is it possible! and am I then despised, neglected—for a wife! Cold, and unloving Woodville! Why did you ever feign a passion for me? Why strive to make me think it still subsisted, in your frozen heart? You cannot bear remorse! Ungrateful man! should not I have shared it with you? Is then my fame less dear, than yours? and did I hesitate, one moment, to sacrifice that, and myself both, to you? Obscurity and infamy were not bars to me, whilst you, infirm of mind, desert the woman you pretend to love, for fear your wife should cry.

True, madam, I replied, I would not give her cause to weep, for worlds—nay, what is more, for you! You have acknowledged, too, that the step your kindness prompted you to take, must be attended with severe regret also, on your own part.—What should I feel, then, from rendering you unhappy! I have not fortitude to brave such two-fold agony.

O! you have half that guilt to answer for, already.—But my pride revolts, at my own meanness. Leave me, Sir—leave me, for *ever,* Woodville! I shall obey you, madam, but before we part, *for ever,* suffer me, at least, to satisfy your pride, by declaring that no man ever loved, with fonder passion, than I now feel for you—how far time and absence may be able to conquer it, I know not; but should they fail of their usual effects, it is impossible that I should bear it long; and now, my Isabelle, one last embrace—may angels guard you!

I rushed out of the house, like a distracted man, but had not walked a quarter of a mile, before the rectitude of my conduct, towards this too lovely woman, began, by flattering my pride, to qualify my passion; and I returned home, in a more rational state of mind, than I have known, for some time.

Rejoice with me, my friend; the conflict's past! and be just enough to acknowledge my triumph more compleat, than the much boasted one of Scipio.[11] He only resigned an *alienated heart*—while I forego *a self-devoted victim!*

I am, this moment, going to step into the coach, for Woodfort, where I shall impatiently long to see you. But, O write soon, to strengthen, and applaud, my growing virtue.

Your's,

WOODVILLE.

# LETTER 44.

## *Lord* SEYMOUR, *To Lord* WOODVILLE.

Hot Wells.

Believe me, Woodville, there is not another event within the power of fortune, which could now give me half the joy that I received from your last letter. I do congratulate my noble friend, myself, and all the world, on that heroic virtue, which has enabled you to pass the *ordeal fire,* unsullied and unhurt. Rather let me say, that like the *Amianthus,*[12] you have gained new whiteness, from the flames, and shine with brighter lustre, than even un-blemished innocence can boast.

I find my stile, perhaps, too much elevated, by my sentiments, but sudden transitions must have strong effects. I had scarce a hope of your es-caping the snare that was laid for you, and mourned your fall from honour, with infinitely more regret, than I should have done your death. Had the latter happened, my grief would have been selfish; but in the other case, I felt for those pangs which you must have inevitably suffered; and for the mis-eries, which your crimes must have inflicted, upon your amiable, and innocent wife.

But I do not wish again to recal this gloomy prospect to your view, you may, now, and ought, to look forward, to a long train of happiness; for surely, if such a thing is to be found on earth, it must arise from a conscious-ness, of having acted rightly. Who then can be better intitled to it, than yourself?

As I have found some little benefit from these waters, I purpose staying here, some time longer—I shall then have some affairs of consequence to my fortune, which I have too long neglected, to settle in London. So that I cannot hope to see you, at Woodfort, in less than two months.

I intreat to hear from you, often, but must insist upon your not men-tioning the subject of our late correspondence; forget it, Woodville, and be happy!

Your's, ever,

SEYMOUR.

*Note,* The journal, promised by lady Woodville, to lady Straffon, is pur-posely omitted, as it contains nothing more, than an account of some of those particulars, that have been already mentioned, which happened during the week they staid at York races.

The Editor.

# LETTER 45.

## *Lady* STRAFFON, *To Lady* WOODVILLE.

I flatter myself that this letter will reach Woodfort, soon after your arrival there, and that it will find my dear Emily rejoicing in the calm delights of domestic happiness, after the scene of hurry and dissipation, she has so lately gone through.

I give you great credit for the lovely picture you have drawn of the marchioness, and also for the tender concern you express, for the accident that befel her—but I am sorry your nerves were so weak, as to occasion your fainting.

I allow much for your present situation, but do not let that, or any thing else, my dear sister, suffer you to indulge, in an habitual lowness of spirits. There is an air of languid discontent, runs through the latter part of the little journal, you were so good to send me, that alarms me much—yet I am certain you endeavoured to conceal your sentiments, even from me; and I approve your caution, as I am persuaded, that by speaking, or writing, on any subject that affects us, we strengthen our own feelings of it; and half the simple girls who are now pining for love, by murmuring rivulets, or in shady groves, would forget the dear objects of their passion, if they had not a female confidante, as silly as themselves, to whom they daily recount the fancied charms of their Adonis,[13] and utter vows of everlasting constancy.

But do not, now, my dear Emily, so perversely misunderstand me, as to suppose that I would wish you to conceal any thing that distresses you, from me, or that I should desire you to let sorrow prey, in silence, on *your heart,* merely to save *mine* the pain of suffering with you. No, I conjure you to speak freely to me, and if I cannot cure, I will at least soothe, your anxiety, if real, and endeavour to laugh you out of it, if imaginary.

We have had a very agreeable visitor, for these ten days past, at Straffon Hill—lord Mount Willis.—He has lived abroad, chiefly in Italy, these ten years; yet is not infected with foreign fopperies, and can relish both the food, and manners, of his native country. Sir John met him last, at Paris, from whence he is but just returned.

He tells us, that Sir James Miller, and his *cara sposa,*[14] are universally ridiculous. Her ladyship affects all the lively galantry, *d'une dame Française,*[15] but is, unfortunately, encumbered, with all the clumsy aukwardness, of a vulgar English-woman. Sir James plays deep,[16] and has lost considerably.

Lucy seems hurt, at the latter part of this account. The goodness of her heart is inexhaustible.

The approach of a certain desirable event,[17] with that of winter, will, I hope, soon afford me the pleasure of embracing my dear Emily, and her lord. We shall return to London, in ten or twelve days. Have you made any discovery, in the *terra incognita*[18] of Sir James Thornton's heart? Does Fanny Weston still sigh in concert with the Æolian lyre? or have the equinoctial blasts so chilled her flame, that she prefers a warm room, and chearful company, to lonely meditation, and soft sounds?

How does lady Harriet bear this second instance, of captain Barnard's perfidy? and how does the poor old gouty knight support the vulgarly called *loss,* of his detestable wife? I find myself in a very impertinent mood; and that I may not ask more questions, in one letter, than you may be inclined to answer, in two, I shall, for the present, bid you adieu.

F. STRAFFON.

## LETTER 46.

### *Lady* WOODVILLE, *To Lady* STRAFFON.

Yes, my dear Fanny, I am now, thank heaven, safely arrived at Woodfort—would I had never left it! I think even the place, and every thing in it, is altered, during a short absence, of twelve days. The trees have lost their verdure, and the birds cease to sing. But though the autumnal season, may have produced these effects, I begin to fear there is a greater change in me, than in any of the objects that surround me.

Yet am I in the spring of life, not ripened even to summer; while like a blasted flower, I shrink, and fade. Say, Fanny, why is this? The animal, and vegetable world bloom in their proper season, youth—while amongst those whom we call rational, grief steals the roses, from the downy cheek, and flowing tears oft dim the brilliant eye. Lord Seymour is unhappy; Thornton sighs; and my loved lord, seems wretched;—need I go on, and close the climax, with my breaking heart!

Chide me, or chide me not, the secret's out; I am undone, my sister! in vain lord Woodville strives, beneath the masque of tenderness, to act a part, which he no longer feels; the piercing eyes of love, detect his coldness—his kind attention is all lost on me, his stifled sighs, belie his face and tongue, and whisper what he suffers, when he smiles.

O, Fanny! tell me how have I offended him! how lost that heart, which formed my utmost bliss! let me blot out that passage, with my tears; it cannot, must not be.—I will not live, if I have lost his love. Why are not you now here, to flatter me—to tell me that my fears are groundless, and that he sighs, from habit, or from chance?

Ah, no! since he whom I adore, has failed to blind me, I cannot, if I would, be now deceived. Yet, if I have erred, why does he not speak out, and tell me I have done wrong? Believe me, Fanny, I have tried my heart, examined every hidden thought that's there, and cannot find out one, that should offend him.

Are all men thus inconstant? I was too young to mark Sir John's behaviour, when you were married, first. A sudden ray of hope, now dawns upon me; perhaps the great exertion of my lord's spirits, while we remained at York, may have occasioned a proportionate degree of languor—perhaps he may again recover his natural chearfulness, and your poor Emily may again be happy—perhaps—I will strive to hope the best.

I have no thoughts of going to London—I always purposed lying in, at Woodfort—I had flattered myself, you would be with me, at that hour of trial; but I do not now expect it—I know Sir John would not consent to your running the hazard of travelling, in your present situation, as it has formerly been of ill consequence, to you, I therefore release my dear Fanny, and desire she may not suffer the least anxiety, on my account.

I find myself much more at ease, than when I began this letter, and I must affirm, though in contradiction to your opinion, that pouring forth our distresses, in the bosom of a friend, affords, at least, a temporary relief, to the afflicted. I am not able to write more, at present, but will answer all your queries, by next post—

Till then, adieu.

E. WOODVILLE.

## LETTER 47.

### *Lady* WOODVILLE, *To Lady* STRAFFON.

My dear FANNY,

There never sure was such a man, as lord Woodville—he is not only determined to preserve my affection, but to rob me of the poor consolation, of complaining that I no longer possess his. In spite of all the pains I have taken, to conceal the anguish of my heart, he has certainly perceived it, and by the most tender and interesting conversation, had well nigh led me into a confession, of my being unhappy.

Thank heaven, I stopped just short of that—had I avowed it, he doubtless would have asked the cause, and artfully have drawn me in, at least tacitly, to reproach his conduct. O never! never, Fanny, can I be capable of that indiscretion.

But were I weak, or mean enough, to do it, I have now no reason for complaint—his tenderness, politeness, and attention, are unabated. No other person, but myself, could possibly perceive the smallest alteration in his conduct; and I begin to hope, that my apprehensions have had no other foundation, than an extremity of delicacy, bordering upon weakness, in myself. A thousand, nay ten thousand women, might, and would be happy, with such an amiable, and tender husband, nor has your Emily a wish ungratified, but that of seeing her dear lord quite happy.

I am sorry to tell you that Sir James Thornton leaves us, to morrow; he is to set out, immediately, on the grand tour. My lord has in vain endeavoured to find out the source of his melancholy; we can discover nothing, but that he is unhappy, which I am sincerely sorry for, as he really is the most agreeable unaccomplished young man, I ever was acquainted with.

Lady Harriet affects to appear thankful, for her escape from captain Barnard; but finds his elopement a cause for sorrow, on his lady's account. Sir Harry is so much enraged, at his son's neglect of him, that he begins to be reconciled to his wife's conduct, and speaks of him, with more acrimony, than of her. Indeed, I think Mr. Ransford highly to blame, for refusing to attend his father, upon such an occasion.

Fanny Weston is *à la mort*,[19] at Sir James Thornton's quitting us. That love is the cause of her mourning, I well know, but I begin now to apprehend that Sir James, and not lord Seymour, is the object of her passion. She has a much better chance, in this case, than the other, for I am persuaded if

Thornton knew of her affection for him, he would endeavour to make her happy.

Alas! if he loves another, how impossible! I fancy he is enamoured, of one of the miss Withers's.—His fortune and family are such, that I do not believe he would be rejected; yet I could not wish him success, for poor Fanny Weston's sake.

Men more easily triumph over an unhappy passion, than women. Dissipation, change of place, and objects, all contribute to their cure; while perhaps the poor sighing fair one is absolutely confined to the same spot, where she first beheld her charmer, and where every object reminds her, that here he sat, walked, or talked.

I am persuaded there is a great deal more in these local memento's, than lovers are willing to allow. I therefore shall not oppose Fanny Weston's going to London, if she should again propose it.

Sir William and lady Lawson are to dine with us, this day.—I will try to muster all my spirits, to receive her. I would not, for the world, make her unhappy, by giving her the least room to suspect, that I am so.

Adieu, my dearest Fanny; to you, and you only, I can, without blushing, discover all the weakness of a heart, that truly, and sincerely loves you.

E. WOODVILLE.

P.S. I have, this moment, received a message from my lord, to let me know that he shall spend three or four days, in hunting, with Sir William Atkinson. I am glad of any thing that can amuse him.

## LETTER 48.

### *Lady* STRAFFON, *To Lady* WOODVILLE.

I cannot express how much my dear Emily's last letters have affected and distressed me.—Your being unhappy is certainly sufficient to render me so; and what adds to my concern, is, my being absolutely incapable of affording you the least consolation, as I am utterly ignorant of the real cause of your affliction. I sometimes think, that it is only a phantom, conjured up by your too delicate apprehensions; and is, of course, merely imaginary.—At other times, the natural inconstancy of men, alarms me with an idea of Lord Woodville's having met, at York, or elsewhere, some object, that may, for a time, divide his heart with you.

Observe, my dearest Emily, that this is mere conjecture;—but we must take certain positions for granted, before we can reason upon any thing. Now do not start, when I tell you, I had much rather your uneasiness should arise, from the latter source, than the former;—though I should consider, even a transitory alienation of his affection, as a misfortune.

Let us now suppose this to be the case, and then see how far you have reason to be distressed, by such an incident. The passions of the human mind, are, I fear, as little under our command, as the motions of our pulse:—you have, therefore, just as much reason, to resent your husband's becoming enamoured, of another person, as you would have to be offended, at his having a fever.

But if, in consequence of that delirium, he should sacrifice your peace to the gratification of his passions, by an open and avowed pursuit of the beloved object; or otherwise render you unhappy, by unkindness, or neglect, you might then have some cause to complain; but if he be unfortunate enough to feel an unwarrantable passion, and keeps that feeling all his own, his merit rises above humanity, and he ought to become almost an object of adoration, to you.

Has he not fled from this alluring charmer? Has he not hid his passion from the world, nor wounded even your pride? Is not his tenderness and kind attention, still unremitted towards you? Indeed, my Emily, allowing these to be matters of fact, you owe him more, than you can ever pay. Consider what his regard to you must be, that can prevail on him to sacrifice his passion, to your peace?

Then do not, I implore you, my dear child, by even the least appearance of distress, aggravate his, but be assured, that from a heart, where honour is the ruling principle, you have every thing to hope, and that the transitory gloom, which now affects him, will be succeeded, by the brightest triumph; and that his reason and his virtue will both join in securing his affection to you, upon a more solid, and permanent foundation, than it could ever have been, if this accident had not happened.

I have gladly laid hold on what you will think the greatest evil, lord Woodville's having conceived an involuntary passion. But formidable as that may appear to you, believe me, Emily, it is of little consequence, compared to what both he, and you must suffer, should there be found no real cause for your distress. A mind so unhappily turned, as yours would then appear to be, must be incapable of receiving or administering content. I am shocked, at the horrid idea, and will not dwell upon it, longer.

As I keep all your letters in a particular drawer of my desk, in looking for your last but one, chance presented me with your first letter, from Wood-fort, where you set out a strenuous advocate, for the existence of terrestrial felicity. Fallacious as the opinion may be, I am truly sorry you have had any reason, to alter your sentiments; but let it, at least, console you, that if you are not an example of your own argument, there is no such thing as an exception to the general rule, that happiness is not, nor ever will be, the lot of human nature, till perfection becomes inherent to it.

The subjects of this letter, have sunk my spirits, so much, that I fear I shall rather increase, than lessen your depression, if I pursue them farther. I will, therefore, change to one that ought to give me pleasure, and will, I hope, afford you some.

Lord Mount Willis, thoroughly apprized of our dear Lucy's former attachment, to Sir James Miller, has declared a passion for her, in the most polite and elegant terms, that can be imagined. Sensibility, he says, is, with him, the highest mark of virtue; and a heart, that could feel what hers has suffered, for an unworthy object, must be capable of the highest tenderness, for one who can, at least, boast the merit of being sensible of her charms.

A little false delicacy has, as yet, prevented Lucy from declaring her sentiments, in favour of this charming man, for such, indeed, he is; though I can see she likes him, full as well, and must necessarily approve him, much more, than she ever did Sir James Miller.

But Lucy declared she would never marry, and that she would leave her fortune, to my Emily.—I know this dwells, on her mind, though it never did, on mine; for I have as little faith, in the vows of disappointed lovers, as in the promises of successful ones. However, I both hope, and believe, that lord Mount Willis will triumph over her scruples, and that I shall have the pleasure of seeing her the happy wife, of that very amiable man.

I am sorry you are to lose Sir James Thornton; but perhaps the want of his company, may induce lord Woodville to come to London; and I should rejoice, at any cause, that could produce that effect, for I cannot bear the thoughts of your lying-in, in the country.

Fanny Weston is not of a temper to break her heart for love; but I would, by all means, have her come to town. Her aunt, lady Weston, talks of going to Bath, next month, and if Fanny chuses to accompany her, I will answer for it, that, that gay scene of dissipation, will soon conquer an hopeless passion, whether lord Seymour, or Sir James Thornton, be the object.

We arrived in Hill-street, last Thursday; to-morrow, Sir John is to place my little Edward, at Eton.[20] The simple mama will feel the loss of her dear play-fellow, but the prudent mother will bless the memory of Henry the Sixth,[21] who instituted that noble foundation.

The accounts we have received of Sir James Miller, are shocking.—He has been obliged to quit Paris, on account of his debts, and is retired into some of the provinces.—His lady remains in the capital, living away upon credit, without character. I begin to pity the unhappy man.

You will easily perceive that this letter has been written, at different periods. The world breaks in upon me. I am embarked in the stream, and must be hurried away by the current, with sticks, straws, and a thousand other insignificant things.

Adieu, my dear Emily: I hope, soon, very soon, to see you—for, if *the mountain will not come to Mahomet, &c.*[22]

F. STRAFFON.

## LETTER 49.

### Lady WOODVILLE, *To Lady* STRAFFON.

I am sincerely sorry, for having given pain to my dear Fanny's gentle heart, as I cannot say that her participation has alleviated my distress. For giving the fullest scope to the arguments you have advanced, what do they prove, but that your Emily is unhappy? and that she knew, too well, before! You set lord Woodville's merits in the fairest light, cruel Fanny! Why could you not find out some fault in him, to make me love him less? But it is impossible; he is, without dispute, the most amiable of mankind.

I told you, in my last, that Sir James Thornton was to leave Woodfort, the day following, which was Tuesday. On Monday night, he took a very polite and affectionate leave, of us all, and I thought appeared more chearful, than he had been, for some time past. When we were at breakfast, on Tuesday, we were told Sir James had set out, at six o'clock; and immediately after, my lord's servant presented him with a letter—he appeared to shew some emotion, while he read it, and soon withdrew to his closet. In less than half an hour, I received the following billet, with the aforesaid letter, inclosed.

### *To Lady* WOODVILLE.

I should be unjust to my unhappy friend, should I conceal the noble and generous sentiments he expresses, for the most lovely, and deserving of her sex; and I should still more highly injure the unbounded confidence I have in my dear Emily, should I prevent her receiving the tribute due to that merit, which could inspire so truly delicate, and sincere a passion. I feel I know not what kind of a mixed sensation, for poor Thornton; I both admire, and pity him.

I would have delivered the inclosed, with my own hand, but feared my presence might distress my Emily, or, perhaps, restrain the pity-flowing tear, which, I confess, I think his sufferings merit.

Adieu, my dearest Emily.

WOODVILLE.

### *Sir* JA. THORNTON, *To Lord* WOODVILLE.

Indebted as I am for many obligations to your lordship, and sensibly awake to the warmest sensations of gratitude, I could not think of quitting Woodfort, and England, for ever, without gratifying that friendly curiosity, which has so often sought the cause of the too visible change, in my manners and appearance. You will, perhaps, be startled, when I tell you, that this alteration is owing to yourself.

Ignorant of every refinement, and elegance of life, dissipated in my temper, and unattached to any particular object, by your lordship's friendly invitation, I arrived at Woodfort.—Heavens! what a scene then opened to my astonished sense! The sudden effect of colours, to a person just restored to sight, could not be felt, more strongly. Every object I beheld, was new, was amiable! yet, in this charming groupe, my lord, there were degrees of merit, and my then vacant heart dared to aspire, at the most perfect of her sex. Need I now tell you, that lady Woodville was its choice! Yes, I avow it! Passion is involuntary; nor would I, if I could, be cured of mine.

Yet witness for me, heaven, that sensual and abandoned, as my past life has been, no gross idea ever mixed with hers, nor did her beauteous form ever raise one thought, that even she need blush to hear.

I do not, my lord, affect to place this purity of sentiment, to the account of my own honour, or even my friendship for you. No, I confess myself indebted for it, to her charming image, which ever appeared to my delighted sense, accompanied by that uncommon delicacy, that graces every word, and action, of her spotless life.—That, like a sacred talisman, has charmed the unruly passions of my mind, and made me only feel the pangs of hopeless love.

Such a confession, as I have now made, my lord, will, I flatter myself, intitle me, both to your regard, and pity. I go, self-banished, from all that I esteem, and love; from you, and lady Woodville.—It would be the heighth of impiety, to doubt of her happiness: and a long continuance of the blessings you now enjoy, is the kindest wish that I can make for you. Felicity like yours, admits of no addition.

When you have read this, my lord, burn, and forget it, but let not the unhappy writer be totally banished from your remembrance. Conceal my presumption, from the too lovely lady Woodville, lest her resentment should be added to the miseries of,

Your unhappy friend,

JAMES THORNTON.

O Fanny, I am distressed, beyond measure, by these two letters! Why did this weak young man place his affections, upon me? Why not bestow them, where they were likely, if not certain, to meet with a return? It is said, that love is involuntary; but I believe it is only so, in very young, or enervated minds.—If we will not struggle with our passions, they will surely overcome us; but they may certainly be weeded out, before they have taken too deep root.

I am doubly distressed, by this unlucky attachment.—Poor Fanny Weston! her passion, for Sir James Thornton, is but too visible;—Would it not be cruel, to attempt her cure, by letting her into this secret? I know not how to act.—Why did my lord reveal his foolish letter? or why did he not sigh, in secret, and conceal his ill-placed love? O these audacious men! they dare do any thing.

There is, however, a degree of modesty, in his keeping the secret, while he was here. I am convinced, if he had given the slightest hint of it, I should have detested him: even as it is, I feel myself offended, and in a very aukward situation. I shall certainly blush, when I see my lord; and yet, why should I be humbled, by another person's folly? What husband, but mine, would have put such a letter, into the hands of a wife? Such a mark of confidence, ought to raise me, in my own opinion, as it is an undoubted proof, that I stand high, in his. Pleasing reflection! dwell upon my mind, and banish every gloomy thought, that has obtruded there.

As Lucy's happiness is of infinite consequence to mine, I hope soon to hear, that she is lady Mount Willis.

Your's, as usual.

E. WOODVILLE.

# LETTER 50.

## *Lady* STRAFFON, *To Lady* WOODVILLE.

I cannot see why my dear Emily should be hurt, or offended, at Sir James Thornton's *innocent* passion? had he dared to avow it, to you, it would have lost *that title,* and should have been considered as an insult; but let the poor youth sigh, in peace, for a few months, and I will venture to promise, that he will get the better of his folly.—Dying for love, is a disorder, that comes not within our bills of mortality.[23]

Not but I believe that a long and habitual fondness, founded on rea-sonable hopes, will, when destroyed, destroy life, with it.

> O the soft commerce! O the tender ties!
> Close twisted with the fibres of the heart,
> Which broken, break it, and drain off the soul
> Of human joy, and make it pain to live.[24]

But these are not the sort of feelings, with which masters and misses, who fancy themselves in love, are commonly affected; for though youth is the season, when we are most capable of receiving strong impressions, it is also the season, when they are most easily erased. I think I might venture to pronounce, that there are not five hundred couples, in the cities of London and Westminster, who are married to their first love, and yet I firmly believe there are, at least, ten times that number, of happy pairs; if so, what becomes of the first passion?

To be sure, we, now and then, meet with a foolish, obstinate heart, that cherishes its own misery, and preserves the image of some worthless object, to the last moment of its existence. Among this simple class, I fear I shall be necessitated to rank my sister Lucy; for though she does not pretend to have the smallest objection, to lord Mount Willis, yet can she not be prevailed upon, to give a final yes.

His behaviour, on this occasion, is truly noble; for though I believe that never man was more in love, he has made it a point, both with Sir John, and me, not to press Lucy, for her consent. I fear Sir John will grow angry, at last, and, perhaps, hurry her into a denial, which she will have reason to repent, all the days of her life.

However, she will now have some time to recollect herself, as Sir John has, this day, received a summons, to attend his aunt, lady Aston, who is dying, and will probably, leave Lucy a large legacy.—That poor idiot, Sir James Miller, has mortgaged the last foot of his estate; but then he has got rid of his wife.—She died, of a fever, at Paris, twelve days ago. Upon the whole, I think fortune has been kinder to him than he deserved.

I am much pleased with lord Woodville's behaviour, in regard to the letter; but, indeed, my dear, you treat these trifling matters, much too seriously; and lest I should myself grow grave upon the subject, I shall bid you, adieu.

F. STRAFFON.

## LETTER 51.

### *Lady* WOODVILLE, *To Lady* STRAFFON.

Dear FANNY,

I have not been well, these three or four days.—Lady Lawson, who is so good to stay with me, and all the *sages femmes,*[25] about me, think that a certain event is nearer, than I apprehended. My lord's foster sister, who has been brought to bed, about five weeks, is now in the house, and every thing is prepared for my *accouchement.*

My lord's tenderness seems doubled, on this occasion.—He scarce ever leaves my apartment; he reads to me, with his eyes oftener fixed on my countenance, than the book, and seems to watch every change in my looks.—What a wretch have I been, Fanny! to suspect this amiable man, of want of love? Would it not be sinning against him, yet more highly, to let him know my crime, by asking his forgiveness, for my unjust suspicions?

No, I will blush in silence, and humble myself before heaven, and you, who alone are conscious of my folly.—Pardon, thou great first Author of my happiness! and thou dear parent-sister, guardian of my youth, excuse my weakness, that had well nigh dashed the cup of blessing from me, or mingled it with bitterness, for ever!

I hear my dear lord's tuneful voice, inquiring for his Emily? I come, my love!

> Adieu, my dearest sister.
>
> E. Woodville.

### Lord Woodville, *To Lady* Straffon.

[With the foregoing letter.]

Joy to my dear lady Straffon, to Sir John, to miss Straffon, and to all who love my Emily! I have the transport to inform you, that she has, this day, made me the happy father, of a lovely boy! and is herself as well, as her situation can admit. My sister Lawson, lady Harriet, and miss Weston, join in congratulations, and compliments to you, with your ever affectionate

> Woodville.

*Note,* The letters from lady Straffon, that immediately follow this, contain only congratulations, and minute inquiries about her sister's, and nephew's health; and as they are, by no means, interesting, the Editor thinks it better to omit them, and return to the correspondence, between lord Seymour, and lord Woodville.

# LETTER 52.

## *Lord* Woodville, *To Lord* Seymour.

My dear Seymour,

I have been at home, now, above a week, yet have purposely avoided writing to you, as your last interdicted me from mentioning the only subject, of which I am capable of thinking. O Seymour! it is in vain to disguise it; my head, and heart, are filled with her, alone! Upon the exertion of any painful act of virtue, we flatter ourselves that we have absolutely conquered its opposite vice, or weakness; our vanity triumphs, and like the *French,* we frequently chant out *Te Deum,*[26] without having gained a victory.

Too much I feel that this has been my case. I begin to fear, that I shall not even be capable of disguising my unhappiness; and of practising that dissimulation, which, in my singular situation, should be deemed a virtue.

I have discovered that lady Woodville has lately wept much; I once surprized her alone, in a flood of tears. I could not bear them; they reproached me, Seymour! but it was with silent anguish. I pressed to know the cause of her distress: had she revealed it, and but once upbraided me, though in the gentlest terms, I fear I should have thrown away the mask, avowed my passion, and quitted her, for ever.

But her soft nature knew not how to chide, and seemed alarmed for fear she had offended. Her suffering gentleness unmanned me quite, or rather, on the instant, it restored all that is worthy of the name of man, my reason, and my virtue: and I dare hope, that, from that time, she has been well deceived, and that I only, am the victim, of my own weakness.

I shall address this letter, to London; I think it is more likely that it should meet you, there, at present, than at the Hot wells. I intreat you will wait upon the marchioness, and tell her, Seymour, what my heart indures; let me, at least, have some merit, from the sacrifice I have made, and not be deemed ungrateful, or insensible, by her.

If you hear any thing of Ransford, let me know it.—His father is outrageous, at his conduct, and even I think he is much to blame.

Adieu, my valued friend.

WOODVILLE.

## LETTER 53.

### *Lord* SEYMOUR, *To Lord* WOODVILLE.

Dear WOODVILLE,

I am sincerely sorry, for your relapsing into a state of weakness, which must be always a state of misery. I confess I thought you in the surest train for happiness, as the having conquered ourselves, is the only subject I know, for real exultation. But as your conduct has been truly noble, and that no person has suffered, from what I now consider as your *own* misfortune, no one can have a right, to reproach you; and it is for your own sake, alone, that I now intreat you to struggle, with your too partial attachment, to an unworthy woman.

You desire me to acquaint her with the state of your heart; can you suppose me so weak, as to comply with your request, were it within my power? But I must travel, some miles, to afford the fugitive conqueror, the triumph you designed.—She set out, from London, five days ago, with your friend Ransford.—I hear they intend to make the tour of Italy, together. Prosperous gales, and calm seas, attend them!—

You see, when a lady is bent upon travelling, she can easily supply herself with a *Cicisbeo;* and I fancy that Ransford will be a much more agreeable companion, upon this party, than your lordship could possibly have been.— He carries not the stings of remorse, about him, the bane of joy, or peace! his neglect of his father, may sometimes, possibly, cloud his gaiety, but one glance from the bright eyes of the marchioness, will quickly dispel the gloom.

Will you forgive me, for owning that I am transported, at their union? Would to heaven, that you could receive joy from it, also! Had she fallen lower than she has done, it might have mortified your pride; but if you can divest yourself of self-love, you must allow that Ransford is more calculated for a lover, than you are. I think he bows, with a better grace, sings charmingly, dances superlatively well, is more *adroit* in his person, is above an inch taller, five years younger, and has ten times your vivacity.

I both hope, and believe, that they are married; and as Ransford does not want penetration, he may possibly have discovered your attachment to her; he will, therefore, probably, prevent her returning to England, for some years. Let her but keep out of your way, and I care not what becomes of her.

Do, my dear Woodville, let me congratulate your escape, from that *Circe!*[27] and rejoice with you in the amiable character of her, whom Providence has designed to bless your future days!

I have business that will detain me, in London, for this month to come; the moment that is finished, I will fly to Woodfort, and hope to find you, and every one there, as happy, as they ought to be; to wish for more, were vain.

SEYMOUR.

# LETTER 54.

## *Lord* WOODVILLE, *To Lord* SEYMOUR.

How could my cruel friend attempt to jest, with misery like mine! It is impossible!—It must not, cannot be! the marchioness gone off with Ransford! by heaven, it is false, though thou, my dearest, truest friend, aver it! You thought to cure my passion, by this legend; but you have blown the sleeping embers, to a flame; and honest indignation, for the injury she sustains, adds fuel to the fire.

Ransford! why Ransford knew her not, six weeks ago.—Their first meeting was at York.—He must have seen her passion.—She could not disguise it; nay, I know she would not—she is above disguise.

Why, Seymour, should you treat me like a child, and strive to impose impossibilities, upon me? how can a heart, that has felt, what yours has done, sport with a lover's anguish? I am impatient, till I send off this, that by the messenger, you may restore my peace, and clear her honour. O! you have set my bosom all on fire! be quick, and quench the blaze, lest it consume the innocent cause of all my wretchedness, along with your distracted friend.

WOODVILLE.

P.S. The servant, who carries this, must neither sleep, or eat, till he brings back your answer. I shall do neither, till I receive it. For pity sake, my friend, trifle no farther, but at once relieve, and excuse the distraction, you have caused.

# LETTER 55.

## *Lord* SEYMOUR, *To Lord* WOODVILLE.

Well mayest thou call thyself distracted, Woodville! and I, as such, can pity, and forgive thee.—Yet must I not become infected by thy folly, and treat thee like a wayward child, indeed.

As I would not have descended to a falsehood, even to have cured you of your weakness, for I cannot call it passion, so neither shall I sooth you, now, by contradicting the truth that I have already asserted; and however impossible, it may appear to you, that the marchioness should so quickly enter into any engagements with Ransford, it is most certain, that they left London, in the same post chaise, on Monday se'ennight,[28] and that she declared her intention of visiting Italy, to my sister Sandford, who was extremely scandalized at her behaviour, with regard to Mr. Ransford, during the short time she staid in town, since they returned from York.

Be assured that I am sincerely affected, by the miserable condition of your mind.—I cannot help considering you as in a state of fascination; for if your reason could operate, at all, you could not possibly be astonished, that a woman, who had jilted you, four years ago, and preferred age, and disease, to you, when she professed to love you, and when it was in your power to marry her, should abandon you, now, that she cannot be your wife, for a lively, agreeable man, who is, probably, as much enamoured of her, though not quite so romantic, as your lordship.

As you are not, at present, in a situation to receive any benefit, from the admonitions of friendship, I shall reserve my sentiments, for a fitter occasion, and not detain your servant longer, than while I subscribe myself

Still yours.

SEYMOUR.


# LETTER 56.

## *Lord* WOODVILLE, *To Lord* SEYMOUR.

Yes, Seymour, I will own I have been mad; I wake, as from a dream: yet why, my kind, my cruel friend, have you recovered me from that delirium, which, like an opiate, while it weakened, soothed my enfeebled sense, and left me scarce a wish, to struggle with my malady! Yes, she is gone! my friend repeats it, and it must be true!

Married to Ransford! Can I yet believe it? "O may the furies light their nuptial torch!"[29] Dissembling, cruel woman! she saw the anguish of my breaking heart, when honour triumphed over my self-love, and prevented my accepting the sacrifice she offered, to her destruction.

Perhaps, that stung her pride; perhaps, she loves me still, but could not bear to be rejected by me.—Perhaps, I have undone her peace, as she has mine.—O no! a younger, gayer, newer lover, absorbs all thoughts of me! I am forgotten, and I will forget

—not Isabelle! my life, my soul, my love!

Do not detest me, Seymour; I would, but cannot conquer, this disease.

The moment I had sent off Williams, with my last to you, I ordered my horses, and rode off, thirty miles, towards London, not only to be so much nearer the return of my express, but to prevent lady Woodville from observing my distraction.

When I had got about five miles, from Woodfort, I sent back my servant, to let her know, that I should spend three or four days, in hunting, with Sir William Atkinson, whom I just then met, going up to London.

I had settled my plan with Williams, who returned, even quicker, than I thought it possible. I have now spent three days, at a wretched inn, where, were it in my choice, I would remain, for ever. Here I can curse, and I can weep—but the innocent lady Woodville may be rendered unhappy, by my stay.—She loves me, as I loved the————Let me not name her.

Sir James Thornton leaves us, in a few days. I must return to Woodfort.—O write soon! and once more say, you pity and forgive,

Your's, ever.

WOODVILLE.

## LETTER 57.

### *Lord* SEYMOUR, *To Lord* WOODVILLE.

Dear WOODVILLE,

I write to you, merely because you desire it; for I am well convinced, that nothing which I, or the greatest philosopher that ever existed, could say to you, would have any effect upon your mind, in its present state; and my own is, at this instant, so extremely agitated, that I am scarce capable of writing, at all.

I have, this day, received a letter, from captain Beaumont.—The contents will amaze you. About six weeks ago, the acknowledged son of madame de Beaumont, was taken ill, of the small pox; and as her daughter had never had it, the general, and she thought proper to send her to a friend's house, lest her beauty be endangered, by the infection.

This young lady, now about fifteen, who had never been out of her mother's sight, before, happened, in the family she was placed in, to become acquainted with a young musqueteer,[30] handsome, and accomplished, but without rank, or fortune. They quickly became enamoured of each other; and, at the end of a fortnight, eloped together, and got safe into Holland. They might, possibly, have been overtaken, and prevented from marrying, if the lady, to whose care Maria Beaumont was entrusted, had not dreaded the violence of madame de Beaumont's temper, so much, that she did not dare to inform her, of the misfortune, till it was past remedy.

In the mean time, the young, and by all accounts, amiable, heir of the family, expired, in his father's arms. The violent agitation, of madame de Beaumont's mind, threw her into a raging fever.—During her delirium, she raved, incessantly, on the ingratitude, and baseness of Maria, and her own inhumanity to the unhappy Charlotte.

The general, who now considered himself as childless, gladly laid hold on the opportunity of endeavouring to recover those, he had formerly, *not lost,* but *thrown away*—he therefore prevailed on madame de Beaumont, to see Charlotte. He went himself to the convent, and having declared his hitherto concealed affinity to Charlotte, he obtained leave from the abbess, to let her visit her dying mother.

But no tongue or pen can express the various emotions, of surprize, grief, and joy, which were occasioned by the sight of his lovely daughter, when she cast herself at his feet, to receive his benediction.—Like poor old Lear,[31] he would have knelt to her, and begged forgiveness.

But when she presented herself on her knees, by the bedside of madame de Beaumont, the unhappy woman, unable to sustain the sight of so much injured beauty, fainted quite away; but the moment she was recovered to her reason, she called for Charlotte, and never let her quit her sight, or ceased to pour forth blessings on her, and implore her pardon, till she expired.

Before she died, she intreated Charlotte to quit the convent, and remain with her unhappy father, while he lived. She desired that a dispensation from her vows, might be immediately solicited, from the Pope, and that captain Beaumont, and lord Seymour might be sent for, in order to obtain their forgiveness. But only one of her wishes, was accomplished.—Captain Beaumont arrived, about two hours before her death; she saw, and blessed him.

He writes me word, that neither his father, nor himself, can prevail on Charlotte, to think of returning into the world again; but that she has consented to go into the country with them, for a couple of months, merely in hopes of reconciling the general, to his youngest daughter. He desires me to *fly* to Bellev: that I may at least see his sister, before she is again secluded from the world, for ever.

O Woodville! I want but *wings,* to obey him! But, hark, my chariot wheels rattle, and my impatient heart, much more than beats responsive, to the horses feet.

Adieu, adieu, my friend.

SEYMOUR.

## LETTER 58.

### *Lord* WOODVILLE, *To Lord* SEYMOUR.

I know not whether to congratulate, or condole, with my dear Seymour, on the very extraordinary events that have happened, in the Beaumont family. His feelings, I know, must arise, from those of his beloved Charlotte; and I am, at present, doubtful, whether she will ever again recover, in the same degree, that peaceful resignation, which we may suppose she had acquired, and was in full possession of, a few weeks ago.

All the passions, of that gentle nature, must now be roused to tumult; the sight of her dear Seymour, must give her joy, transporting joy! which is as much an enemy to peace, as the most poignant misery. And yet, again, must she be torn, from all the social ties of human life; again be buried in that *quick* sepulchre, a convent!

Do not, my friend, indulge a single thought of her returning back, into the world.—It cannot be: Charlotte Beaumont will not be prevailed upon, even by the man she loves, to break her vows to heaven: for though I believe her possessed of the most exalted virtue, she cannot, possibly, be free from superstition, as she is both a woman, and a catholick.

You will, perhaps, be surprized, at my writing to you, in this strain; but I would wish you to guard your heart, against its greatest foe, against self-delusion, Seymour! that sly, slow, underminer of our reason, and our peace! that, lying, whispered to my weak presumption, I might behold the marchioness, unmoved! Fatal, fatal error! it has undone me, Seymour! But I will think, I mean speak, of her, no more.

I have an anecdote to tell you, which convinces me, that Adam's curse is intailed, on all his offspring.

> For either,
> He never shall find out fit mate, but such
> As some misfortune brings him, or mistake;
> Or whom he wishes most, shall seldom gain,
> Through her perverseness; but shall see her gained,
> By a far worse; or, if she love, withheld
> By parents; or, his happiest choice, too late
> Shall meet, already linked and wedlock-bound,
> To a fell adversary, his hate, or shame:
> Which infinite calamity shall cause
> To human life, and household peace confound.[32]

Thornton quitted Woodfort, three days ago.—The morning he went off, he left a letter for me, which contained an absolute declaration, of the most ardent passion, for lady Woodville! You may, perhaps, think he was a little out, in the choice of a confidant—by no means, I assure you. I inclosed his letter, immediately, to my wife, and felt myself really concerned, for his misfortune. Emily is certainly capable of inspiring the most delicate passion; Thornton was a second Cymon, when he first saw her; and I may, with great truth, say, that with all the beauties of an Iphigenia,[33] she is possessed of every amiable virtue, that can inspire esteem, and respect.—I would give millions, to change passions with him.

I can scarce hope to hear from you, while the charming delirium of your happiness, lasts; but when you return again to reason and misery, I shall then be a proper companion, for your affliction. But in every situation of life, I shall remain, unalterably,

Your's,

WOODVILLE.

## LETTER 59.

### *Lady* STRAFFON, *To Lady* WOODVILLE.

As my dear Emily may yet be considered as an invalid, I think myself bound to write, every day, and every thing that can possibly contribute to her amusement, without expecting, or waiting for, any acknowledgement of my letters.

Sir John returned, last night, from paying his last duty, to his aunt, lady Aston, and very well she has paid him, for his attendance. She has bequeathed to him, the pleasant manor of Ashfield, which is worth, between eight and nine hundred pounds, a year; and made him her residuary legatee,[34] when he has paid her bequests, of twelve thousand pounds to Lucy, a thousand pounds, a-piece, to my children, and some few legacies, to old servants.

As soon as Sir John had acquainted us, with this agreeable news, he asked Lucy, if she was yet determined, with regard to lord Mount Willis? when, to my great pleasure and surprize, she answered, Yes, I think I shall be ready to give him my hand, before this day se'nnight; though I cannot, positively, fix the day, as lawyers are dilatory folks.

Sir John then began to rally her, on what he imagined to be her attention to settlements,[35] &c. and told her that my lord and he would take care of all those matters, without her assistance.—She answered, with a very steadfast countenance, and determined air, You will pardon me, brother; for once, and only once, in my life, I am resolved to act for myself.—Now hear my resolution, which I desire you will communicate to lord Mount Willis, tomorrow morning.

When his lordship did me the honour to address me, I had then but five thousand pounds, a fortune much too small to be an object of consideration, to him; but neither he, nor you, knew, at that time, that I had but a use,[36] even in that small sum, for life.

Sir John attempted to interrupt her, by inquiring what she meant? she begged that he would suffer her to proceed, without interruption, and went on.—The severe treatment I met with, from Sir James Miller, made me, at that time, resolve, that I would never marry.—We little know our own hearts, in many particulars of life; but least of all, in this.

But the extreme kindness, I met with, at the same time, from lady Straffon, laid me under such indelible obligations, as no time, nor circumstance, can ever efface. I then determined, nay declared, that I would bequeath[37] my fortune, to my niece Emily; and no power on earth, shall make me alter my resolution.

From my aunt's unmerited goodness to me, it is now in my power, to fulfil my intentions, before my death, and to give a proof, of that gratitude, which I owe to my more than sister. Again both Sir John and I would have broken in on her discourse, but she beckoned silence.

When this, the first wish of my heart, is accomplished, I shall still have a much better fortune, than lord Mount Willis first expected with me.—But it must not be all his. Sir James Miller has been, in some degree, conducive to that happiness, which I expect, and hope for, from an union with his lordship. Sir James is poor, and wretched; justly punished, for his crimes, but not rewarded, for the benefits, he has conferred on me.—Some small provision must be made, for him, without his ever knowing, from whom he receives it. I formerly looked upon him, with horror, and aversion; I now consider him, as my benefactor; and the saving him from the miseries of extreme poverty, will relieve my mind, from a sort of mental debt.

Sir John could forbear, no longer, but clasping her in his arms, said, Providence had made him rich, indeed, when it bestowed such treasures on him, as his wife, and sister. Both he and I said every thing, to dissuade her, from her intended gift to Emily, but in vain.

Sir John seemed to hint, as if he thought it would be better, that her generous intentions, towards Sir James Miller, should be executed, by lord Mount Willis, rather than herself. By no means, brother, replied Lucy; were there a remain of tenderness, for him, in my heart, the world should not bribe me, to marry its sole lord. Generosity should flow, from principle, not passion; and, as I can truly boast, that this action, with regard to Sir James Miller, arises from the first source, nothing must change the current of it. My conduct, on this occasion, is, I think, the highest compliment, that I can pay, to lord Mount Willis, and I have not a doubt, of his considering it, in that light.

We both acquiesced, in her opinion, and Sir John waited on lord Mount Willis, this morning, to inform him, of Lucy's intentions. He says he never saw any person so transported, as his lordship; he said he had ever looked upon Lucy, as the most amiable of women, but that her generosity, to Sir James Miller, made him now look up to her, as to a superior being; and that if she gave thousands, he ought to give ten thousands, to the unhappy man, who had been, in any degree, instrumental, to his felicity.

This will be a whimsical contest, I think, Emily, but I do not fancy that Lucy will consent to my lord's interfering, with her designs. At present, she intends to lay out four thousand pounds, in an annuity, for Sir James; which, if he continues to live abroad, may support him, decently.

I have been, this day, to bespeak a pair of diamond shoe buckles, and a very fine egrette,[38] which Sir John and I mean to present her with. I know lord Mount Willis's family jewels are very rich, but my dear Lucy's virtues will outshine them all.—Indeed she is an honour, not only to her sex, but to human nature!

She joins with me, in intreating yours, and lord Woodville's company, at her wedding. Surely my Emily will not refuse us both! you can have no doubts but that your little boy will be taken every possible care of, and even a little month's absence, from that dear face, on which your dotage hangs, will make an amazing change for the better, in it—He will be as handsome again, by the time you return to Woodfort.

Lucy writes, this night, to lady Harriet, and Fanny Weston, to attend her nuptials.—All girls will fly to a wedding; so that you will be left totally alone, if you are so ill-natured, as to deny our request.

Who knows what a good example may do?—The pensive lady Harriet, may, perhaps, be prevailed upon, to sigh, no more,[39] for her perjured swain, but may, possibly, be inclined to make some worthy man happy. As to Fanny Weston, I am persuaded that the festivity of a wedding, will intirely conquer her hopeless passion, for the wandering Thornton. She is no Penelope,[40] believe me; and I fancy Mr. Willis, my lord's brother, will be able to banish the errant knight, quite out of her mind.

Adieu, my dear Emily. I hope you will make me happy, in your next, by telling me that I shall soon have the pleasure of seeing you. Indeed I want nothing else, at present, to compleat my felicity.

F. STRAFFON.

# LETTER 60.

## *Lady* WOODVILLE, *To Lady* STRAFFON.

My dear FANNY,

I am extremely charmed, but not surprized, at Lucy's conduct.—There is every thing to be expected, from *sensibility, and delicacy,* joined; but, indeed, I have scarce ever known them separated, in a female heart. Refined manners are the natural consequences of fine feelings, which will, even in an untutored mind, form a species both of virtue, and good breeding, higher than any thing that is to be acquired, either in courts, or schools; but when these *two qualities* receive every addition, that education, and example can bestow,

> When youth makes such bright objects still more bright,
> And fortune sets them in the strongest light;
> 'Tis all of Heaven that we below may view,
> And all, but adoration, is their due.[41]

Thus do I think of our dear Lucy; yet I must say that she has been uncommonly fortunate, in having such an opportunity, of exerting the noble qualities of her heart, and proving how much superior she is to the detestable meanness, of malice, or revenge. Charming girl! may she be as happy, as she deserves!

She, as well as you, has intreated me to partake her happiness.—Alas, Fanny! though grief is contagious, we cannot always sympathize with joy— strange perverseness of our natures, that accepts the evil, and rejects the good! Do not, from this, suspect me of malevolence, or suppose that I do not truly rejoice, in Lucy's felicity. But there is, I know not why, a kind of weight, that hangs upon my mind, which I find it impossible to remove. Perhaps, change of place, may help to shake it off.—Be that as it may, I shall, certainly, comply with your's, and Lucy's request.

My lord has kindly promised to accompany me, and our sweet little babe is to be left at lady Lawson's. Indeed, Fanny, you scarce can think what a sacrifice I make, to quit him, for a day; but he will be under the protection of the best of women.

I fear there is a scene preparing, that will trouble her repose. That bad miss Fanning! what a heart must hers be? how void of gratitude! and where that virtue is wanting, there can subsist no other.—Neither precept, nor example, can operate, on base minds.

Is it not strange, that nature should vary, so much, in the human genus, as to create a Lucy Straffon, and a Mary Fanning? so nearly of the same age, too; both descended from good families; and both well educated. The animal creation do not differ thus, from their own species. There are no furious sheep, nor mild tigers.—Nature is uniform, in all her works, but man.—Hapless variety! sad source of misery! the tiger, and the lamb, are not less similar, than the betrayer, and the betrayed—yet both wear the same form, and only by experience, is the difference found.—Nay, sometimes, we have seen the fairest face conceal the vilest heart; as lurks the serpent, underneath the rose.—This is a mortifying subject; I will no more of it.

Fanny Weston, as you guessed, is in high spirits, at the idea of Lucy's wedding.—She talks of nothing, but dress, equipage, and jewels, ever since it has been mentioned—but a new subject is of infinite use, in the country; and I do not know whether a great funeral, would not have entertained her, quite as much.—Nodding plumes, and painted escutcheons will amuse the imagination, when gilt coaches, and gay liveries do not come in the way.—

Happy triffler! how I envy her—yet I am sure she loves Lucy, and fancies that she is really enamoured, of Sir James Thornton, too.—I am certain, that lady Harriet would gladly be excused, from going to London, but I will not seem to see which way her inclinations tend.

> The silent heart, which grief assails,
> Treads soft, and lonesome, o'er the vales.
> Sees daisies open, rivers run,
> And seeks (as I have vainly done)
> Amusing thought; but learns to know,
> That solitude's a nurse of woe.[42]

And a soft, and tender nurse it is—but dissipation may, perhaps, be good for us all, and lady Harriet shall try the recipe, as well as
    Your affectionate, &c.

                                                    E. Woodville.

# Letter 61.

## *Lady* Straffon, *To Lady* Woodville.

I think myself extremely obliged to my dear Emily, for her compliance with her friends request.—You cannot conceive what delightful effects the hopes of seeing you have produced, in Hill-street.—Sir John talks of nothing else, but the *sparkler;* you know he used to call you so.—Lucy is all gratitude, for your kindness, and my little Emily holds up her head, most amazingly, that her aunt may observe what a fine carriage she has, and how much she is grown, since she saw her.—The servants are all transported, with double joy, for Lucy's wedding, and your arrival. In short, every one wears a smiling face, and I shall not pardon it, if there should appear the smallest trace of gloom, on your's.

I am very sorry, for what you hint at, with regard to lady Lawson—but be assured, that a woman should be thoroughly convinced, not only of her husband's attachment, but of his morals, also, before she introduces a female inmate, younger, though perhaps not fairer, than herself.

The caution should be equally attended to, with regard to male intimates.—I have seldom known an habitual friendship, that did not kindle, into what is called love, where there has been youth, beauty, and un-ceasing opportunity, to fan the flame.

I think, if I were in lady Lawson's case, I should not feel much—for the heart of a man, who is capable of seducing a young creature, that is immedi-ately under his protection, can never be worth regretting. I have always heard, that Sir William is a very debauched man; and a truly delicate woman cannot preserve her affection, for such a one, long.—Contempt must follow vice; and where we once despise, we soon must cease to love.

Nor do I look upon miss Fanning, as an object of pity—bred up, as she has been, with so excellent a woman, one should suppose her heart replete, with every virtue;—but she cannot, possibly, be possessed, even of the common merits, which we expect from a chambermaid, when she can de-scend to prostitution, without temptation.

Had she been led astray, by an agreeable young man, I could have pitied, nay, perhaps, have loved, and even esteemed her; for I am not such an Amazon, in ethics, as to consider a breach of chastity, as the highest crime, that a woman can be guilty of; though it is, certainly, the most unpardonable folly; and I believe there are many women, who have erred, in that point, who may have more real virtue, aye, and delicacy too, than half the sainted dames, who value themselves on the preservation of their chastity; which, in all probability, has never been assailed. She alone, who has withstood the solicitations, of a man she fondly loves, may boast her virtue; and I will venture to say, that such an heroine will be more inclined to pity, than despise, the unhappy victims of their own weakness.

I have sported my opinion, upon this subject, very freely; you must, therefore, allow me to explain myself, more clearly. I know your delicacy will be hurt, if I do not; and I may expect to be severely attacked, by my dear little prude.

First then, I confine my fair penitents, to their first choice; a second error of this sort, is never to be pardoned.—Passion is the only excuse, that can possibly be made, for such a transgression; and a woman, who has made such a sacrifice, to love alone, may be perfectly satisfied, that she can never be subject to that passion, in the same degree, again. For there never is above one human creature, that we can love *better than ourselves.*

The woman, who receives two galants, is, in my mind, quite upon a footing, with the most venal beauties; whose capacious hearts scorn to be limited, to any number. All married ladies I absolutely exclude, from my order of amiable unfortunates—they cannot even pretend, to be deceived;—whereas a simple girl, however mean her condition, may flatter herself, that her lover's intentions are honourable. Old legends tell of king Cophetua, and the beggar maid; and your Pamelas, and your Mariannes,[43] encourage hope, in young, untutored minds, which perhaps the artful destroyer takes the utmost pains to encrease; "till they can trust, and he betray, no more."

This is, I confess, a nice subject, for a woman to treat upon; but I promise you I will indeavour to make my girl distinguish, between vice, and weakness; and I hope, while she detests the one, she will be always ready to pity, and, if in her power, to protect, the other.—There is no character, I so heartily abominate, as that of the *outrageously virtuous.* I have seen a lady render herself hateful, to a large company, by repeating, perhaps a forged tale, of some unhappy frail one, with such a degree of rancour, and malevolence, as is totally inconsistent, with the calm dignity of real virtue.

Have you ever read a fable, which is bound up with Mr. Moore's, but was written by Mr. Brooke, called The Female Seducers?[44] I think it the prettiest thing, that ever was written, upon this subject.—To that I refer you, for my sentiments, at large.

Your remark, upon the diversity of natures, amongst the human species, is pretty, and ingenious;—but when we consider the amazing variety there is, in the animal creation, and how many of them are noxious, we cannot wonder that there should be some difference, in human kind.—Had we been all formed, with equal virtues, those very virtues would have been rendered useless;—an insipid sameness would have prevented emulation, and life would have become a perfect sinecure.

On the other hand, were we all vicious, disorder and confusion must take place, and this world be quickly reduced, to its primitive chaos. Without temptation, there could be no virtue; and, without virtue, this world could not subsist.—We should not be so much pleased with the gentleness of the lamb, if there was no animal more fierce, nor should we feel the sweetness of the woodlark's note, so sensibly as we do, if we had never heard the screech-owl's voice, or the croaking of the raven. It is by comparison, alone, that we are capable of estimating good and evil, both in the moral, and natural sense.

I could illustrate my argument, as fully amongst our own species, as in the brute creation; but I have drawn this letter to such an immoderate length, that I must, at least, defer the remainder of my discourse, parson-like, to another opportunity.

Every thing is settled, to Lucy's mind; and lord Mount Willis's happy day is fixed, for Saturday fortnight. I hope you will come to town, next week; till then,

Adieu, my ever dear Emily.

F. STRAFFON.

## LETTER 62.

## *Lady* WOODVILLE, *To Lady* STRAFFON.

Dear FANNY,

I should have answered your letter, by last post, but was prevented, by having company. The two miss Withers's spent three days, with us.—I told you before, they were charming women; but agreeable, as I first thought them, I now think them ten times more so.

The eldest is extremely sensible, and perfectly accomplished, but of a grave turn; the youngest has every merit of her sister, with the most engaging vivacity, imaginable. She is soon to be married, to an Irish nobleman.—Happy man, who is to be blessed with such a companion!

She seems to feel some regret, at the thoughts of quitting her friends, and England; but says, she is sure that her lord will be so good, to let her visit them, sometimes; and she would, by no means, wish to detach him, intirely, from his native country, or prevent his spending that fortune, in it, which he derives, from it.

Miss Withers is to go to Ireland, with her sister. I am almost sorry that I ever was acquainted with these sweet girls, since I am to lose the pleasure of their society, so soon. They told me a piece of news, which though it surprized, did not displease me.—Mr. Ransford is married, to the marchioness of St. Aumont, and they are now, in France, together.

Is it not odd, that my lord never mentioned this particular, as it is no secret, in the country? and he must certainly know it, as he has been, once, or twice, to see Sir Harry Ransford. But I think you desired me never to pry into his motives, for any thing; and I obey.

Indeed, Fanny, you appear to me to affect the stoic, too much, from what you say about lady Lawson; but we can all bear the misfortunes of others, with great fortitude,

> When they are lash'd, we kiss the rod,
> Resigning to the will of God.[45]

In my mind, lady Lawson's trial is a fiery one.—She is, she must be, doubly distressed. As to the slight infidelities of husbands, I think the wife must be contemptible, who resents them; but every woman, that truly loves her husband, wishes to preserve his heart; and a consciousness of his attachment, to another object, must be productive of the most poignant anguish. Happy, happy sister! that have never felt that "Hydra of calamity."

I grant that Sir William Lawson has ever been a debauched man, but he has always had, except in this instance, so much regard to his lady, to decency, and humanity, as to conceal his vices, from her: He, therefore, had not forfeited her esteem, though she had lost his love.—O loss, beyond repair! Then her affection for that wretch, miss Fanning, must add to her distress. Not having been blessed with children, she looked upon this worthless girl, as her own daughter—and can she, in a moment, forget the tenderness, she has indulged, so long, and detest the wicked couple, as she ought?—impossible!

I am really angry, at your philosophic insensibility, upon this occasion.—for my part, I can scarcely behave, with common civility, either to Sir William, or miss Fanning. But lady Lawson, who is a saint, behaves with her usual kindness, to them both, nor has ever seemed to have discovered, or hinted the least suspicion, of what is already too visible to the whole country.—Yet her lovely face is emaciated, and pale; and, sometimes, involuntary sighs, and tears, escape her.

I know my lord is extremely distressed, on this occasion; he loves his sister, tenderly; but fears his interposing, might, possibly, make Sir William lay aside all restraint, and, perhaps, occasion a separation, from his wife. I am glad, for this reason, that we are leaving the country, as I imagine miss Fanning's situation will make her removal necessary, before we return to Woodfort.

You need not have apprehended my dissenting from your generous sentiments, with regard to the unhappy victims of love.—Nay, I carry my humanity farther, and feel for those, who, without strong passion, fall a sacrifice to the vile arts of their seducer, and their own weakness. That unsuspecting confidence, which is, too frequently, the cause of womens ruin, must certainly arise from a generous disposition; and I should look upon a young, innocent girl, who was armed, at all points, like Moor of Moor-hall,[46] to be a most unnatural character.

At the same time, I detest a vicious woman, more than any being, in the creation; and, for this reason, my compassion does not extend, to married ladies, in general, any more than yours.—They have always a protector, to fly to; who, upon that occasion, if upon no other, will, with open arms, receive them—for, though every man may not love his wife, every man is certainly jealous of his honour; and the false notions of the world, are, at present, so constituted, that the failure of a woman, brings infamy, upon her husband; while, in a much more pitiable case, it rests, solely, upon the injured unfortunate.

However, Fanny, I agree with you, that this is too nice a subject, for a female pen; though one is insensibly led into reflections, that are humiliating to an honest mind. But when he, who knew the frailty of our natures, adjudged the convict criminal, his sentence was not severe; for well he knew it was impossible there could be found a wretch, so lost to humanity, as to throw a stone.[47]

Let not the young, the gay, the rich, the fortunate, whose situations in life, have prevented their being liable to temptation, like an herd of deer, turn their armed brows, against their wounded friend, and give her to the hunters!

Miss Withers and I, were last night, talking upon this subject, and she repeated a little poem, that lord Digby, her sister's lover, had shewn her. It was written, upon a particular occasion, at a water drinking place, in Ireland, called Mallow, some years ago.—The unfortunate subject of it, had been a much admired character, in that place, a few seasons before, and dignified by the title of Sappho.[48]

The lines are extremely pretty; turn over, and you will find them in the next page.

VERSES,

WRITTEN AT THE

FOUNTAIN AT MALLOW, IN THE COUNTY OF

CORKE, IN IRELAND[49]

Thou azure fount, whose chrystal stream,
Was once a nobler poet's theme,
While to inspire the tuneful strain,
Sappho was called, nor called in vain.
Ah let the good forgive! if here,
I pay the tribute of a tear,
In tender grief for Sappho's fate,
The wonder of thy banks so late,
So many virtues were thy share,
Thou most accomplished, ruined fair!
One error sure may be forgiven,
And pardon find from Earth and Heaven.
That sovereign power who made us all,
Suffered the sons of light to fall!
And oft, to mortify our pride,
From virtue lets the wisest slide.
Ye fair, no more her faults proclaim;
For your own sakes, conceal her shame;
Since if a nymph so wise could fail,
We well may think Ye all are frail!

A truce, for the present, with this, and every other subject, but the pleasing thought of our meeting, which I hope will be on Tuesday evening, next,

Till then, adieu.

E. WOODVILLE.

P.S. We have got a furnished house, in St. James's Street;[50] and I am strongly tempted to bring my sweet little Harry, with me.—Cruel Fanny, never to mention my little cherub! but *I'll be revenged, and love him better for it.*

# Letter 63.

## *Lady* Woodville, *To Lady* Lawson.

London, Jan[ry] 18.

A thousand thanks to my dear lady Lawson, for the pleasing account she has given me, of herself, and my dear little boy. You will, perhaps, think me ill-natured, for rejoicing that you have no other companion, at present; but I am not so selfish, as you may imagine, upon this occasion; for I well know that the most agreeable company in the world, could not abate your affectionate attention to him.

But there are certain situations in life, when our dearest friends become irksome to us, from an apprehension that they may possibly discover, what we wish to hide.—There needs no other illustration of my opinion, than a fair confession, that I have, sometimes, seen you under these very circumstances, with your brother, and myself.—But I hope, and believe you will never again experience them. I may now speak freely upon a subject, which though your virtue and goodness concealed, Sir William has thought proper to mention to my lord, with every eulogium, on your conduct, which, noble as it has been, it could deserve.

Miss Fanning set out for Yorkshire, this morning, truly sensible of your goodness, and her own unworthiness. Sir William says he is certain, that it is not in your nature, to detest her, as much as she does herself. He told my lord that this affair was, by no means so unfortunate an event, with regard to you two, as it might, at first, have appeared to be; as your behaviour had not only made him esteem, and admire, but love you also, a thousand degrees more, than he ever had done before.

He declared, that he felt the impatience of a lover, to throw himself at your feet, and said he never should forgive himself, for having rendered you unhappy, by his infamous conduct. Joy, joy, to my dear sister! will you forgive my saying, that I envy your situation?

I would give you an account of lady Mount Willis's wedding, dress, equipage, &c. &c. did I not know that your full heart can have no room to entertain such triffling ideas. But I am certain it will give you pleasure to hear that lord Mount Willis, is as amiable, and accomplished, as his charming bride, and that I think they have the fairest prospect of a long uninterrupted course of happiness.

As the house of lords are now sitting, your brother purposes staying in town, till March; but I may whisper to you, what I would not have him hear, that I cannot help regretting so long an absence from Woodfort, from my child, and from yourself.

Lady Harriet, my sister Straffon, and Fanny Weston, present their more than compliments, and my lord joins, in love, and sincere congratulations, with your

Truly affectionate,

E. WOODVILLE.

## LETTER 64.

### *Lord* WOODVILLE, *To Lord* SEYMOUR.

Is it possible that my dear Seymour can be so totally absorbed in his own felicity, as to make him intirely forget his absent, his unhappy friend. I have been, above two months, in London, without hearing from you! Miss Straffon's marriage with lord Mount Willis, brought lady Woodville and me, to town.

I confess I flattered myself that a change of objects, and a scene of dissipation, would have assisted me, in conquering the gloomy disease, that hangs upon my mind. Far from it! I think it has rather increased my malady, by laying me under greater restraints, than I experienced, at Woodfort; as all humours, both of the mind, and body, acquire additional force, if they are denied a vent.

As my ill fortune would have it, we are lodged in the same house the marchioness lived in; and, to add to my distress, there is a picture of hers, which was not finished, when she went away, that is hung up, in my dressing room. As lady Woodville was coming to speak to me, yesterday morning, she overheard me earnest in discourse, with the fair shadow; she immediately retired, supposing there was company with me.

When we met, at dinner, she smiling asked me, who the lady was, that had been to visit me, in the morning. I could not, for some time, conceive the meaning of her question; but when, from the naïveté of her discourse, I understood it, I was all confusion, and your sister, lady Sandford, who was at table with us, gave me a look, that perfectly convinced me she was acquainted with my folly.

The inhuman marchioness must have revealed my weakness to her,—Seymour could not betray his friend! Yet may I not, from hence, deduce a kind of tacit compliment, to myself, by supposing she must have been vain of her conquest, when she proclaimed it? weak consolation! like a drowning wretch, I catch at rushes!

Why, why can I not tear her fatal image, from my breaking heart! Have you seen her, Seymour? It is a thousand years, since I beheld her—Have age and ugliness yet overtaken her, or is she lovely still? Excuse my raving—such, I know, it will appear to you.

I know not whether I told you that lady Woodville had presented me with a son, before we left the country, and appears, if possible, still more amiable, in the character of a mother, than before she was one.—I rejoice to think that her being a parent, has added to her happiness, as well as her merit. Our virtue, and our felicity are both increased, by the diffusion of our affections.—What a wretch am I, then, Seymour, who feel all mine concentred, in one object, where they must rest for ever!

This reflection on myself, is too severe, nay most unjust! for I declare, that I am sensible of the utmost tenderness, for the lovely, the unoffending lady Woodville; and I would die, rather than render her unhappy—At the same instant, I adore the cruel, insolent, ungrateful marchioness—What tortures must arise, from such a state of contradiction!

I am truly impatient to know whether you have prevailed with your fair vestal, to renounce her vows, and enter, once again, into this world of cares? be assured I am sincerely interested, in every thing that relates to you; and this, the most momentous point of your life, is of the utmost consequence,

To your ever affectionate,

WOODVILLE.

## LETTER 65.

### *Lord* SEYMOUR, *To Lord* WOODVILLE.

Yes, Woodville, I confess it, I have been absorbed, entranced, in the most delightful delusion, that ever lulled the restless heart of man! I have passed three months, in paradise! I thought not of the world, nor of its cares—I even grudged the hours which nature claimed for rest, they robbed me of my Charlotte's tuneful voice, though her loved form oft visited my slumbers—But the gay vision is now flown, and I indeed awake, as from a dream!

You may suppose I reached Belleveüe, in as short a space of time, as it was possible—My Charlotte was prepared to meet me. At our first interview, through all the agonizing joy I felt, I perceived a steady calmness in her manner, that spoke the tender, the indulgent friend, not the fond mistress: the gravity of her dress, added dignity to her deportment, and awed even my tumultuous wishes, into silence. I looked up to her, as to a superior being; and felt myself grow little in her sight. She took advantage of my first impressions, and spoke to me, in the following manner.

You see before you, Sir, the happiest of her sex, now first permitted to indulge those fond sensations, which nature plants in every human heart, filial, and sisterly affection.—I will confess myself still farther gratified, by seeing you, the first, the only object of a passion, which took its rise, in youth and innocence, but which has been long since matured, into the firmest friendship, and rendered you—pardon me, my father!—the first, the constant object, of my prayers.

But let not the fond wishes of a father, or your own desires, tempt you to think that ought on earth, can move me to exchange the state of tranquil happiness, I now enjoy, for any other, less pure, and more precarious. My vows were heard in Heaven; they passed not forth, from feigning, or forced lips; for, in the very moment I pronounced the words, my heart assented to the pious sounds, nor would I then have changed my situation, even to be lord Seymour's wife.

Nor do I now repent the choice I made, though fully satisfied both of your worth, and love. Providence seemed to have planted insuperable bars between us, at the sad hour when I fixed my purpose to renounce the world; and my then torn heart found its sole peace, in humble acquiescence to his will.

Now mark me, Henry, this is the last time that I shall ever speak upon the subject, and it is in order to save your heart the pain of fruitless solicitation, that I explain my resolution. Should his holiness be prevailed upon, by my father's intreaties, to grant me the indulgence he has requested, thus far I will, on my part, comply with the general's desire.—I will spend one, two, or three months, with him, in this house, whenever he shall command me; but my place of residence, must be the convent.—There I have sworn to live, and there I mean to die.

There was something so commanding, and determined, in Charlotte's voice and manner, even while she denounced a sentence so severe, that neither her brother, who was present, nor I, attempted once to interrupt her. When she had finished, I found my heart subdued, and ready to sacrifice its every wish, to whatever seemed most conducive to her happiness. I was, alas! the fatal cause, of the vows she had made, how then should I dare to solicit the breach of them!

Truth, Woodville, flashes conviction, even upon our passions, as swift as light obtrudes upon the eyes. I, instantly, felt the delicate impossibility of her being happy, in the world, and as quickly resolved never to importune her to be wretched. It was not, however, without the sincerest regret, that I beheld my most sanguine hopes of happiness, vanish, once more, into air.

She received my acquiescence with her determination, as the highest mark of my affection, and told me that she now considered me, in a light, where the tenderest regard for my welfare, was compatible with her duty; and that, henceforward, she should know no difference, in her affection, for captain Beaumont, and lord Seymour.

From that time, Woodville, our days have been spent in the most delightful intercourse, and have stolen away, almost unperceived by me. Charlotte's voice, which was ever charming, is now so highly improved, that no melody on earth can equal it. The good old general, who absolutely adores her, is frequently melted into tears, while she sings; and upon all occasions, gazes on her, with a look of repentant sorrow and delight, as if conscious of the injury, he has done to the world, by robbing it of such an ornament; while her charming countenance is lighted up, with the most animated looks, of filial love.

She has prevailed on the general, to be reconciled to his youngest daughter, and her husband.—He has obtained the young man's release, and is to purchase him a commission, immediately.—As soon as that can be effected, they will come here, and Charlotte will again retire into the convent—how do I dread the fatal hour of separation! and blush to think, that even Charlotte's mind should be so far superior to my own.

Within these few days, she has frequently mentioned her going to Paris, with a look, and manner, almost expressive of impatience, yet chastened by the pain she sees it gives her father, brother, and the unhappy Seymour.—Must she again be torn from my fond eyes! Have I not sacrificed my wishes to her will, and will she rob me of the last, sole delight, of sometimes gazing on her?

Her brother tried to prevail on her, to let me visit her, at the convent, but she has peremptorily refused; nor will she even consent to see him, except on particular business. Her father is the only person she will admit, within those walls.—This is a self-imposed restraint, for the abbess is perfectly inclined to grant her every indulgence, she can ask.

I know nothing of the marchioness, Ransford, nor of any other person, at Paris. I shall certainly accompany Charlotte thither; and, when there, shall acquaint you with every thing I hear, about them. I am truly concerned, that your infatuation, for that worthless woman, should still continue.— O Woodville! had you lost such a treasure, as I have, and by your own fault, too, what would your situation now have been! I will think of my miseries, no more—but endeavour to enjoy the small portion of happiness, that yet remains for me.

I congratulate you, on being a father—may that tender tie awaken every pleasing sensation, in your mind, and restore your heart to the amiable lady Woodville, who only can deserve it.

Direct your next, to the hotel de ———, at Paris; and till I arrive there,

    Adieu.

SEYMOUR.

## LETTER 66.

### *Lord* WOODVILLE, *To Lord* SEYMOUR.

Once more returned to Woodfort's peaceful shades, escaped from crouds and noise, to gentle converse, and the sweet music of my vocal woods; yet can I not enjoy the pleasing scene, I have so much longed for—the cause of my coming hither, embitters the satisfaction I hoped to find, in being here. My Emily is in a bad state of health, occasioned, as her physicians think, by the foggy air, and hurry of London.

But, O Seymour! to you I will confess the secret woundings of my troubled soul. I fear that sorrow preys upon her tender heart; for from the time of our being at York, I have frequently imagined her mind was distressed; but whenever she seemed to perceive that idea rising in my thought, she has instantly banished it, by assuming an air of chearfulness and vivacity; and the transition was made with such amazing ease, that I thought it impossible she should be insincere, and that the gloomy medium of my own reflections, and not hers, had tinctured her appearance with an air of sorrow. Can it be possible, Seymour, that a creature, so young, and innocent, as lady Woodville, can be capable of disguising her sentiments, and hiding her grief, in smiles!

I begin to fear that women are our superiors, in every thing. If she has perceived my passion for the marchioness, and concealed the anguish, which such a discovery must occasion, to a heart like hers, for well I know she fondly loves me, the story of the Spartan boy,[51] should no longer be repeated; but lady Woodville be, henceforth, considered as the first example, of human fortitude.—In what a light, then, must *her lord* appear! I cannot bear the thought.

When the physicians first attended her, they advised her setting out, immediately, for the south of France, but she refused to go, with a more determined air, and manner, than I had ever seen her assume before. I imagined her dislike arose from the thought of being separated from her son, and immediately assured her that he should go with us. She thanked me for my condescension, but said it had only removed one of her objections, and that not the strongest.

Then, with a tear, just starting from her eye, she intreated that I would not press her, farther. I kissed away the pearly fugitive, as it stole down her cheek, which was instantly lighted up, by the soft glow of joy, and modesty.—She told me, then, she wished to return to Woodfort, and, if I pleased, she would go to Bristol, when the season came on.

I acquiesced in every thing she desired; and would, at that instant, as I would at this, have laid down my life, to procure her health and happiness. We set out, immediately, for this place.—For the first three or for days, I thought her better; since that, I too plainly perceive, that she declines.

If she should die, Seymour, I shall consider myself as her murderer. Surely, you would, then, allow me the painful preeminence of wretchedness, and acknowledge your situation, when compared to mine, to be like beds of roses, to the rack. O no! it must not be—she shall not die.

I never was so impatient for any æra, as for the month of June.—I have great hopes, from the Hot-wells, my Emily's youth, and naturally good constitution.

I had not the least expectation, that your Charlotte would have been prevailed on, to quit the convent; indeed, I scarcely hoped that she would have condescended, as far as she has done, by consenting to spend a portion of every year, at Belleveüe. Happy Seymour! to have such a subject, for expectation, before you.—It is surely one of the highest degrees of human felicity, to look forward with hope.

You will pardon me if I think there is some faint trait of the coquette, in her refusing to see you, at the convent. She certainly wishes to keep your flame alive; and as she does not mean to feed it, with any thing more substantial, than her conversation, she wisely thinks, that that, like all other enjoyments, might possibly pall upon the taste, if too often repeated.

She has, therefore enjoined you a long fast, in order to heighten your relish for the "feast of reason."[52] You, I dare say, as a still passionate lover, may, probably think this little *ruse d'amour*[53] unnecessary; but I am firmly persuaded, that abstinence will enhance the value of our mental, as well as corporeal pleasures.

A servant has just informed me, that lady Woodville is ready to ride out.—I attend her, on horseback, every day.

Adieu, my friend.

WOODVILLE.

P.S. I hope this will be a letter of credit for me, in your books, as I have not once drawn upon your patience, by mentioning the marchioness.—Be generous, then, my dear Seymour, and reward my self-denying virtue.

## LETTER 67.

### *Lord* SEYMOUR, *To Lord* WOODVILLE.

Paris.

My dear WOODVILLE,

I have made an exchange, directly opposite to yours, having just quitted the sweet scenes of Belleveüe, and my Charlotte's delightful converse, for the irksome crouds and noise, of this great city.

The young musqueteer, and his lady, arrived at general Beaumont's, about a fortnight ago. Charlotte had fixed the time of her return to the convent, for the tenth day after they came, but her sister, madame de Carignon, being taken violently ill, made her postpone her journey, and made me hasten mine.

From the time that Maria complained, Charlotte never quitted her apartment.—Belleveüe became a desart to me, and I fancied I should feel less regret, at being separated from her, by distance, than accident.—But the effects are the same, be the cause what it may; for there is no place, or situation, that can afford me happiness, in her absence.

You treat Charlotte, very severely, nay unjustly, by charging the highest proof of her delicate affection, to the account of coquetry. She is too sensible not to perceive that my passion for her, renders me unhappy, and she, though vainly, flatters herself, that time and absence may effect a cure.

This she, in confidence, declared to captain Beaumont, when pressed by him to receive my visits.—Alas! she little knows I would not change my malady, for health; and yet, I will conform to her prescription, and drink the bitter draught, without a murmur. O Woodville! when we truly love, it is our highest transport, to obey!

I am truly concerned, for the account you give of lady Woodville, but find a secret consolation, for her sufferings, in your sensibility, as I am almost certain, that your tenderness, properly exerted towards her, will restore, both her health, and happiness.—I dare not trust myself with a doubt, of your conduct, upon this occasion.

I think nothing can be plainer, than her knowledge of your attachment to the marchioness.—Her positive refusal of going to France, marks it, too strongly. Woodville, I fear—but I will not reproach you—your own generous heart must sting you, too severely.

I have, this moment, received a letter, from captain Beaumont.—Madame de Carignon's disorder appears to be the small pox; and as she is pretty far advanced in her pregnancy, they think her life in danger. What has been gained, by making her fly from that disease, a few months ago!

But I have not time, now, to moralize. I shall send off a physician, immediately, and shall follow him, myself, in a few hours; my Charlotte must want consolation, and is, at the same time, the only person capable of administering it, to her unhappy father.

Yours, ever.

SEYMOUR.

P.S. I should give you credit, for not mentioning the marchioness, in your letter, if I had not often heard that ladies, and lovers, generally postpone their most material business, to their postscripts. Be that, as it may, I can only tell you that the marchioness, and her *Caro Sposo*,[54] are in this town; but where, I know not. Captain Barnard and lady Ransford are also here.

# LETTER 68.

## *Lord* WOODVILLE, *To Lord* SEYMOUR.

Dear SEYMOUR,

Lady Woodville is much better—Sir John and lady Straffon, lord and lady Mount Willis, have been here, this fortnight.—The polite chearfulness of their society, has, I believe, been of infinite service to Emily; but I still flatter myself, that my attention, and tenderness, have contributed more to her recovery, than any thing else.

I have now the real happiness to think, that every apprehension of her mind, is intirely removed; I can, therefore, scarcely doubt, but that health and peace will return, together; for I am but too clearly convinced, that the privation of the latter, occasioned the loss of the former.

There certainly never was a more amiable creature, than lady Woodville—so gentle, so unassuming, in her manners, so fearful of giving pain, that she would, if possible, conceal her complaints, even from her domestics, who all adore her.

Is it not amazing, Seymour, that perfectly sensible, as I am, of her uncommon merits, there should be found a being, upon earth, who holds a higher place, in my affection? How falsely do they flatter our understandings, who say that esteem is the basis of love! If that were true, I should be the happiest of men, should think no more of the ungrateful Isabelle, should no longer feel the reproaches of a wayward heart, which would then be intirely devoted, to the charming Emily.

But though I may never be able, intirely, to eradicate this fatal disease from my mind, I have great pleasure in perceiving, that the constant exertion of my tenderness, towards Emily, is attended with the sincerest delight, to myself; as it fulfills a duty, and flatters my humanity with the idea of conferring happiness, upon an amiable and deserving object.

The practice of any virtue, is not so difficult, as we are apt to imagine.—There requires nothing more, than resolution to commence.—Habit will soon make it easy, if not pleasant, to us.—Yet still must I envy those, who have no need to struggle; and when I behold the ingenuous fondness of lord Mount Willis, and Sir John Straffon, to their wives, I curse my fate, and despise my own weakness, for having reduced me to the contemptible necessity of feigning, what they are happy enough to feel.

We are to return the visits of our present guests, in our way to Bristol.—Lord Mount Willis has a very fine seat, in Somersetshire.—He is a very agreeable, accomplished man. His wife, before her marriage, loved Sir James Miller—passionately loved him—and yet, she has withdrawn her ill-placed fondness, and doats upon her lord. Shall I be weaker, than a puny girl? and shall the voice of reason, always plead in vain? I dare not reply to these mortifying queries.

I most sincerely pity the unhappy general de Beaumont; his misfortunes have been multiplied on him, at a time when he is least able to encounter them. There is a spring in youth, which makes us capable of resisting almost any pressure; but when a body, which has been nursed in the soft lap of prosperity, becomes enfeebled by years, the mind also partakes of its enervation; and we have still less reason to expect a vigorous exertion, of the mental powers, than of muscular strength, at threescore.

The wisdom, therefore, that is, in general, attributed to age, arises more from a privation of passion, than from experience, or any other cause. As the nerves grow rigid, the heart is, insensibly, rendered callous. The exquisite sensations, both of pain, and pleasure, after a certain time of life, are imperceptibly blunted, by each returning day; and we, at last, become solely indebted to memory, for informing us, that we were ever capable of feeling the extremes of joy, or sorrow.

The only passion, which nature seems to design should remain in its full force, in our declining age, is parental affection; and as the others subside, I should imagine that gains strength.—There is a mixture, too, of self-love, in it, which generally makes its existence equal with our own. The objects of this affection, are gradually maturing, under our fostering care; each day, they make some advances, towards our idea of perfection, a likeness to ourselves; with anxious hopes we watch the tender bud, look with delight upon the opening blossom, and gaze enraptured on the blooming fruit!—It is our own, we planted, and we reared it! In this most tender point, then, the poor old general is now wounded; his armour and his breast-plate thrown aside, the barbed arrow sinks into his heart.

Should madame de Carignon die, which I hope she will not, there are abundance of good christians, who would, immediately, conclude her death to be a judgment on him, for his inhuman treatment of Charlotte. But I, who confess myself a sinner, have not a doubt of his having already atoned his passive guilt, towards her, by his contrition.—You are the single person, who appear to be injured by it,—for I am fully satisfied, that Charlotte is, no longer, unhappy.

I have philosophized and moralized upon this subject, to the extent of my time and paper, perhaps to prevent my entering again, upon another, on which I am neither philosopher, nor moralist.—I shall, therefore, fly from it, by bidding you,

Adieu.

WOODVILLE.

# LETTER 69.

## *Lord* SEYMOUR, *To Lord* WOODVILLE.

Dear WOODVILLE,

Madame de Carignon is recovered, if it can be called a recovery, for a fine young woman to survive her beauty.—That is, indeed, absolutely destroyed; but, as her husband's fondness seems unabated by the loss, her homeliness may possibly become an advantage, rather than a misfortune.—Few, very few women, or men either, have strength of mind, sufficient, to bear universal admiration; and when that is derived from beauty alone, there is scarce a young person who thinks it necessary, to attain any other qualification, or accomplishment, that does not tend to the embellishment of their charms.

I have observed, through life, that we seldom meet with an agreeable man, or woman, who have been remarkably handsome. But, perhaps, this may be philosophically accounted for.—As Providence acts by the simplest means, and beauty is alone sufficient, to procure the love and admiration of mankind, great qualities would be unnecessary to the purpose, and perhaps mar the original design; for we should be more apt to fear, than love, *a human being,* that we considered as absolutely perfect.

I, therefore, think, with Milton, that where there is

> bestowed
> Too much of ornament, in outward shew
> Elaborate, the inward's less exact—[55]

which may be a kind of consolation to those, whom nature has dealt her personal favours to, with a scanty hand.

In the country where I am, at present, neither youth or beauty are of much value. The grandmother and grand-daughter are, pretty near, upon the same footing.—What little difference there may be, is, generally, in the dowager's favour; as she may, probably, be possessed of more knowledge and experience, and a better fortune.—No woman is ever young, or old, at Paris; for the same paint, that fills up the furrows, of the aged cheek, hides the soft down, upon the youthful one.

You see that a word to the wise, is enough, and that I have followed your plan of philosophizing, upon indifferent subjects, to avoid recurring to painful ones.—I must, however, acquaint you, that I am to attend Charlotte, to Paris, in three days. She has insisted on my returning to England, as soon as she enters the cloister; and I have consented, on her promising to meet me here, next spring, provided the general be then living.

The poor old man has insisted on captain Beaumont's quitting the army, and taking possession of his fortune, except a small annuity, which he reserves for charitable uses. He has behaved nobly, to monsieur and madame de Carignon, and presented twenty thousand crowns to the convent of St. Anthony, as a reward for their kindness to his beloved Charlotte. You would pity him, sincerely, if you were to behold his distress, at the idea of parting with his favourite child; but

What are, alas! his woes, compared to mine!

Adieu, my friend; if I were capable of joy, I should feel it for lady Woodville's recovery. I shall write to you, from Paris; and am,

Ever your's,

SEYMOUR.

## LETTER 70.

### *Lord* SEYMOUR, *To Lord* WOODVILLE.

Paris.

I have, once more, bid adieu, to my dear Charlotte.—But painful as the hour of separation, was, the recollection of what I had formerly endured, from her entrance into the convent, with the fond hope of our re-meeting, in a few months, have abated its anguish; and some very extraordinary accidents, which have happened, within these few hours, have taken up my whole attention, and carried me, as it were, out of myself.

The count de Clerembaut, for whom you know I have a sincere friendship, came to see me, yesterday morning.—He told me he was just come from the tennis court, where there had been a very warm *brouillerie*[56] between two English gentlemen. One of their names, he said, was Ransford, who had quitted the field to his antagonist, but with a look, and manner, that seemed to say, he was determined to meet him, elsewhere.

I was alarmed, at this account, and immediately ordered my chariot, and drove to the marchioness's.—Ransford was not at home.—I came back to my hôtel, and wrote to him; expatiated on the ill consequences of fighting a duel, in Paris; begged him to defer his resentments, till his opponent, whom I understood to be an Englishman, and he, should meet in their own country; but, if he should be so circumstanced, as to be under a necessity of rejecting my advice, I hoped he would, at least, accept of my service, to attend him to the field, or command me, in whatever way he thought proper.

In about three hours, I received the following answer.

### *To Lord* Seymour.

My dear Lord,

I am truly thankful, for your kind attention to me; but I am, at present, too far embarked, to recede; and even your admonition must, therefore, come too late. Let the consequence be what it will, I cannot think of heightening my distress, by involving you, in it. But I have a much more material act of friendship, to implore from you.—The marchioness will stand in need of your protection.—I need say no more—hasten to her; the affair will be over, before you receive this. I have the satisfaction to think that captain Barnard deserves his fate, if he should fall, by my hand, as he has, this day, added fresh insult, to former injury.

Adieu, perhaps, for ever.

William Ransford.

I instantly ran, or rather flew, to the marchioness, whom I found waiting dinner for Mr. Ransford.—She seemed surprized, at my entrance, as she had heard that I had been there, in the morning.—The anxiety of my countenance, became contagious; and she inquired, with the greatest earnestness, if I knew any thing, about Mr. Ransford? before I could frame a reply, the lieutenant de Police was on the stairs, and I rushed out of the room, to prevent his coming into it. He passed me by, and entered.—She did not appear to be alarmed.

It seems there is a law-suit, between her, and her late husband's heir, for a part of her jointure;[57] and she, I suppose, concluded, that he came to execute some order of court, relative to that affair. But long before he could fully explain the real motives of his coming, she ceased to hear, and had sunk, motionless, upon the sofa where she sat.

Barnard is dead, and Ransford, by this time, I hope, out of the French dominions. My heart bleeds for the gentle lady Harriet, for Ransford, for the marchioness.—It has not now, one pang to spare, to its own miseries.

The lieutenant, and his myrmidons, took possession of every thing, *au nom du roi*,[58] and assured us that diligent search would be made, for the murderer. I intreated him to leave the unhappy lady's apartment, to herself, and that I would be answerable, for every thing in it. He retired, with infinite politeness, which is the best substitute to humanity: and, in this country, which abounds with shew and delusion, is frequently mistaken for it.

As the marchioness is five months gone with child, it was thought proper to have her blooded.—Every possible care has been, and shall be, taken of her. She is distressingly grateful, for my small attentions toward her. But a mind, subdued by affliction, is apt to over-rate every little mark of kindness.

I staid with her, till eleven at night, and then left her fully determined to follow Mr. Ransford, the moment she was informed of his retreat. He cannot, possibly, think of returning to England, which, I own, does not displease me.—I can wish happiness to the marchioness and him, in any other country.

This unhappy affair will detain me here, for some time longer.—I will not quit the post of guardian to the afflicted fair, till I resign her into Ransford's hands. You shall hear, daily, from me.

Adieu.

SEYMOUR.

## LETTER 71.

### *Lord* SEYMOUR, *To Lord* WOODVILLE.

Yesterday passed away, in forming melancholy conjectures, on the recent cause of quarrel, between captain Barnard, and Mr. Ransford; in indeterminate ideas, whither he would bend his course, and in listening to various reports, which were variously repeated, by the friends, acquaintance, and servants, of the unhappy combatants.

We had, however, the satisfaction to discover, that Ransford had made some provision for his escape, as he had converted above three hundred pounds, into post bills,[59] the morning of the duel, and had ordered a Swiss servant, who has lived with him, for five years, and is remarkably attached to him, to attend, at a particular place, with a couple of the fleetest horses, he could hire, or purchase. From hence, I conclude he will travel to Switzerland, and take up his abode, at Berne, till he can return with honour and safety, into England.

You will, perhaps, say, why at that particular place, more than any other? I grant the idea is formed upon a vague conjecture; but André was born at Berne, and the Swiss are of all nations, the Scotch not excepted, the most smitten with the love of their country. Ransford's mind must be unhinged by this sad accident, torn from its props, and ready to recline itself on the first friendly stay, that will support it. The honest Swiss looks back, with transport, on those barren hills, where first his mind found joy, his body strength; and leads his master there, to share the gifts which he received from nature, and the soil. I say he will not stop, till he arrives at Berne.

The marchioness does not agree with my opinion; she thinks Brussels, Holland, Italy, nay England, more agreeable. That is, she could like to fix her residence, in any of those places, rather than at Berne.—They are all equal to me, except England, where I am pretty sure he will not go.

There were two sealed letters found in captain Barnard's pocket, the one addressed to lady Ransford, the other to the man who killed him. I will wait upon her ladyship, to morrow, to obtain the latter; it must certainly throw some extraordinary light, upon the affair.

I had written so far, when I received a summons from the marchioness, to attend her, instantly. A thousand apprehensions crouded on my mind; I feared Ransford might not have escaped, and I knew the vindictive spirit of his step-mother, too well, to hope that she would not prosecute. I found the marchioness in a state little short of madness—her expressions were such as made me rather fear, than feel—her eyes darted fire, and she traversed the circumference of her dressing room, with the air and pace of distraction: she seemed to be unsexed.

Where is he, madam? said I. Let me fly to him, and try what gold can do, to purchase his enlargement. This must be our only resource? let them take it all, said she, but let me go—a *lettre de cachet!*[60] no monarch, nor no minister dare sign it—I will fly to Versailles[61]—it is already granted, and you see me a prisoner, at this moment—dare you rescue me?

Amazement took away the power of speech; I did not understand her, it was impossible I should.—At that instant, a person of a very gentleman-like and engaging appearance, entered the chamber.—He seemed to be astonished at her beauty, and perturbation, and gazed, for an instant, first at her, and then at me—at last, seeming to recollect himself, he addressed me, in the following words.

I am sorry your indiscretion has permitted our meeting, Sir.—It is true I have received no particular information against you; you are, therefore, at liberty to depart; which I beg you will do, instantly, as you cannot be safe, in this house, a single moment.

I immediately perceived he had mistaken me for Mr. Ransford, and readily accepting all the good will he had shewn to my friend's unhappy situation, returned him thanks for his intended humanity, and assured him of my gratitude, for a favour, which I did not stand in need of. He blushed at his mistake, and said that he had been twelve years in office, and had never exceeded his commission, but in that way. Strange, that a man should blush, that had been, twelve years, in such an office!

He then explained his business.—He had a *lettre de cachet*, against madame, which the marquis de St. Aumont, her husband's nephew, had obtained, to prevent her quitting the kingdom, till the suit between them, should be determined.

Her rage is not to be described; she accused the laws of injustice, and its officers of insolence, and cruelty. Asked to what prison a peeress should be led, and whether she was to be handcuffed, like a malefactor? to all this intemperate language, the officer replied with great calmness, that her ladyship might put an end to her distress, by giving security to the court, for her stay in Paris. She told him she would not stay, for all the courts in Europe. He then said something, in a low voice, about her being confined.

She had sent for her lawyer, who arrived critically, and prevailed, on her, at last, to pass her word, jointly with us, that she would not quit Paris, without leave of the court, which he said he would apply for, the next day.

The agitation of her spirits, now subsiding, she fell into violent passions of tears; bewailed her fate, and said she was the most wretched of human beings. I fear she has more reason to think so, than she is yet acquainted with. For after she withdrew to her chamber, her lawyer, at my request, explained the nature of the process against her, and assured me that the late marquis de St. Aumont, had no power over those lands, which he settled on her for a jointure; that he was, therefore, very glad to find she was married to an English gentleman of fortune, as he had great reason to believe, the cause would go against her.—That he feared she was extremely in debt, and that all her personalities[62] were already forfeited to the crown, as being the supposed property of Mr. Ransford. What a scene of distress, Woodville! and what will become of this unhappy pair?

Before I left the house, the marchioness sent for her lawyer, into her chamber.—I took that opportunity of retiring to write to you, and shall now close this melancholy narrative, with wishing you good night.

SEYMOUR.

## LETTER 72.

### Lord SEYMOUR, *To Lord* WOODVILLE.

Dear WOODVILLE,

Both my mind and body are so extremely harrassed, that I am scarce able to give you an account of the distresses, in which I am involved.

Just as I had sealed my last letter to you, I received a billet from captain Beaumont, to inform me, that the general, and he, were, that moment, arrived at Paris, and that their coming was occasioned by a very alarming account they had received, of my ever-dear Charlotte's being extremely indisposed.

I flew, directly, to the general's house, and found the poor old man sinking under the double weight, of years, and sorrow. He shewed me the abbess's letter to him, which said, "that from the time of Charlotte's return into the convent, a fever had preyed upon her spirits; that she had concealed her illness, for several days, and even made light of it, when it was too visible; that she was now reduced to such a state of weakness, that the physicians had declared medicine could be of no use to her, and that an immediate change of air, was the only chance she had for life."

No words can express what I felt, on reading this sad letter; yet will I candidly confess, that her father's anguish seemed to surpass even mine. He called himself her murderer! and said if she should die, he never could have hopes of mercy, or salvation.—Alas! am I not guilty, as himself! My fatal rashness made her take those vows, which her fond love for me, in any other case, would have rejected!

The general determined to remove Charlotte out of the convent, the next day, and convey her as far out of Paris, as her strength would permit. He intreated me to accompany them, in their melancholy and slow progress to Belleveüe. Judge of my distress, at being obliged to refuse! But my honour was passed to a wretch, who has none—the marchioness.—Captain Beaumont promised to bring me a faithful account of his sister's situation, in the morning, and I retired home—not to rest.

Captain Beaumont was punctual to his word; he came to me, before eight o'clock, and told me that his father and he had seen Charlotte, and found her in a very weak state; that she had consented to set out with them, for Belleveüe, but that he did not believe they should be able to carry her farther than three or four leagues, that day, and intreated me to go with them. I readily consented, and determined that I would return to Paris, that night, as soon as ever Charlotte should retire to bed.

The captain and I agreed to meet, at the general's house, at eleven o'-clock, to follow our fair fugitive, who was to set out with her father, from the convent. He told me that Charlotte had made a thousand tender inquiries, about my health; that she rejoiced at my being still in Paris, and seemed delighted at the thought of seeing me, that day. I needed not these new proofs of her regard, to increase my ardour for her; my soul was on the wing to meet her, yet still the claims of friendship, were not unheard.

I resolved to go, immediately, to lady Ransford, for the letter that was addressed to her step-son, and found in Barnard's pocket. Then, to wait on *the marchioness,* and make my excuse, for absenting myself from her, the remainder of that day: but though *she* had left Paris, it was fated, that I should not quit it, for some time.

As I was coming out of my apartment, I was met by the lieutenant de police, who arrested me as an accomplice with the marchioness, in having defrauded his majesty, by conveying away her most valuable effects, which were confiscated to his use, and having fled herself, though under an *arrêt.*[63]—Never was astonishment greater than mine.

In vain I pleaded my ignorance of the fact, or the innocence of my intentions, or offered to give ample security, for those effects, which had been secreted by that mean, that worthless woman! The officer told me he was not quite such an idiot, as the person who had taken my word before, and that no argument I could urge, would have the least weight with him.

As the last, and most prevailing rhetoric, I offered him my purse, if he would go with me to general Beaumont's, and take his bail, for my appearance, the next day; but he withstood my gold, and even refused to let me return into my apartment, to write an apology for not attending my beloved Charlotte.

This was the first time, I had ever felt "the insolence of office."[64]—I submitted to it, though reluctantly, and was immediately conveyed to the Châtelet.[65]—I sent off a servant to captain Beaumont, to desire him to come to me; but as soon as I was lodged in prison, I was informed that no person would be admitted to see me, as they considered me as a delinquent of state.

I then demanded to be confronted with my accusers, and brought before a judge. They smiled at my ignorance, and told me, that as I was not in England, I must submit to their laws, which were not quite so expeditious as ours, and that patience would be my best resource, for the present.

Though my temper is naturally gentle, and my passions have been long subdued by affliction, it was with difficulty I could command my rage—yet on whom should I vent it? on wretches, brazed[66] by custom, to the wild ravings of resentment, or the soft plaints of sorrow!

As soon as I was capable of reasoning with myself, I considered that a consciousness of my own integrity, ought to support me, under the disagreeable circumstances I was involved in, by another's fault; and am certain it would have done so, had I not been disappointed of the painful pleasure, of seeing the lovely, languid Charlotte! I lamented the uneasiness, which she must feel, from hearing of my confinement, unknowing of the cause; and the apprehension of her thinking me guilty of some criminal action, and her suffering from that thought, almost distracted me. I cursed the marchioness, a thousand times—Yes, Woodville, from my heart I cursed her. Bane of your happiness! disturber, now, of mine!

When I grew a little calm, I desired to see the keeper of the prison, as I wanted to know whether I was at liberty to write to the English ambassador, who I knew was then at Versailles, and to the rest of my friends. The governor du Châtelet, was immediately annonced, and on his entering, my eye was struck, with the most graceful figure, and engaging countenance, I had ever seen. He seemed to be turned of fifty, but had such a softness of features, and complexion, as is rarely to be met with, but in extreme youth. His appearance filled me with surprize; I was amazed that such a man should be capable of accepting such an office, which I supposed could only be suited to the most insensible, or brutal natures.

His conversation was as pleasing, as his person; he readily assented to my request, and said he would take care that my letters should be delivered. He then gave orders that my own servants should be permitted to attend me, and that any person whom I desired to see, should be immediately admitted. I thanked him for his humanity, in removing every unnecessary restraint, and assured him I should make no other use of his indulgence, than that of indeavouring to procure my liberty, by the most legal means.

He encreased my astonishment, by replying to me, in English, that he could not have any doubts of lord Seymour's honour; and that he hoped I would do him and his family the favour to dine with them, and allow them as much of my company, as was convenient to me, while I remained in the Châtelet.

My curiosity to know something more of him and his family, made me accept his invitation; though heaven knows how little inclined to mix with strangers, or enter into any plan of dissipation. I have written to the ambassador, and to my dear Charlotte. By removing her anxiety, I have lessened my own.

I am not apprehensive that my confinement can last, many hours; I will therefore endeavour to keep up my spirits, with the fond hope of flying to my Charlotte, the moment I am released. In the mean time, I attend the governor's summons to dinner, and, for the present, bid my dear Woodville
   Adieu, your's.

SEYMOUR.

P.S. What is the reason, that I do not hear from you? whilst at liberty, I regretted, but, in my confinement, shall lament, your silence. My affectionate compliments to lady Woodville.

## LETTER 73.

### *Lord* SEYMOUR, *To Lord* WOODVILLE.

"Hope travels thro', nor quits us, till we die."[67]

And without that charming companion, I think I should not now survive to tell my dear Woodville, that I am just released from a confinement of fifteen tedious days. But let me be methodical in my relation.—No, it is impossible! my chariot waits to carry me to Belleveüe, to my adored Charlotte! She is better, I am happy, and

most sincerely yours.

SEYMOUR.

## LETTER 74.

### *Lord* SEYMOUR, *To Lord* WOODVILLE.

Belleveüe.

Charlotte recovers, daily; my fears for her precious life are abated. Your silence, now, alarms me.—Why must I never be free from apprehensions, for those I truly love? But I will, for the present, indulge your impatience, and restrain my own.

On the first day of my confinement, I was shewn into the governor's apartment, which was elegantly furnished, and received by him, and his lady, with the utmost politeness. She was surrounded by five beautiful children, the eldest, a girl about sixteen. I will confess it, Woodville! my eyes were insensibly rivetted to this young creature's lovely form; and for the first time of my life, *my heart* received delight, from gazing on the charms of another woman, besides Charlotte!

I did not long indulge the dangerous pleasure, without calling *the wanderer* to account, and soon perceived that the fair Maria's chief attraction was owing to her remarkable likeness to my Charlotte. This observation quieted my scruples, and left me the innocent satisfaction of admiring her beauty, with a brother's eye. Yet still my curiosity was increased, by the resemblance;

and as soon as I was left alone with the governor, I took the liberty of asking him, if he was related to general Beaumont?

He answered, no; but said his wife, was sister to the late madame de Beaumont, though much unlike her, both in mind, and person; that he could well allow madame D'Angueville inferior, in respect to beauty, but that her understanding and her heart were fraught with every charm, and virtue, that could adorn a woman.

I asked him, had he ever seen his niece, Charlotte Beaumont? he answered, with an honest warmth, yes, Sir, when it was too late, to make her happy, or reward your merit—would to heaven I had known her sooner! I bowed, and thanked him, even for fruitless wishes, and, for a time, forgot my being a prisoner, from the delight I felt, at being with one, who knew, and loved my Charlotte.

We became totally unreserved; and the governor informed me, that he was of the N—— family, descended from one of those infatuated men,[68] who had sacrificed their fortunes, and renounced their country, to serve a weak, and worthless prince, who had neither inclination, or power, to reward their attachment.

He told me, that his father had died of a broken heart, while he was but a child; that his friends had, with difficulty, obtained him a commission, in the Irish brigade, where he had served, above twenty years, without arriving to the rank of captain; and that he might still have remained, in that situation, but that general Beaumont, by his interest, had procured him the post, he then enjoyed, when he and his family had been reduced to the greatest distress.

That he hoped he had acquitted himself in his office, with humanity, and compassion; and by many circumstances which he related, convinced me, that none, but a person of a noble, and generous nature, was fit to preside over the number of unfortunates, that guilt or accident impels to that gloomy mansion. Sad reflection! that those, who are fittest for that charge, are most averse to accept, and least thought of, for the office.

About seven o'clock, in the evening, captain Beaumont inquired for me, and was immediately admitted. His uncle, monsieur D'Angueville, had never seen him, before.—They were mutually charmed with each other. The captain told me that as soon as my servant had acquainted him with my situation, he wrote a line to the general, to inform him of it, and set out, on the instant, for Versailles; that he had seen the English ambassador, who promised to wait on monsieur le duc de N——, the premier minister, next morning, and obtain my release, as soon as possible.

I thanked my generous friend, for his kind attention to my interests, and passed the evening with tolerable chearfulness. The next day, about noon, I received a visit, from Mr. S—— secretary to our ambassador. He told me that his excellency had been with the minister, and desired that I might be set at liberty, immediately. That the duc de N—— had informed him it was impossible to comply with his request, as there was a criminal process instituted against me, for aiding and abetting the marchioness de St. Aumont, in open violation of the laws; and the only favour, that could be indulged me, was the allowing me counsel, and bringing the affair to a trial, with the utmost expedition.

I endeavoured to make a virtue of necessity, and affected to appear contented, with the very small favour that his excellency had obtained for me. But not to make the repetition of my confinement, as tedious to you, as the time was to me, the day of trial came, and by the joint testimony of the marchioness's lawyer, her servants, and my own, I was acquitted of being concerned in her escape, but obliged to give bail, for four thousand pounds, which is the value set upon the jewels, plate, &c. which she either carried off, or secreted.

Thus have I been injured, in my honour, person, and property, by my humane attention to that most worthless of humankind. But, no matter; and if the meanness of her conduct towards me, sets her in the light, in which I wish you to behold her, I shall think myself overpaid, for every injury I have sustained, on her account.

The moment I recovered my liberty, I waited on the ambassador, who had come to Paris, on purpose, to know if he could be any way serviceable to me. I made my acknowledgments to him, and set out, that evening, with my dear, and indefatigable friend, captain Beaumont, for the loved place where my heart's treasure lay. I have already told you that I had the happiness of finding her much better; and the joy, which she felt, at seeing her brother, and me, has, I flatter myself, contributed to her recovery.

The marchioness's lawyer told me he had received a letter from her, dated Brussels, wherein she exulted, at her own cleverness, in getting out of the power of the laws, and gave some dark hints, of her not being married to Ransford. Heaven grant this may be true! The suit with her husband's nephew, will certainly go against her; and for her contempt of the *arrêt,* she will be outlawed, and her whole fortune confiscated;—so that if, as I hope, she is not Ransford's wife, she may possibly be reduced to her original poverty, and meet the contempt due to her vices, from all mankind.

This is the fifth letter I have written to you, without receiving a line from you. I have certainly reason to apprehend that some fatal accident has occasioned your silence, for I can never doubt the sincerity of your attachment, to yours,

Most truly,

SEYMOUR.

## LETTER 75.

### *Lady* WOODVILLE, *To Lady* STRAFFON.

Pity me! pray for me, my dearest sister! for heaven but mocks my prayers! had they been heard, lord Woodville's life had never been in danger. I am distracted, Fanny! O no! I would I were. Though anguish, such as mine, strains every sense, and racks my tortured brain, it will not crack! No, I am still awake to all the miseries, a wretch can feel, who doats, and who despairs!

On Tuesday se'ennight, fatal day! my lord received a letter from lord Seymour, while I was present. I observed that he was strongly agitated, while he read it, even to a change of countenance, and colour. I thought there must be some extraordinary cause for his emotion, which perhaps he wished to conceal from me; I, therefore, rose, softly from my seat, and attempted to retire.

O, Fanny! can I ever forget the look of sorrow, which he wore, when taking me by the hand, he said, you must not leave me, Emily! but share a painful office with your lord.—You must endeavour to console poor lady Harriet, for Barnard's death; Ransford has killed him, and is fled from Paris.

He then turned quick away, as if to hide his grief. It could not be for Barnard that he wept; and Ransford, he, as well as I, believed was safe.—O, there is another cause! let me not think of it, lest it divide my tears, which should all flow for him, not for my worthless self.

He told me he would go directly, to Sir Harry Ransford, to acquaint him with his son's misfortune, and as he could not do it abruptly, said it was possible he might stay to dinner there, and begged I would take the most immediate opportunity of informing lady Harriet, of this unhappy affair. His horses were immediately ordered, and he rode off.

I sent for Fanny Weston, to assist me in the painful task I had undertaken. But why do I waste a moment in thinking of any object upon earth, but one? About two hours after my lord left Woodfort, one of the servants, who had attended him, gallopped into the court yard, ordered the chariot to be got ready, instantly, and bid my woman tell me, that my lord, had fallen from his horse, and was much hurt.

I was sitting in lady Harriet's dressing room, when the sound of the chariot passing hastily under the window, alarmed me.—I rang to know the cause, when a servant, pale as death, told me that my lord had met with a sad accident. I cried, where is he? and rushed out of the room. I was met by my woman, on the stairs. Lady Harriet, Fanny Weston, and she, prevented my running into the high way; they poured drops, and water, down my throat. I knew not what they did, or said to me.

An express was sent off, for a surgeon, who arrived, in less than half an hour after my lord was brought home senseless. They would not suffer me to see him, till he had been bled, and his wounds dressed.—But, gracious heaven, when I beheld him!

Let me try to banish the sad idea—Alas! I fear it will never be effaced! never, my sister! never, unless I live to see his natural form restored to my fond wishes, and my ardent prayers!—Oh, join with me, my Fanny! in earnest supplication, for his precious life!

The humane, the tender-hearted surgeon, said every thing that could amuse, but not dispel, my fears. That his wounds, though dangerous, in his poor judgment, were not mortal; but that he wished for better help, than his own.

An express was dispatched for Middleton, or Ranby.

I cannot, but I would not, if I could, describe the night I passed—my lord remained quite senseless; enviable state! yet, now-and-then, his languid eyes seemed fixed on me. About five in the morning, he fell into a kind of dose, and remained in that situation, till near seven, when he awoke in the most violent delirium—he raved, incessantly—*but not of me.*

In this most melancholy state has he continued, eleven days—"a burning fever, and a broken heart!" O Fanny, it is too much! but should he recover it, I never shall.

Mr. Ranby, and the surgeon, who first attended my dear lord, have both assured me, that the hurt which he received from his fall, could not endanger his life. But neither they, nor the physicians, who visit him daily, can pretend to say what turn his fever will take. Strong opiates have been given, and, at length, have taken effect; he sleeps, my Fanny! while I, who have never closed my eyes, since this sad accident, indulge them now in their once pleasing task, of writing to my friend, my more than sister! grief weighs my eye-lids down, but not with the soft pressure of an healthful slumber.

Adieu, adieu, my Fanny!

E. WOODVILLE.

## LETTER 76.

### *Lady* STRAFFON, *To Lady* WOODVILLE.

Let not my dearest Emily condemn her sincerely affectionate, and afflicted Fanny, for not having instantly replied, in person, to her most affecting letter.

O, my Emily! my child! my sister! how does my heart bleed, for you! tears dim my sight, and yet perhaps your eyes are dry! the burning balls fixed on your dying lord! would you could weep, as I do.

As my spirits have been rather weak, and languid, since my lying in, even while I was at Woodfort, lady Mount Willis, whose attention and tenderness to me, is without bounds, prevailed upon Sir John and me, to pass a few weeks with her, at a house which my lord has hired, near Windsor, while his family seat is repairing. The old topics, of change of air, and moderate exercise, were exhausted, both by Sir John, and her, before I would consent.

At length, I most reluctantly complied. I knew not then, why I should feel reluctance; but I now begin to think with you, that our presages should be listened to—Would I had hearkened then, to mine! I should now, be with my dearest Emily, and by sharing her anguish, and fatigue, perhaps, in some degree, might lessen both—but we now must feel the sad addition to our present miseries, of knowing that each other is unhappy.

About two hours before the post brought your letter to Windsor, lord Mount Willis and Sir John, set out for his lordship's seat in Oxfordshire; and while Lucy and I were sitting, at breakfast, after they were gone, we heard a violent scream—I knew the voice to be my little Emily's—I ran up stairs to her chamber, without recollecting that she had been some time dressed, and playing with the house-keeper's daughter, a child of her own age, in the garden.

Lady Mount Willis followed the sound, and found my poor little angel lying on the ground, with her right leg broken—the only words she spoke, were, "Do not let my mama be frighted," and fainted quite away.

In this condition, she was brought into the house; I will not attempt to describe mine. Your situation is by far more dreadful, yet sure it was a scene of deep distress. Suffice it now to say, that the very moment she is out of danger, I will fly to share, or alleviate, my dearest Emily's affliction. The fond, the tender claims, of child, and sister, now divide my heart—it almost breaks that I must say,
  Adieu.

F. Straffon.

## Letter 77.

### Lady Woodville, To Lady Straffon.

My dearest Fanny,

  This is the one-and-twentieth day, of my lord's illness; and on this day, be it for ever blessed, by me! the physicians have observed a change in his disorder, attended with many favourable symptoms, that give hopes of life. He lay, for many days, in a state of insensibility, had ceased to rave, and hardly moved his limbs.

  At eleven o'clock, this morning, he sighed, extremely; O Fanny! those sad sighs too long have pierced my heart! then seemed to wake, as from a trance. The first object he took notice of, was me, and with a languid voice, he said, my Emily, have you sat up, all night? O, go to bed, my love. Then closed his eyes, and fell into a little slumber.

I could not answer him, tears came to my relief, and drowned my utterance. Yes, Fanny, I have wept, most bitterly, and my poor heart is much relieved. Doctor Fenton insists on bleeding me, immediately. I know he thinks that I have caught the fever, from my lord; blessed contagion! may it not, Fanny, lighten his disease? would I not die, to lessen, or remove, his heart-felt pains! but I much fear that even my death would not, now, heal his griefs.—She is another's; and never can be his.—I fear I rave, my thoughts are wild; I do not wish that you should comprehend them.

Your poor, dear Emily! I hope she will recover.—A broken limb is dreadful! but a broken heart far worse! They snatch away the pen. Well! well! I will be blooded. Aye, and I will go to bed; my limbs no longer can support my weight.

Farewel, my Fanny.

E.W.

## LETTER 78.

### *Miss* WESTON, *To Lady* STRAFFON.

My dear Lady STRAFFON.

I know not how to acquaint you with the additional misfortune, that is fallen upon us all. Our dear lady Woodville lies dangerously ill, of a fever. My heart almost breaks while I tell you, that the physicians have but little hopes of her life. During the first one-and-twenty days, of her lord's illness, she never left his chamber, nor could even be prevailed upon to rest herself, except for a few minutes, when quite exhausted, on a couch.

What surprized lady Harriet, and me, most, was, that she never shed a tear, till lord Woodville first recovered his reason, and spoke to her. The servants who attended in his chamber, have told me, that while he remained insensible, she used, frequently, to lay her cheek upon his pillow, and kiss his poor parched lips, as if she wished to catch the fever from him. O, madam! why were you not here, to save her precious life?

Lady Harriet and I have been so much used to look up to her, with respect, as well as love (and sure no human being ever deserved them, more) that we could not attempt to oppose her resolution, farther than by fruitless intreaties, though we knew it must be hurtful, to herself. Lady Lawson was, unfortunately, gone upon a visit, into Lincolnshire, two days before my lord Woodville's accident; she returned, yesterday, and is almost distracted, at lady Woodville's illness. But what is hers, or any other persons grief, to what my lord endures? no words can describe his sorrow; and I am convinced, if she should die, he never will recover.

He insisted on being taken out of bed, this day, and carried to her chamber. Doctor Fenton finding him peremptory, consented, though reluctantly. Good God! what a pale, and emaciated figure! Lady Woodville, at first, did not know him; but when he spoke to her, she started up, clasped her arms round his neck, and cried out, with unnatural strength! My dearest lord! this, this is kind! she shall not part us, now! yes, we will go together; indeed I will not stay, for any thing on earth; no not for *little Harry!*

Her spirits became quite exhausted, at these words; and she sunk down in a flood of tears. We thought lord Woodville would have expired, on the instant. He fainted, and was carried back to his chamber, in that situation. This was the first time that lady Woodville had mentioned her *child,* since my lord's illness.

The Doctor thinks it a good symptom, and would have the little cherubim brought into her sight—but who can answer for the consequence, if he should catch the fever from her. At this moment, she sleeps, and lady Lawson is determined to make the experiment, as soon as she awakes.— God grant it may succeed!

I hope my little cousin has got the better of her sad accident, and that I shall not hear from, but see, you, as soon as possible. I send this, by a special messenger, and shall write, every day, till you come.

I am, dear lady Straffon,
Your afflicted, and affectionate,

F. Weston.

## LETTER 79.

### *Lady* STRAFFON, *To Miss* WESTON.

O Fanny! humbled in the dust, by the Almighty's chastening hand, I strive, in vain, to bow my heart to his all-wise decrees, and bless the arrow, that inflicts the wound!

How have I, vainly, vaunted my own fortitude, and thought it proof against the severest trials! Perhaps it is to show me my own weakness, that my loved sister, and my child, are doomed to suffer.—I fear there is impiety, in that thought. Gracious heaven, look down on my distraction! The first, the tenderest object of my youthful fondness, my Emily! my sister! given to my care by a much honoured, and a dying parent—for her I felt a mother's tenderness, a sister's love! Why were the ties thus doubly twined around my sad heart, if they must thus be broken! My daughter, too, child of my wedded love! dear to me, for her father's sake, as for my own—Both! both, my Emilys, at once! Sure I may dare to say, the infliction is severe!

Nothing can be more alarming, than your account of my dear sister's situation; I would fly to her, this moment, but that my poor little girl is, also, in a fever—my heart is torn to pieces, for the two dear sufferers; nor does lord Woodville want his share of my compassion.—Sinful, weak, and repining as I am, I will still look up to the throne of mercy, and hope for the recovery of these dear, dear friends! Write to me, Fanny, every hour, if possible: and, O! may your next bring comfort to

The truly afflicted,

F. STRAFFON.

P.S. Sir John returned here, this morning, and is almost distracted.

## LETTER 80.

### *Miss* WESTON, *To Lady* STRAFFON.

Dear Madam,

A ray of consolation beams upon us: lady Woodville's fever is abated; she raves no more. The disorder seems now to have fallen upon her nerves;

and her extreme weakness is, at present, the principal source of our apprehensions for her. When she awoke out of the slumber she was in, during my last letter, her recollection returned; she knew lady Lawson, and every person near her; but seemed particularly anxious to remember, what she had said to her lord; and expressed great uneasiness, at doctor Fenton's having suffered him to run the hazard of leaving his chamber.

Lady Lawson never quits her bed-side; and lady Harriet, who seems to have forgotten all her own distresses, hardly ever leaves my lord.—I am a sort of courier, between both; and, by flattering each, in my accounts of the other, hope to forward both their recoveries.—My lord expresses the strongest impatience, to see lady Woodville: doctor Fenton will not consent to their meeting, for some days; nor even suffer my lord's letters to be delivered to him. I am called to receive a visitor—who can it be, at this improper time?

What a flutter am I in? You would never guess who this guest was— Sir James Thornton! but so altered, as I never saw any creature! I began to fear he was married; though what is it to me, if he were? He has been poring his eyes out, at Geneva, ever since he left us; and looks as grave, and as wise, as an old professor of philosophy.

Do not be angry with me, for trifling, a little, my dear lady Straffon. I confess, I was very glad to see him; and as lord and lady Woodville have had, each of them, a tolerable night, I think I may be allowed this small indulgence. I have a presentiment, too, that my cousin Emily is better.—In short, every thing seems to wear a more chearful aspect, than it did, yesterday.

Poor Thornton was so much affected at his friend's illness, that the tears stood in his eyes; and he offered up an ejaculation, for their recovery, with almost as much devotion, as your ladyship could; though he is just come from a place, where, they say, religion is not much in fashion: but he is the best-natured creature breathing, and I am sure he prayed, from his heart.

He told me, that a vexatious law-suit had brought him to England, and that he meant to have returned to Geneva, without seeing lord Woodville, or any of his friends; but being informed of the situation of this family, he had come from London, on purpose, to make the most minute inquiries.

He begged I would not let lord, or lady Woodville know, that he had been here; said he would stay, a couple of days, at Sir William Lawson's, in hopes of hearing they were out of danger; then return to town, to pursue his law-suit; and as soon as that was over, he would go back to Geneva—but I shall use my best crow-quill,[69] to try to persuade him to visit Woodfort, once more, before he crosses the sea again; and if I succeed in that, I may, perhaps, try a little farther.

This is the last express that I shall send, as, I hope, by next post, to be able to give you a still more satisfactory account, of our dear, dear friends. Lady Woodville is very anxious, about her niece.—I tell her, I hope with truth, that the sweet little Emily is much better. I intreat you to confirm my assertion, in your next; and to believe me,

Most affectionately your's,

F. WESTON.

## LETTER 81.

### *Lady* STRAFFON, *To Miss* WESTON.

Dear FANNY,

The manner, more than the matter, of your last letter, has been a cordial to my heart. You could not surely write, in such a chearful strain, if our dear lady Woodville was in danger; and yet your account is, by no means, satisfactory; except where you say, that her reason is returned, and that she had a good night—your thoughts were diverted, to another object, and your letter is confused. Pray, be more explicit, in your next.

I am very happy, to be able to confirm your assertion, in favour of my child.—She is, thank God, much better, though still in a dangerous state, as the bone of her leg knits slowly, and she suffers much, but with the patience of an angel.—She has made me blush, at my own impatience; but though I may not be able to learn fortitude, from her example, I have, at least, acquired humility, from seeing that a natural mildness of disposition, can better enable us to support the accidental miseries of this life, than all our boasted reason, and philosophy.

I am ashamed of the intemperate lamentations I made use of, in my last letter; and I intreat you to burn it, if you have not already done so.

I shall continue to offer up my fervent prayers and wishes, for the recovery of my dear sister, and her lord; and am, dear Fanny,

Sincerely your's,

F. Straffon.

## Letter 82.

### *Miss* Weston, *To Lady* Straffon.

Upon my word, my dear lady Straffon, if I had not very good news to send you, and was not very good natured, I do not think I should write to you—how you huff[70] one, for being glad to see an old acquaintance. If I did not know that your ladyship is married, I should have thought your last letter had been written by an old maid: but I am so overjoyed, at being able to tell you that lady Woodville is infinitely better, that I cannot keep up my resentment against you, any longer.

Yes, I am sincerely glad, too, that the little Emily has verified my prediction, and recovers, daily.—Now, do not expect me to be methodical, for I will never be so; no, nor will I burn the letter you desire, for I really do not think there is any thing in it, that you need be ashamed of.

Our affections are not given us intirely for our amusement; they were certainly designed to make us feel our mutual dependance upon each other, and the total insufficiency of individuals, to create their own happiness. They are the links, which form society; and though, by being stretched, or broken, they may give us pain, I am certain we could have no pleasure, without them.

I think I have got off, of this subject, very well, considering that this is my first *coup d'essai*,[71] in the moralizing strain.—Now for particulars— Lady Woodville sat up, two hours, this day—She looks weak, and languid, but is, I really think, more beautiful than ever.

My lord wrote her a few lines, which I had the honour of presenting to her; she seemed transported with them, but, churl as she is, she did not let any body see them. The doctor would not permit her answering them, till to-morrow.—If she sends her letter by me, I shall be mightily tempted to peep—but I will not—for I should not like to be served so, myself; and I think that is the best way of determining all doubtful matters.

I saw Sir James Thornton, again, last night—You see I mention him, last, that you may not say he has diverted my thoughts from more interesting subjects. He persists in not having his visits annonced to lord, or lady Woodville. I have promised to keep his secret, and write to him by every post, till they are quite recovered. I shall begin my correspondence, this night; therefore,

Adieu, my dear lady Straffon.

F. WESTON.

## LETTER 83.

### Miss WESTON, *To Lady* STRAFFON.

Encore, my dear lady Straffon! do not you really think me very good-natured? but this is now the house of joy; and we, poor things, who have no character of our own, camelion-like, catch the hue of our next neighbour.—No letter from you, by last post—but, no matter.—I have a little familiar,[72] who tells me that Emily is better—thank you, good spirit, for the pleasing news—and now let me tell you, that lady Woodville is so much recovered, that doctor Fenton is to leave us, to-morrow.

I think I shall be sorry when he goes; he is a pure chatty man, and I have some reason to imagine, that he likes me, vastly. Whenever I happen to be sick, I will certainly send for him.

Well! matrimony is a fine thing, to be sure! and it is very hard, that I, who am so well inclined to enter into that holy state, cannot find an help-mate, meet for me. Though I have my doubts, whether there be many such husbands, as lord Woodville. I declare he appears to be infinitely more in love with his wife, than he ever was. Such tender attention, such unaffected fondness, I never beheld.—He is never out of her chamber, but when he is obliged to leave her to her repose, which seems now, to be perfectly uninterrupted.

Sir James Thornton is a better correspondent, than your ladyship.—I received a letter from him, in answer to mine, with some very pretty compliments interspersed through it, upon my easy manner of writing. Travelling, I find, has improved him; for I do not recollect that he ever said a civil thing to me, before he went abroad. *Better late, than never,* is a good proverb. Poor lady Harriet! her spirits are very low, though she has behaved surprizingly well, on Barnard's death; but I fear her calmness, on that occasion, was owing to the alarming situation, of lord and lady Woodville; and that her grief will return, with their health. I wish she would think of marrying—a good husband would make her forget Barnard. Dear, good Thornton! another letter from him, and more flattery! *quelle douceur! quel charme!* [73] Adieu, my dear lady Straffon, I must indulge my vanity, this very moment, by shewing his epistle to lord, and lady Woodville.

Your's, ever.

F. WESTON.

## LETTER 84.

### *Lady* STRAFFON, *To Miss* WESTON.

Thank you, my good Fanny, for your two lively letters—they have been of infinite use to my poor weak spirits; and though I may not be able to compliment, as agreeably, as Sir James Thornton, I will venture to say that I am as well pleased, as he, with the ease, and chearfulness, of your writing. I hope my heart is truly grateful to the Almighty, for the recovery of my dear sister, and her lord, as well as for the restoration of my little Emily, whom we now think past danger.

You say, very justly, that "our affections were not given us, for amusement." No, Fanny! they were meant to humble the proud heart; to shew us our own weakness, and fallibility, by our frequently bestowing them, on unworthy, or improper objects; and even when directed by nature, and reason, into their right course, to all the tender charities of life, they should remind us of our intire dependence, on the great Author of our being, by making us sensible that the most delightful attachments, which can be formed, by love, or friendship, serve but to enlarge our vulnerary part, and encrease our capacity, of feeling pain.

You, perhaps, may think this moral too severe; but it is not meant to restrain us from the indulgence of those fond sensations, which are natural to every good heart, but to raise our gratitude, to the great Giver of all our blessings, and to remind us, that we hold them, by grant, from his bounty, and not from any right, or merit of our own.

As my Emily gains strength, every day, we purpose going into Essex, in a short time; and as soon as Sir John can settle some necessary affairs, there, we shall all set out, for Bristol, in hopes of meeting lord and lady Woodville there.—What a joyful meeting will it be to me! my eyes run over, at the delightful idea.

Though lady Mount Willis took every possible precaution, to conceal her generosity to Sir James Miller, from himself, the unhappy man has discovered that he is indebted to her, for his subsistence, and has written her a most affecting letter, acknowledging his own unworthiness, and intreating her to withdraw her bounty, as he declares he could better support the most abject poverty, than the receiving of favours from one, whom he had so highly injured, and offended. There is something in this sentiment, that inclines me to forgive, even his former baseness, and to pity his present misery. Sure there can be nothing so truly humiliating, as receiving obligations, from those we have wronged.

I sincerely wish that your epistolary correspondence, with Sir James Thornton, may answer all your expectations.—But, remember, Fanny, that flattery costs men nothing; and that women are apt to over-rate it, and frequently bestow their love and esteem, in exchange, for what has no intrinsic worth.—I grant, that in the general commerce of the world, the person whose politeness and attention is most marked to us, deservedly obtains a preference, in our regard: vanity is, in some degree, inherent to all human kind, and the being rated above our fellows, is a species of flattery, which the most delicate creature in the world is never, offended at. But, in a particular intercourse, between man and woman, we should take great care, that our own self-love, does not impose upon us, and magnify the common forms, or expressions, of politeness, into a particular address.—Do not be angry, at this hint, Fanny, as it is only meant to save your vanity, for I hope your heart is not yet concerned, from the mortification of a disappointment.

Tell my dear lady Woodville, that I most impatiently long for a line from her, and that I mutually congratulate her lord, and her, on their recovery.

I am, dear Fanny,

Your's sincerely.

F. STRAFFON.

# LETTER 85.

## *Lady* WOODVILLE, *To Lady* STRAFFON.

Where, Fanny, shall I find words, to express my gratitude to the *Almighty,* for the blessings I have received from him? the smallest of which, is my own recovery from the borders of the grave! Words are inadequate to what I feel, but *He* can read my heart! Life is a common blessing given to all; and sure there was a time, now not long past, when I would most willingly have yielded mine, into *His* hands that gave it—but happiness, my sister! such bliss as mine, is but the lot of few. O, how shall I deserve it! teach me, Fanny; teach me every honest art, to keep the treasure I have so lately found—lord Woodville's heart.

How little, alas! are we capable of judging, for ourselves? my lord's late illness, which I considered as the severest infliction of Providence, has been the blessed means, of all my present, and, I hope, future happiness! His generous nature, struck with the sufferings I endured, by one rich gift, has over paid them all—but I must not, dare not, enter into the charming detail of my felicity—my spirits will not bear it, but you shall know it all. For the present, let it suffice to tell you, I have not now a wish ungratified, but that of being able to render myself worthy, of the happiness I enjoy.

My lord, lady Harriet, who is a mirror of resignation, and Fanny Weston, all join with me, in sincere congratulations to you, and Sir John, on Emily's recovery. How truly thankful ought I to be, for the dear child's preservation! for indeed, I could not have been happy, had you been otherways.

Adieu, my Fanny, I am, as ever,

Your's,

E. WOODVILLE.

## LETTER 86.

### *Miss* WESTON, *To Lady* STRAFFON.

[Inclosed in the foregoing.]

I hope your ladyship will believe me perfectly sincere, when I tell you that I rejoice at lady Woodville's being able to release me from the office of her secretary, by answering for herself. For, though I am highly sensible of the great honour, which your ladyship confers upon such a mad-cap as me, by condescending to write to me, I must beg leave to observe *que la rose a ses picques*[74]–for indeed, your ladyship's kind and friendly admonitions, upon the subject of Sir James Thornton's politeness, and my vanity, are rather humiliating. But in order to make your mind, as well as my own, easy, upon this subject, I will venture to assure you, that I shall require stronger proofs of Sir James Thornton's regard, than a little flimsy flattery, before I suffer my self-love to persuade me, that the baronet is enamoured, of your ladyship's

Most humble servant,

F. WESTON.

P.S. Pray, my dear lady Straffon, do not fancy I am in a huff, for I never was in greater harmony of spirits, than at present; having, this moment, received a letter from Sir James Thornton, in answer to an invitation, which lord and lady Woodville commissioned me to make, and which he will accept, in a few days. It is lucky that flattery *costs men nothing*, for the poor dear baronet would certainly be a bankrupt, if he were to purchase all that he bestows, upon

Your ever affectionate,

F.W.

## LETTER 87.

### *Lady* STRAFFON, *To Lady* WOODVILLE.

Like the rich gales from the Arabian coast, my Emily's last letter came fraught with health and joy.—What an high cordial must it have been to a fond sister's heart, who long has mourned, without affecting to perceive, those secret sorrows, which she could not heal, to hear that they, at length, are vanished?

I know not which of us is, at present, happiest; but were the charming contest to be determined, by the merit of the competitors, the precious palm would be adjudged to you. Long may my Emily enjoy the triumph, she so well deserves!

I will not, cannot, wait for a detail of your felicity; I will behold, and share it.—It is possible to be circumstantial, under the severest affliction; but happiness is, by much, too volatile for narrative—like a fine and subtle essence, it evaporates, through the activity of its own spirit; we cannot paint the expressive looks, which are lighted up by a glad heart; the *eye* alone can catch the brilliant beam, which brightens by reflection.—Therefore, expect to meet *mine,* in less than four-and-twenty hours, after you receive this. Sir John, and my girl, will accompany me.

I have had a very pleasing letter, from lady Somerville.—Lodovico, Laura, and she, arrived safely, at Genoa; her friends received them all, with open hearts and arms.—The young people have been intirely taken up, with feasts, balls, and masquerades. To avoid giving offense, by refusing to partake in these amusements, lady Somerville has retired to the very house, which she quitted upon her marriage, which is twenty leagues from Genoa.—She there continues to indulge that melancholy, which time has been only able to soften, not subdue—amiable relict!

Tell Fanny Weston that the present harmony of my spirits, prevents my answering her letter, as I ought; but she must not flatter herself, that I do not mean to take any farther notice of it; for the moment I become acquainted with Sir James Thornton, I will insist upon his devising a proper punishment for her pertness, and he shall be at once the judge, and executioner.

Adieu, my dear Emily: I quit you, with pleasure, at *this* moment, to hasten *that* of our meeting.

F. Straffon.

## LETTER 88.

### *Lord* WOODVILLE, *To Lord* SEYMOUR.

The apprehensions, which my dear Seymour expresses, on account of my silence, have been but too well founded.—I have been upon the verge of

> That undiscovered country, from whose bourn
> No traveller returns.[75]

But how do I now rejoice, at not having passed the irremediable bounds, in a state of insensibility to the virtues of my now truly dear, and I hope happy, wife! She is an angel, Seymour!

I know what true delight these words will give you; they are sincere, my friend—they flow from my full heart. Blinded as I have been, to her perfections, you will, surely, pardon the transports of a man, who, waking from a dream of misery, finds himself in Elysium[76]–such is my present state; what was my former one, you, and you, only, know, too well.

You are, doubtless, impatient to hear what has wrought this happy change; with pleasure will I dwell on every circumstance, that must endear my Emily to my heart, and render her still more amiable, in my friend's eyes.

It is now above two months, since I received your first account of Ransford's duel, and the marchioness's distress. No words can paint the strong emotions of my mind—a thousand various schemes to succour her, rushed, instantly, through my disturbed imagination. My wife was present, while I read your letter, and saw the agitation of my mind.—Her delicacy prompted her to retire; I prevented her, and told her, I know not how, of Barnard's death, and begged her to inform lady Harriet of it, in the tenderest manner—needless caution.

I then told her, I would go and acquaint Sir Harry Ransford, with the affair; and ordered my horses to be got ready, immediately.

I set out, directly, on that purpose—but before I had rode a quarter of a mile, a sudden impulse seized me, a certain foreign and irresistible force, that impelled me to fly to the instant relief of the marchioness.

The baseness, and madness of such a resolve, sprang forward to my view, at the same moment; but the passions triumphed, as they always must do, at the first onset, over the feebler reason.

I considered, that Ransford might, probably, call me to account, for interfering in his affairs; and I felt a kind of gloomy satisfaction, in thinking that the loss of my life, might be deemed an atonement, for the cruelty of my conduct, towards Emily.

I then traversed the road, in order to return home through my park, and got into my closet, unperceived by any of my family.

I there took out the marchioness's picture, and hung it round my neck, as a kind of talisman, against that remorse which I must certainly feel, for abandoning my wife. I then sat down, and wrote a letter to my Emily; and, though at that time under the influence of the strongest delirium, I am pleased, and proud, to own, that my tears flowed, faster than my ink, while I reflected on the pain which she must suffer, when she read those lines.—I resolved to travel, night and day, and not to put my letter into the post-office, till I came to Canterbury.

As I was stepping out of my library, which you know looks into the parterre, I saw my little boy, at play, close by the window, with his maid.—The sight of my son, startled me.—The order of nature seemed reversed—The child admonishing the parent. I felt all this, but felt myself, at the same time, like one in a dream, labouring under an impression of the imagination, without reason to correct, or free-will to controul, it. I could not pass into the park, without being seen by them;—the private manner of my return, would have alarmed the family. I was ashamed to be detected by my servant, and spent above an hour, which appeared a summer's day to me, in a state of the most restless impatience. I have since thought, that this little accident seemed as if kindly designed by Providence, to give me time for reflection. But alas! the delay only quickened the vehemence of my purpose, to pursue my scheme.

The moment I was at liberty, I flew back to the park, bid my servants follow me, and set off, with all the speed my horse could make.—But I had not got three miles, from my own demesne, when by some *fortunate* accident, my horse made a false step, which he was incapable of recovering, and threw me senseless, to the ground.

How long I continued there, or what passed, during an interval of one-and-twenty days, has left no trace upon my memory; at the end of that period, I awaked, as from unquiet rest.—Gracious heaven! how shall I ever be able to express my astonishment, at beholding lady Woodville, seated by my bedside, the statue of despair; pale, wan, and faded was her youthful cheek, her eyes were raised to heaven, as if in fervent, though in hopeless prayer! O, Seymour! what a train of horrid images, broke in, at once, upon my burning brain; my unsettled reason fluttered on the wing, and seemed as if it would depart again, for ever.

The striking object that appeared before me, impressed my senses with a kind of awe; yet I had power to speak to her! she could not answer—A flood of tears, but they were tears of joy, suppressed the power of speech. She was carried out of the room, by doctor Fenton's orders, and I then feigned a slumber, in hopes that recollection would afford some clue, to lead me through the labyrinth of my situation.

The first circumstance that presented itself to my memory, was, my having quitted Woodfort, with a design of abandoning that amiable creature, whom I now beheld reduced to the state I have already described, by her tenderness for me;—the next thing, that occurred to me, was my having had the marchioness's picture round my neck, which I now searched for in vain.—I instantly ordered every person to leave the room, except Williams, and demanded from him, an account of my present situation, and what was become of the picture, which I had placed next my heart? I could have no doubt of his faith, or sincerity—he has lived with me ever since I was a *child*, and loved me, as if I had been *his*.

He fell upon his knees, by my bedside, and begged me not to hurry, or exhaust my spirits, which he was sure must be extremely weak, as this was the first moment the fever had left me, for one-and-twenty days; during which time, he told me lady Woodville had never quitted my apartment, for a single hour, nor closed her lovely eyes.

That on the night I was brought home, the surgeon had me stripped, in order to know if I had received any wound or bruise, in my body; that he had taken off the picture, and given it to my wife, supposing it to be hers; that at that time she took no notice of it, but that he had often, since, seen her gaze upon it, most intently, and sigh, as if her heart would break.

He said, that Thomas had also brought her the papers, which were found in my pockets; that she gave them all, without looking at them, to him, to lock up; but that Mrs. Winter, her woman, who was present, told her ladyship there was a letter, sealed and directed for her, which she then took, and left the room.

That she returned, in a few minutes, as pale as death, but never disclosed the contents; though Mrs. Winter took as much pains, as she dared, to find them out, as she could not conceive, what I could have to say to lady Woodville, when I had but just left her.

He told me, Seymour, that Emily has knelt by my bedside, for hours, in speechless agony; has kissed my feverish lips, and bathed my burning hands, with her most precious tears; and yet she knew I had inhumanly determined to forsake her! to leave such worth as hers, a prey to pining grief, and discontent! For whom?—You have too justly named her, the most unworthy of her sex.

You may suppose, that during Williams's recital, my reason tottered in its feeble seat; but I had still enough left, to rouse my slumbering virtue, and to resolve, that if I should recover, my future life should be devoted to love, to gratitude, to Emily. This, bear me witness, heaven! I had determined, before I knew, or even thought it possible, I ever should despise the marchioness.

As soon as I had heard all that Williams had to say, I begged to see my wife. Doctor Fenton absolutely refused my request. I acquiesced, upon his telling me she had lain down to rest.

The next day, I repeated my intreaties, without success.—On the third, I became so impatient, that Williams thought it most prudent to let me know the sad truth, which every one else concealed from me, which was, that lady Woodville lay dangerously ill of the fever, she had caught, from me.

I was no longer sensible of my own weak state.—The tumult of my passions, gave me a momentary strength.—I rushed out of bed, upon the *instant;* never, Seymour, did I experience such *another!* All lady Woodville's merits, which I had before but coldly admired, appeared to me, now, in the warmest colors, and rose even to perfection. But when contrasted, with my ingratitude towards her, they overcame me.—I sunk into my servant's arms, and shed a flood of tears.

In spite of all opposition, I would be carried into my wife's apartment.—I had resolved to implore her pity, and forgiveness, for my past follies, and to assure her of my future conduct, which I could no longer entertain a doubt of; as the sincere and tender affection, I then felt for her would, I hoped, ensure her happiness, and that I should date mine, from her recovery.

Think of my situation, Seymour, when I approached her bedside—she was delirious! yet the dear angel knew me, though she raved, and in such terms, that her words struck daggers to my heart—My strength forsook me; I fainted, and was carried back to my own chamber, the unhappiest wretch that breathed upon the earth.

In pity to you, I will draw a veil, over the wild ravings of my tortured mind, and make you happy, by telling you, that I am truly so, by knowing that my dearest Emily is out of danger.

This letter has been the work of two days; to-morrow, I am to see my wife.—I count the moments, Seymour, and think them hours, till then!

I have heard that persons who have been once mad, never recover the perfect use of their reason; or, at least, are liable to some returns of insanity. This thought shocks me! for if I could suppose it possible, I should ever again sink into that shameful, that now-detested delirium, which so long possessed me, I would not wish to live another hour—but it is impossible.— My Emily's virtues have subdued my heart, and time, instead of lessening, must increase their power.

It is high time that I should condole with you, on the sufferings you have endured, from your generous friendship towards the marchioness. The meanness of her behaviour to you, makes me rejoice in the hope of her not being Ransford's wife.—Yet contemptible as her conduct has made her appear, even in my once-partial eyes, she must not know distress, I mean with regard to her circumstances: and while Sir Harry Ransford lives, it will not be in his son's power, to support her, in the rank which she has held, for some years past.—Let me, therefore, intreat you to inform me of the event of her law-suit with the marquis of St. Aumont.

Be not alarmed, at this request, Seymour. It is not passion, but compassion, that makes me wish to serve her; for I here solemnly declare, that if I were not certain, of having intirely conquered the phrensy, which had so long possessed my enfeebled reason, I have still virtue enough left, to restrain myself, from ever mentioning her name. But the real lustre of my Emily's virtues, has triumphed over the false glare of Isabella's charms, that fatal *ignis fatuus*,[77] which has so long dazzled and misled my benighted senses.

I sincerely rejoice in your fair vestal's recovery;—may she live to make you as happy, as your uncommon situation will admit.

I am truly concerned for Ransford, and earnestly wish to know what course he has pursued.—I think, with you, that he is now in Switzerland; and suppose he has written to you, before this time. What is become of Lady Ransford? But I forget that you were prevented from seeing her, before you left Paris.

Adieu, my friend;—let me, once more, congratulate you, upon my Emily's recovery, and my own restoration, to more than life!

I am, most truly, your's.

WOODVILLE.

## LETTER 89.

### *Lord* WOODVILLE, *To Lord* SEYMOUR.

The wished-for, the charming interview, is over! but where, Seymour, shall I find words to express the delicacy of my Emily's conduct? when I would have fallen at her feet, and implored her to forgive my having made her miserable, she caught me in her arms, with that modest sensibility, which accompanies her every action, and said that all the misery she had ever suffered, arose from considering herself, as the fatal, though innocent cause, of my unhappiness.

That she should ever be truly grateful, for the pains I had taken to prevent her being wretched, by endeavouring to conceal a passion, which she was sure it was as impossible for me to conquer, as it had been to disguise.

That she had long known of my attachment to the marchioness, and that her utmost wish, for many months past, was, to be considered as my first friend; that she should never make an improper use of my confidence, but that her utmost tenderness should be exerted, to soothe the sorrows, which she could not heal.—A flood of tears opposed her farther utterance.

I took that opportunity, of assuring her, that it was in her power, and hers alone, to render me the happiest of men.

She wiped away her tears, and gazed on me, with looks of joy, and doubt. Let not your kindness, said she, tempt you to deceive me. I feel, too well, the impossibility of conquering a fond, a real passion! but I will strive, my lord.

I caught her trembling hand, and pressed it to my lips. O no! I cried, my Emily! my love! indulge your virtuous fondness, and deeply as my heart appears to be indebted to you, like a poor bankrupt, it shall give its all, though it can never pay you what it owes.—She quick exclaimed, O I am overpaid, in this blest moment, for years of misery! your heart! but can you give it? is it yours, my lord? No, Emily! unworthy as it is, it is already yours, and shall be ever so.

Tears and embraces closed this charming scene; and now, with truth, my Seymour, I can boast, I never knew what heart-felt rapture was, before that hour.

The conferring happiness, on any creature, is certainly the highest enjoyment, of the human mind; but the paying it to an amiable, and deserving object, must heighten the sentiment, even to transport.

Sir James Thornton has been obliged to return to England, on account of a law-suit. He purposed keeping himself concealed, but upon hearing of mine, or rather my Emily's illness, he posted down from London, to Sir William Lawson's, and remained there, till she was pronounced out of danger. Since that time, he has had frequent accounts of our recovery, from Fanny Weston, with whom he corresponds, in a very galant stile.

I know *she* likes the young baronet, and as I flatter myself he is cured of his hopeless passion, for lady Woodville, or at least, am well assured that he will never presume to pursue it, I have prevailed upon my wife, to consent to his making us a visit; but neither his being at Woodfort, nor any thing else, shall prevent our going to Bristol, in a few days; for though my lovely invalid is surprizingly recovered, from her late illness, the shock, which her constitution has received, has rendered it almost as delicate, as her charming mind. I will watch over them both, and hope soon to restore them to their natural state, which is almost perfection.

I have shewn Emily all your letters, and told her the story of my connection with the marchioness, without concealing a single circumstance which passed, either at Paris, or York. During my narrative, "I often did beguile her of her tears"[78]—they flowed sincerely, when I informed her of the struggles, of my then tortured mind.

I well knew that the confession of my past weakness, must give her pain; but I was certain she would receive it as the strongest mark, of my present sincerity. The tenderness and delicacy of her expressions, upon this trying subject, have, if possible, raised her in my esteem, by convincing me that her understanding is as excellent, as her heart; and that her mind and person constitute a treasure, almost too great for the most worthy man. Sensible as I am of my own demerits, can I ever be sufficiently grateful, for such a blessing? but I will endeavour to deserve it, Seymour, by devoting every hour of my future life, to her happiness.

Since the recovery of my reason, I have received infinite pleasure, from playing with my little boy. How could I be insensible to the natural and innocent endearments, of such a lovely creature? but I find happiness and pleasure crouding in upon me, through a thousand avenues, that my delirium had rendered impervious to their soft attacks; and I begin to think that I have been *new formed,* as well as *reformed,* since my redemption.

Lady Woodville, who is sincerely grateful for your kind attachment to her, entreats you will, at your return to Paris, endeavour to find out Sir James Miller, and purchase for him, either a commission, employment, or annuity, which may be sufficient for his support, as the unhappy man has absolutely refused to accept lady Mount Willis's bounty, from the moment he discovered, that it was to her he owed it. There is something like greatness of mind, in this circumstance, which renders him an interesting object. What mixtures are we compounded of! You may guess your pay-mistress *incog.*[79]

I impatiently long for the pleasure of hearing from you, and am, with the warmest affection of friendship,

> Ever yours,

> WOODVILLE.

# LETTER 90.

## *Lord* SEYMOUR, *To Lord* WOODVILLE.

My dear WOODVILLE,

This letter will probably reach England, but a few days before the writer of it; but I would not, for a moment, delay pouring forth my acknowlegements, for the sincere pleasure I have received, from your two last letters; and my warmest congratulations, on the charming subject of them.

Yes, thank Heaven, my friend is restored to life, to reason, and to happiness! can Seymour sigh, while he repeats that sound. O Woodville! my cup has been severely dashed with sorrow, nor has there ever yet one joy unmixed, e'er reached my heart. Yet let me not complain; my own imprudence formed the fatal web, that has ensnared my peace; the unhappy duel that I fought with captain Beaumont, sealed its ruin!

But why should I distress you, by tracing my misfortunes to their source? it is too much for you to know, that I am wretched—no matter from what cause.

The length of time that has elapsed, since my last letter to you, has been fertile of sad events; which I shall relate to you, in as succinct a manner, as I can.

When I had been, about a week, at Belleveüe, the good old general was attacked with a disorder in his stomach, which had most alarming symptoms. He was sensible of his situation, but seemed to wish to conceal it, from his children, who vied with each other, in their tenderness and affliction, for him. It is impossible to do justice to their merits, or describe the affecting scene.

At the end of twelve days, he expired, and left the most disconsolate family, I ever beheld: but Charlotte's grief surpassed even credibility. Neither her brother, sister, nor I, could prevail upon her, to leave the chamber, where the body lay, till the moment it was to be interred. She passed the nights and days, in prayers, and tears.—Judge what I suffered, from my apprehensions for her.

As soon as the funeral was over, she requested that we would indulge her, with the liberty of passing a few days, without interruption, in her chamber. We had no right to trespass on her grief; but yet our fears, for her too delicate constitution, made us reluctantly comply with her desire.

On the fourth evening of her retirement, she sent for madame de Carignon, who flew to obey her summons, but returned, in a few minutes, to captain Beaumont and me, and, with an air of distraction, cried out, our miseries are but begun, O hasten, quickly, or her angelick spirit will be fled! And can I paint the sad, the solemn scene! no, Woodville, no! it will live for ever, graved upon my heart—but words would wrong my feelings.

Charlotte! my once beloved, my now adored, and sainted maid! sighed out her soul to heaven.

Grief will not kill us, Woodville, or I should not survive, to tell her death—I can no more,

Adieu, my friend.

SEYMOUR.

## LETTER 91.

### Lord SEYMOUR, To Lord WOODVILLE.

My dear WOODVILLE,

It was impossible for me to have added another word, to my last letter. I have but a very few more to say, with regard to the Beaumont family; and then the dear, the fatal name, shall no more pass my lips, but remain, treasured up, in my sad heart, a precious hoard, for everlasting grief to brood upon.

I told you, in some of my former letters, that captain Beaumont visited me, every day, during my confinement, in the Châtelet. He there beheld, and became enamoured of, the fair Maria D'Angueville. When we had been about ten days, at Belleveüe, he acquainted me with his passion, and in-treated me to speak to his father, upon the subject. Accident prevented my having an opportunity of obeying him, till the general's illness rendered it improper—and the real affliction, which he has since felt, seemed to have quenched the new enkindled flame.

But a few days, after our return to Paris, he again re-assumed the sub-ject, and begged me to apply to his fair cousin, and his uncle, for leave to pay his addresses to her. I told him, truly, that the situation of my mind, ren-dered me totally unfit, to be the ambassador of love or joy; but that I was de-termined, before I should leave Paris, to pay a visit, at the Châtelet, to return my thanks, for the humane, and generous treatment, I had met with, from the governor, and his family, and to intreat Maria's acceptance, of the legacy, which her uncle, the general had bequeathed me, of twenty thousand livres.[80]

I thought that captain Beaumont appeared displeased, at my intention; as he, coolly, replied, that he did not want a fortune, with his wife, and thought I had better bestow the legacy I did not chuse to accept, upon some of the younger children of the family, who might possibly stand in need of my bounty. I told him that Maria's likeness to his beloved sister, had made her the principal object, of my present attention, and that I would put it in her power, to dispose of the sum, in question, as she thought proper.

Soon after this conversation, the captain withdrew, and I remained for several days, so intirely absorbed in my grief, that I reflected not upon the unkindness of my friend's conduct, who neither came, nor sent, to me, for near a fortnight.

At length, he entered my chamber, one morning, without being an-nonced, and found me gazing so intently, upon Charlotte's picture, that I saw him not, till he exclaimed, with a voice of distraction, what unmerited affliction, and distress, has the unhappy Seymour brought on all the Beau-mont race?

Though the severity of this reproach, might have roused my resent-ment, at another time, I was so much softened, by the object then before me, my angel Charlotte's face! that, bursting into tears, I answered—O Beau-mont! cannot grief, like this, atone for my involuntary crimes? and does my friend upbraid my misery?

At these words, he rushed into my arms, and cried, forgive me, Seymour. Then started wildly from me, and went on—but wherefore flow these tears, upon a senseless object, lost and forgotten in the grave, when there is now, a fairer, and a kinder maid, ready to heal your sorrows.

I could not avoid expressing my astonishment, at this unintelligible discourse, and it was a long time, before he explained himself, by telling me, that the lovely and innocent Maria D'Angueville, had conceived a passion for me, during the time I remained a prisoner in the Châtelet; and that, upon being pressed by her father, and mother, to receive her cousin's hand, she had declared, that she would rather pass her days, in a cloister, than with any other man, but lord Seymour. I was extremely affected with this intelligence, as it concerned my friend, the unhappy girl, and my own honour.

I assured captain Beaumont, that I never had spoken to her, upon the subject of love, or made the least attempt to gain her affections; and that I was ready to do every thing, in my power, to assist in conquering Maria's weak partiality to me, that might not injure her delicacy, or my own character.

The frankness and sincerity of my manner, soon got the better of his ill-grounded suspicions; he asked my pardon, a thousand times, for having entertained a doubt of my affection to his dear dead sister; but hoped, as I had been myself a lover, I would forgive his rashness.

It was, at last agreed upon, between us, that I should write to Maria, directly, and acquaint her with the real state of my heart; which must be, for ever, incapable of love, for any earthly object; that I should not see her, before I left Paris; and at my setting out, should take an everlasting leave of her, by letter. That neither her father, nor any other person, should press her to marry, till time and reason might enable her to triumph over a passion, which opposition would certainly increase. That captain Beaumont should continue his assiduities, without mentioning his love.—That she should not know of the present, I designed her, till a year was elapsed; but if at that time, she refused to marry captain Beaumont, I should be at liberty, to put her in possession, of the twenty thousand livres; and that she should be allowed to dispose of them, as she pleased.

This affair, thus settled, my friend took his leave, with a thousand acknowlegements, for what he called a sacrifice, and I sat down to fulfil my promise, of writing to Maria—when Wilson announced a very unexpected visitor; it was madame de St. Far, the marchioness's mother, whom I had never seen, or heard of, since the time that you first became acquainted with her daughter.

She was then, you may recollect, an agreeable figure, rather comely, than handsome, and plumper than the generality of her countrywomen. She is now emaciated, to a skeleton, and I could not help feeling some apprehensions, that she would expire, before she left my apartment, as she was frequently much agitated, during the time she staid.

She told me, that her daughter had suffered her to want, even the common necessaries of life, and had absolutely refused to see her, from the moment she became a widow. Though I detest the marchioness, I could not avoid observing to madame de St. Far, that I imagined the first part of her accusation, must be unjust, as she had formerly, appeared in the world, as a woman of fortune; and therefore, must certainly be able to support herself, independant of her daughter's bounty.

She told me, I was much deceived, and as she had no longer any terms to keep, with the ungrateful marchioness, she would reveal her real situation.—She then informed me, that she had lived, for several years, with a monsieur de Verville, at Dijon, by whom she had Isabella; that, at length, by the persuasion of his friends, monsieur de Verville determined to marry, and parted with her, and her daughter; but allowed them a decent support, and took every proper care of his child's education.

That as she grew up extremely handsome, madame de St. Far, determined to bring her to Paris, in hopes of making her fortune; and, for that purpose, assumed the name she now used, and endeavoured to appear like a person of distinction. That the marchioness was perfectly acquainted with their circumstances, and readily entered into the scheme; but, in order to carry it on, she was obliged to run considerably in debt, though they were not above six months in Paris, before the marchioness had the good fortune, to charm both you, and the marquis de St. Aumont.

She added, that the only reason, her daughter ever gave, for preferring the marquis, to you, was the probability of becoming her own mistress, by his death, for that she knew her own disposition, so perfectly, that she was certain she could not confine her affections, to any one person, long.

O, Woodville! what an happy escape, have you had, from this vile woman! but to make an end of this tedious tale. She told me, that monsieur de Verville died, without a will, soon after the marchioness's marriage; and that she was, by that means, deprived even of the small income, which he had allowed her. She implored me to assist her, in getting into some convent, where she might pass the remainder of her days, without hearing of her un-dutiful, and unnatural daughter. I have desired her to fix upon a proper place, for her retirement, and I will readily pay the sum necessary to her admission. I presented her with my purse, and desired to hear from her, as soon as possible.

This affair, and lady Woodville's commands, to find out Sir James Miller, will detain me, a few days longer, in Paris. How earnestly do I long, to quit it? yet are not all places alike, to the unhappy! no, there is one asylum, and but one, for wretchedness like mine—the peaceful grave!

Forgive me, Woodville, for talking in this melancholy strain, to my now happy friend—may he be long so, is the warmest wish of

SEYMOUR.

P.S. I know not whether I told you that I have sought lady Ransford, in vain, ever since my return to Paris. She quitted her hôtel, in a few days after Barnard's death, and has left no trace behind her.

## LETTER 92.

### *Lord* WOODVILLE, *To Lord* SEYMOUR.

My dear SEYMOUR,

Your remark, that neither happiness, nor pleasure, can come to us unmixed, is but too aptly verified, in me; for the real and tender concern which your situation gives me, is a strong alloy to that tranquil happiness, I should, at present, enjoy, if the friend of my heart were not wretched.—There is something so uncommonly distressful, in your circumstances, that to attempt to lessen your affliction, would be an insult to humanity;—for who that has a heart to feel another's loss, would wish to stop the graceful tears that flow, "where reason, and where virtue o'er the tomb, are fellow mourners."

I am sorry for captain Beaumont's disappointment in love, but I have infinitely more pity, for the young and innocent Maria. You and I both know how difficult it is to struggle with the first fond impressions of the heart; and women, in general, from a principle of delicacy, are much more inclined, than men, to cherish their first passion, even when hope is fled.

I have a melancholy proof of this truth, too near me—poor lady Harriet Hanbury! She still laments the unworthy Barnard, and, I fear will soon follow him to an untimely grave.—While Sir James Thornton seems to have transferred the passion he felt for lady Woodville, to Miss Weston, who kindly receives his vows, and will, I hope, soon crown his wishes.

I cannot help being extremely shocked, at the infamous conduct of the marchioness, towards her mother.—Why need we become volunteers, in vice? Our passions but too strongly, and frequently, impel us to break the bounds prescribed by virtue; but then those passions may, I humbly hope, in some degree, alleviate our transgressions; but her unnatural behaviour, to the unhappy woman who gave her birth, admits of no extenuation. This could not have proceeded from any passion, and must, therefore, be a double vice.

I wish I had been informed of this particular, before, as I now think it would have been a powerful antidote, against the poison of her charms. For though a man may love a woman, that has ten thousand faults, and follies, those faults and follies should be feminine.—Avarice, and inhumanity, are sufficient to unsex the loveliest woman, and strip her of her every charm.

I am, however, much better pleased to owe my cure to my Emily's virtues, than to Isabella's vices, as the knowledge of the former, is a perpetual source of happiness to me, while the discovery of the latter, must, for ever, reflect on my own weakness, in being so grossly deceived.

Madame de St. Far's establishment in the convent, must not be at your expence. My Emily! my lovely, generous girl! insists on paying her pension. She must not be refused whatever she desires, by Woodville, or his friend.

I most impatiently long, for your return to England; I wish you would meet us, at Bristol, where we purpose going, in a few days: for though my Emily is so much recovered, that neither her physician, nor herself think she has occasion to drink the waters, I will not be satisfied, unless she does; as I flatter myself they may assist, in confirming that health, which her present happiness seems to have perfectly restored.

Sir John, lady Straffon, and their daughter, are now at Woodfort; they, and my sister Lawson, are to accompany us to the Hot-wells. Lady Mount Willis has lain in, at her house in Somersetshire—we are to pay her a visit, *en passant*[81]–she has got a son, and is as happy, as she is amiable.—We are all *anxious* to know what is become of Ransford, of his step-mother, and Sir James Miller: but I am much more *so,* to embrace my ever valued friend, and if I cannot heal, to soothe his sorrows—may that, at least, be in the power of Seymour's most affectionate,

WOODVILLE.

## LETTER 93.

### *Lord* SEYMOUR, *To Lord* WOODVILLE.

Yes, Woodville, I will take your counsel, and hasten to lay hold on the possession of the only good, that is now left me, your generous friendship! I will meet you, at the Hot-wells, in a short time; but I will not live in the same house with you, nor return from thence to Woodfort. I know the value of your regard too well, to suffer it to be productive of misery to you, or your deservedly happy wife.—No! Seymour's sorrows shall not cast a shade, on the bright sunshine of your future days! nor subject you to the unavailing pain, of endeavouring to erase the dark engrained tints of melancholy, which must form the colour of my life to come. Yet I will frequently behold my friend, and with sincere delight, contemplate his felicity.

I have, at last, had a letter from Ransford. Sure there is fascination in the marchioness's charms! He raves, and is distracted, at her having disowned him, as a husband, which she has formally done, by her solicitor, in order to recover the remainder of those effects, which were confiscated on account of his duel with Barnard. She has carried her point; they were restored to the marchioness de St. Aumont, but her creditors have seized on every thing she left. Her husband's nephew has carried his suit against her, but has allowed her an annuity of four thousand livres, while she remains unmarried, in respect to his uncle's memory.—I think this income is quite sufficient for her wants, and infinitely beyond her merits. I therefore intreat you to reserve your generosity, for some more worthy object.

The now happy St. Far is settled in a convent, at Dijon; where she purposes leading an exemplary life. Lady Woodville's expence, for she must be obeyed, will not amount to more than forty pounds, a year.

About ten days ago, a monk came to my apartments, and desired to speak with me. He told me there was a lady, in the Carmelites convent, who begged to see me, upon an affair of the utmost importance to one of my friends. I enquired, very particularly, who the lady was: he said he knew nothing more of her, than that she was an Englishwoman, and was called Jefferson. He added, that, at her request, he had been often to seek for me, while I was absent from Paris; that he had given up all hopes of meeting me; but rejoiced at his being more fortunate than he expected, and intreated me to obey the lady's summons.

This affair would have been matter of speculation to me, if my mind had been sufficiently at ease, to think about it; but without reflecting, at all, upon the subject, I entered the Carmelite's convent, at ten o'clock, the next morning, and enquired for Mrs. Jefferson.—I did not wait long, in the parlour, when a lady, dressed in deep mourning, approached the grate.—I fixed my eyes intently upon her, and knew her to be lady Ransford.—A crimson glow overspread her cheek, when she saluted me, and, at that moment, she appeared a most interesting object.

To save her the confusion of apologizing for sending for me, I told her how much I had been disappointed, at not being able to discover her retreat, at my return to Paris, and begged to know if I could be, any way, serviceable to her; and, at the same time, intreated she would inform me, of every thing she knew, in relation to the unhappy affair, between captain Barnard, and my friend.

Her tears flowed fast, and silent, while I spoke.—When she perceived that I waited for her reply, she took out her pocket book, and presenting it to me, said, your lordship will there find two letters, which will render any conversation with me, upon this painful subject, needless.—I commit them to your care, in order that every possible use may be made of them, for Mr. Ransford's advantage. I bear no enmity to his father, or to him, nor do I wish to make him an exile, from that country, to which I never more will return.

I asked her, with as much delicacy as I possibly could, what scheme of life she intended to pursue, and again repeated the offer of my services to her. She thanked me, and said, that captain Barnard's death had made her think differently, from what she had ever done before; that she was too conscious of the enormity of her conduct, to think of returning into the world; that she, therefore, determined to pass her days in a convent, but would always have it in her power, to quit it, as she did not mean to make any vows.

I really admired the rationality of her sentiments, and, of course, approved them; but was ignorant by what means she could be supported, even in a convent; till she told me that, at her marriage with Sir Harry Ransford, he had signed an article, allowing her, in case of separation, a power over three thousand pounds, or an annuity, of a hundred and fifty pounds, a year, during his life; and a jointure, of four hundred pounds, a year, at his death. She said the annuity would be sufficient for her maintenance; that she desired no favour from a person she was supposed to have injured, though the fatal connection, between Sir Harry and her, had been the source of all her miseries.

She begged me to forward Barnard's letter, to Ransford, and to send copies of it, to the captain's friends, in England, in order to pave the way, for Ransford's return. I promised to obey her, and took my leave; as I now must of you, in order to hasten my setting out.—You will, probably, hear from me, once more, before you see your unhappy, but

Truly affectionate,

SEYMOUR.


## LETTER 94.

### *Lord* SEYMOUR, *To Lord* WOODVILLE.

Amiens.

I have, at length, taken an everlasting leave, of Paris, and have got so far, on my way to my native land, but without being sensible of that charming enthusiasm, which is stiled the Amor Patriæ,[82] and which I believe has been oftener described, than felt, by voluntary exiles; for I confess that I have very little idea of local attachments; persons, and not places, have engrossed all the affections, of which my heart is capable; and, though the sight of Albion's chalky cliffs,[83] may not inspire me with much delight, I shall certainly feel true pleasure, when I behold my dear Woodville, and his amiable wife.

I should not stop on my journey, to tell you this, because I am sure you must know it untold, but my worthy, my faithful Wilson, whom I have long considered as my friend, though he still acts as my servant, left Paris, with a slight fever on him: travelling has, perhaps, increased his malady, and I purpose halting here, till he is quite recovered.

I gave you an account of my interview, with lady Ransford, in my last, and will now inform you, of the purport of those letters, which were found in captain Barnard's pocket, after the duel. That, which was addressed to her ladyship, was filled with tender adieus, and soft contrition for having involved her in distress, and leaving her probably exposed to misery, in a foreign land; with the most solemn intreaties not to prosecute Mr. Ransford, in case he should survive, as he there acknowleged, that he had drawn the duel on himself.

That, which he wrote to Ransford, was short, yet contained the fullest declaration, of his having sought the quarrel, and its consequences, from a weariness of life, which he said must be forever embittered, by reflecting on the baseness of his behaviour, towards lady Harriet Hanbury, as well as on the unworthy part he had acted, in seducing lady Ransford from her duty. He implored his forgiveness, for the injury he had committed, against the honour of his family, and for having engaged him to hazard his life, from a too earnest desire, of getting rid of his own.

How inconsistent is the conduct of this unfortunate man! his attention to the preservation of his antagonist's life, is certainly noble; but what an act of inhumanity, was it, to lay Ransford under the fatal necessity, of becoming his executioner? or how are we to reconcile the spirit, of this last action, with the unworthy tenor, of his former life?

I am convinced there is no human creature, so intirely lost to virtue, as not to be possessed of one good quality, at least; which if known, and properly cultivated, might, in some measure, counter-balance its owner's vices to society; but we are all too apt, to reprobate a faulty character; too indolent to search out the latent virtues of another's heart; and find it more for our ease, to take it for granted, that a vicious person, must be vicious throughout, than to seek for a grain of wheat, in a bushel of chaff.

After many fruitless inquiries, I am informed that Sir James Miller has obtained a commission, in the Hungarian service, by the interest of some of his friends here, and that he left Paris, about three weeks ago, in order to join his regiment. Ransford is at Brussels, but the marchioness and he do not live together. I have forwarded Barnard's letter to him, and flatter myself we shall soon see him, in England.

My parting, with the dear remains of the Beaumont family, was truly affecting, madame de Carignon came to Paris, on purpose to bid me adieu. Captain Beaumont presented me with his and his father's pictures; he had before given me Charlotte's portrait—alas! it was an useless gift, as her dear image is too strongly graved, on my sad heart!

I will not dwell upon this subject, longer; but it is impossible that I should turn my thoughts to any other, now.—I can, therefore, only say,

Farewel,

SEYMOUR

END OF THE SECOND VOLUME.

# Appendix

## A List of the Subscribers.

### A
The Countess of Albemarle
Right Hon. Francis Andrews
George Ayscough, Esq;
James Agar, Esq;
Miss Agar
Welbore Agar, Esq;
Miss Aston
Lieutenant Adams

### B
Earl of Blessington
Earl of Belvidere
Walter Butler, Esq;
John Butler, Esq;
Captain Henry Butler
Counsellor Pierce Butler
Amyas Bushe, Esq;
Gervis P. Bushe, Esq;
Rev. Thomas Bushe
John Bambrick, Esq;
Edmund Burke, Esq;
Archdeacon Browne
Doctor Edward Barry
Mrs. Jane Barry
Richard Barrett, Esq;
Mrs. Barrett
Captain Basset

Major Brownrigg
Walter Bermingham, Esq;
Charles Boucher, Esq;
Captain Barclay
Rev. Peter Bristow
Rev. George Berkley
Mrs. Barnard
Cornet Badcock
Mrs. Bishopp
Mrs. Berkley
Mrs. Brooke
Rev. James Blair
Mr. John Braodley
Mrs. Browne
Mrs. Balfour

### C
Earl of Clanricarde
Earl of Charlemont
Bishop of Clogher
Bishop of Corke
Bishop of Cloyne
Hon. and Rev. Mr.
    Cholmondely
Hon. General Cholmondely
Hon. Mrs. Cholmondely
George Cholmondely, Esq;
Miss Cholmondely

Mrs. Cartwright
Mrs. Clive
Doctor Cadogan
General Carnac
Anthony Chamier, Esq;
Captain Alured Clarke
Rev. Robert Clarke, M.A.
Rev. Mr. Cocks
Rev. John Cliffe
Monsieur Le Chevalier
    Depiennes
Mrs. Crewe
Miss Cuffe
Cornet Callender
Miss Coningham
Mrs. Cockburn
Captain John Cooke

### D
Sir Robert Deane, Bar.
Joseph Deane, Esq;
William Davis, Esq;
James Lenox Dutton, Esq;
Mrs. Townley Dawson
Counsellor William Doyle

### E
Colonel Thomas Eyre

Captain Ellis

F

Sir William Founes, Bart.
William Fitzherbert, Esq;
Lady Frances Flood
Henry Flood, Esq;
Charles Flood, Esq;
John Flood, Esq;
Miss Flood
Councellor James Fitzgerald
John Fitzgibbon, Esq;
Mrs. M. Forth

G

John Greene, Esq;
William Greene, Esq;
Councellor Godfrey Greene
David Garrick, Esq;
Mr. Garston
Major Edward Griffith
Mrs. Griffith
Doctor Goldsmith
Mrs. Gore
Miss Gore
Mrs. Grady

H

Reverend Dean Handcock
Gustavus Handcock, Esq;
John Hanbury, Esq;
Edward Hunt, Esq;
Robert Hartpole, Esq;
General Haviland
Mrs. Haviland
John Hobson, Esq;
Mrs. Hobson
Thomas Hodges, Esq;
Gorges Edmond Howard,
    Esq;
Captain Hugonin
Hon. Mrs. Hamilton
Rev. James Hamilton
Captain Hamilton

Cornet Hamilton
Archibald Roan Hamilton,
    Esq;
Mungo Haldane, Esq;
Mrs. Hopkins
Miss Hamilton
Miss Haughton

I

William Izod, Esq;
William Johnson, Esq;
Mr. Jennings
Rev. William Jephson

K

Mrs. Kavanah
Miss Keppel
James Kearney, Esq;
Mrs. Elizabeth Kelly

L

Hercules Langrishe, Esq;
Rev. Dean Lewis
Gustavus Lambart, Esq;
Henry Lyons, Esq;
Mrs. Lumm
Mr. Edward Lord
Rev. Smyth Loftus

M

Earl of Mornington
Lord Viscount Mountgarret
Lord Mountmorres
Sir George Macartney
John M. Mason, Esq;
Mr. William Mitford
Justin Macarthy, Esq;
Mrs. Christian Macarthy
Thomas Paul Monck, Esq;
Captain Percy Monck
Thomas Monck, Esq;
Major James Mansergh, late
    of the eighth regiment of
    dragoons

Lieutenant Bryan Mansergh,
    of the second regiment
    of horse
John Manship, Esq;
Mrs. Maunsell
Captain Luke Mercer

N

Duke of Northumberland
Brockhill Newburgh, Esq;
Edward North, Esq;
Captain Nicholson

O

Murrough Obrien, Esq; *3
sets*
Bishop of Ossory
Robert Orme, Esq;

P

Lord Pigot
Miss Parry
Mrs. Pery
Rev. Thomas Pack
Henry James Pye, Esq;
Robert Hamden Pye, Esq;
Mrs. Hamden Pye
Mrs. Robert Pye
Rev. Mr. Penrick, of the
    Musæum

Q

Doctor Quin

R

Lady Rich
Right Hon. Richard Rigby
Sir John Russel, Bart.
George Rochfort, Esq;
John Rochfort, Esq;
Dudley Ryves, Esq;
Mrs. Reade
Mr. William Richardson
Mr. John Richardson

S

Earl of Shannon
Sir Richard St. George, Bart.
Mrs. St. George
Mons. Le Baron Van
    Staaden
Rev. Thomas Stephens
Walter Synnot, Esq;
Marks Synnot, Esq;
Luke Scrafton, Esq;
William Smyth, Esq;
Mrs. Smyth
Mr. Thomas Stagg
Rev. Doctor Sandford
Ralph Schomberg, M. D.
    F. S. A.
Richard Supple, Esq;
Rev. Anthony Sterling
Mrs. Spooner
Miss Swan
Edward B. Swan, Esq;
John Steare, Esq;

T

Mrs. Tilson
Richard Tyson, Esq;
William Tighe, Esq;
John Tickell, Esq;
William Talbot, Esq;

V

Mrs. Victor

W

Earl of Wandesford
Patrick Welch, Esq;
Mrs. Walker
Mrs. Margaret Wybrants
Miss Wybrants
Miss Elizabeth Wybrants
Mr. Stephen Wybrants
Mrs. Wilmot
Colonel Ward
Mrs. Williams
Mrs. Jane White

Miss Elizabeth Warren
Folliot Warren, Esq;
Edward Walsh, Esq;
Rev. Samuel Woodroffe
Lieutenant Webb
Mrs. Rose Whitwell

Y

Mr. Young

ADDITIONAL
    SUBSCRIBERS
Henry Harvey Aston, Esq.
Colonel Brent Butler.
Thomas Cobbe, Esq.
Miss Foley.
Robert Fanshawe, Esq.
Doctor Samuel Johnson.
Mrs. Keck.
Mrs. Kettleby.
William Mowbray, Esq.
James Martin.

# EMENDATIONS

~

The following sigla appear in this list: E (list of errata printed in the London edition of 1769); H (Harvard copy of London edition of 1769); D (Harvard copy of Dublin edition of 1769). Numbers given are for the page and line numbers in the present edition. The reading of our critical text is then followed by a rejected reading of the Illinois copy of the London edition of 1769, our copy text. The subscript caret (ₐ) indicates the absence of a mark of punctuation. Statements in boldface represent editorial commentary.

The copies of the London edition we have collated represent several states, the best being represented by the Illinois copy [X823.G874t] in which lines of *Leonidas* (p. 107) are printed in verse; in other states, they are printed in prose.

## TITLE PAGE.

1.7: délicate] delicate

## PREFACE.

4.26: the novel] novel
4.26: *épopée*] *epopée*
5.7: Trublet] Troublet
5.9: *défaut*] *defaut*
5.9: *médiocre*] *mediocre*
5.10: *différent*] *different*
5.10: *défaut*] *defaut*

## LETTER 2.

10.15: *cap-à-pie*] cap-à-pie
10.19: tête-à-tête] tête-à-tête
11.19–20: affectionately   D; affection/ately

## LETTER 3.

12.6: *un bel esprit,* than as *une belle dame.*] un bel esprit, than as une belle dame.
14.3: *grands ballets*] grands balets
14.36: paragraph.] D; paragraph<sub>∧</sub>

## LETTER 5.

16.31: *quantum sufficit*] quantum sufficit
17.3: lady] D; la d
17.13–14: from / Your's] D; from Your's

## LETTER 8.

20.12: Hanbury] E, D; Hartston

## LETTER 9.

21.21: *Lord*] E; *Lady*

## LETTER 11.

25.6: Lady STRAFFON] *From* Lady STRAFFON
25.11–12: that "the mind that hath any cast towards devotion, naturally flies to it in its afflictions."] that "a mind, which has the least turn to religion, naturally flies to it, in affliction."
25.30: emotions... have] emotions... has
26.31–32: /Like... tribe./] "like the base Indian, thrown a pearl away, richer than all his tribe."
27.13: writing,] E, D; writing to
27.32: What] E, D; Whan

## LETTER 12.

30.22: receive it, I] receive, I
30.22: Pray] D; pray

## LETTER 13.

34.2, 4, 6, 8, 19, 21, 23: **[lines of verse indented]**
34.4: That] Which

34.31–33: I think not on my father,/ And these great tears grace his remembrance, more, / Than those I shed for him.] "I think not on my father, and these great tears do grace his memory, more, than those I shed for him."

36.22: and feared I should] E, D; I feared and should

38.2: allotted] E, D; allowed

39.23: Lord] D; lord

40.27–28: *petit tour*] petit tour

41.4: Montpellier] Montpelier

41.6: *grand monde*] grande monde

44.2: how] E; why

45.33: to] D; *to*

## LETTER 14

48.27: Your's] D; your's

## LETTER 16

50.14: *mélange*] *melange*

50.28: duchess] D; duchess of

51.8: Tuileries] Tuilleries

## LETTER 17

53.35: "at grief."] D; "in grief."

54.12: tears.] D; tears,

55.34: wishes/ Your] D; wishes          Your

## LETTER 18

56.26: *Grève*] *Greve*

56.33: and provoked] E, D; provoked

57.4: "proud and melancholy and gentleman-like:"] "proud, melancholy, and gentleman-like:"

## LETTER 21

60.21: *Hélas*] *Helas*

60.25: You have been brought] Brought

## LETTER 22

64.23: violoncello] D; violencello

64.35: passed.—We] passed.—we

## LETTER 23

67.23: curiosity] D; curi-/sity
68.18: *grand*] *grande*
68.31: such] sucn
68.32: The] While the
68.33-34: the sight of him. We] sight of him, We
69.18: *Belleveüe*] *belle veue*
70.12: arrival.—] D; arrival —
70.38: *accouchement*] D; *accouchment*
72.23: madame] mademoiselle
73.2: madame] mademoiselle
73.5: Madame] mademoiselle
73.10: promised] D; promissed
73.16: madame] mademoiselle
73.27: madame] mademoiselle
73.30: madame] mademoiselle
74.4: Madame] Mademoiselle
74.15: Madame] Mademoiselle
74.26: ever] even
74.36: madame] mademoiselle
75.6: Madame] mademoiselle
75.13: madame] mademoiselle
75.27: madame] mademoiselle
76.11: Madame] Mademoiselle
76.15: madame] mademoiselle
76.24: madame] mademoiselle
77.4: madame] mademoiselle
77.17: following letter] D; followingletter
77.19: Madame] Mademoiselle
77.25: prince.] D; prince<sub>∧</sub>
78.31: Sybil's] Sybils
81.5: madame] mademoiselle
81.8: madame] mademoiselle
83.16: would] may
84.6: quiet] qniet
87.1: Laval] de Beaumont
87.22: be restrained] E, D; restrained
88.12: astonished,] astonished.
88.31: page 52, para. 3] Page 110, part 4.
89.6: Laval] de Beaumont
89.34: *Salpêtrière*] *Salpetriere*

90.6: *Salpêtrière*] *Salpetriere*
92.20: hope] D; hopes
92.23: merely] D; meerly
94.4: page 51] page 110
94.17: that] which

## Letter 26

98.11: to a man] D; to man
98.20: makes] make

## Letter 28

101.14: Hill] hill
104.19: a great] great

## Letter 29

107.17: the] H; he

## Letter 30

111.10: her distress] D; het distress
113.37: welfare] E, D; welware

## Letter 32

114.19: account] D; acconnt

## Letter 33

116.27: depends] depend
116.31: separation] D; separa/tion

## Letter 34

118.22: friendship] D; friend/ship

## Letter 35

120.9: *séjour*] sejour

## Letter 39

126.15: Tisiphone] Tisiphoné
126.23: complexion] D; compiexion

## Letter 40

127.14: the repetition] D; repetition

## Letter 45

140.34: Française] Françoise

## Letter 48

145.17: render] E, D; rendered
146.38: month, and] D; month, and
146.38: her,] D; her.

## Letter 54

155.5: aver] D; averr

## Letter 58

160.14: love] loves
160.27: Iphigenia] Iphigene

## Letter 60

164.15: all,] all$_\wedge$
165.24: whom] which
165.27: (as] ,as
165.27: done)] done,
165.29: a] the
165.31: recipe] recipé

## Letter 61

167.36: The Female Seducers] the female seducers

## LETTER 62

170.37: herd] E, D; heard
172.1: St. James's St.] D; St. James St.

## LETTER 64

173.32: morning,] E, D; morning.

## LETTER 66

178.30: she intreated] D; intreated
178.32: cheek, which ] cheek. which

## LETTER 67

180.2–3: Paris. / My dear Woodville,] My dear Woodville, Paris

## LETTER 68

181.22: but I still flatter myself] E, D; but still flatter myself

## LETTER 69

184.18–22: is / bestowed / Too much of ornament, in outward shew / Elaborate, the inward's less exact—] is "bestowed too much of ornament, in outward shew elaborate, the inward's less exact:" which

## LETTER 71

189.23: Asked] D; , Asked

## LETTER 72

192.10: Châtelet] Chatelet
192.34: Châtelet] Chatelet
193.14: Châtelet] Chatelet

## LETTER 74

194.21: sixteen.] H, D; sixteen,

## Letter 75

197.14: tortured] D; tutored

## Letter 80

204.22: may be] D; may he

## Letter 81

205.25–26: though I may not] D; though I ay not

## Letter 82

207.3: subjects.] subjects,

## Letter 83

208.6: Barnard.] D; Barnard⌃

## Letter 84

209.32: that I] D; that

## Letter 86

211.14–15: ladyship's / Most] ladyship's Most
213.4–5: of /That] of "that
213.5–6: bourn / No] bourn no
213.6: returns.] returns."

## Letter 88

214.26: I was] D; Iwas
216.29: her,] D; her⌃
217.24: has] have

## Letter 89

219.19: tears"—] tears,"

## LETTER 90

221.14: Carignon] Carignan

## LETTER 91

222.2: Châtelet] Chatelet
222.13: Châtelet] Chatelet
223.8: Châtelet] Chatelet
223.24: setting] D; settiug
225.17: is] are
226.20: must ] D; mnst

## SUBSCRIPTION LIST

233.17: Supple,] Supple∧

# EXPLANATORY NOTES

~

The following abbreviations are used in these explanatory notes: *SJD* = Samuel Johnson, *A Dictionary of the English Language* (1765), facsimile ed. (London: Times Books, 1979); *OED* = *The Oxford English Dictionary*, 2d ed., 20 vols. (Oxford: Clarendon Press, 1989). In defining French words and phrases we have relied heavily on Able Boyer, *Dictionnaire Royal François-Anglois et Anglois-François, tiré des meilleurs auteurs . . . ,* 2 vols. (Lyon, 1768). Biblical quotations are quoted from the King James Version (Oxford: Oxford Univ. Press, n.d.).

## VOLUME I

1. L'amour . . . plaisirs. /Recueil Anonyme.] Fr.: Love can never live without pain, in a delicate soul, but its very pains are, sometimes, the source of love's sweetest pleasures. Anonymous Collection.

2. Bedford] John Russell, fourth Duke of Bedford (1700–1771), an English politician who served as Lord Lieutenant of Ireland from 1756 to 1761 and as Ambassador to France in 1762–63. In 1760, the Duke had given Richard Griffith a customs post. Elizabeth dedicated her translation, *Memoirs of Ninon de L'Enclos* (1761), and her comedy, *The Platonic Wife* (1765), to the Duchess of Bedford.

3. *épopée]* Fr.: an epic or heroic poem. *SJD* lists "epopee."

4. Trublet] Nicolas-Charles-Joseph Trublet (1697–1770) was the author of *Essais sur divers sujets de littérature et de morale* (6 vols., Paris, 1735–60). Educated by the Jesuits, he took the side of the moderns in the quarrel between the ancients and moderns. From 1736 to 1739 editor of the *Journal des Savants,* he then from 1758 to 1760 worked for the *Journal Crétien.*

5. *"Si un ouvrage . . . médiocre."]* Fr.: "If a work without flaw were possible, it would be possible only to an ordinary man."

6. *"Il n'y a rien . . . parfait."]* Fr.: "A work without fault and a perfect work are utterly different."

7. *with all its imperfections on its head]* Adapting the lament of the Ghost of Hamlet's father that he was murdered suddenly:

> Thus was I, sleeping, by a brother's hand,
> Of life, of Crown, of Queen at once dispatcht;
> Unhousel'd, disappointed, unaneal'd:
> No reck'ning made, but sent to my account
> With all my imperfections on my head.
> Oh, horrible! oh, horrible! most horrible!

[William Shakespeare, *Hamlet, Prince of Denmark*, Act 1, scene 8; vol. 8, pp. 167–68.] Unless otherwise indicated, all our citations of Shakespeare are from Samuel Johnson's edition, *The Plays of William Shakespeare*, 8 vols. (London, 1765).

8. hymeneals] marriage songs.

9. parterres] A parterre is "a level division of ground, that, for the most part, faces the south and best front of an house and is generally furnished with greens, flowers, etc." *SJD*.

10. lappets] "The parts of a head dress that hang loose." *SJD*.

11. closet] "A small room of privacy and retirement." *SJD*.

12. inoculate] as a safeguard against smallpox. According to *SJD*, "The practice of transplanting the small-pox, by infusion of the matter from ripened pustules into the veins of the uninfected, in hopes of procuring a milder sort than what frequently comes by infection. *Quincy.*" This procedure, called "variolation," could be unreliable and dangerous, although, given the death-rate from smallpox, many judged the risks worthwhile. Edward Jenner did not publish his account of a safer procedure using the cowpox until 1798.

13. Ranelagh] One of the fashionable London pleasure gardens. After paying an admission fee, usually half a crown, people could enter to enjoy walking in the formal gardens, listening to the music and other entertainments provided, and partaking of refreshments that included tea, coffee, bread, and butter.

14. Strephon] A common name for a shepherd in pastoral poetry. Lady Straffon puns.

15. *cap-à-pie*] Fr.: head to toe.

16. umpire] "An arbitrator; one who, as a common friend, decides disputes." *SJD*.

17. *un bel . . . dame*] Fr.: as a wit rather than as a beautiful woman.

18. grand tour] The grand tour was intended to be the capstone of the upperclass gentleman's education. The young gentleman, accompanied by a tutor, traveled through France, Italy (especially Rome), and, ideally, Germany and Holland as well. He was supposed to perfect his skill in languages, compare governments and manners, study the arts, meet distinguished foreigners, develop his judgment of men, and acquire urbanity.

19. where there are most words, there is generally the least sense] Probably recalling Alexander Pope's poem, "An Essay on Criticism" (ll. 309–10): "Words are like leaves; and where they most abound, / Much fruit of sense, beneath is rarely found." *The Works of Alexander Pope, Esq. In Nine Volumes, Complete. With His Last Correc-*

*tions, Additions, and Improvements* . . . . ed. William Warburton (London, 1757), vol. 1, p. 126. Subsequent Pope citations are from this edition.

20. saluted] Kissed.

21. *mauvaise honte]* Fr.: bashfulness, self-consciousness.

22. Hymen] The god of marriage.

23. *grands ballets]* Fr.: ballets.

24. twenty-fifth of March] Since he can be fairly sure that the roads will be passable and daylight more abundant after this date, Sir Harry prefers not to sleep elsewhere when he is within driving distance of his own bed.

25. *Carte du Païs]* Fr.: the lay of the land, how matters stand.

26. *quantum sufficit]* Latin: as much as is necessary.

27. Shakespear] The Shakespeare's Head in Covent Garden was one of the better London taverns.

28. Covent Garden] The London area where there was a market for flowers, fruit, and vegetables. A fashionable district in the early seventeenth century, by the mid-eighteenth century many of the houses had been converted into brothels.

29. Calypso] The beautiful goddess and enchantress who rescues Odysseus from the sea after his ship and men are lost between Scylla and Charybdis. Calypso takes Odysseus as her lover on the island of Ogygia until a stern command from Zeus forces her, reluctantly, to send him on his way home to his wife Penelope.

30. sharpers] "tricking fellows, petty thieves, rascals." *SJD.*

31. food of love] Alluding to the opening lines of Shakespeare's *Twelfth Night; or, What you Will,* lines spoken by the lovesick Orsino, Duke of Illyria, to musicians:

> If musick be the food of love, play on;
> Give me excess of it; that, surfeiting,
> The appetite may sicken, and so die. [Act 1, scene 1; vol. 2, p. 353]

32. "Days of ease, and nights of pleasure"] A quotation from Alexander Pope's "Two Chorus's to the Tragedy of Brutus" (1717). Pope wrote these poems to fit into the Duke of Buckingham's adaptation of Shakespeare's *Julius Caesar;* both were set to music by the Italian composer G. B. Bononcini in 1723. The second "Chorus of Youths and Virgins" is sung to Love and concludes:

> Hence guilty joys, distastes, surmises,
> Hence false tears, deceits, disguises,
> Dangers, doubts, delays, surprises;
>    Fires that scorch, yet dare not shine:
> Purest love's unwasting treasure,
> Constant faith, fair hope, long leisure,
> Days of ease, and nights of pleasure;
>    Sacred Hymen! these are thine.
> [*Works,* ed. Warburton (1757), vol. 1, p. 83.]

33. Syren] In Greek myth, a female creature who had the power of drawing men to destruction by her song. In Homer's *Odyssey,* Odysseus fills the ears of his crew with wax so they can row without being lured off course by the sirens, but he leaves his own ears unblocked and lashes himself to the mast to hear the song.

34. "good breeding . . . sense."] Quoting from "Satire V. On Women" (1727) by Edward Young (1683–1765):

> Few to good-breeding make a just pretence,
> Good-breeding is the blossom of good sense;
> The last result of an accomplisht mind,
> With outward grace, the *body's virtue,* joined.

[*Love of Fame, The Universal Passion. In Seven Characteristical Satires,* 2d ed. (London, 1728), p. 112.]

35. Hottentot] Literally, a person of one of the tribes of Southern Africa; in the transferred sense here intended, a person ignorant of the usages of civilized society.

36. Mr. Addison . . . afflictions."] Joseph Addison (1672–1719), poet, dramatist, and essayist, was a proprietor of and a principal contributor to the periodical the *Spectator.* Initially popular as a periodical, the *Spectator* continued to be read throughout the century as a compilation of essays in book form. Here quoting Addison in *Spectator* 163 (1711). Addison's reflections are prompted by a letter purporting to be from a young woman whose lover has suddenly died and who asks for consolation.

37. source, from whence our blessings flow] God. Recalling the "Morning Hymn" of Bishop Thomas Ken (1636–1711): "Praise God, from whom all blessings flow / Praise Him, all creatures here below!" *A Manual of Prayers for the Use of the Scholars of Winchester College. And all other Devout Christians. To which is added three Hymns for Morning, Evening, and Midnight* (London, 1695), p. 144. The lines, often used as a doxology, also conclude the Evening and Midnight hymns.

38. Lethe] In Roman mythology, a river in Hades; its waters were drunk by souls about to be reincarnated, who then forgot their previous lives. "Oblivion; a draught of oblivion." *SJD.*

39. "like the base Indian . . . tribe."] Adapting lines from Othello's penultimate speech in Shakespeare's *Othello:*

> one, whose hand,
> Like the base *Indian,* threw a pearl away
> Richer than all his tribe . . . .

These lines contain a famous crux; Johnson prints and argues for *Judean* instead of *Indian.* Here we quote from the edition of Edward Capell, *Mr. William Shakespeare. His Comedies, Histories, and Tragedies . . . .* 10 vols. (London, 1767–68), vol. 10, p. 119.

40. to an account] That is, Sir John Straffon would be tempted to defend the

honor of his family, injured by Sir James's jilting his sister Lucy, by challenging him to a duel.

41. Henry and Emma] Matthew Prior's long poem, "Henry and Emma" (1709), was based on the ballad of "The Nut-Brown Maid." The nobly born Henry disguises himself in various lowly garbs and courts the nobly born Emma until she is in love with him. Devising a test of "The Faith of Woman, and the Force of Love," he announces that he is guilty of murder and must flee from justice and from her. She volunteers to flee with him, but he elaborates on the evils that must attend that choice: loss of reputation, loss of beauty as she must disguise herself too, hunger, danger of death, and so on. He defines her choice as between virtue and love for him. As she persists in her wish to flee with him, he accuses her of a "roving Fancy" that would yield to any man's temptation and even (falsely) tells her that he now loves another; abject, she persists in her love, asking only to attend her rival as a servant and to be remembered by Henry at her death as one "whom Love abandon'd to Despair." Henry then confesses that all his stories were false; Emma has passed his tests and rejoices in his love. *The Literary Works of Matthew Prior,* ed. H. Bunker Wright and Monroe K. Spears, 2d ed. (Oxford: Clarendon Press, 1971), vol. 1, pp. 278–300.

"Henry and Emma" was extremely popular, beloved by many, but was also controversial. William Cowper, for instance, thought Samuel Johnson's condemnation of the poem showed Johnson had never understood love. *The Letters and Prose Writing of William Cowper,* ed. James King and Charles Ryskamp, 4 vols. (Oxford: Clarendon Press, 1984), vol. 2, pp. 4–5.

42. "to mention, is to suffer pain"] Lady Harriet prefaces her recital of her history with a reference to Matthew Prior's most serious long poem, *Solomon on the Vanity of the World* (1718). In Book 2, entitled "Pleasure," and quoted three times in *The Delicate Distress,* the Biblical King Solomon explores the possibilities of finding happiness through pleasures, including the construction of magnificent buildings and gardens, music, and love. His hand-maiden and slave, Abra, begs leave to tell Solomon of her growing passion for him:

> Mine to obey; Thy Part is to ordain:
> And tho' to mention, be to suffer Pain;
> If the King smiles, whilst I my Woe recite;
> If weeping I find Favour in His Sight;
> Flow fast my Tears, full rising his Delight. [ll. 398–402]
> [*The Literary Works of Matthew Prior,* vol. 1, p. 344.]

43. involved] That is, the Earl's estate had many liens upon it, such as mortgages, and he required cash for debt service and to avoid foreclosure.

44. portion] A girl's portion was the share of her parents' estate, often expressed as a lump sum of money, to which she was entitled, normally by the terms of the marriage settlement of her parents.

45. entailed] The Colonel might have left her more, but, as was often the case in the upper classes, he was not legally entitled to control the disposition of his entire estate. The cash and other chattel (personal) property he could and did devise to Harriet, but the real estate had previously been entailed or settled on his male heirs, probably by the Colonel's own marriage settlement. Harriet's account suggests that the Colonel is worried that his son and heir, Harriet's father, will fail to provide appropriately for her.

46. soliciting a ship] Although the navy was closer to being a meritocracy than the army, officers and their families and friends did solicit patronage from men who had influence over appointments. Captain Barnard's father lobbies for his son to have command of a ship and succeeds.

47. A mutual flame . . . a foe.] Lady Harriet quotes, slightly altering, a literary ballad, *Edwin, and Emma* (1760), by the Scottish poet, David Mallet (1705?-1765). Mallet's original lines read "home-felt bliss" rather than "heart-felt bliss." The love of Edwin and Emma, begun so happily, is opposed by Edwin's "sordid" father, who thinks Emma too poor, and by Edward's envious sister. Edwin dies of his love, and, when Emma hears his death knell, she dies of a broken heart. *Edwin, and Emma* (Birminghamshire: Printed by John Baskerville for A. Millar, 1760), p. 61.

48. Arcadian] Ideally rural. Arcadia is a mountainous region in Greece whose inhabitants claimed to be the oldest people in Greece; in poetry, Arcadia was frequently chosen as the place for pastoral.

49. not a shilling for me] As her grandfather feared, Harriet's father settled his estate on the children of the second marriage, omitting provision for Harriet. Also, as her father and guardian he was in receipt of the £6,000 that was hers under her grandfather's will. But at his death his debts exceeded his assets; apparently Harriet's stepmother has used Harriet's £6,000 to help pay off these debts. Harriet has a legal right to the £6,000, but, as a pious and moral child she scruples to sue her stepmother to enforce the right.

50. "I think . . . him."] Quoting Helena in Shakespeare's *All's Well that Ends Well* (Act 1, scene 2, 11. 1–3; vol. 3, p. 282). Helena, daughter of the physician Gerard de Nabron, now dead, soliloquizes that her present tears, taken by others for tears of mourning, are actually tears of her frustrated love for Count Bertram, who does not love her.

51. Bristol] The spa at Bristol Hot Wells, smaller than its more famous neighbor, the spa at Bath.

52. Downs] "The treeless undulating chalk uplands of the south and southeast of England. . . ." *OED*, s.v. "down."

53. splendid sum] Harriet writes ironically, thinking the sum paltry rather than splendid. If £4,000 were conservatively invested to yield 4 percent, a common yield for conservative investments in the period, she would have £160 a year, an income roughly equivalent to the stipends of the better-off clergy of the period.

54. echo] In classical mythology, Echo was a nymph who used her endless flow of talk to detain Juno when Juno might have discovered her consort Jupiter

sleeping with other female spirits. When Juno caught on to Echo's trick, she punished her by making it impossible for her to initiate speech, but only to repeat the last words spoken by another. Echo then fell in love with Narcissus and followed him; she could not declare her love until Narcissus happened to utter words, some of which she could repeat. Narcissus fled from her. Scorned and shamed, she withdrew into the woods, and withered away until only her voice remained. The story is told in Book 3 of Ovid's *Metamorphoses*.

55. Niobe] Ovid in *Metamorphoses,* Book 4, tells the story of how the goddess Leto becomes enraged at Niobe, who, although human, boasts that she is more beautiful than Leto and more blessed, in part because she has fourteen children while Leto has only two. After Niobe forces the Phrygians to cease their worship of Leto and worship her instead, Leto retaliates by having all Niobe's children killed. Niobe's grief turns her to stone; she is carried away by a whirlwind to a mountain top, where tears continually fall from her marble face.

56. peace] The Treaty of Paris, signed in 1763, brought an end to the Seven Years War between England and France.

57. Montpellier] A city in the south of France, near the Mediterranean, frequented in this period by those in search of health.

58. *grand monde]* Fr.: persons of quality.

59. *gens d'armes]* Fr.: armed men, soldiers.

60. own religion] She is, presumably, a Protestant and a member of the Church of England.

61. With thee . . . of art.] Apparently adapting a couplet from "To Mr. George Grenville. Elegy XV" of James Hammond (1710–1742):

> With thee I scorn the low Constraint of Art,
> Nor fear to trust the Follies of my Heart.
> [*Love Elegies Written in the Year 1732*, 3d ed. (London, 1752), p. 30).]

62. *la belle passion]* Fr.: the beautiful passion, a periphrasis for "love."

63. willow] The willow tree was associated with grief over lost love.

64. *chef d'œvre]* Fr.: masterpiece.

65. Tuileries] Notable Parisian gardens, open to the public, first designed in an Italian style in the sixteenth century, then redesigned in the French style by André Le Nôtre in 1661.

66. Rousseau] The French philosopher Jean-Jacques Rousseau in 1761 published his epistolary novel, *La Nouvelle Héloïse.* One of the greatest and most controversial works of late eighteenth-century sentimentalism, the novel offered letters of great "tenderness" written by both its heroine, Julie, and her lover, Saint-Preux.

67. Gazette] The newspaper of record, printing government notices, accounts of ceremonies, and lists, as well as diplomatic and foreign news.

68. "smiling at grief"] Again quoting Shakespeare's *Twelfth Night: Or, What You Will,* this time the scene in which the Duke and Viola, disguised as a boy, debate

whether women have as much capacity to love as men. Viola, arguing that women are "as true of heart" as men, offers as evidence a "history" which, though the Duke does not know it, is her own:

> She never told her love,
> But let concealment, like a worm i'th'bud,
> Feed on her damask cheek: She pin'd in thought;
> And, with a green and yellow melancholy,
> She sat like Patience on a monument,
> Smiling at Grief. [Act 2, scene 6; vol. 2, p. 391]

69. bravo] "A man who murders for hire." *SJD.*

70. "above life's . . . too"] From Alexander Pope's very famous and eminently quotable philosophical poem, *An Essay on Man* (1733–34). This fourth epistle considers the "Nature and State of Man, with respect to Happiness," and reviews the debate over the relationship of virtue and happiness. Here, wisdom is said not to be a guarantor of happiness:

> 'Tis but to know how little can be known;
> To see all others faults, and feel our own
> . . . . . . . . . . . . . . . . . . . . . .
> Painful preheminence! yourself to view
> Above life's weakness, and its comforts too. [Book 4, ll. 261–62, 267–68]
> [*Works,* ed. Warburton (1757), vol. 3, p. 152.]

71. *Grève*] Criminals were executed in La place de Grève in Paris, in front of the Hôtel-de-Ville and near the Seine.

72. "proud . . . gentleman-like"] Quoting Ben Jonson's comedy, *Every Man in his Humour,* popular in the mid-eighteenth century in David Garrick's adaptation. Stephen, a "Country Gull" who aspires to fashionable gentility, is teased by his more sophisticated cousin, Edward Knowell, to hold up his head "and let the Idea of what you are be portrayed, i' your face. . . ." Stephen replies, ". . . . I will be more proud and melancholy and gentleman-like than I have been, I'll insure you." *The Plays of David Garrick,* ed. Harry William Pedicord and Fredrick Louis Bergman, 7 vols. (Carbondale and Edwardsville: Southern Illinois Univ. Press, 1982), vol. 6, p. 66.

73. Aeolian harp] Aeolus, a friend of the gods, in the *Odyssey* gave Odysseus a bag of winds; later he came to be regarded as the god of the winds. The Aeolian harp was a stringed instrument sounded by natural wind, requiring no human player. The sound boxes were of various shapes, usually with four to twelve strings, though sometimes more. A correspondent in the *Gentleman's Magazine* 24 (1754):74, observing that the instrument is not yet "thoroughly known," provides a diagram and directions for making an Aeolian harp designed to be fitted into a window. James Thomson, in "An Ode on Aeolus's Harp" (1748) speculated:

> Those tender notes, how kindly they upbraid!
>> With what soft woe they thrall the lover's heart!
> Sure from the hand of some unhappy maid
>> Who died of love these sweet complainings part.

But the appeal of the harp in the age of sensibility is best conveyed by three stanzas in Thomson's *Castle of Indolence* (Canto I, xxxix–xli), where the Wizard of Indolence holds his captives in thrall with soft pleasures, including the music of an Aeolian harp:

> Aerial music in the warbling wind,
> At distance rising oft, by small degrees,
> Nearer and nearer came, till o'er the trees
> It hung, and breathed such soul-dissolving airs
> As did, alas! with soft perdition please:
> Entangled deep in its enchanting snares,
>> The listening heart forgot all duties and all cares.

[James Thomson, *Liberty, The Castle of Indolence, and Other Poems,* ed. James Sambrook (Oxford: Clarendon Press, 1986), pp. 314–15, 176–77.]

74. *Au contraire]* Fr.: on the contrary.

75. *faire la guerre]* Fr.: to banter about a thing.

76. first mother] Eve. The "first mother" of all women, Eve showed her curiousity in the Garden of Eden when the serpent tempted her to eat the fruit of the one tree God had forbidden Adam and Eve to enjoy. When the serpent tells her that to eat of this fruit will open their eyes and make them "as gods, knowing good and evil," Eve wishes to be wise, but in succumbing to the serpent's temptation brings death and sin to mankind. Genesis 3:5.

77. *the fly upon the chariot wheel]* A fable that became proverbial. According to Bacon in "Of Vain-glory": "It was prettily devised of *Aesop, The Fly sate upon the Axletree of the Charriot-wheel, and said, What a Dust do I raise?—.* So there are some *Vain Persons,* that whatsoever goeth alone, or moveth upon greater Means, if they have never so little Hand in it, they think it is they that carry it." *The Essays or Counsels, Civil and Moral, of Sir Francis Bacon, Lord, Verulam, Viscount St. Alban . . .* (London, 1673), p. 230. In Matthew Prior's version, "The Flies" (1721): "(Says t'other, perch'd upon the Wheel:) / Did ever any mortal Fly / Raise such a Cloud of Dust, as I?" *The Literary Works of Matthew Prior,* vol. 1, p. 453.

78. quarte or tierce] Two of the positions in fencing; the third and the fourth parries in sword-play.

79. *Hélas, ma pauvre enfant!]* Fr.: Alas, my poor child!

80. *badinage]* Fr.: light, trifling raillery or humorous banter.

81. *quelque chose de nouveau]* Fr.: something new.

82. Apollo] The son of Zeus, who was worshiped by the Greeks and Romans as a god of healing, of music, of poetry, and of prophecy. A number of great eighteenth-

century estates were adorned with classicizing architecture, including temples to gods and goddesses. For example, Stourhead in Wiltshire, Henry Hoare's estate, boasted a Temple of Flora, a Pantheon, and, at the top of a hill, a circular Temple of Apollo, this last designed by Flitcroft in 1765 and derived from the Temple of Venus at Baalbec.

83. Shenstone's elegies] In 1743 the poet William Shenstone wrote to his friend, Richard Jago, "I send you my pastoral elegy (or ballad, if you think the name more proper) . . . ." As "A Pastoral Ballad," in four parts, the poem was first published in Dodsley's *Collection,* vol. 4 (1755), where it was mistakenly attributed to Thomas Arne, who composed music for it. Subsequently, it appeared in Shenstone's *Works* I (1764), pp. 189–98. The four parts, in each of which the shepherd speaks, are entitled: "Absense," "Hope," "Solicitude," and "Disappointment." The lines Lord Woodville sings are from the first stanza of the last part:

> She was fair—and my passion begun;
> She smil'd—and I could not but love:
> She is faithless—and I am undone.

[*The Works in Verse and Prose of William Shenstone, Esq; . . .,* 2 vols. (London, 1764), p. 196.]

Arne's music appears in *Numb. VII. The Agreeable Musical Choice. A Pastoral Collection of Songs Sung at the Publick Gardens. Composed by Mr. Arne* (London, 175?), pp. 4–5.

84. nurse] A wet nurse, a woman who was hired to suckle and nurse Lord Woodville when he was an infant. Upper-class women in the earlier eighteenth century often did not nurse their own children.

85. lye in] Give birth.

86. foster sister] The nurse's daughter has become the "foster sister" of Lord Woodville because he was "fostered" or nursed by the same mother. That he honors this relationship, however archly, is intended as a sign of his benevolence and sensibility.

87. sumpter car] A wheeled vehicle for carrying provisions.

88. *Languedoc]* The southernmost region of France, bordering on the Mediterranean; Montpellier and Toulouse are principal cities.

89. Dian's modesty] Dian or Diana was a Roman goddess, sister of Apollo, especially worshiped by women. At her request, her father Jupiter gave her permission to be a perpetual virgin.

90. desart rose] Probably an allusion to Thomas Gray's famous "Elegy Written in a Country Churchyard" (1751): "Full many a flower is born to blush unseen / And waste its sweetness on the desert air" (ll. 55–56). *The Poems of Thomas Gray, William Collins, Oliver Goldsmith,* ed. Roger Lonsdale (London: Longman's, 1969), p. 127.

91. *accouchement]* Fr.: child-bed, a woman's delivery.

92. Aurora] Aurora, the goddess of dawn, was the mother of Memnon, for whose death at the hands of Achilles she was thought to shed tears in the form of dew.

93. *fierté*] Fr.: haughtiness.

94. heretic] "When a papist uses the word *hereticks,* he generally means Protestants; when a Protestant uses the word, he means any persons wilfully and contentiously obstinate in fundamental errours." Watt's *Logick,* quoted in *SJD.*

95. devoted her to heaven] Decided to commit her to a convent.

96. Pandora's box] Pandora in Greek mythology was the name of the first woman, created on Zeus's orders to avenge Prometheus's theft of fire from heaven and destined to bring misery to humankind. In one version of the myth, the gods give her a gift, a casket or sealed jar containing all the evils that were to plague mankind. Curiosity led her to open it and loose the evils on the world.

97. Sybil's leaves] The Sybil was an oracle; the prophecies of the Cumaean Sibyl were inscribed on palm leaves. In Virgil's *Aeneid,* Book 6, Aeneas consults the Sybil to learn what awaits him in Italy and she prophesies future wars. In John Dryden's translation, Aeneas pleads with her:

> But, oh! commit not thy prophetick Mind
> To flitting Leaves, the sport of ev'ry Wind:
> Lest they disperse in Air our empty Fate:
> Write not, but what the Pow'rs ordain, relate. [11. 116–19]

[*The Works of John Dryden. Vol. 5. Poems. The Works of Virgil in English (1697),* ed. William Frost and Vinton A. Dearing (Berkeley: Univ. of California Press, 1987), p. 530]

98. deaf adder] Psalm 58:4: "They are like the deaf adder that stoppeth her ear."

99. *farouche*] Fr.: wild, fierce, unsociable.

100. *La Salpêtrière*] On the site of a place where saltpeter, an ingredient of gunpowder, was manufactured, Louis XIV in 1656 founded an asylum for the indigent; a house of correction for women was added in 1684.

101. broke] Demoted in rank.

102. Aaron's rod] In Exodus 7, the magicians of the Egyptian Pharaoh try to show that their powers are stronger than the power of the Lord in his priest Aaron. Aaron casts down his rod and it becomes a serpent. The Egyptian magicians transform their rods into serpents too, "but Aaron's rod swallowed up their rods."

103. "sweet peace . . . ever"] An apposite quotation from Milton's *Comus* (1. 368). The Elder Brother in Milton's masque expresses his confidence that his sister, the virtuous Lady, although lost in the dark woods, can come to no real harm:

> I do not think my sister so to seek,
> Or so unprincipled in virtue's book,
> And the sweet peace that goodness bosoms ever,
> As that the single want of light and noise
> (Not being in danger, as I trust she is not)
> Could stir the constant mood of her calm thoughts,

And put them into mis-becoming plight.
Virtue could see to do what Virtue would
By her own radiant light, though sun and moon
Were in the flat sea sunk. And wisdom's self
Oft seeks to sweet retired solitude,
Where with her best nurse Contemplation,
She plumes her feathers, and lets grow her wings . . . .
[11. 366–78]

["A Mask Presented at Ludlow-Castle, 1634," in *Paradise Regain'd. A Poem in Four Books. To which is added Samson Agonistes; And Poems upon Several Occasions. The Author John Milton,* ed. Thomas Newton, D.D. (London, 1752).]

104. hanging sleeves] Loose open sleeves, hanging down from the arms; worn by children and young persons.

105. *les petits soins*] Fr.: small cares.

106. *Cecisbeo*] Var. *cacisbeo*. In Italy, the recognized gallant or *cavalier servente* of a married woman. Lady Mary Wortley Montagu described the custom in a letter to her sister, wryly observing that it kept the young men occupied and prevented them from cutting "one another's throats *pour passer le temps*":

These are Gentlemen that devote themselves to the service of a particular Lady (I mean a marry'd one, for the virgins are all invisible, confin'd to convents). They are oblig'd to wait on her to all public places, the Plays, Operas, and Assemblies . . . , where they wait behind her Chair, take care of her fan and Gloves if she plays, have the privelege of Whispers, etc. . . . In short, they are to spend all their time and Money in her service who rewards them according to her Inclination (for Opportunity they want none), but the husband is not to have the Impudence to suppose 'tis any other than pure platonic Friendship.
[Genoa, 28 August 1718]
[*The Complete Letters of Lady Mary Wortley Montagu,* ed. Robert Halsband, 3 vols. (Oxford: Clarendon Press, 1965–67), vol. 1, pp. 429–30.]

107. woodhouse] A woodhouse is a figure of a wild man of the woods or of a satyr, used as a decoration. (*OED* s.v., "woodwose, woodhouse")

108. Arcadian star] In Milton's masque, *Comus,* the Elder Brother, lost in the wood, asks for a star to guide them and promises:

And thou shalt be our star of Arcady,
Or Tyrian Cynosure. [11. 341–42]

The star of Arcady was the constellation of the Great Bear, by which Greek mariners steered, and the Tyrian Cynosure was the North Pole Star in the Little Bear, by which Tyrians navigated. Callisto, the daughter of an Arcadian king, loved by Zeus, was changed into the Great Bear; her son Arcas became the Little Bear.

109. felucca] "A small vessel propelled by oars or lateen sails, or both, used chiefly on the Mediterranean, for coasting voyages." *OED*.

110. But . . . care and pain.] Very slightly adapting lines from the blank verse epic *Leonidas. A Poem* (London, 1737), p. 210, by Richard Glover (1712–1785). The poem is based on the Greek historian Herodotus's narrative of the Persian effort to conquer Greece and Sparta and of the heroic defence of the pass at Thermopylae by the Spartan Leonidas in 480 B.C. In the lines quoted, the royal maid Ariana addresses Leonidas on the occasion of the death of her lover, the Persian general Teribazus; she subsequently kills herself.

111. *piasters]* "An Italian coin, about five shillings sterling in value." *SJD*.

112. in Italian] The Italian word for "summer" is "estate."

113. *séjour]* Fr.: an adobe, a residence.

114. "*Obedience* is better than SACRIFICE."] The title of one of the *Psalms of David* (1719) by Isaac Watts (1674–1748): "Obedience is better than Sacrifice (Psalm 50. v. 10, 1, 14, 15, 23. Second Part [Common Meter])." Although Watts's *Psalms* use elements of the Old Testament Psalms, they are not translations or even close paraphrases, but rather Christian interpretations.

## Volume II

1. methodist's chapel] Lord Woodville teases his friend by suggesting that his gloominess and his warnings of dire evils are in the spirit of preachers to be found at methodist chapels. In the 1760's, the religious movement called methodism was still a movement within the Church of England, but one criticized as potentially schismatic. Its leader, John Wesley, was a clergyman of the Church of England who preached salvation through faith and inspired evangelical preaching throughout Britain and America. The warmth of Wesley's preaching, sometimes out of doors and often in other men's parishes, and his recruiting laymen to preach disturbed many and provoked satire.

2. Pseudo-magus] A "magus" was a member of an ancient Persian priestly caste; in a wider sense, it referred to one skilled in oriental magic and astrology, a magician or sorcerer. A "pseudo-magus" is a false magician.

3. Tisiphone] One of the Furies, who were, according to Hesiod, primal beings born from the blood of the castrated Uranus. They were avengers of crime, especially crimes against the ties of kinship. Lord Woodville refers back to Seymour's image of an Emily enraged by jealousy. Ovid's Tisiphone is a frightful creature: "Then, stretching out her arms, round which the serpents were knotted and coiled, she gave her head a toss. The snakes of her hair hissed as they were disturbed: some lay upon her shoulders, some slipped down around her breast, uttering sibilant sounds, vomiting gore and flickering their tongues." *The Metamorphoses of Ovid*, trans. Mary M. Innes (Harmondsworth, Middlesex: Penguin Books, 1953), Book 4, p. 116.

4. Pharo-bank] "Pharo" or "Faro" was "a gambling game at cards, in which the players bet on the order in which certain cards will appear when taken singly from the top of the pack." A "pharo-bank" is "the banker's deposit of money against which the other players put their stakes." *OED,* s.v. faro.

5. *salique]* Or Salic law. The "allegedly fundamental law of the French monarchy, by which females were excluded from the succession to the crown; hence generally a law excluding females from dynastic succession." *OED,* s.v. Salic.

6. Diana . . . and moves.] Lord Woodville adapts lines from Matthew Prior's *Solomon on the Vanity of the World,* earlier quoted by Lady Harriet Hanbury (Letter 13). King Solomon has allowed himself to fall in love with his female slave Abra; he shocks his subjects by publicly indulging her every whim. Bejeweled and on a "Milk-white Steed," Abra appears to hunt with the King and his court:

> DIANA, Huntress, Mistress of the Groves,
> The fav'rite ABRA speaks, and looks, and moves.
> Her, as the present Goddess, I obey:
> Beneath her Feet the captive Game I lay. [Bk. 2, ll. 629–32]

7. Apelles] A painter of the 4th century B.C., considered the greatest painter of antiquity. He was noted for the grace and charm of his portraits. His most famous picture was that of Aphrodite just rising from the sea.

8. *en Turk]* Fr.: in the Turkish way; here, like a Turk with a seraglio of women.

9. "and live . . . love alone"] In Prior's *Solomon on the Vanity of the World,* previously quoted by Lord Woodville in Letter 40, Solomon repents the infamy into which his passion for Abra has led him and turns her away. Yet even after her death he longs for her:

> How oft, all Day, recall'd I ABRA's Charms,
> Her Beauties press'd, and panting in my Arms?
> . . . . . . . . . . . . . . . . . . . .
> How oft desir'd to fly from ISRAEL's Throne,
> And live in Shades with her and Love alone? [Bk. 2, ll. 835–36, 839–40]

10. Brutus . . . a name."] "A Vertuous Unbeliever, who lies under the Pressure of Misfortunes, has reason to cry out, as they say *Brutus* did a little before his Death, *O Vertue, I have worshipped thee as a Substantial Good, but I find thou art an empty Name."* Addison, *Spectator* 293 (1712).

11. Scipio] Publius Cornelius Scipio, Africanus Major (236–183 B.C.); Roman conqueror of Spain and victor in the second Punic War. He was said to have restored a captive princess to her lover, Alleucius, and given the money her parents brought for a ransom to add to her portion. Oliver Goldsmith tells the story in his *Roman History, From the Foundation of the City of Rome, To the Destruction of the Western Empire,* 2 vols. (London, 1769), vol. 1, chap. 16, pp. 282–83.

12. Amianthus] Or amiantus. The first edition offers a footnote: *"The Asbestos, or Salamander's wool."* According to the *OED,* "a mineral, a variety of asbestos, splitting into long flexible pearly white fibers. . . ." Also called "earth flax" and "salamander's hair."

13. Adonis] In classical mythology, an extraordinarily handsome human born of an incestuous union between Cinyras, king of Cyrus, and his daughter, Myrrha. Penitent and pregnant, Myrrha begs the gods to change her into another form. They change her into a tree, from which Adonis is born. The goddess Venus falls in love with him, but cannot prevent his being killed by a wild boar.

14. *cara sposa]* Italian: dear wife.

15. *d'une dame Française]* Fr.: of a French lady.

16. plays deep] gambles for high stakes.

17. a certain desirable event] A periphrastic way of referring to the birth of a child.

18. *terra incognita]* Latin: unknown territory.

19. *à la mort]* Fr.: dying.

20. Eton] A prestigious boys' school in Eton, Berkshire.

21. Henry the Sixth] The king who founded Eton in 1440–41.

22. *the mountain . . . Mahomet]* "Mahomet" was a common earlier spelling of "Muhammad," the prophet and founder of Islam. The saying was proverbial. Frances Bacon, for example, in "Boldness," wrote: *"Mahomet* called the Hill to him . . . .And when the Hill stood still, he was never a whit abashed, but said; *If the Hill will not come to* Mahomet, Mahomet *will go to the Hill." The Essays or Counsels,* p. 49.

23. bills of mortality] Periodically published lists of the number of deaths in particular districts of London, often sorted by cause of death.

24. O the soft . . . pain to live.] Quoting, with slight alteration, from Edward Young's important religious poem, *The Complaint, or Night Thoughts on Life, Death, and Immortality* (1742–54). Night V, "The Relapse," contemplates the early death of an innocent young girl whom the poet has known and also the deaths of Lysander, who dies at sea in a storm on his wedding day, and his bride Aspasia, who drowns "without the furious Ocean's Aid, / In suffocating Sorrows." In the concluding lines, the poet envies the fate of those who die "undivorc'd by Death!" and exclaims:

> O the soft Commerce! O the tender Tyes,
> Close-twisted with the Fibres of the Heart!
> Which broken, break them; and drain off the Soul
> Of Human Joy; and make it Pain to Live—

[*Night Thoughts,* ed. Stephen Cornford (Cambridge: Cambridge Univ. Press, 1989), Night V, ll. 1063–66.]

25. *sages femmes]* Fr.: midwives.

26. *Te Deum]* From the opening words of the Latin original, *Te Deum laudamus,* "Thee, God, we praise." "An ancient Latin hymn of praise in the form of

a psalm, sung as a thanksgiving on special occasions, as after a victory or deliverance . . ." *OED*.

27. *Circe]* In Greek mythology, a goddess whose magic has the power to turn men into beasts and to make them forget their native lands. Odysseus, although protected from her tranformative powers by a magic herb, nevertheless stays with her on her island for one year in *Odyssey,* Book 10.

28. se'nnight] "(Contracted from *sevennight*) The space of seven nights and days, a week." *SJD*.

29. "O may . . . torch!"] Adapting a line from James Thomson's popular tragedy, *Tancred and Sigismunda* (1745). Tancred, although in love with Sigismunda, has signed a pledge to marry Constantia. Sigismunda, although in love with Tancred, has been commanded by her father to marry Osmond. Sigismunda, distraught, briefly allows her love to turn to rage and utters a curse upon Tancred's approaching marriage and upon her own:

> O may the Furies light his Nuptial Torch!
> Be it accurs'd as mine! [Act 3, scene 3, ll. 69–70]
> [*The Plays of James Thomson, 1700–1748,* ed. John C. Greene, 2 vols. (New York: Garland, 1987,) vol. 2, p. 438.]

30. musketeer] "A soldier whose weapon is his musket." *SJD*.

31. Lear] Shakespeare's *Lear* was most familiar in the eighteenth century in Nahum Tate's adaptation, *The History of King Lear* (1681), a version in which Cordelia lives to become Queen and marry Edgar. Lear says to Cordelia in the Tate version:

> Come, Kent, Cordelia come,
> We too will sit alone, like birds i'th'cage.
> Then thou dost ask me blessing, I'll kneel down
> And ask of thee forgiveness. [Act 5, scene 4, ll. 69–72]
> [Nahum Tate, *The History of King Lear,* ed. James Black (Lincoln: Univ. of Nebraska Press, 1975), p. 84.]

David Garrick dominated the role at mid-century and gradually brought back more Shakespearian elements, though without altering the happy ending.

32. For either . . . peace confound.] Quoting Milton, *Paradise Lost,* Book 10, ll. 898–908. *Paradise Lost. A Poem in Twelve Books. The Author John Milton, The Third Ed.,* ed. Thomas Newton, D.D., 2 vols. (London, 1754), vol. 2, pp. 110–11.

33. Cymon and Iphigenia] Characters in a tale of Giovanni Boccaccio, well known to English readers in John Dryden's translation in his *Fables Ancient and Modern; Translated into Verse* (1700). Although wellborn, Cymon is awkward and clownish, unimproved by the instruction his father provides for him, preferring rustic company to the company of gentlemen. Only when he sees and falls in love with the

beautiful Iphigenia does he begin to dress like a gentlemen, study the liberal arts, and learn to move "with graceful Ease." Garrick wrote a "dramatic romance" on the subject, *Cymon,* which premiered on 2 January 1767 with music by Charles Dibden. *The Poems and Fables of John Dryden,* ed. James Kinsley (London: Oxford Univ. Press), "Cymon and Iphigenia. From Boccace," pp. 815–31.

34. residuary legatee] The person entitled by a will to take that part of the estate which is left after other legacies and devises have been paid and all legal claims against the estate discharged.

35. settlements] The prenuptial contracts normally negotiated before upper-class marriages. Family lawyers and male relatives of the bride and groom normally participated in these negotiations; brides did not.

36. use] A legal term: the equitable right to receive the profit or benefit of real property divorced from the legal ownership thereof. Lucy understands that she has only an entitlement to enjoy an income for her life from the underlying asset; she does not own it in the sense of being able to sell it, and she cannot control the disposition of it after her death.

37. bequeath] Lucy correctly understands the law. As a single woman she is entitled to make a will leaving her money to whomever she likes; once she is married, she will be able to make a valid will only with the consent of her husband.

38. shoe buckles . . . egrette] Jeweled shoe-buckles were fashionable ornaments for both men and women in this period. An "egrette" or "aigrette" was a jeweled ornament worn in the hair or headdress, most often in the form of a feather or feathers, or supporting a feather. It was named after the egret, or lesser white heron, whose head is adorned with a beautiful crest of feathers. Lady Straffon probably understands that these jewels she gives Lucy will fall into the legal category of paraphernalia, that is, goods, consisting of her apparel and ornaments, suitable to her rank and degree, which a wife, after the death of her husband, legally owns; widows could devise paraphernalia.

39. sigh, no more] Perhaps alluding to the song in Shakespeare's *Much Ado about Nothing:*

> *Sigh no more, ladies, sigh no more,*
> *    Men were deceivers ever;*
> *One foot in sea, and one on shore,*
> *    To one thing constant never . . . .* [Act 2, scene 9; vol. 3, p. 206]

40. Penelope] The wife of Odysseus in Homer's *Odyssey.* She remains faithful to him during the twenty years of his absense despite the blandishments of many suitors.

41. When youth . . . their due.] Slightly adapting lines from *The Force of Religion* (1714) by Edward Young. The poem celebrates the heroism of Lady Jane Grey (1537–1554), Queen of England for nine days. In Young's version, despite Queen

Mary's offer to spare her life and that of her husband, Lord Guilford, if she will renounce her Protestant faith and convert to Roman Catholicism, Lady Jane elects to remain true to her faith and is beheaded. *The Force of Religion; or, Vanquish'd Love. A Poem. In Two Books* (London, 1714), p. 2.

42. The silent Heart . . . nurse of woe.] Quoting, with slight variation, lines from "A Hymn to Contentment" by the Irish poet Thomas Parnell (1679–1718). The poem was first posthumously published in Parnell's *Poems on Several Occasions* (1721).

43. king Cophetua . . . Mariannes] In British legend, king Cophetua was an African king who never loved until a dart from Cupid makes him fall in love with a beggar maid, Penelophon, he sees before his palace. He marries her and they live happily until they die. The story is told in "King Cophetua and the Beggar Maid," one of the ballads collected in Thomas Percy's *Reliques of Ancient English Poetry* (1765). Pamela was the heroine of Samuel Richardson's novel, *Pamela; or, Virtue Rewarded* (1740). A servant in the house of Mr. B., she resists all his attempts at seduction until he eventually marries her. Marianne was the heroine of a long, but tantalizingly uncompleted French novel, *La Vie de Marianne* (1731–34), by Pierre Carlet de Chamblain de Marivaux. Orphaned at age two, Marianne believes herself, with some justification, to be an upper-class person, but she cannot prove who her parents were. She struggles to be virtuous and to be accepted into polite society, resisting the attempt of M. de Climal, a supposedly religious and charitable man, to seduce her into becoming his mistress. She is close to marrying the upper-class Valville, whom she loves, when she is virtually kidnapped and given choices that include entering a convent or marrying a lower-class man. She again resists, but Valville proves weak and unfaithful.

44. Female Seducers] Henry Brooke's "The Female Seducers" in Edward Moore's *Fables for the Female Sex* (London, 1744). More like an allegory than a fable, the poem tells of fifteen-year-old Chastity, whose parents tell her she must go on a dangerous journey to climb a mountain in the province of virtue and warn her that "if once thy sliding foot should stray":

> Reproach, scorn, infamy, and hate,
> On thy returning steps shall wait,
> Thy form be loath'd by ev'ry eye,
> And ev'ry foot thy presence fly. [pp. 127–28]

As she reaches the heights of the mountain, Sirens sing to tempt her to "fierce delights" and Curiosity and Pleasure come to pull her down. Honour, her former companion, looks on helplessly and addresses "fair ones":

> Nor, with the guilty world, upbraid
> The fortunes of a wretch betray'd,
> But o'er her failing cast a veil,
> Remembering, you yourselves are frail. [p. 138]

As Slander and Contempt assail her, a remorseful Chastity attempts to return to the land of virtue. Virtue speaks from the sky to summon the penitent to find forgiveness and happiness in heaven.

45. "When they . . . God."] Quoting Jonathan Swift's "Verses on the Death of Dr. Swift." Swift, imagining various reactions to news of his death, imagines that some few of those he loves will grieve, but:

> The rest will give a Shrug and cry,
> I'm sorry; but we all must dye.
> Indifference clad in Wisdom's Guise,
> All Fortitude of Mind supplies:
> For how can stony Bowels melt,
> In those who never Pity felt;
> When *We* are lash'd, *They* kiss the Rod;
> Resigning to the Will of God. [ll. 211–18]

[*The Poems of Jonathan Swift*, ed. Harold Williams, 3 vols. (Oxford: Clarendon Press, 1958), vol. 2, p. 561.]

46. Moor of Moor-hall] A legendary hero who armed himself with spiked armor to fight the Dragon of Wantley. The story was told in a ballad in *Pills to Purge Melancholy*, but more famously in a popular burlesque opera, *The Dragon of Wantley* (1737), with libretto by Henry Carey and music by John Frederick Lampe. According to the ballad, printed with the libretto, Moor got new armor at Sheffield:

> With Spikes all about, not within but without,
> Of Steel so sharp and strong,
> Both behind and before, Arms, legs, and all o'er,
> Some five or six Inches long.

[*Burlesque Plays of the Eighteenth Century*, ed. Simon Trussler (Oxford: Oxford Univ. Press, 1969), p. 244.]

47. stone] Alluding to the New Testament story of Jesus and the woman taken in adultery. The scribes and Pharisees remind Jesus that the Mosaic law requires that the adulteress be stoned. Jesus challenges: "He that is without sin among you, let him first cast a stone at her." The men, "convicted by their own conscience," walk away, one by one. Jesus tells the woman, "Go, and sin no more." John 8:1–11.

48. Sappho] A female poet of ancient Greece who wrote nine books of odes, epithalamia, elegies, and hymns, of which only fragments survive. Later women writers, including Griffith herself, were often referred to as Sappho.

49. VERSES . . . IRELAND] This poem appears in *The Memoirs of Mrs. Laetitia Pilkington* (1748) under the title "Mr Worsdale to Mrs Pilkington" (*Memoirs of Mrs. Letitia Pilkington, 1712–1750. Written by Herself*, ed. Iris Barry [London: George Routledge, 1928]). Pilkington was divorced in 1737 by her husband, the clergyman Matthew Pilkington, who claimed to have discovered her committing adultery with a Mr. Adair. She denied the adultery (and other accusations of

subsequent unchastity) but was not generally believed. Pilkington was an Irish writer who made money writing poems not only for herself but also, she plausibly claimed, for men, including James Worsdale, who wished to be thought poets. In the *Memoirs* she prints a set of poems she says she wrote for Worsdale to use while at Mallow. In return, he sent her two poems, upon herself, including this one, which he claimed he wrote. She prints them, but denies that he could have written them: "Who wrote these lines I know not; but, as I am certain the author need not blush to acknowledge them, I hope he will not only pardon my vanity in making them public but also subscribe to my writings." Although this poem may have been published elsewhere, with or without association with Pilkington (for instance, in an Irish newspaper we have not discovered), we think it probable that Griffith knew it was associated with the infamous Pilkington.

50. St. James's Street] A London street noted for coffee houses, clubs, and fashionable shops.

51. Spartan boy] Plutarch gives an account of the regime for educating Spartan boys in his life of Lycurgus. Taken from their parents at seven, they were enrolled in "companies or classes" led by young men, lodged together, and told to forage or steal food so as "to exercise their energy and address": "If they were taken in the fact, they were whipped without mercy, for thieving so ill and awkwardly . . . . So seriously did the Lacedæmonian children go about their stealing, that a youth, having stolen a young fox and hid it under his coat, suffered it to tear out his very bowels with its teeth and claws, and died upon the place, rather than let it be seen." *Plutarch's Lives. The Translation called Dryden's. Corrected from the Greek and Revised*, 5 vols., ed. A. H. Clough (Boston: Little, Brown, 1891) 1:107–8.

52. "feast of reason"] Not an uncommon phrase in the Enlightenment, but perhaps here quoting Alexander Pope's "The First Satire of the Second Book of Horace Imitated" (1733), in which Pope declares himself "TO VIRTUE ONLY and HER FRIENDS, A FRIEND" (1. 121) and celebrates the delights of his Twickenham grotto, a retreat graced by "the best Companions":

> There *ST. JOHN* mingles with my friendly bowl
> The Feast of Reason and the Flow of soul. [ll. 127–28]
> [*Works*, ed. Warburton (1757), vol. 4 p. 71.]

53. *ruse d'amour*] Fr.: trick of love.

54. *Caro Sposo*] Italian: Dear husband.

55. "bestowed . . . exact"] Adapting lines from Milton's *Paradise Lost* (1667). Adam recalls and reflects upon God's creation of Eve out of his rib, noting that no earlier created thing had the power to arouse "passion" in him:

> here only weak
> Against the charm of beauty's pow'rful glance.
> Or nature fail'd in me, and left some part

> Not proof enough such object to sustain,
> Or from my side subducting, took perhaps
> More than enough; at least on her bestow'd
> Too much of ornament, in outward shew
> Elaborate, of inward less exact.
> For well I understand in the prime end
> Of nature her th' inferior, in the mind
>   And inward faculties, which most excel . . . . [Book 8, ll. 532–42]
>         [*Paradise Lost,* vol. 2, pp. 110–11]

56. *brouillerie]* Fr.: a quarrel.

57. jointure] According to Sir Edward Coke (1628), "A competent livelihood of freehold for the wife of lands or tenements, &c to take effect presently in possession or profit after the decease of her husband for the life of the wife at the least." *The First Part of the Institutes of the Laws of England; or a Commentary upon Littleton,* ed. Charles Butler, 2 vols. (London, 1832), 36b. Normally a provision of land or income made in the marriage settlement for the wife should she survive her husband.

58. *au nom du roi]* Fr.: in the name of the king.

59. post bills] Bills, "usually at seven days' sight, issued by the Bank of England for convenience of transmission through the post." *OED,* s.v. bank-bill. The first bank post bills were issued in 1754.

60. *lettre de cachet]* Fr.: under the ancien régime, a sealed letter of the king, containing an order for imprisonment or exile without trial or judicial sentence.

61. Versailles] The site of the French king's court.

62. personalities] Personal property.

63. *arrêt]* Fr.: a judgment of a court of justice.

64. "the insolence of office"] Quoting Hamlet's "To be or not to be" soliloquy:

> For who would bear the whips and scorns of time,
> Th' oppressor's wrong, the proud man's contumely,
> . . . . . . . . . . . . . . . . . . . . . . . .
> The insolence of office, and the spurns
> That patient merit of th' unworthy takes . . . . [*Hamlet,* Act 3, scene 2; vol. 8, pp.
>                          208–9]

65. Châtelet] A fortress in Paris, built in 1131 on the right bank of the Seine. It originally protected the access to the city and later housed a court and a prison.

66. brazed] Brazened, rendered shameless. *OED.*

67. "Hope . . . die."] Adapting Alexander Pope's *Essay on Man* (1733–34), Epistle II, where the poet argues that the passions are useful to individuals:

> Whate'er the Passion, knowledge, fame, or pelf,
> Not one will change his neighbor with himself . . . .
>   See some strange comfort ev'ry state attend,

And pride bestow'd on all, a common friend:
See some fit passion ev'ry age supply,
Hope travels thro', nor quits us when we die.
[*Works,* ed. Warburton (1757), vol. 3, pp. 76–78.]

68. infatuated men] Presumably Jacobites, that is, followers of the Stuart dynasty after the Glorious Revolution of 1688 which removed the Roman Catholic James II from the throne. One armed Jacobite rebellion in Great Britain was mounted in 1715 on behalf of the son of James II, James Francis Edward, later called "The Old Pretender," and another in 1745 on behalf of his son, Charles Edward, called "The Young Pretender." James II took refuge in France; France in various ways continued to aid and abet Jacobitism.

69. crow-quill] The feather of a crow formed into a pen by pointing and slitting the lower end of the barrel.

70. huff] To blow or puff up.

71. *coup d'essai]* Fr.: attempt.

72. familiar] helpful spirit. Miss Weston is probably referring to Lucy Mount Willis, her friend.

73. *quelle douceur! quel charme!]* Fr.: what sweetness! what allurement!

74. *que la rose a ses picques]* Fr.: that the rose has its thorns.

75. Again quoting Hamlet's "To be or not to be" soliloquy:

But that dread of something after death,
That undiscover'd country, from whose bourne
No traveller returns, puzzles the will . . . . [*Hamlet,* Act 3, scene 2; vol. 2, p. 209]

76. Elysium] "The place assigned by the heathens to happy souls; any place exquisitely pleasant." *SJD.*

77. *ignis fatuus]* Latin: literally, a foolish fire; a deluding light.

78. "I often . . . tears,"] Adapting a line from Othello's defense of himself before the senate in Venice. Othello repudiates charges that he has used magic to woo Desdemona and explains that his narratives of his earlier life have won her. Desdemona asked that he speak of his adventures:

I did consent,
And often did beguile her of her tears,
When I did speak of some distressful stroke
That my youth suffer'd [*Othello,* Act 1, scene 8; vol. 8, p. 344]

79. *incog.]* Colloquial abbreviation for "incognito" or "incognita"; having one's identity concealed or disguised.

80. livres] The *livre* was a unit of French money roughly equivalent to the British pound.

81. *en passant]* Fr.: on the way.

82. Amor Patriæ] Latin: love of one's country.

83. Albion's chalky cliffs] "Albion" is a name for England; the cliffs of Dover on the south coast, a usual landfall after crossing the Channel from France, are chalky white.

# Suggested Reading

~

Diderot, Denis. *Selected Writings on Art and Literature*, trans. Geoffrey Bremner. London: Penguin Books, 1994.

Eshleman, Dorothy Hughes. *Elizabeth Griffith: A Biographical and Critical Study*. Philadelphia: Univ. of Pennsylvania Press, 1949.

Harris, Marla. "'How Nicely Circumspect Must Your Conduct Be': Double Standards in Elizabeth Griffith's *The History of Lady Barton*." In *Eighteenth-Century Women and the Arts,* ed. Frederick M. Keener and Susan E. Lorsch, pp. 277-82. New York and Westport, Conn.: Greenwood Press, 1985.

Milton, John. "A Mask" (Comus). In *John Milton: Complete Poems and Major Prose,* ed. Merritt Y. Hughes, pp. 86-114 (Indianapolis, Ind.: Odyssey Press, 1957).

Napier, Elizabeth R. "Griffith, Elizabeth." In *Dictionary of Literary Biography: Vol. 39. British Novelists, 1660-1800. Part 1: A-L,* ed. Martin Battestin. Detroit, Mich.: Gale Research, 1985.

Prior, Matthew. "Henry and Emma, a Poem, Upon the Model of the Nut-Brown Maid" and "Solomon on the Vanity of the World. A Poem in Three Books." In *The Literary Works of Matthew Prior,* ed. H. Bunker Wright and Monroe K. Spears. 2 vols. Oxford: Clarendon, 1971.

Rizzo, Betty. "'Depressa Resurgam': Elizabeth Griffith's Playwriting Career." In *Curtain Calls: British and American Women and the Theater, 1660-1820,* ed. Mary Anne Schofield and Cecilia Macheski, pp. 120-42. Athens: Ohio Univ. Press, 1991.

———. "Elizabeth Griffith." In *A Dictionary of British and American Writers, 1660-1800,* ed. Janet Todd. Totowa, N.J.: Rowman and Allanheld, 1986.

Rousseau, Jean-Jacques. *La Nouvelle Héloïse; Julie, or the New Eloise,* trans. and abridged by Judith H. McDowell. University Park: Univ. of Pennsylvania Press, 1968.

Staves, Susan. "French Fire, English Asbestos: Ninon de Lenclos and Elizabeth Griffith." *Studies on Voltaire and the Eighteenth Century* 314 (1993): 193-205.

———. "Griffith, Elizabeth." *Dictionary of Literary Biography: Vol. 89. Restoration and Eighteenth-Century Dramatists.* Detroit: Gale Research, 1989.

Stewart, Joan Hinde. *The Novels of Mme Riccoboni.* Chapel Hill: Univ. of North Carolina Press, 1976.

Todd, Janet. *Sensibility: An Introduction.* London and New York: Methuen, 1986.
————. *The Sign of Angellica: Women, Writing and Fiction, 1600-1800.* London: Virago, 1989.
Tompkins, J.M.S. *The Polite Marriage.* Cambridge: Cambridge Univ. Press, 1938. Pp. 1-40.
————. *The Popular Novel in England, 1770-1800.* 1932 Reprint, Lincoln: Univ. of Nebraska Press, 1961.